50
GREATEST
LOVE
STORIES

Terry O'Brien is a bestselling author of several books, an academician, a freelance broadcaster, a quiz enthusiast and a motivational trainer. He is a man of many parts, a language expert, a connoisseur of literature, a versatile writer on a plethora of subjects and a trainer's trainer.

50

GREATEST
LOVE
STORIES

Selection and Introduction by

TERRY O'BRIEN

RUPA

Published by
Rupa Publications India Pvt. Ltd 2023
7/16, Ansari Road, Daryaganj
New Delhi 110002

Sales Centres:
Allahabad Bengaluru Chennai
Hyderabad Jaipur Kathmandu
Kolkata Mumbai

P-ISBN: 978-93-5702-070-1
E-ISBN: 978-93-5702-049-7

First impression 2023

10 9 8 7 6 5 4 3 2 1

Printed in India

CONTENTS

INTRODUCTION

'Some say love's a little boy,
And some say it's a bird,
Some say it makes the world go round,
And some say that's absurd,
And when I asked the man next door,
Who looked as if he knew,
His wife got very cross indeed,
And said it wouldn't do.'

—W.H. Auden

Some love stories are not epic novels—they are short stories—but that doesn't make them less filled with love. Love stories always seem to have a spark. A love story has the nature of love and cares not for the age of lovers. Sometimes grief is the price one pays for love but this grief has a loud and clear message beneath: 'Let us go where souls do couch on flowers.'

Who does not enjoy reading inspiring love stories from all over the world? Indeed, literature holds the mirror to nature—after all, life scripts the most beautiful love stories possible. They are heartbeats—to love is nothing; to be loved is something; but to love and be loved is *everything*. There is an element of magic, when one falls in love, the world looks like an enchanted place.

The structure of a love story mostly has three convincing elements: the lover, the beloved and the adventure they have together. To love 'very much' is to love inadequately; *we love—that is all*. Love cannot be modified without being nullified. Love is a short word but it contains everything. Love means the body, the soul, the life, the entire being. We feel love as we feel the warmth of our blood. We breathe love as we breathe the air. We hold it in ourselves as we hold our thoughts. Nothing more exists for us.

Love is not a word; it is a wordless state indicated by four letters. Love is not an adjective; it is a verb. It is not something that hangs from the cloud for a poet's eye. Is it just moonshine or is it like a 'red, red rose'? It indeed has many shades, hues and nuances:

- It may be romantic entanglement in myriad forms.
- To begin with, it can be first love.
- It can be either an infatuation or obsession.
- In relationships, it could be unrequited love, marriage or adultery.
- It may sometimes be the 'green eyed monster' or jealousy
- Time is no factor—it can also be a complicated bond for those who have lived together for long.

Love can evoke a variety of moods, from raw emotions, erotic passion or cynical comedy to agonizing madness of jealousy or the yearnings of romantic illusions. Writers of short stories on love explore the elemental force of love in fascinatingly different ways. They deal with the solar plexus and the cerebral cortex. Love could be a strong desire for an alternate life; it could also mean feeling of listlessness.

This anthology makes an enticing gift for lovers at any stage of life. One of the salient features of this anthology is that it has not just *love* as a common theme but *rhythm*: repetition with variations—incidentally we have three stories titled, 'The Kiss' yet each stands out for their sincerity, authenticity and approach to the theme.

The pages of this edited book can trace *Eros* that denotes romantic, passionate love. It may also be *Phila*, affectionate friendly love or *Storge* which indicates familial love. It may also be *Agape*, selfless universal love. It could be *Ludus* or playful, flirtatious love or *Pragma,* committed lasting love or even *Philautia* or self love. It seems to be timeless. It will exist till the mountains jump over the ocean; till Africa and China meet...

In which ever shade love may be, the lover will continue to sing: *love has no ending!*

As the anthem for lovers goes—

We are the music makers,
We are the dreamer of dreams...

Happy reading,

Terry O'Brien

THE KISS

Kate Chopin

A kiss can be a comma, a question mark, or an exclamation mark!

It was still quite light out of doors, but inside with the curtains drawn and the smouldering fire sending out a dim, uncertain glow, the room was full of deep shadows.

Brantain sat in one of these shadows; it had overtaken him and he did not mind. The obscurity lent him courage to keep his eyes fastened as ardently as he liked upon the girl who sat in the firelight.

She was very handsome, with a certain fine, rich colouring that belongs to the healthy brune type. She was quite composed, as she idly stroked the satiny coat of the cat that lay curled in her lap, and she occasionally sent a slow glance into the shadow where her companion sat. They were talking low, of indifferent things which plainly were not the things that occupied their thoughts. She knew that he loved her—a frank, blustering fellow without guile enough to conceal his feelings, and no desire to do so. For two weeks past he had sought her society eagerly and persistently. She was confidently waiting for him to declare himself and she meant to accept him. The rather insignificant and unattractive Brantain was enormously rich; and she liked and required the entourage which wealth could give her.

During one of the pauses between their talk of the last tea and the next reception the door opened and a young man entered whom Brantain knew quite well. The girl turned her face toward him. A stride or two brought him to her side, and bending over her chair—before she could suspect his intention, for she did not realize that he had not seen her visitor—he pressed an ardent, lingering kiss upon her lips.

Brantain slowly arose; so did the girl arise, but quickly, and the newcomer stood between them, a little amusement and some defiance struggling with the confusion in his face.

'I believe,' stammered Brantain, 'I see that I have stayed too long. I—I had no idea—that is, I must wish you good-by.' He was clutching his hat with both hands, and probably did not perceive that she was extending her hand to him, her presence of mind had not completely deserted her; but she could not have trusted herself to speak.

'Hang me if I saw him sitting there, Nattie! I know it's deuced awkward for you. But I hope you'll forgive me this once—this very first break. Why, what's the matter?'

'Don't touch me; don't come near me,' she returned angrily. 'What do you mean by entering the house without ringing?'

'I came in with your brother, as I often do,' he answered coldly, in self-justification. 'We came in the side way. He went upstairs and I came in here hoping to find you. The explanation is simple enough and ought to satisfy you that the misadventure was unavoidable. But do say that you forgive me, Nathalie,' he entreated, softening.

'Forgive you! You don't know what you are talking about. Let me pass. It depends upon—a good deal whether I ever forgive you.'

At that next reception which she and Brantain had been talking about she approached the young man with a delicious frankness of manner when she saw him there.

'Will you let me speak to you a moment or two, Mr Brantain?' she asked with an engaging but perturbed smile. He seemed extremely unhappy; but when she took his arm and walked away with him, seeking a retired corner, a ray of hope mingled with the almost comical misery of his expression. She was apparently very outspoken.

'Perhaps I should not have sought this interview, Mr Brantain; but—but, oh, I have been very uncomfortable, almost miserable since that little encounter the other afternoon. When I thought how you might have misinterpreted it, and believed things'—hope was plainly gaining the ascendancy over misery in Brantain's round, guileless face—'Of course, I know it is nothing to you, but for my own sake I do want you to understand that Mr Harvy is an intimate friend of long standing. Why, we have always been like cousins—like brother and sister, I may say. He is my brother's most intimate associate and often fancies that he is entitled to the same privileges as the family. Oh, I know it is absurd, uncalled for, to tell you this; undignified even,' she was almost weeping, 'but it makes so much difference to me what you think of—of me.' Her voice had grown very low and agitated. The misery had all disappeared from Brantain's face.

'Then you do really care what I think, Miss Nathalie? May I call you Miss Nathalie?' They turned into a long, dim corridor that was lined on either side with tall, graceful plants. They walked slowly to the very end of it. When they turned to retrace their steps Brantain's face was radiant and hers was triumphant.

Harvy was among the guests at the wedding; and he sought her out in a rare moment when she stood alone.

'Your husband,' he said, smiling, 'has sent me over to kiss you.'

A quick blush suffused her face and round polished throat. 'I suppose it's natural for a man to feel and act generously on an occasion of this kind. He tells me he doesn't want his marriage to interrupt wholly that pleasant intimacy which has existed between you and me. I don't know what you've been telling him,' with an insolent smile, 'but he has sent me here to kiss you.'

She felt like a chess player who, by the clever handling of his pieces, sees the game taking the course intended. Her eyes were bright and tender with a smile as they glanced up into his; and her lips looked hungry for the kiss which they invited.

'But, you know,' he went on quietly, 'I didn't tell him so, it would have seemed ungrateful, but I can tell you. I've stopped kissing women; it's dangerous.'

Well, she had Brantain and his million left. A person can't have everything in this world; and it was a little unreasonable of her to expect it.

2

A SERVICE OF LOVE

O. Henry

Life of sacrifice is the pinnacle of love.

When one loves one's Art no service seems too hard.
    That is our premise. This story shall draw a conclusion from
it, and show at the same time that the premise is incorrect. That
will be a new thing in logic, and a feat in story-telling somewhat
older than the Great Wall of China.

Joe Larrabee came out of the post-oak flats of the Middle West
pulsing with a genius for pictorial art. At six he drew a picture
of the town pump with a prominent citizen passing it hastily.
This effort was framed and hung in the drug store window by
the side of the ear of corn with an uneven number of rows. At
twenty he left for New York with a flowing necktie and a capital
tied up somewhat closer.

Delia Caruthers did things in six octaves so promisingly in a
pine-tree village in the South that her relatives chipped in enough
in her chip hat for her to go 'North' and 'finish'. They could not
see her f—but that is our story.

Joe and Delia met in an atelier where a number of art and
music students had gathered to discuss Chiaroscuro, Wagner, music,
Rembrandt's works, pictures, Waldteufel, wallpaper, Chopin and
Oolong.

Joe and Delia became enamoured one of the other, or each of
the other, as you please, and in a short time were married—for
(see above), when one loves one's Art no service seems too hard.

Mr and Mrs Larrabee began housekeeping in a flat. It was

a lonesome flat—something like the A sharp way down at the left-hand end of the keyboard. And they were happy; for they had their Art, and they had each other. And my advice to the rich young man would be—sell all thou hast, and give it to the poor—janitor for the privilege of living in a flat with your Art and your Delia.

Flat-dwellers shall indorse my dictum that theirs is the only true happiness. If a home is happy it cannot fit too close—let the dresser collapse and become a billiard table; let the mantel turn to a rowing machine, the escritoire to a spare bedchamber, the washstand to an upright piano; let the four walls come together, if they will, so you and your Delia are between. But if home be the other kind, let it be wide and long—enter you at the Golden Gate, hang your hat on Hatteras, your cape on Cape Horn and go out by the Labrador.

Joe was painting in the class of the great Magister—you know his fame. His fees are high; his lessons are light—his highlights have brought him renown. Delia was studying under Rosenstock—you know his repute as a disturber of the piano keys.

They were mighty happy as long as their money lasted. So is every—but I will not be cynical. Their aims were very clear and defined. Joe was to become capable very soon of turning out pictures that old gentlemen with thin side-whiskers and thick pocketbooks would sandbag one another in his studio for the privilege of buying. Delia was to become familiar and then contemptuous with music, so that when she saw the orchestra seats and boxes unsold she could have sore throat and lobster in a private dining room and refuse to go on the stage.

But the best, in my opinion, was the home life in the little flat—the ardent, voluble chats after the day's study; the cozy dinners and fresh, light breakfasts; the interchange of ambitions—ambitions interwoven each with the other's or else inconsiderable—the mutual help and inspiration; and—overlook my artlessness—stuffed olives and cheese sandwiches at 11.00 p.m.

But after a while Art flagged. It sometimes does, even if some switchman doesn't flag it. Everything going out and nothing coming in, as the vulgarians say. Money was lacking to pay Mr Magister and Herr Rosenstock their prices. When one loves one's Art no service seems too hard. So, Delia said she must give music lessons to keep the chafing dish bubbling.

For two or three days she went out canvassing for pupils. One evening she came home elated.

'Joe, dear,' she said, gleefully, 'I've a pupil. And, oh, the loveliest people! General—General A. B. Pinkney's daughter on Seventy-first street. Such a splendid house, Joe—you ought to see the front door! Byzantine I think you would call it. And inside! Oh, Joe, I never saw anything like it before.

'My pupil is his daughter Clementina. I dearly love her already. She's a delicate thing—dresses always in white; and the sweetest, simplest manners! Only eighteen years old. I'm to give three lessons a week; and, just think, Joe! $5 a lesson. I don't mind it a bit; for when I get two or three more pupils I can resume my lessons with Herr Rosenstock. Now, smooth out that wrinkle between your brows, dear, and let's have a nice supper.'

'That's all right for you, Dele,' said Joe, attacking a can of peas with a carving knife and a hatchet, 'but how about me? Do you think I'm going to let you hustle for wages while I philander in the regions of high art? Not by the bones of Benvenuto Cellini! I guess I can sell papers or lay cobblestones, and bring in a dollar or two.'

Delia came and hung about his neck.

'Joe, dear, you are silly. You must keep on at your studies. It is not as if I had quit my music and gone to work at something else. While I teach I learn. I am always with my music. And we can live as happily as millionaires on $15 a week. You mustn't think of leaving Mr Magister.'

'All right,' said Joe, reaching for the blue scalloped vegetable dish. 'But I hate for you to be giving lessons. It isn't Art. But you're a trump and a dear to do it.'

'When one loves one's Art no service seems too hard,' said Delia.

'Magister praised the sky in that sketch I made in the park,' said Joe. 'And Tinkle gave me permission to hang two of them in his window. I may sell one if the right kind of a moneyed idiot sees them.'

'I'm sure you will,' said Delia, sweetly. 'And now let's be thankful for General Pinkney and this veal roast.'

During all of the next week the Larrabees had an early breakfast. Joe was enthusiastic about some morning-effect sketches he was doing in Central Park, and Delia packed him off breakfasted, coddled, praised and kissed at seven o'clock. Art is an engaging mistress. It was most times seven o'clock when he returned in the evening.

At the end of the week Delia, sweetly proud but languid, triumphantly tossed three five-dollar bills on the 8×10 inches centre table of the 8×10 feet flat parlour.

'Sometimes,' she said, a little wearily, 'Clementina tries me. I'm afraid she doesn't practise enough, and I have to tell her the same things so often. And then she always dresses entirely in white, and that does get monotonous. But General Pinkney is the dearest old man! I wish you could know him, Joe. He comes in sometimes when I am with Clementina at the piano—he is a widower, you know—and stands there pulling his white goatee. "And how are the semiquavers and the demisemiquavers progressing?" he always asks.

'I wish you could see the wainscoting in that drawing-room, Joe! And those Astrakhan rug portières. And Clementina has such a funny little cough. I hope she is stronger than she looks. Oh, I really am getting attached to her, she is so gentle and high bred. General Pinkney's brother was once Minister to Bolivia.'

And then Joe, with the air of a Monte Cristo, drew forth

a ten, a five, a two and a one—all legal tender notes—and laid them beside Delia's earnings.

'Sold that watercolour of the obelisk to a man from Peoria,' he announced overwhelmingly.

'Don't joke with me,' said Delia, 'not from Peoria!'

'All the way. I wish you could see him, Dele. Fat man with a woollen muffler and a quill toothpick. He saw the sketch in Tinkle's window and thought it was a windmill at first. He was game, though, and bought it anyhow. He ordered another—an oil sketch of the Lackawanna freight depot—to take back with him. Music lessons! Oh, I guess Art is still in it.'

'I'm so glad you've kept on,' said Delia, heartily. 'You're bound to win, dear. Thirty-three dollars! We never had so much to spend before. We'll have oysters to-night.'

'And filet mignon with champignons,' said Joe. 'Where is the olive fork?'

On the next Saturday evening Joe reached home first. He spread his $18 on the parlour table and washed what seemed to be a great deal of dark paint from his hands.

Half an hour later Delia arrived, her right hand tied up in a shapeless bundle of wraps and bandages.

'How is this?' asked Joe after the usual greetings. Delia laughed, but not very joyously.

'Clementina,' she explained, 'insisted upon a Welsh rabbit after her lesson. She is such a queer girl. Welsh rabbits at five in the afternoon. The General was there. You should have seen him run for the chafing dish, Joe, just as if there wasn't a servant in the house. I know Clementina isn't in good health; she is so nervous. In serving the rabbit she spilled a great lot of it, boiling hot, over my hand and wrist. It hurt awfully, Joe. And the dear girl was so sorry! But General Pinkney!—Joe, that old man nearly went distracted. He rushed downstairs and sent somebody—they said the furnace man or somebody in the basement—out to a drug store for some oil and things to bind it up with. It doesn't hurt so much now.'

'What's this?' asked Joe, taking the hand tenderly and pulling at some white strands beneath the bandages.

'It's something soft,' said Delia, 'that had oil on it. Oh, Joe, did you sell another sketch?' She had seen the money on the table.

'Did I?' said Joe; 'just ask the man from Peoria. He got his depot to-day, and he isn't sure but he thinks he wants another parkscape and a view on the Hudson. What time this afternoon did you burn your hand, Dele?'

'Five o'clock, I think,' said Dele, plaintively. 'The iron—I mean the rabbit came off the fire about that time. You ought to have seen General Pinkney, Joe, when—'

'Sit down here a moment, Dele,' said Joe. He drew her to the couch, sat beside her and put his arm across her shoulders.

'What have you been doing for the last two weeks, Dele?' he asked.

She braved it for a moment or two with an eye full of love and stubbornness, and murmured a phrase or two vaguely of General Pinkney; but at length down went her head and out came the truth and tears.

'I couldn't get any pupils,' she confessed. 'And I couldn't bear to have you give up your lessons; and I got a place ironing shirts in that big Twenty-fourth street laundry. And I think I did very well to make up both General Pinkney and Clementina, don't you, Joe? And when a girl in the laundry set down a hot iron on my hand this afternoon I was all the way home making up that story about the Welsh rabbit. You're not angry, are you, Joe? And if I hadn't got the work you mightn't have sold your sketches to that man from Peoria.'

'He wasn't from Peoria,' said Joe, slowly.

'Well, it doesn't matter where he was from. How clever you are, Joe—and—kiss me, Joe—and what made you ever suspect that I wasn't giving music lessons to Clementina?'

'I didn't,' said Joe, 'until to-night. And I wouldn't have then, only I sent up this cotton waste and oil from the engine-room this afternoon for a girl upstairs who had her hand burned with a smoothing-iron. I've been firing the engine in that laundry for the last two weeks.'

'And then you didn't—'

'My purchaser from Peoria,' said Joe, 'and General Pinkney are both creations of the same art—but you wouldn't call it either painting or music.'

And then they both laughed, and Joe began:

'When one loves one's Art no service seems—'

But Delia stopped him with her hand on his lips. 'No,' she said—'just "When one loves".'

3

ABOUT LOVE

Anton Chekhov

Love can be a great mystery that nobody understands.

At lunch next day there were very nice pies, crayfish, and mutton cutlets; and while we were eating, Nikanor, the cook, came up to ask what the visitors would like for dinner. He was a man of medium height, with a puffy face and little eyes; he was close-shaven, and it looked as though his moustaches had not been shaved, but had been pulled out by the roots. Alehin told us that the beautiful Pelagea was in love with this cook. As he drank and was of a violent character, she did not want to marry him, but was willing to live with him without. He was very devout, and his religious convictions would not allow him to 'live in sin'; he insisted on her marrying him, and would consent to nothing else, and when he was drunk he used to abuse her and even beat her. Whenever he got drunk she used to hide upstairs and sob, and on such occasions Alehin and the servants stayed in the house to be ready to defend her in case of necessity.

We began talking about love.

'How love is born,' said Alehin, 'why Pelagea does not love somebody more like herself in her spiritual and external qualities, and why she fell in love with Nikanor, that ugly snout—we all call him "The Snout"—how far questions of personal happiness are of consequence in love—all that is known; one can take what view one likes of it. So far only one incontestable truth has been uttered about love: "This is a great mystery." Everything else that has been written or said about love is not a conclusion, but only a statement of questions which have remained unanswered. The explanation which would seem to fit one case does not apply in a dozen others, and the very best thing, to my mind, would be to explain every case individually without attempting to generalize. We ought, as the doctors say, to individualize each case.'

'Perfectly true,' Burkin assented.

'We Russians of the educated class have a partiality for these questions that remain unanswered. Love is usually poeticized, decorated with roses, nightingales; we Russians decorate our loves with these momentous questions, and select the most uninteresting of them, too. In Moscow, when I was a student, I had a friend who shared my life, a charming lady, and every time I took her in my arms she was thinking what I would allow her a month for housekeeping and what was the price of beef a pound. In the same way, when we are in love we are never tired of asking ourselves questions: whether it is honourable or dishonourable, sensible or stupid, what this love is leading up to, and so on. Whether it is a good thing or not I don't know, but that it is in the way, unsatisfactory, and irritating, I do know.'

It looked as though he wanted to tell some story. People who lead a solitary existence always have something in their hearts which they are eager to talk about. In town bachelors visit the baths and the restaurants on purpose to talk, and sometimes tell the most interesting things to bath attendants and waiters; in the country, as a rule, they unbosom themselves to their guests. Now from the window we could see a grey sky, trees drenched in the rain; in such weather we could go nowhere, and there was nothing for us to do but to tell stories and to listen.

'I have lived at Sofino and been farming for a long time,' Alehin began, 'ever since I left the University. I am an idle gentleman by education, a studious person by disposition; but there was a big debt owing on the estate when I came here, and as my father was in debt partly because he had spent so much on my education,

I resolved not to go away, but to work till I paid off the debt. I made up my mind to this and set to work, not, I must confess, without some repugnance. The land here does not yield much, and if one is not to farm at a loss one must employ serf labour or hired labourers, which is almost the same thing, or put it on a peasant footing—that is, work the fields oneself and with one's family. There is no middle path. But in those days I did not go into such subtleties. I did not leave a clod of earth unturned; I gathered together all the peasants, men and women, from the neighbouring villages; the work went on at a tremendous pace. I myself ploughed and sowed and reaped, and was bored doing it, and frowned with disgust, like a village cat driven by hunger to eat cucumbers in the kitchen-garden. My body ached, and I slept as I walked.

'At first it seemed to me that I could easily reconcile this life of toil with my cultured habits; to do so, I thought, all that is necessary is to maintain a certain external order in life. I established myself upstairs here in the best rooms, and ordered them to bring me there coffee and liquor after lunch and dinner, and when I went to bed I read every night the Yyesnik Evropi. But one day our priest, Father Ivan, came and drank up all my liquor at one sitting; and the Yyesnik Evropi went to the priest's daughters; as in the summer, especially at the haymaking, I did not succeed in getting to my bed at all, and slept in the sledge in the barn, or somewhere in the forester's lodge, what chance was there of reading? Little by little I moved downstairs, began dining in the servants' kitchen, and of my former luxury nothing is left but the servants who were in my father's service, and whom it would be painful to turn away.

'In the first years I was elected here an honourary justice of the peace. I used to have to go to the town and take part in the sessions of the congress and of the circuit court, and this was a pleasant change for me. When you live here for two or three months without a break, especially in the winter, you begin at last to pine for a black coat. And in the circuit court there were frock-coats, and uniforms, and dress-coats, too, all lawyers, men who have received a general education; I had some one to talk to. After sleeping in the sledge and dining in the kitchen, to sit in an arm-chair in clean linen, in thin boots, with a chain on one's waistcoat, is such luxury!

'I received a warm welcome in the town. I made friends eagerly. And of all my acquaintanceships the most intimate and, to tell the truth, the most agreeable to me was my acquaintance with Luganovitch, the vice-president of the circuit court. You both know him: a most charming personality. It all happened just after a celebrated case of incendiarism; the preliminary investigation lasted two days; we were exhausted. Luganovitch looked at me and said:

'"Look here, come round to dinner with me."

'This was unexpected, as I knew Luganovitch very little, only officially, and I had never been to his house. I only just went to my hotel room to change and went off to dinner. And here it was my lot to meet Anna Alexyevna, Luganovitch's wife. At that time she was still very young, not more than twenty-two, and her first baby had been born just six months before. It is all a thing of the past; and now I should find it difficult to define what there was so exceptional in her, what it was in her attracted me so much; at the time, at dinner, it was all perfectly clear to me. I saw a lovely young, good, intelligent, fascinating woman, such as I had never met before; and I felt her at once some one close and already familiar, as though that face, those cordial, intelligent eyes, I had seen somewhere in my childhood, in the album which lay on my mother's chest of drawers.

'Four Jews were charged with being incendiaries, were regarded as a gang of robbers, and, to my mind, quite groundlessly. At dinner I was very much excited, I was uncomfortable, and I don't know what I said, but Anna Alexyevna kept shaking her head and saying to her husband:

'"Dmitry, how is this?"

'Luganovitch is a good-natured man, one of those simple-hearted people who firmly maintain the opinion that once a man is charged before a court he is guilty, and to express doubt of the correctness of a sentence cannot be done except in legal form on paper, and not at dinner and in private conversation.

'"You and I did not set fire to the place," he said softly, "and you see we are not condemned, and not in prison."

'And both husband and wife tried to make me eat and drink as much as possible. From some trifling details, from the way they made the coffee together, for instance, and from the way they understood each other at half a word, I could gather that they lived in harmony and comfort, and that they were glad of a visitor. After dinner they played a duet on the piano; then it got dark, and I went home. That was at the beginning of spring.

'After that I spent the whole summer at Sofino without a break, and I had no time to think of the town, either, but the memory of the graceful fair-haired woman remained in my mind all those days; I did not think of her, but it was as though her light shadow were lying on my heart.

'In the late autumn there was a theatrical performance for some charitable object in the town. I went into the governor's box (I was invited to go there in the interval); I looked, and there was Anna Alexyevna sitting beside the governor's wife; and again the same irresistible, thrilling impression of beauty and sweet, caressing eyes, and again the same feeling of nearness. We sat side by side, then went to the foyer.

'"You've grown thinner,' she said; "have you been ill?"

'"Yes, I've had rheumatism in my shoulder, and in rainy weather I can't sleep."

'"You look dispirited. In the spring, when you came to dinner, you were younger, more confident. You were full of eagerness, and talked a great deal then; you were very interesting, and I really must confess I was a little carried away by you. For some reason you often came back to my memory during the summer, and when I was getting ready for the theatre today I thought I should see you."

'And she laughed.

"'But you look dispirited today," she repeated; "it makes you seem older."

'The next day I lunched at the Luganovitchs'. After lunch they drove out to their summer villa, in order to make arrangements there for the winter, and I went with them. I returned with them to the town, and at midnight drank tea with them in quiet domestic surroundings, while the fire glowed, and the young mother kept going to see if her baby girl was asleep. And after that, every time I went to town I never failed to visit the Luganovitchs. They grew used to me, and I grew used to them. As a rule I went in unannounced, as though I were one of the family.

"'Who is there?" I would hear from a faraway room, in the drawling voice that seemed to me so lovely.

"'It is Pavel Konstantinovitch," answered the maid or the nurse.

'Anna Alexyevna would come out to me with an anxious face, and would ask every time:

' "Why is it so long since you have been? Has anything happened?"

'Her eyes, the elegant refined hand she gave me, her indoor dress, the way she did her hair, her voice, her step, always produced the same impression on me of something new and extraordinary in my life, and very important. We talked together for hours, were silent, thinking each our own thoughts, or she played for hours to me on the piano. If there were no one at home I stayed and waited, talked to the nurse, played with the child, or lay on the sofa in the study and read; and when Anna Alexyevna came back I met her in the hall, took all her parcels from her, and for some reason I carried those parcels every time with as much love, with as much solemnity, as a boy.

'There is a proverb that if a peasant woman has no troubles she will buy a pig. The Luganovitchs had no troubles, so they made friends with me. If I did not come to the town I must be ill or something must have happened to me, and both of them were extremely anxious. They were worried that I, an educated man with a knowledge of languages, should, instead of devoting myself to science or literary work, live in the country, rush round like a squirrel in a rage, work hard with never a penny to show for it. They fancied that I was unhappy, and that I only talked, laughed, and ate to conceal my sufferings, and even at cheerful moments when I felt happy I was aware of their searching eyes fixed upon me. They were particularly touching when I really was depressed, when I was being worried by some creditor or had not money enough to pay interest on the proper day. The two of them, husband and wife, would whisper together at the window; then he would come to me and say with a grave face:

'"If you really are in need of money at the moment, Pavel Konstantinovitch, my wife and I beg you not to hesitate to borrow from us."

'And he would blush to his ears with emotion. And it would happen that, after whispering in the same way at the window, he would come up to me, with red ears, and say:

'"My wife and I earnestly beg you to accept this present."

'And he would give me studs, a cigar-case, or a lamp, and I would send them game, butter, and flowers from the country. They both, by the way, had considerable means of their own. In early days I often borrowed money, and was not very particular about it—borrowed wherever I could—but nothing in the world would have induced me to borrow from the Luganovitchs. But why talk of it?

'I was unhappy. At home, in the fields, in the barn, I thought of her; I tried to understand the mystery of a beautiful, intelligent young woman's marrying some one so uninteresting, almost an old man (her husband was over forty), and having children by him; to understand the mystery of this uninteresting, good, simple-hearted man, who argued with such wearisome good sense, at balls and evening parties kept near the more solid people, looking listless and superfluous, with a submissive, uninterested expression, as though he had been brought there for sale, who yet believed in his right to be happy, to have children by her; and I kept trying to understand why she had met him first and not me, and why such a terrible mistake in our lives need have happened.

'And when I went to the town I saw every time from her eyes that she was expecting me, and she would confess to me herself that she had had a peculiar feeling all that day and had guessed that I should come. We talked a long time, and were silent, yet we did not confess our love to each other, but timidly and jealously concealed it. We were afraid of everything that might reveal our secret to ourselves. I loved her tenderly, deeply, but I reflected and kept asking myself what our love could lead to if we had not the strength to fight against it. It seemed to be incredible that my gentle, sad love could all at once coarsely break up the even tenor of the life of her husband, her children, and all the household in which I was so loved and trusted. Would it be honourable? She would go away with me, but where? Where could I take her? It would have been a different matter if I had had a beautiful, interesting life—if, for instance, I had been struggling for the emancipation of my country, or had been a celebrated man of science, an artist or a painter; but as it was it would mean taking her from one everyday humdrum life to another as humdrum or perhaps more so. And how long would our happiness last? What would happen to her in case I was ill, in case I died, or if we simply grew cold to one another?

'And she apparently reasoned in the same way. She thought of her husband, her children, and of her mother, who loved the husband like a son. If she abandoned herself to her feelings she would have to lie, or else to tell the truth, and in her position either would have been equally terrible and inconvenient. And she was tormented by the question whether her love would bring me happiness—would she not complicate my life, which, as it was, was hard enough and full of all sorts of trouble? She fancied she was not young enough for me, that she was not industrious nor energetic enough to begin a new life, and she often talked to her husband of the importance of my marrying a girl of intelligence and merit who would be a capable housewife and a help to me—and she would immediately add that it would be difficult to find such a girl in the whole town.

'Meanwhile the years were passing. Anna Alexyevna already had two children. When I arrived at the Luganovitchs' the servants smiled cordially, the children shouted that Uncle Pavel Konstantinovitch had come, and hung on my neck; every one was overjoyed. They did not understand what was passing in my soul, and thought that I, too, was happy. Every one looked on me as a noble being. And grown-ups and children alike felt that a noble being was walking about their rooms, and that gave a peculiar charm to their manner towards me, as though in my presence their life, too, was purer and more beautiful. Anna Alexyevna and I used to go to the theatre together, always walking there; we used to sit side by side in the stalls, our shoulders touching. I would take the opera-glass from her hands without a word, and feel at that minute that she was near me, that she was mine, that we could not live without each other; but by some strange misunderstanding, when we came out of the theatre we always said good-bye and parted as though we were strangers. Goodness knows what people were saying about us in the town already, but there was not a word of truth in it all!

'In the latter years Anna Alexyevna took to going away for frequent visits to her mother or to her sister; she began to suffer from low spirits, she began to recognize that her life was spoilt and unsatisfied, and at times she did not care to see her husband nor her children. She was already being treated for neurasthenia.

'We were silent and still silent, and in the presence of outsiders she displayed a strange irritation in regard to me; whatever I talked about, she disagreed with me, and if I had an argument she sided with my opponent. If I dropped anything, she would say coldly:

'"I congratulate you."

'If I forgot to take the opera-glass when we were going to the theatre, she would say afterwards:

'"I knew you would forget it."

'Luckily or unluckily, there is nothing in our lives that does not end sooner or later. The time of parting came, as Luganovitch was appointed president in one of the western provinces. They had to sell their furniture, their horses, their summer villa. When they drove out to the villa, and afterwards looked back as they were going away, to look for the last time at the garden, at the green roof, every one was sad, and I realized that I had to say goodbye not only to the villa. It was arranged that at the end of August we should see Anna Alexyevna off to the Crimea, where the doctors were sending her, and that a little later Luganovitch and the children would set off for the western province.

'We were a great crowd to see Anna Alexyevna off. When she had said good-bye to her husband and her children and there was only a minute left before the third bell, I ran into her compartment to put a basket, which she had almost forgotten, on the rack, and I had to say good-bye. When our eyes met in the compartment our spiritual fortitude deserted us both; I took her in my arms, she pressed her face to my breast, and tears flowed from her eyes. Kissing her face, her shoulders, her hands wet with tears—oh, how unhappy we were! I confessed my love for her, and with a burning pain in my heart I realized how unnecessary, how petty, and how deceptive all that had hindered us from loving was. I understood that when you love you must either, in your reasonings about that love, start from what is highest, from what is more important than happiness or unhappiness, sin or virtue in their accepted meaning, or you must not reason at all.

'I kissed her for the last time, pressed her hand, and parted for ever. The train had already started. I went into the next compartment—it was empty—and until I reached the next station I sat there crying. Then I walked home to Sofino…'

While Alehin was telling his story, the rain left off and the sun came out. Burkin and Ivan Ivanovitch went out on the balcony, from which there was a beautiful view over the garden and the mill-pond, which was shining now in the sunshine like a mirror. They admired it, and at the same time they were sorry that this man with the kind, clever eyes, who had told them this story with such genuine feeling, should be rushing round and round this huge estate like a squirrel on a wheel instead of devoting himself to science or something else which would have made his life more pleasant; and they thought what a sorrowful face Anna Alexyevna must have had when he said good-bye to her in the railway-carriage and kissed her face and shoulders. Both of them had met her in the town, and Burkin knew her and thought her beautiful.

4

THE HORSE DEALER'S DAUGHTER

D.H. Lawrence

'If passion drives you, let reason hold the reins.'

'Well, Mabel, and what are you going to do with yourself?' asked Joe, with foolish flippancy. He felt quite safe himself. Without listening for an answer, he turned aside, worked a grain of tobacco to the tip of his tongue, and spat it out. He did not care about anything, since he felt safe himself.

The three brothers and the sister sat round the desolate breakfast table, attempting some sort of desultory consultation. The morning's post had given the final tap to the family fortunes, and all was over. The dreary dining-room itself, with its heavy mahogany furniture, looked as if it were waiting to be done away with.

But the consultation amounted to nothing. There was a strange air of ineffectuality about the three men, as they sprawled at table, smoking and reflecting vaguely on their own condition. The girl was alone, a rather short, sullen-looking young woman of twenty-seven. She did not share the same life as her brothers. She would have been good-looking, save for the impassive fixity of her face, 'bull-dog', as her brothers called it.

There was a confused tramping of horses' feet outside. The three men all sprawled round in their chairs to watch. Beyond the dark holly-bushes that separated the strip of lawn from the highroad, they could see a cavalcade of shire horses swinging out of their own yard, being taken for exercise. This was the last time. These were the last horses that would go through their hands.

The young men watched with critical, callous look. They were all frightened at the collapse of their lives, and the sense of disaster in which they were involved left them no inner freedom.

Yet they were three fine, well-set fellows enough. Joe, the eldest, was a man of thirty-three, broad and handsome in a hot, flushed way. His face was red, he twisted his black moustache over a thick finger, his eyes were shallow and restless. He had a sensual way of uncovering his teeth when he laughed, and his bearing was stupid. Now he watched the horses with a glazed look of helplessness in his eyes, a certain stupor of downfall.

The great draught-horses swung past. They were tied head to tail, four of them, and they heaved along to where a lane branched off from the highroad, planting their great hoofs floutingly in the fine black mud, swinging their great rounded haunches sumptuously, and trotting a few sudden steps as they were led into the lane, round the corner. Every movement showed a massive, slumbrous strength, and a stupidity which held them in subjection. The groom at the head looked back, jerking the leading rope. And the cavalcade moved out of sight up the lane, the tail of the last horse, bobbed up tight and stiff, held out taut from the swinging great haunches as they rocked behind the hedges in a motionlike sleep.

Joe watched with glazed hopeless eyes. The horses were almost like his own body to him. He felt he was done for now. Luckily he was engaged to a woman as old as himself, and therefore her father, who was steward of a neighbouring estate, would provide him with a job. He would marry and go into harness. His life was over, he would be a subject animal now.

He turned uneasily aside, the retreating steps of the horses echoing in his ears. Then, with foolish restlessness, he reached for the scraps of bacon-rind from the plates, and making a faint whistling sound, flung them to the terrier that lay against the fender. He watched the dog swallow them, and waited till the creature looked into his eyes. Then a faint grin came on his face, and in a high, foolish voice he said:

'You won't get much more bacon, shall you, you little b—?'

The dog faintly and dismally wagged its tail, then lowered his haunches, circled round, and lay down again.

There was another helpless silence at the table. Joe sprawled uneasily in his seat, not willing to go till the family conclave was dissolved. Fred Henry, the second brother, was erect, clean-limbed, alert. He had watched the passing of the horses with more *sang-froid*. If he was an animal, like Joe, he was an animal which controls, not one which is controlled.

He was master of any horse, and he carried himself with a well-tempered air of mastery. But he was not master of the situations of life. He pushed his coarse brown moustache upwards, off his lip, and glanced irritably at his sister, who sat impassive and inscrutable.

'You'll go and stop with Lucy for a bit, shan't you?' he asked. The girl did not answer.

'I don't see what else you can do,' persisted Fred Henry.

'Go as a skivvy,' Joe interpolated laconically.

The girl did not move a muscle.

'If I was her, I should go in for training for a nurse,' said Malcolm, the youngest of them all. He was the baby of the family, a young man of twenty-two, with a fresh, jaunty *museau*.

But Mabel did not take any notice of him. They had talked at her and round her for so many years, that she hardly heard them at all.

The marble clock on the mantel-piece softly chimed the half-hour, the dog rose uneasily from the hearthrug and looked at the party at the breakfast table. But still they sat on in ineffectual conclave.

'Oh, all right,' said Joe suddenly, *à propos* of nothing. 'I'll get a move on.'

He pushed back his chair, straddled his knees with a downward jerk, to get them free, in horsy fashion, and went to the fire. Still he did not go out of the room; he was curious to know what the others would do or say. He began to charge his pipe, looking down at the dog and saying, in a high, affected voice:

'Going wi' me? Going wi' me are ter? Tha'rt goin' further than tha counts on just now, dost hear?'

The dog faintly wagged its tail, the man stuck out his jaw and covered his pipe with his hands, and puffed intently, losing himself in the tobacco, looking down all the while at the dog with an absent brown eye. The dog looked up at him in mournful distrust. Joe stood with his knees stuck out, in real horsy fashion.

'Have you had a letter from Lucy?' Fred Henry asked of his sister.

'Last week,' came the neutral reply.

'And what does she say?'

There was no answer.

'Does she ask you to go and stop there?' persisted Fred Henry.

'She says I can if I like.'

'Well, then, you'd better. Tell her you'll come on Monday.'

This was received in silence.

'That's what you'll do then, is it?' said Fred Henry, in some exasperation.

But she made no answer. There was a silence of futility and irritation in the room. Malcolm grinned fatuously.

'You'll have to make up your mind between now and next Wednesday,' said Joe loudly, 'or else find yourself lodgings on the kerbstone.'

The face of the young woman darkened, but she sat on immutable.

'Here's Jack Fergusson!' exclaimed Malcolm, who was looking aimlessly out of the window.

'Where?' exclaimed Joe, loudly.

'Just gone past.'

'Coming in?'

Malcolm craned his neck to see the gate.

'Yes,' he said.

There was a silence. Mabel sat on like one condemned, at the head of the table. Then a whistle was heard from the kitchen. The dog got up and barked sharply. Joe opened the door and shouted:

'Come on.'

After a moment a young man entered. He was muffled up in overcoat and a purple woollen scarf, and his tweed cap, which he did not remove, was pulled down on his head. He was of medium height, his face was rather long and pale, his eyes looked tired.

'Hello, Jack!' 'Well, Jack!' exclaimed Malcolm and Joe. Fred Henry merely said, 'Jack!'

'What's doing?' asked the newcomer, evidently addressing Fred Henry.

'Same. We've got to be out by Wednesday—Got a cold?'

'I have—got it bad, too.'

'Why don't you stop in?'

'Me stop in? When I can't stand on my legs, perhaps I shall have a chance.' The young man spoke huskily. He had a slight Scotch accent.

'It's a knock-out, isn't it,' said Joe, boisterously, 'if a doctor goes round croaking with a cold. Looks bad for the patients, doesn't it?'

The young doctor looked at him slowly.

'Anything the matter with you, then?' he asked sarcastically.

'Not as I know of. Damn your eyes, I hope not. Why?'

'I thought you were very concerned about the patients, wondered if you might be one yourself.'

'Damn it, no, I've never been patient to no flaming doctor, and hope I never shall be,' returned Joe.

At this point Mabel rose from the table, and they all seemed to become aware of her existence. She began putting the dishes together. The young doctor looked at her, but did not address her. He had not greeted her. She went out of the room with the tray, her face impassive and unchanged.

'When are you off then, all of you?' asked the doctor.

'I'm catching the eleven-forty,' replied Malcolm. 'Are you goin' down wi'th' trap, Joe?'

'Yes, I've told you I'm going down wi' th' trap, haven't I?'

'We'd better be getting her in then—So long, Jack, if I don't see you before I go,' said Malcolm, shaking hands.

He went out, followed by Joe, who seemed to have his tail between his legs.

'Well, this is the devil's own,' exclaimed the doctor, when he was left alone with Fred Henry. 'Going before Wednesday, are you?'

'That's the orders,' replied the other.

'Where, to Northampton?'

'That's it.'

'The devil!' exclaimed Fergusson, with quiet chagrin.

And there was silence between the two.

'All settled up, are you?' asked Fergusson.

'About.'

There was another pause.

'Well, I shall miss yer, Freddy, boy,' said the young doctor.

'And I shall miss thee, Jack,' returned the other.

'Miss you like hell,' mused the doctor.

Fred Henry turned aside. There was nothing to say. Mabel came in again, to finish clearing the table.

'What are you going to do, then, Miss Pervin?' asked Fergusson. 'Going to your sister's, are you?'

Mabel looked at him with her steady, dangerous eyes, that always made him uncomfortable, unsettling his superficial ease.

'No,' she said.

'Well, what in the name of fortune *are* you going to do? Say what you mean to do,' cried Fred Henry, with futile intensity.

But she only averted her head, and continued her work. She folded the white table-cloth, and put on the chenille cloth.

'The sulkiest bitch that ever trod!' muttered her brother.

But she finished her task with perfectly impassive face, the young doctor watching her interestedly all the while. Then she went out.

Fred Henry stared after her, clenching his lips, his blue eyes fixing in sharp antagonism, as he made a grimace of sour exasperation.

'You could bray her into bits, and that's all you'd get out of her,' he said, in a small, narrowed tone.

The doctor smiled faintly.

'What's she going to do, then?' he asked.

'Strike me if I know!' returned the other.

There was a pause. Then the doctor stirred.

'I'll be seeing you tonight, shall I?' he said to his friend.

'Ay—where's it to be? Are we going over to Jessdale?'

'I don't know. I've got such a cold on me. I'll come round to the Moon and Stars, anyway.'

'Let Lizzie and May miss their night for once, eh?'

'That's it—if I feel as I do now.'

'All's one—'

The two young men went through the passage and down to the back door together. The house was large, but it was servantless now, and desolate.

At the back was a small bricked house-yard, and beyond that a big square, gravelled fine and red, and having stables on two sides. Sloping, dank, winter-dark fields stretched away on the open sides.

But the stables were empty. Joseph Pervin, the father of the family, had been a man of no education, who had become a fairly large horse dealer. The stables had been full of horses, there was a great turmoil and come-and-go of horses and of dealers and grooms. Then the kitchen was full of servants. But of late things had declined. The old man had married a second time, to retrieve his fortunes. Now he was dead and everything was gone to the dogs, there was nothing but debt and threatening.

For months, Mabel had been servantless in the big house, keeping the home together in penury for her ineffectual brothers. She had kept house for ten years. But previously, it was with unstinted means. Then, however brutal and coarse everything was, the sense of money had kept her proud, confident. The men might be foul-mouthed, the women in the kitchen might have bad reputations, her brothers might have illegitimate children. But so long as there was money, the girl felt herself established, and brutally proud, reserved.

No company came to the house, save dealers and coarse men. Mabel had no associates of her own sex, after her sister went away. But she did not mind. She went regularly to church, she attended to her father. And she lived in the memory of her mother, who had died when she was fourteen, and whom she had loved. She had loved her father, too, in a different way, depending upon him, and feeling secure in him, until at the age of fifty-four he married again. And then she had set hard against him. Now he had died and left them all hopelessly in debt.

She had suffered badly during the period of poverty. Nothing, however, could shake the curious sullen, animal pride that dominated each member of the family. Now, for Mabel, the end had come. Still she would not cast about her. She would follow her own way just the same. She would always hold the keys of her own situation. Mindless and persistent, she endured from day to day. Why should she think? Why should she answer anybody? It was enough that this was the end, and there was no way out. She need not pass any more darkly along the main street of the small town, avoiding every eye. She need not demean herself any more, going into the shops and buying the cheapest food. This was at an end. She thought of nobody, not even of herself. Mindless and persistent, she seemed in a sort of ecstasy to be coming nearer to her fulfilment, her own glorification, approaching her dead mother, who was glorified.

In the afternoon she took a little bag, with shears and sponge and a small scrubbing brush, and went out. It was a grey, wintry day, with saddened, dark-green fields and an atmosphere blackened by the smoke of foundries not far off. She went quickly, darkly along the causeway, heeding nobody, through the town to the churchyard.

There she always felt secure, as if no one could see her, although as a matter of fact she was exposed to the stare of everyone who passed along under the churchyard wall. Nevertheless, once under the shadow of the great looming church, among the graves, she felt immune from the world, reserved within the thick churchyard wall as in another country.

Carefully she clipped the grass from the grave, and arranged the pinky-white, small chrysanthemums in the tin cross. When this was done, she took an empty jar from a neighbouring grave, brought water, and carefully, most scrupulously sponged the marble headstone and the coping-stone.

It gave her sincere satisfaction to do this. She felt in immediate contact with the world of her mother. She took minute pains, went through the park in a state bordering on pure happiness, as if in performing this task she came into a subtle, intimate connexion with her mother. For the life she followed here in the world was far less real than the world of death she inherited from her mother.

The doctor's house was just by the church. Fergusson, being a mere hired assistant, was slave to the countryside. As he hurried now to attend to the outpatients in the surgery, glancing across the graveyard with his quick eye, he saw the girl at her task at the grave. She seemed so intent and remote, it was like looking into another world. Some mystical element was touched in him. He slowed down as he walked, watching her as if spellbound.

She lifted her eyes, feeling him looking. Their eyes met. And each looked again at once, each feeling, in some way, found out by the other. He lifted his cap and passed on down the road. There remained distinct in his consciousness, like a vision, the memory of her face, lifted from the tombstone in the churchyard, and looking at him with slow, large, portentous eyes. It was portentous, her face. It seemed to mesmerize him. There was a heavy power in her eyes which laid hold of his whole being, as if he had drunk some powerful drug. He had been feeling weak and done before. Now the life came back into him, he felt delivered from his own fretted, daily self.

He finished his duties at the surgery as quickly as might be, hastily filling up the bottles of the waiting people with cheap drugs. Then, in perpetual haste, he set off again to visit several cases in another part of his round, before teatime. At all times he preferred to walk, if he could, but particularly when he was not well. He fancied the motion restored him.

The afternoon was falling. It was grey, deadened, and wintry, with a slow, moist, heavy coldness sinking in and deadening all the faculties. But why should he think or notice? He hastily climbed the hill and turned across the dark-green fields, following the black cinder track. In the distance, across a shallow dip in the country, the small town was clustered like smouldering ash, a tower, a spire, a heap of low, raw, extinct houses. And on the nearest fringe of the town, sloping into the dip, was Oldmeadow, the Pervins' house. He could see the stables and the outbuildings distinctly, as they lay towards him on the slope. Well, he would not go there many more times! Another resource would be lost to him, another place gone: the only company he cared for in the alien, ugly little town he was losing. Nothing but work, drudgery, constant hastening from dwelling to dwelling among the colliers and the iron-workers. It wore him out, but at the same time he had a craving for it. It was a stimulant to him to be in the homes of the working people, moving as it were through the innermost body of their life. His nerves were excited and gratified. He could come so near, into the very lives of the rough, inarticulate, powerfully emotional men and women. He grumbled, he said he hated the hellish hole. But as a matter of fact it excited him, the contact with the rough, strongly-feeling people was a stimulant applied direct to his nerves.

Below Oldmeadow, in the green, shallow, soddened hollow of fields, lay a square, deep pond. Roving across the landscape, the doctor's quick eye detected a figure in black passing through the gate of the field, down towards the pond. He looked again. It would be Mabel Pervin. His mind suddenly became alive and attentive.

Why was she going down there? He pulled up on the path on the slope above, and stood staring. He could just make sure of the small black figure moving in the hollow of the failing day. He seemed to see her in the midst of such obscurity, that he was like a clairvoyant, seeing rather with the mind's eye than with ordinary sight. Yet he could see her positively enough, whilst he kept his eye attentive. He felt, if he looked away from her, in the thick, ugly falling dusk, he would lose her altogether.

He followed her minutely as she moved, direct and intent, like something transmitted rather than stirring in voluntary activity, straight down the field towards the pond. There she stood on the bank for a moment. She never raised her head. Then she waded slowly into the water.

He stood motionless as the small black figure walked slowly and deliberately towards the centre of the pond, very slowly, gradually moving deeper into the motionless water, and still moving forward as the water got up to her breast. Then he could see her no more in the dusk of the dead afternoon.

'There!' he exclaimed. 'Would you believe it?'

And he hastened straight down, running over the wet, soddened fields, pushing through the hedges, down into the depression of callous wintry obscurity. It took him several minutes to come to the pond. He stood on the bank, breathing heavily. He could see nothing. His eyes seemed to penetrate the dead water. Yes, perhaps that was the dark shadow of her black clothing beneath the surface of the water.

He slowly ventured into the pond. The bottom was deep, soft clay, he sank in, and the water clasped dead cold round his legs. As he stirred he could smell the cold, rotten clay that fouled up into the water. It was objectionable in his lungs. Still, repelled and yet not heeding, he moved deeper into the pond. The cold water rose over his thighs, over his loins, upon his abdomen. The lower part of his body was all sunk in the hideous cold element. And the bottom was so deeply soft and uncertain, he was afraid of pitching with his mouth underneath. He could not swim, and was afraid.

He crouched a little, spreading his hands under the water and moving them round, trying to feel for her. The dead cold pond swayed upon his chest. He moved again, a little deeper, and again, with his hands underneath, he felt all around under the water. And he touched her clothing. But it evaded his fingers. He made a desperate effort to grasp it.

And so doing he lost his balance and went under, horribly, suffocating in the foul earthy water, struggling madly for a few moments. At last, after what seemed an eternity, he got his footing, rose again into the air and looked around. He gasped, and knew he was in the world. Then he looked at the water. She had risen near him. He grasped her clothing, and drawing her nearer, turned to take his way to land again.

He went very slowly, carefully, absorbed in the slow progress. He rose higher, climbing out of the pond. The water was now only about his legs; he was thankful, full of relief to be out of the clutches of the pond. He lifted her and staggered on to the bank, out of the horror of wet, grey clay.

He laid her down on the bank. She was quite unconscious and running with water. He made the water come from her mouth, he worked to restore her. He did not have to work very long before he could feel the breathing begin again in her; she was breathing naturally. He worked a little longer. He could feel her live beneath his hands; she was coming back. He wiped her face, wrapped her in his overcoat, looked round into the dim, dark-grey world, then lifted her and staggered down the bank and across the fields.

It seemed an unthinkably long way, and his burden so heavy he felt he would never get to the house. But at last he was in the stable-yard, and then in the house-yard. He opened the door and went into the house. In the kitchen he laid her down on the hearthrug, and called. The house was empty. But the fire was burning in the grate.

Then again he kneeled to attend to her. She was breathing regularly, her eyes were wide open and as if conscious, but there seemed something missing in her look. She was conscious in herself, but unconscious of her surroundings.

He ran upstairs, took blankets from a bed, and put them before the fire to warm. Then he removed her saturated, earthy-smelling clothing, rubbed her dry with a towel, and wrapped her naked in the blankets. Then he went into the dining-room, to look for spirits. There was a little whisky. He drank a gulp himself, and put some into her mouth.

The effect was instantaneous. She looked full into his face, as if she had been seeing him for some time, and yet had only just become conscious of him.

'Dr. Fergusson?' she said.

'What?' he answered.

He was divesting himself of his coat, intending to find some dry clothing upstairs. He could not bear the smell of the dead, clayey water, and he was mortally afraid for his own health.

'What did I do?' she asked.

'Walked into the pond,' he replied. He had begun to shudder like one sick, and could hardly attend to her. Her eyes remained full on him, he seemed to be going dark in his mind, looking back at her helplessly. The shuddering became quieter in him, his life came back in him, dark and unknowing, but strong again.

'Was I out of my mind?' she asked, while her eyes were fixed on him all the time.

'Maybe, for the moment,' he replied. He felt quiet, because his strength had come back. The strange fretful strain had left him.

'Am I out of my mind now?' she asked.

'Are you?' he reflected a moment. 'No,' he answered truthfully, 'I don't see that you are.' He turned his face aside. He was afraid now, because he felt dazed, and felt dimly that her power was stronger than his, in this issue. And she continued to look at him fixedly all the time. 'Can you tell me where I shall find some dry things to put on?' he asked.

'Did you dive into the pond for me?' she asked.

'No,' he answered. 'I walked in. But I went in overhead as well.'

There was silence for a moment. He hesitated. He very much wanted to go upstairs to get into dry clothing. But there was another desire in him. And she seemed to hold him. His will seemed to have gone to sleep, and left him, standing there slack before her. But he felt warm inside himself. He did not shudder at all, though his clothes were sodden on him.

'Why did you?' she asked.

'Because I didn't want you to do such a foolish thing,' he said.

'It wasn't foolish,' she said, still gazing at him as she lay on the floor, with a sofa cushion under her head. 'It was the right thing to do. I knew best, then.'

'I'll go and shift these wet things,' he said. But still he had not the power to move out of her presence, until she sent him. It was as if she had the life of his body in her hands, and he could not extricate himself. Or perhaps he did not want to.

Suddenly she sat up. Then she became aware of her own immediate condition. She felt the blankets about her, she knew her own limbs. For a moment it seemed as if her reason were going. She looked round, with wild eye, as if seeking something. He stood still with fear. She saw her clothing lying scattered.

'Who undressed me?' she asked, her eyes resting full and inevitable on his face.

'I did,' he replied, 'to bring you round.'

For some moments she sat and gazed at him awfully, her lips parted.

'Do you love me then?' she asked.

He only stood and stared at her, fascinated. His soul seemed to melt.

She shuffled forward on her knees, and put her arms round him, round his legs, as he stood there, pressing her breasts against his knees and thighs, clutching him with strange, convulsive certainty, pressing his thighs against her, drawing him to her face, her throat, as she looked up at him with flaring, humble eyes, of transfiguration, triumphant in first possession.

'You love me,' she murmured, in strange transport, yearning and triumphant and confident. 'You love me. I know you love me, I know.'

And she was passionately kissing his knees, through the wet clothing, passionately and indiscriminately kissing his knees, his legs, as if unaware of every thing.

He looked down at the tangled wet hair, the wild, bare, animal shoulders. He was amazed, bewildered, and afraid. He had never thought of loving her. He had never wanted to love her. When he rescued her and restored her, he was a doctor, and she was a patient. He had had no single personal thought of her. Nay, this introduction of the personal element was very distasteful to him, a violation of his professional honour. It was horrible to have her there embracing his knees. It was horrible. He revolted from it, violently. And yet—and yet—he had not the power to break away.

She looked at him again, with the same supplication of powerful love, and that same transcendent, frightening light of triumph. In view of the delicate flame which seemed to come from her face like a light, he was powerless. And yet he had never intended to love her. He had never intended. And something stubborn in him could not give way.

'You love me,' she repeated, in a murmur of deep, rhapsodic assurance.

'You love me.'

Her hands were drawing him, drawing him down to her. He was afraid, even a little horrified. For he had, really, no intention of loving her. Yet her hands were drawing him towards her. He put out his hand quickly to steady himself, and grasped her bare shoulder. A flame seemed to burn the hand that grasped her soft shoulder. He had no intention of loving her: his whole will was against his yielding. It was horrible. And yet wonderful was the touch of her shoulders, beautiful the shining of her face. Was she perhaps mad? He had a horror of yielding to her. Yet something in him ached also.

He had been staring away at the door, away from her. But his hand remained on her shoulder. She had gone suddenly very still. He looked down at her. Her eyes were now wide with fear, with doubt, the light was dying from her face, a shadow of terrible greyness was returning. He could not bear the touch of her eyes' question upon him, and the look of death behind the question.

With an inward groan he gave way, and let his heart yield towards her. A sudden gentle smile came on his face. And her eyes, which never left his face, slowly, slowly filled with tears. He watched the strange water rise in her eyes, like some slow fountain coming up. And his heart seemed to burn and melt away in his breast.

He could not bear to look at her any more. He dropped on his knees and caught her head with his arms and pressed her face against his throat. She was very still. His heart, which seemed to have broken, was burning with a kind of agony in his breast. And he felt her slow, hot tears wetting his throat. But he could not move.

He felt the hot tears wet his neck and the hollows of his neck, and he remained motionless, suspended through one of man's eternities. Only now it had become indispensable to him to have her face pressed close to him; he could never let her go again. He could never let her head go away from the close clutch of his arm. He wanted to remain like that for ever, with his heart hurting him in a pain that was also life to him. Without knowing, he was looking down on her damp, soft brown hair.

Then, as it were suddenly, he smelt the horrid stagnant smell of that water. And at the same moment she drew away from him and looked at him. Her eyes were wistful and unfathomable. He was afraid of them, and he fell to kissing her, not knowing what he was doing. He wanted her eyes not to have that terrible, wistful, unfathomable look.

When she turned her face to him again, a faint delicate flush was glowing, and there was again dawning that terrible shining of joy in her eyes, which really terrified him, and yet which he now wanted to see, because he feared the look of doubt still more.

'You love me?' she said, rather faltering.

'Yes.' The word cost him a painful effort. Not because it wasn't true. But because it was too newly true, the saying seemed to tear open again his newly-torn heart. And he hardly wanted it to be true, even now.

She lifted her face to him, and he bent forward and kissed her on the mouth, gently, with the one kiss that is an eternal pledge. And as he kissed her his heart strained again in his breast. He never intended to love her. But now it was over. He had crossed over the gulf to her, and all that he had left behind had shrivelled and become void.

After the kiss, her eyes again slowly filled with tears. She sat still, away from him, with her face drooped aside, and her hands folded in her lap. The tears fell very slowly. There was complete silence. He too sat there motionless and silent on the hearthrug. The strange pain of his heart that was broken seemed to consume him. That he should love her? That this was love! That he should be ripped open in this way!Him, a doctor! How they would all jeer if they knew! It was agony to him to think they might know.

In the curious naked pain of the thought he looked again to her. She was sitting there drooped into a muse. He saw a tear fall, and his heart flared hot. He saw for the first time that one of her shoulders was quite uncovered, one arm bare, he could see one of her small breasts; dimly, because it had become almost dark in the room.

'Why are you crying?' he asked, in an altered voice.

She looked up at him, and behind her tears the consciousness of her situation for the first time brought a dark look of shame to her eyes.

'I'm not crying, really,' she said, watching him half frightened.

He reached his hand, and softly closed it on her bare arm.

'I love you! I love you!' he said in a soft, low vibrating voice, unlike himself.

She shrank, and dropped her head. The soft, penetrating grip of his hand on her arm distressed her. She looked up at him.

'I want to go,' she said. 'I want to go and get you some dry things.'

'Why?' he said. 'I'm all right.'

'But I want to go,' she said. 'And I want you to change your things.'

He released her arm, and she wrapped herself in the blanket, looking at him rather frightened. And still she did not rise.

'Kiss me,' she said wistfully.

He kissed her, but briefly, half in anger.

Then, after a second, she rose nervously, all mixed up in the blanket. He watched her in her confusion, as she tried to extricate herself and wrap herself up so that she could walk. He watched her relentlessly, as she knew. And as she went, the blanket trailing, and as he saw a glimpse of her feet and her white leg, he tried to remember her as she was when he had wrapped her in the blanket. But then he didn't want to remember, because she had been nothing to him then, and his nature revolted from remembering her as she was when she was nothing to him.

A tumbling, muffled noise from within the dark house startled him. Then he heard her voice: 'There are clothes.' He rose and went to the foot of the stairs, and gathered up the garments she had thrown down. Then he came back to the fire, to rub himself down and dress. He grinned at his own appearance when he had finished.

The fire was sinking, so he put on coal. The house was now quite dark, save for the light of a street-lamp that shone in faintly from beyond the holly trees. He lit the gas with matches he found on the mantel-piece. Then he emptied the pockets of his own clothes, and threw all his wet things in a heap into the scullery. After which he gathered up her sodden clothes, gently, and put them in a separate heap on the copper-top in the scullery.

It was six o'clock on the clock. His own watch had stopped. He ought to go back to the surgery. He waited, and still she did not come down. So he went to the foot of the stairs and called:

'I shall have to go.'

Almost immediately he heard her coming down. She had on her best dress of black voile, and her hair was tidy, but still damp. She looked at him—and in spite of herself, smiled.

'I don't like you in those clothes,' she said.

'Do I look a sight?' he answered.

They were shy of one another.

'I'll make you some tea,' she said.

'No, I must go.'

'Must you?' And she looked at him again with the wide, strained, doubtful eyes. And again, from the pain of his breast, he knew how he loved her. He went and bent to kiss her, gently, passionately, with his heart's painful kiss.

'And my hair smells so horrible,' she murmured in distraction. 'And I'm so awful, I'm so awful! Oh, no, I'm too awful.' And she broke into bitter, heart-broken sobbing. 'You can't want to love me, I'm horrible.'

'Don't be silly, don't be silly,' he said, trying to comfort her, kissing her, holding her in his arms. 'I want you, I want to marry you, we're going to be married, quickly, quickly—to-morrow if I can.'

But she only sobbed terribly, and cried:

'I feel awful. I feel awful. I feel I'm horrible to you.'

'No, I want you, I want you,' was all he answered, blindly, with that terrible intonation which frightened her almost more than her horror lest he should not want her.

5

THE SPECTACLES

Edgar Allan Poe

Love at first sight! Beauty lies in the eyes of the beholder, indeed.
But then take the question: Is beauty just skin deep...

Many years ago, it was the fashion to ridicule the idea of 'love at first sight'; but those who think, not less than those who feel deeply, have always advocated its existence. Modern discoveries, indeed, in what may be termed ethical magnetism or magnetoesthetics, render it probable that the most natural, and, consequently, the truest and most intense of the human affections are those which arise in the heart as if by electric sympathy — in a word, that the brightest and most enduring of the psychal fetters are those which are riveted by a glance. The confession I am about to make will add another to the already almost innumerable instances of the truth of the position.

My story requires that I should be somewhat minute. I am still a very young man—not yet twenty-two years of age. My name, at present, is a very usual and rather plebeian one—Simpson. I say 'at present', for it is only lately that I have been so called—having legislatively adopted this surname within the last year in order to receive a large inheritance left me by a distant male relative, Adolphus Simpson, Esq. The bequest was conditioned upon my taking the name of the testator—the family, not the Christian name; my Christian name is Napoleon Bonaparte—or, more properly, these are my first and middle appellations.

I assumed the name, Simpson, with some reluctance, as in my true patronym, Froissart, I felt a very pardonable pride—

believing that I could trace a descent from the immortal author of the Chronicles. While on the subject of names, by the bye, I may mention a singular coincidence of sound attending the names of some of my immediate predecessors. My father was a Monsieur Froissart, of Paris. His wife—my mother, whom he married at fifteen—was a Mademoiselle Croissart, eldest daughter of Croissart the banker, whose wife, again, being only sixteen when married, was the eldest daughter of one Victor Voissart. Monsieur Voissart, very singularly, had married a lady of similar name—a Mademoiselle Moissart. She, too, was quite a child when married; and her mother, also, Madame Moissart, was only fourteen when led to the altar. These early marriages are usual in France. Here, however, are Moissart, Voissart, Croissart, and Froissart, all in the direct line of descent. My own name, though, as I say, became Simpson, by act of Legislature, and with so much repugnance on my part, that, at one period, I actually hesitated about accepting the legacy with the useless and annoying proviso attached.

As to personal endowments, I am by no means deficient. On the contrary, I believe that I am well made, and possess what nine tenths of the world would call a handsome face. In height I am five feet eleven. My hair is black and curling. My nose is sufficiently good. My eyes are large and grey; and although, in fact they are weak a very inconvenient degree, still no defect in this regard would be suspected from their appearance. The weakness itself, however, has always much annoyed me, and I have resorted to every remedy—short of wearing glasses. Being youthful and good-looking, I naturally dislike these, and have resolutely refused to employ them. I know nothing, indeed, which so disfigures the countenance of a young person, or so impresses every feature with an air of demureness, if not altogether of sanctimoniousness and of age. An eyeglass, on the other hand, has a savour of downright foppery and affectation. I have hitherto managed as well as I could without either. But something too much of these merely personal details, which, after all, are of little importance. I will content myself with saying, in addition, that my temperament is sanguine, rash, ardent, enthusiastic—and that all my life I have been a devoted admirer of the women.

One night last winter I entered a box at the P— Theatre, in company with a friend, Mr Talbot. It was an opera night, and the bills presented a very rare attraction, so that the house was excessively crowded. We were in time, however, to obtain the front seats which had been reserved for us, and into which, with some little difficulty, we elbowed our way.

For two hours my companion, who was a musical fanatico, gave his undivided attention to the stage; and, in the meantime, I amused myself by observing the audience, which consisted, in chief part, of the very elite of the city. Having satisfied myself upon this point, I was about turning my eyes to the prima donna, when they were arrested and riveted by a figure in one of the private boxes which had escaped my observation.

If I live a thousand years, I can never forget the intense emotion with which I regarded this figure. It was that of a female, the most exquisite I had ever beheld. The face was so far turned toward the stage that, for some minutes, I could not obtain a view of it—but the form was divine; no other word can sufficiently express its magnificent proportion—and even the term 'divine' seems ridiculously feeble as I write it.

The magic of a lovely form in woman—the necromancy of female gracefulness—was always a power which I had found it impossible to resist, but here was grace personified, incarnate, the beau ideal of my wildest and most enthusiastic visions. The figure, almost all of which the construction of the box permitted to be seen, was somewhat above the medium height, and nearly approached, without positively reaching, the majestic. Its perfect fullness and tournure were delicious. The head of which only the back was visible, rivalled in outline that of the Greek Psyche, and was rather displayed than concealed by an elegant cap of *gaze aérienne*, which put me in mind of the *ventum textilem* of Apuleius. The right arm hung over the balustrade of the box, and thrilled every nerve of my frame with its exquisite symmetry. Its upper portion was draperied by one of the loose open sleeves now in fashion. This extended but little below the elbow. Beneath it was worn an under one of some frail material, close-fitting, and terminated by a cuff of rich lace, which fell gracefully over the top of the hand, revealing only the delicate fingers, upon one of which sparkled a diamond ring, which I at once saw was of extraordinary value. The admirable roundness of the wrist was well set off by a bracelet which encircled it, and which also was ornamented and clasped by a magnificent aigrette of jewels—telling, in words that could not be mistaken, at once of the wealth and fastidious taste of the wearer.

I gazed at this queenly apparition for at least half an hour, as if I had been suddenly converted to stone; and, during this period, I felt the full force and truth of all that has been said or sung concerning 'love at first sight'. My feelings were totally different from any which I had hitherto experienced, in the presence of even the most celebrated specimens of female loveliness. An unaccountable, and what I am compelled to consider a magnetic, sympathy of soul for soul, seemed to rivet, not only my vision, but my whole powers of thought and feeling, upon the admirable object before me. I saw—I felt—I knew that I was deeply, madly, irrevocably in love—and this even before seeing the face of the person beloved. So intense, indeed, was the passion that consumed me, that I really believe it would have received little if any abatement had the features, yet unseen, proved of merely ordinary character, so anomalous is the nature of the only true love—of the love at first sight—and so little really dependent is it upon the external conditions which only seem to create and control it.

While I was thus wrapped in admiration of this lovely vision, a sudden disturbance among the audience caused her to turn her head partially toward me, so that I beheld the entire profile of the face. Its beauty even exceeded my anticipations—and yet there was something about it which disappointed me without my being able to tell exactly what it was. I said 'disappointed', but this is not altogether the word. My sentiments were at once quieted and exalted. They partook less of transport and more of calm enthusiasm of enthusiastic repose. This state of feeling arose, perhaps, from the Madonna-like and matronly air of the face; and yet I at once understood that it could not have arisen entirely from this. There was something else—some mystery which I could not develope—some expression about the countenance which slightly disturbed me while it greatly heightened my interest. In fact, I was just in that condition of mind which prepares a young and susceptible man for any act of extravagance. Had the lady been alone, I should undoubtedly have entered her box and accosted her at all hazards; but, fortunately, she was attended by two companions—a gentleman, and a strikingly beautiful woman, to all appearance a few years younger than herself.

I revolved in my mind a thousand schemes by which I might obtain, hereafter, an introduction to the elder lady, or, for the present, at all events, a more distinct view of her beauty. I would have removed my position to one nearer her own, but the crowded state of the theatre rendered this impossible; and the stern decrees of Fashion had, of late, imperatively prohibited the use of the opera-glass in a case such as this, even had I been so fortunate as to have one with me—but I had not—and was thus in despair.

At length I bethought me of applying to my companion.

'Talbot,' I said, 'you have an opera-glass. Let me have it.'

'An opera-glass! No! What do you suppose I would be doing with an opera-glass?' Here he turned impatiently toward the stage.

'But, Talbot,' I continued, pulling him by the shoulder, 'listen to me will you? Do you see the stage—box? There! No, the next!

Did you ever behold as lovely a woman?'

'She is very beautiful, no doubt,' he said.

'I wonder who she can be?'

'Why, in the name of all that is angelic, don't you know who she is? Not to know her argues yourself unknown. She is the celebrated Madame Lalande—the beauty of the day par excellence, and the talk of the whole town. Immensely wealthy too—a widow, and a great match—has just arrived from Paris.'

'Do you know her?'

'Yes; I have the honour.'

'Will you introduce me?'

'Assuredly, with the greatest pleasure; when shall it be?'

'To-morrow, at one, I will call upon you at B—'s.'

'Very good; and now do hold your tongue, if you can.'

In this latter respect I was forced to take Talbot's advice; for he remained obstinately deaf to every further question or suggestion, and occupied himself exclusively for the rest of the evening with what was transacting upon the stage.

In the meantime I kept my eyes riveted on Madame Lalande, and at length had the good fortune to obtain a full front view of her face. It was exquisitely lovely—this, of course, my heart had told me before, even had not Talbot fully satisfied me upon the point—but still the unintelligible something disturbed me. I finally concluded that my senses were impressed by a certain air of gravity, sadness, or, still more properly, of weariness, which took something from the youth and freshness of the countenance, only to endow it with a seraphic tenderness and majesty, and thus, of course, to my enthusiastic and romantic temperment, with an interest tenfold.

While I thus feasted my eyes, I perceived, at last, to my great trepidation, by an almost imperceptible start on the part of the lady, that she had become suddenly aware of the intensity of my gaze. Still, I was absolutely fascinated, and could not withdraw it, even for an instant. She turned aside her face, and again I saw only the chiselled contour of the back portion of the head. After some minutes, as if urged by curiosity to see if I was still looking, she gradually brought her face again around and again encountered my burning gaze. Her large dark eyes fell instantly, and a deep blush mantled her cheek. But what was my astonishment at perceiving that she not only did not a second time avert her head, but that she actually took from her girdle a double eyeglass—elevated it—adjusted it—and then regarded me through it, intently and deliberately, for the space of several minutes.

Had a thunderbolt fallen at my feet I could not have been more thoroughly astounded—astounded only—not offended or disgusted in the slightest degree; although an action so bold in any other woman would have been likely to offend or disgust. But the whole thing was done with so much quietude—so much nonchalance—so much repose–with so evident an air of the highest breeding, in short—that nothing of mere effrontery was perceptible, and my sole sentiments were those of admiration and surprise.

I observed that, upon her first elevation of the glass, she had seemed satisfied with a momentary inspection of my person, and was withdrawing the instrument, when, as if struck by a second thought, she resumed it, and so continued to regard me with fixed attention for the space of several minutes—for five minutes, at the very least, I am sure.

This action, so remarkable in an American theatre, attracted very general observation, and gave rise to an indefinite movement, or buzz, among the audience, which for a moment filled me with confusion, but produced no visible effect upon the countenance of Madame Lalande.

Having satisfied her curiosity—if such it was—she dropped the glass, and quietly gave her attention again to the stage; her profile now being turned toward myself, as before. I continued to watch her unremittingly, although I was fully conscious of my rudeness in so doing. Presently I saw the head slowly and slightly change its position; and soon I became convinced that the lady, while pretending to look at the stage was, in fact, attentively regarding myself. It is needless to say what effect this conduct, on the part of so fascinating a woman, had upon my excitable mind.

Having thus scrutinized me for perhaps a quarter of an hour, the fair object of my passion addressed the gentleman who attended her, and while she spoke, I saw distinctly, by the glances of both, that the conversation had reference to myself.

Upon its conclusion, Madame Lalande again turned toward the stage, and, for a few minutes, seemed absorbed in the performance. At the expiration of this period, however, I was thrown into an extremity of agitation by seeing her unfold, for the second time, the eye-glass which hung at her side, fully confront me as before, and, disregarding the renewed buzz of the audience, survey me, from head to foot, with the same miraculous composure which had previously so delighted and confounded my soul.

This extraordinary behaviour, by throwing me into a perfect fever of excitement—into an absolute delirium of love—served rather to embolden than to disconcert me. In the mad intensity of my devotion, I forgot everything but the presence and the majestic loveliness of the vision which confronted my gaze. Watching my opportunity, when I thought the audience were fully engaged with the opera, I at length caught the eyes of Madame Lalande, and, upon the instant, made a slight but unmistakable bow.

She blushed very deeply—then averted her eyes—then slowly and cautiously looked around, apparently to see if my rash action had been noticed—then leaned over toward the gentleman who sat by her side.

I now felt a burning sense of the impropriety I had committed, and expected nothing less than instant exposure; while a vision of pistols upon the morrow floated rapidly and uncomfortably through my brain. I was greatly and immediately relieved, however, when

I saw the lady merely hand the gentleman a play-bill, without speaking, but the reader may form some feeble conception of my astonishment—of my profound amazement—my delirious bewilderment of heart and soul—when, instantly afterward, having again glanced furtively around, she allowed her bright eyes to set fully and steadily upon my own, and then, with a faint smile, disclosing a bright line of her pearly teeth, made two distinct, pointed, and unequivocal affirmative inclinations of the head.

It is useless, of course, to dwell upon my joy, upon my transport, upon my illimitable ecstasy of heart. If ever man was mad with excess of happiness, it was myself at that moment. I loved. This was my first love—so I felt it to be. It was love supreme—indescribable. It was 'love at first sight', and at first sight, too, it had been appreciated and returned.

Yes, returned. How and why should I doubt it for an instant. What other construction could I possibly put upon such conduct, on the part of a lady so beautiful—so wealthy—evidently so accomplished—of so high breeding—of so lofty a position in society—in every regard so entirely respectable as I felt assured was Madame Lalande? Yes, she loved me—she returned the enthusiasm of my love, with an enthusiasm as blind—as uncompromising—as uncalculating—as abandoned—and as utterly unbounded as my own! These delicious fancies and reflections, however, were now interrupted by the falling of the drop-curtain. The audience arose; and the usual tumult immediately supervened. Quitting Talbot abruptly, I made every effort to force my way into closer proximity with Madame Lalande. Having failed in this, on account of the crowd, I at length gave up the chase, and bent my steps homeward; consoling myself for my disappointment in not having been able to touch even the hem of her robe, by the reflection that I should be introduced by Talbot, in due form, upon the morrow.

This morrow at last came, that is to say, a day finally dawned upon a long and weary night of impatience; and then the hours until 'one' were snail-paced, dreary, and innumerable. But even Stamboul, it is said, shall have an end, and there came an end to this long delay. The clock struck. As the last echo ceased, I stepped into B—'s and inquired for Talbot.

'Out,' said the footman—Talbot's own.

'Out!' I replied, staggering back half a dozen paces—'let me tell you, my fine fellow, that this thing is thoroughly impossible and impracticable; Mr Talbot is not out. What do you mean?'

'Nothing, sir; only Mr Talbot is not in, that's all. He rode over to S—, immediately after breakfast, and left word that he would not be in town again for a week.'

I stood petrified with horror and rage. I endeavoured to reply, but my tongue refused its office. At length I turned on my heel, livid with wrath, and inwardly consigning the whole tribe of the Talbots to the innermost regions of Erebus. It was evident that my considerate friend, il fanatico, had quite forgotten his appointment with myself—had forgotten it as soon as it was made. At no time was he a very scrupulous man of his word. There was no help for it; so smothering my vexation as well as I could, I strolled moodily up the street, propounding futile inquiries about Madame Lalande to every male acquaintance I met. By report she was known, I found, to all–to many by sight—but she had been in town only a few weeks, and there were very few, therefore, who claimed her personal acquaintance. These few, being still comparatively strangers, could not, or would not, take the liberty of introducing me through the formality of a morning call. While I stood thus in despair, conversing with a trio of friends upon the all absorbing subject of my heart, it so happened that the subject itself passed by.

'As I live, there she is!' cried one.

'Surprisingly beautiful!' exclaimed a second.

'An angel upon earth!' ejaculated a third.

I looked; and in an open carriage which approached us, passing slowly down the street, sat the enchanting vision of the opera, accompanied by the younger lady who had occupied a portion of her box.

'Her companion also wears remarkably well,' said the one of my trio who had spoken first.

'Astonishingly,' said the second; 'still quite a brilliant air, but art will do wonders. Upon my word, she looks better than she did at Paris five years ago. A beautiful woman still—don't you think so, Froissart—Simpson, I mean.'

'Still!' said I, 'and why shouldn't she be? But compared with her friend she is as a rush—light to the evening star—a glow worm to Antares.'

'Ha! ha! ha! Why, Simpson, you have an astonishing tact at making discoveries—original ones, I mean.' And here we separated, while one of the trio began humming a gay vaudeville, of which I caught only the lines—

Ninon, Ninon, Ninon a bas—
A bas Ninon De L'Enclos!

During this little scene, however, one thing had served greatly to console me, although it fed the passion by which I was consumed. As the carriage of Madame Lalande rolled by our group, I had observed that she recognized me; and more than this, she had blessed me, by the most seraphic of all imaginable smiles, with no equivocal mark of the recognition.

As for an introduction, I was obliged to abandon all hope of it until such time as Talbot should think proper to return from the country. In the meantime I perseveringly frequented every reputable place of public amusement; and, at length, at the theatre, where I first saw her, I had the supreme bliss of meeting her, and of exchanging glances with her once again. This did not occur, however, until the lapse of a fortnight. Every day, in the interim, I had inquired for Talbot at his hotel, and every day had been thrown into a spasm of wrath by the everlasting 'Not come home yet' of his footman.

Upon the evening in question, therefore, I was in a condition little short of madness. Madame Lalande, I had been told, was a Parisian—had lately arrived from Paris—might she not suddenly return? Return before Talbot came back—and might she not be thus lost to me forever? The thought was too terrible to bear. Since my future happiness was at issue, I resolved to act with a manly decision. In a word, upon the breaking up of the play, I traced the lady to her residence, noted the address, and the next morning sent her a full and elaborate letter, in which I poured out my whole heart.

I spoke boldly, freely—in a word, I spoke with passion. I concealed nothing—nothing even of my weakness. I alluded to the romantic circumstances of our first meeting—even to the glances which had passed between us. I went so far as to say that I felt assured of her love; while I offered this assurance, and my own intensity of devotion, as two excuses for my otherwise unpardonable conduct. As a third, I spoke of my fear that she might quit the city before I could have the opportunity of a formal introduction. I concluded the most wildly enthusiastic epistle ever penned, with a frank declaration of my worldly circumstances—of my affluence— and with an offer of my heart and of my hand.

In an agony of expectation I awaited the reply. After what seemed the lapse of a century it came.

Yes, actually came. Romantic as all this may appear, I really received a letter from Madame Lalande—the beautiful, the wealthy, the idolized Madame Lalande. Her eyes—her magnificent eyes, had not belied her noble heart. Like a true Frenchwoman as she was she had obeyed the frank dictates of her reason—the generous impulses of her nature—despising the conventional pruderies of the world. She had not scorned my proposals. She had not sheltered herself in silence. She had not returned my letter unopened. She had even sent me, in reply, one penned by her own exquisite fingers. It ran thus:

Monsieur Simpson vill pardonne me for not compose de butefulle tong of his contrée so vell as might. It is only de late dat I am arrive, and not yet ave do opportunité for to—l'étudier.

Vid dis apologie for the manière, I vill now say dat, hélas! Monsieur Simpson ave guess but de too true. Need I say de more? Hélas! Am I not ready speak de too moshe?

—Eugenie Laland

This noble -spirited note I kissed a million times, and committed, no doubt, on its account, a thousand other extravagances that have now escaped my memory. Still Talbot would not return. Alas! Could he have formed even the vaguest idea of the suffering his absence had occasioned his friend, would not his sympathizing nature have flown immediately to my relief? Still, however, he came not. I wrote. He replied. He was detained by urgent business—but would shortly return. He begged me not to be impatient—to moderate my transports—to read soothing books—to drink nothing stronger than Hock—and to bring the consolations of philosophy to my aid. The fool! If he could not come himself, why, in the name of everything rational, could he not have enclosed me a letter of presentation? I wrote him again, entreating him to forward one forthwith. My letter was returned by that footman, with the following endorsement in pencil. The scoundrel had joined his master in the country:

Left S— yesterday, for parts unknown—did not say where— or when be back—so thought best to return letter, knowing your handwriting, and as how you is always, more or less, in a hurry.

Yours sincerely,

Stubbs

After this, it is needless to say, that I devoted to the infernal deities both master and valet—but there was little use in anger, and no consolation at all in complaint.

But I had yet a resource left, in my constitutional audacity. Hitherto it had served me well, and I now resolved to make it avail me to the end. Besides, after the correspondence which had passed between us, what act of mere informality could I commit, within bounds, that ought to be regarded as indecorous by Madame Lalande? Since the affair of the letter, I had been in the habit of watching her house, and thus discovered that, about twilight, it was her custom to promenade, attended only by a negro in livery, in a public square overlooked by her windows. Here, amid the luxuriant and shadowing groves, in the grey gloom of a sweet midsummer evening, I observed my opportunity and accosted her.

The better to deceive the servant in attendance, I did this with the assured air of an old and familiar acquaintance. With a presence of mind truly Parisian, she took the cue at once, and, to greet me, held out the most bewitchingly little of hands. The valet at once fell into the rear, and now, with hearts full to overflowing, we discoursed long and unreservedly of our love.

As Madame Lalande spoke English even less fluently than she wrote it, our conversation was necessarily in French. In this sweet tongue, so adapted to passion, I gave loose to the impetuous enthusiasm of my nature, and, with all the eloquence I could command, besought her to consent to an immediate marriage.

At this impatience she smiled. She urged the old story of decorum—that bug-bear which deters so many from bliss until the opportunity for bliss has forever gone by. I had most imprudently made it known among my friends, she observed, that I desired her acquaintance—thus that I did not possess it—thus, again, there was no possibility of concealing the date of our first knowledge of each other. And then she adverted, with a blush, to the extreme recency of this date. To wed immediately would be improper—would be indecorous—would be outre. All this she said with a charming air of naivete which enraptured while it grieved and convinced me. She went even so far as to accuse me, laughingly, of rashness—of imprudence. She bade me remember that I really even know not who she was—what were her prospects, her connections, her standing in society. She begged me, but with a sigh, to reconsider my proposal, and termed my love an infatuation—a will o' the wisp—a fancy or fantasy of the moment—a baseless and unstable creation rather of the imagination than of the heart. These things she uttered as the shadows of the sweet twilight gathered darkly and more darkly around us—and then, with a gentle pressure of her fairy-like hand, overthrew, in a single sweet instant, all the argumentative fabric she had reared.

I replied as best I could—as only a true lover can. I spoke at length, and perseveringly of my devotion, of my passion—of her exceeding beauty, and of my own enthusiastic admiration. In conclusion, I dwelt, with a convincing energy, upon the perils that encompass the course of love—that course of true love that never did run smooth—and thus deduced the manifest danger of rendering that course unnecessarily long.

This latter argument seemed finally to soften the rigour of her determination. She relented; but there was yet an obstacle, she said, which she felt assured I had not properly considered. This was a delicate point—for a woman to urge, especially so; in mentioning it, she saw that she must make a sacrifice of her feelings; still, for me, every sacrifice should be made. She alluded to the topic of age. Was I aware—was I fully aware of the discrepancy between us? That the age of the husband, should surpass by a few years—even by fifteen or twenty—the age of the wife, was regarded by the world as admissible, and, indeed, as even proper, but she had always entertained the belief that the years of the wife should never exceed in number those of the husband. A discrepancy of this unnatural kind gave rise, too frequently, alas! To a life of unhappiness. Now she was aware that my own age did not exceed two and twenty; and I, on the contrary, perhaps, was not aware that the years of my Eugenie extended very considerably beyond that sum.

About all this there was a nobility of soul—a dignity of candour—which delighted—which enchanted me—which eternally riveted my chains. I could scarcely restrain the excessive transport which possessed me.

'My sweetest Eugenie,' I cried, 'what is all this about which you are discoursing? Your years surpass in some measure my own. But what then? The customs of the world are so many conventional follies. To those who love as ourselves, in what respect differs a year from an hour? I am twenty-two, you say, granted: indeed, you may as well call me, at once, twenty-three. Now you yourself, my dearest Eugenie, can have numbered no more than—can have numbered no more than—no more than—than—than—than—'

Here I paused for an instant, in the expectation that Madame Lalande would interrupt me by supplying her true age. But a Frenchwoman is seldom direct, and has always, by way of answer to an embarrassing query, some little practical reply of her own. In the present instance, Eugenie, who for a few moments past had seemed to be searching for something in her bosom, at length let fall upon the grass a miniature, which I immediately picked up and presented to her.

'Keep it!' she said, with one of her most ravishing smiles. 'Keep it for my sake—for the sake of her whom it too flatteringly represents. Besides, upon the back of the trinket you may discover, perhaps, the very information you seem to desire. It is now, to be sure, growing rather dark—but you can examine it at your leisure in the morning. In the meantime, you shall be my escort home to-night. My friends are about holding a little musical *levée*. I can promise you, too, some good singing. We French are not nearly so punctilious as you Americans, and I shall have no difficulty in smuggling you in, in the character of an old acquaintance.'

With this, she took my arm, and I attended her home. The mansion was quite a fine one, and, I believe, furnished in good taste. Of this latter point, however, I am scarcely qualified to judge; for it was just dark as we arrived; and in American mansions of the better sort lights seldom, during the heat of summer, make their appearance at this, the most pleasant period of the day. In about an hour after my arrival, to be sure, a single shaded solar lamp was lit in the principal drawing-room; and this apartment, I could thus see, was arranged with unusual good taste and even splendour; but two other rooms of the suite, and in which the company chiefly assembled, remained, during the whole evening, in a very agreeable shadow. This is a well-conceived custom, giving the party at least a choice of light or shade, and one which our friends over the water could not do better than immediately adopt.

The evening thus spent was unquestionably the most delicious of my life. Madame Lalande had not overrated the musical abilities of her friends; and the singing I here heard I had never heard excelled in any private circle out of Vienna. The instrumental performers were many and of superior talents. The vocalists were chiefly ladies, and no individual sang less than well. At length, upon a peremptory call for Madame Lalande she arose at once, without affectation or demur, from the chaise longue upon which she had sat by my side, and, accompanied by one or two gentlemen and her female friend of the opera, repaired to the piano in the main drawing-room. I would have escorted her myself, but felt that, under the circumstances of my introduction to the house, I had better remain unobserved where I was. I was thus deprived of the pleasure of seeing, although not of hearing, her sing.

The impression she produced upon the company seemed electrical but the effect upon myself was something even more. I know not how adequately to describe it. It arose in part, no doubt, from the sentiment of love with which I was imbued; but chiefly from my conviction of the extreme sensibility of the singer.

It is beyond the reach of art to endow either air or recitative with more impassioned expression than was hers. Her utterance of the romance in Otello—the tone with which she gave the words 'Sul mio sasso', in the Capuletti—is ringing in my memory yet. Her lower tones were absolutely miraculous. Her voice embraced three complete octaves, extending from the contralto D to the D-upper soprano, and, though sufficiently powerful to have filled the San Carlos, executed, with the minutest precision, every difficulty of vocal composition—ascending and descending scales, cadences, or fiorituri. In the final of the Somnambula, she brought about a most remarkable effect at the words:

Ah! non guinge uman pensiero
Al contento ond 'io son piena.

Here, in imitation of Malibran, she modified the original phrase of Bellini, so as to let her voice descend to the tenor G, when, by a rapid transition, she struck the G above the treble stave, springing over an interval of two octaves.

Upon rising from the piano after these miracles of vocal execution, she resumed her seat by my side; when I expressed to her, in terms of the deepest enthusiasm, my delight at her performance. Of my surprise I said nothing, and yet was I most unfeignedly surprised; for a certain feebleness, or rather a certain tremulous indecision of voice in ordinary conversation, had prepared me to anticipate that, in singing, she would not acquit herself with any remarkable ability.

Our conversation was now long, earnest, uninterrupted, and totally unreserved. She made me relate many of the earlier passages of my life, and listened with breathless attention to every word of the narrative. I concealed nothing—felt that I had a right to conceal nothing—from her confiding affection. Encouraged by her candour upon the delicate point of her age, I entered, with perfect frankness, not only into a detail of my many minor vices, but made full confession of those moral and even of those physical infirmities, the disclosure of which, in demanding so much higher a degree of courage, is so much surer an evidence of love. I touched upon my college indiscretions—upon my extravagances—upon my carousals—upon my debts—upon my flirtations. I even went so far as to speak of a slightly hectic cough with which, at one time, I had been troubled—of a chronic rheumatism—of a twinge of hereditary gout—and, in conclusion, of the disagreeable and inconvenient, but hitherto carefully concealed, weakness of my eyes.

'Upon this latter point,' said Madame Lalande, laughingly, 'you have been surely injudicious in coming to confession; for, without the confession, I take it for granted that no one would have accused you of the crime. By the by,' she continued, 'have you any recollection—' and here I fancied that a blush, even through the gloom of the apartment, became distinctly visible upon her chee —'have you any recollection, mon cher ami of this little ocular assistant, which now depends from my neck?'

As she spoke she twirled in her fingers the identical double eye-glass which had so overwhelmed me with confusion at the opera.

'Full well—alas! Do I remember it,' I exclaimed, pressing passionately the delicate hand which offered the glasses for my inspection. They formed a complex and magnificent toy, richly chased and filigreed, and gleaming with jewels, which, even in the deficient light, I could not help perceiving were of high value.

'Eh bien! Mon ami!' she resumed with a certain empressment of manner that rather surprised me—'Eh bien! Mon ami, you have earnestly besought of me a favour which you have been pleased to denominate priceless. You have demanded of me my hand upon the morrow. Should I yield to your entreaties—and, I may add, to the pleadings of my own bosom—would I not be entitled to demand of you a very—a very little boon in return?'

'Name it!' I exclaimed with an energy that had nearly drawn upon us the observation of the company, and restrained by their presence alone from throwing myself impetuously at her feet. 'Name it, my beloved, my Eugenie, my own—name it! But, alas! It is already yielded ere named.'

'You shall conquer, then, mon ami,' said she, 'for the sake of the Eugenie whom you love, this little weakness which you have at last confessed—this weakness more moral than physical—and which, let me assure you, is so unbecoming the nobility of your real nature—so inconsistent with the candour of your usual character—and which, if permitted further control, will assuredly involve you, sooner or later, in some very disagreeable scrape. You shall conquer, for my sake, this affectation which leads you, as you yourself acknowledge, to the tacit or implied denial of your infirmity of vision. For, this infirmity you virtually deny, in refusing to employ the customary means for its relief. You will understand me to say, then, that I wish you to wear spectacles—ah, hush—you have already consented to wear them, for my sake. You shall accept the little toy which I now hold in my hand, and which, though admirable as an aid to vision, is really of no very immense value as a gem. You perceive that, by a trifling modification thus —or thus—it can be adapted to the eyes in the form of spectacles, or worn in the waistcoat pocket as an eye-glass. It is in the former mode, however, and habitually, that you have already consented to wear it for my sake.'

This request— must I confess it? Confused me in no little degree. But the condition with which it was coupled rendered hesitation, of course, a matter altogether out of the question.

'It is done!' I cried, with all the enthusiasm that I could muster at the moment. 'It is done—it is most cheerfully agreed. I sacrifice every feeling for your sake. To-night I wear this dear eye-glass, as an eye-glass, and upon my heart; but with the earliest dawn of that morning which gives me the pleasure of calling you wife, I will place it upon my—upon my nose—and there wear it ever afterward, in the less romantic, and less fashionable, but certainly in the more serviceable, form which you desire.'

Our conversation now turned upon the details of our arrangements for the morrow. Talbot, I learned from my betrothed, had just arrived in town. I was to see him at once, and procure a carriage. The soiree would scarcely break up before two; and by this hour the vehicle was to be at the door, when, in the confusion occasioned by the departure of the company, Madame L. could easily enter it unobserved. We were then to call at the house of a clergyman who would be in waiting; there be married, drop Talbot, and proceed on a short tour to the East, leaving the fashionable world at home to make whatever comments upon the matter it thought best.

Having planned all this, I immediately took leave, and went in search of Talbot, but, on the way, I could not refrain from stepping into a hotel, for the purpose of inspecting the miniature; and this I did by the powerful aid of the glasses. The countenance was a surpassingly beautiful one! Those large luminous eyes—that proud Grecian nose—those dark luxuriant curls! 'Ah!' said I, exultingly to myself, 'this is indeed the speaking image of my beloved!' I turned the reverse, and discovered the words—'Eugenie Lalande—aged twenty-seven years and seven months.'

I found Talbot at home, and proceeded at once to acquaint him with my good fortune. He professed excessive astonishment, of course, but congratulated me most cordially, and proffered every assistance in his power. In a word, we carried out our arrangement to the letter, and, at two in the morning, just ten minutes after the ceremony, I found myself in a close carriage with Madame Lalande—with Mrs Simpson, I should say—and driving at a great rate out of town, in a direction Northeast by North, half-North.

It had been determined for us by Talbot, that, as we were to be up all night, we should make our first stop at C—, a village about twenty miles from the city, and there get an early breakfast and some repose, before proceeding upon our route. At four precisely, therefore, the carriage drew up at the door of the principal inn. I handed my adored wife out, and ordered breakfast forthwith. In the meantime we were shown into a small parlour, and sat down.

It was now nearly if not altogether daylight; and, as I gazed, enraptured, at the angel by my side, the singular idea came, all at once, into my head, that this was really the very first moment since my acquaintance with the celebrated loveliness of Madame Lalande, that I had enjoyed a near inspection of that loveliness by daylight at all.

'And now, mon ami,' said she, taking my hand, and so interrupting this train of reflection, 'and now, mon cher ami, since we are indissolubly one—since I have yielded to your passionate entreaties, and performed my portion of our agreement—I presume you have not forgotten that you also have a little favour to bestow—a little promise which it is your intention to keep. Ah! let me see! Let me remember! Yes; full easily do I call to mind the precise words of the dear promise you made to Eugenie last night. Listen! You spoke thus: "It is done! It is most cheerfully agreed! I sacrifice every feeling for your sake. To-night I wear this dear eye-glass as an eye-glass, and upon my heart; but with the earliest dawn of that morning which gives me the privilege of calling you wife, I will place it upon my—upon my nose—and there wear it ever afterward, in the less romantic, and less fashionable, but certainly in the more serviceable, form which you desire." These were the exact words, my beloved husband, were they not?'

'They were,' I said; 'you have an excellent memory; and assuredly, my beautiful Eugenie, there is no disposition on my part to evade the performance of the trivial promise they imply. See! Behold! They are becoming—rather—are they not?' And here, having arranged the glasses in the ordinary form of spectacles, I applied them gingerly in their proper position; while Madame Simpson, adjusting her cap, and folding her arms, sat bolt upright in her chair, in a somewhat stiff and prim, and indeed, in a somewhat undignified position.

'Goodness gracious me!' I exclaimed, almost at the very instant that the rim of the spectacles had settled upon my nose—'My goodness gracious me—why, what can be the matter with these glasses?' and taking them quickly off, I wiped them carefully with a silk handkerchief, and adjusted them again.

But if, in the first instance, there had occurred something which occasioned me surprise, in the second, this surprise became elevated into astonishment; and this astonishment was profound— was extreme—indeed I may say it was horrific. What, in the name of everything hideous, did this mean? Could I believe my eyes? Could I? That was the question. Was that—was that—was that rouge? And were those—and were those—were those wrinkles, upon the visage of Eugenie Lalande? And oh! Jupiter, and every one of the gods and goddesses, little and big! What—what— what—what had become of her teeth? I dashed the spectacles violently to the ground, and, leaping to my feet, stood erect in the middle of the floor, confronting Mrs Simpson, with my arms set a-kimbo, and grinning and foaming, but, at the same time, utterly speechless with terror and with rage.

Now I have already said that Madame Eugenie Lalande—that is to say, Simpson—spoke the English language but very little better than she wrote it, and for this reason she very properly never attempted to speak it upon ordinary occasions. But rage will carry a lady to any extreme; and in the present care it carried Mrs Simpson to the very extraordinary extreme of attempting to hold a conversation in a tongue that she did not altogether understand.

'Vell, Monsieur,' said she, after surveying me, in great apparent astonishment, for some moments—'Vell, Monsieur? And vat den? Vat de matter now? Is it de dance of de Saint Itusse dat you ave? If not like me, vat for vy buy de pig in the poke?'

'You wretch!' said I, catching my breath—'you—you—you villainous old hag!'

'Ag? Ole? Me not so ver ole, after all! Me not one single day more dan de eighty-doo.'

'Eighty-two!' I ejaculated, staggering to the wall—'eighty-two hundred thousand baboons! The miniature said twenty-seven years and seven months!'

'To be sure! Dat is so! Ver true! But den de portraite has been take for dese fifty-five year. Ven I go marry my segonde usbande, Monsieur Lalande, at dat time I had de portraite take for my daughter by my first usbande, Monsieur Moissart!'

'Moissart!' said I.

'Yes, Moissart,' said she, mimicking my pronunciation, which, to speak the truth, was none of the best—'and vat den? Vat you know about de Moissart?'

'Nothing, you old fright—I know nothing about him at all; only I had an ancestor of that name, once upon a time.'

'Dat name! And vat you ave for say to dat name? 'Tis ver goot name; and so is Voissart—dat is ver goot name too. My daughter, Mademoiselle Moissart, she marry von Monsieur Voissart— and de name is bot ver respectaable name.'

'Moissart?' I exclaimed, 'and Voissart! Why, what is it you mean?'

'Vat I mean? I mean Moissart and Voissart; and for de matter of dat, I mean Croissart and Froissart, too, if I only tink proper to mean it. My daughter's daughter, Mademoiselle Voissart, she marry von Monsieur Croissart, and den again, my daughter's grande daughter, Mademoiselle Croissart, she marry von Monsieur Froissart; and I suppose you say dat dat is not von ver respectaable name.'

'Froissart!' said I, beginning to faint, 'why, surely you don't say Moissart, and Voissart, and Croissart, and Froissart?'

'Yes,' she replied, leaning fully back in her chair, and stretching out her lower limbs at great length; 'yes, Moissart, and Voissart, and Croissart, and Froissart. But Monsieur Froissart, he vas von ver big

vat you call fool—he vas von ver great big donce like yourself—
for he lef la belle France for come to dis stupide Amerique—and
ven he get here he went and ave von ver stupide, von ver, ver
stupide sonn, so I hear, dough I not yet av ad de plaisir to meet
vid him—neither me nor my companion, de Madame Stephanie
Lalande. He is name de Napoleon Bonaparte Froissart, and I
suppose you say dat dat, too, is not von ver respectable name.'

Either the length or the nature of this speech, had the effect of
working up Mrs Simpson into a very extraordinary passion indeed;
and as she made an end of it, with great labour, she lumped up
from her chair like somebody bewitched, dropping upon the floor
an entire universe of bustle as she lumped. Once upon her feet,
she gnashed her gums, brandished her arms, rolled up her sleeves,
shook her fist in my face, and concluded the performance by tearing
the cap from her head, and with it an immense wig of the most
valuable and beautiful black hair, the whole of which she dashed
upon the ground with a yell, and there trammpled and danced a
fandango upon it, in an absolute ecstasy and agony of rage.

Meantime I sank aghast into the chair which she had vacated.
'Moissart and Voissart!' I repeated, thoughtfully, as she cut one of
her pigeon-wings, and 'Croissart and Froissart!' as she completed
another—'Moissart and Voissart and Croissart and Napoleon
Bonaparte Froissart! Why, you ineffable old serpent, that's me—
that's me—d'ye hear? That's me!' Here I screamed at the top of
my voice—'that's me-e-e! I am Napoleon Bonaparte Froissart! And
if I havn't married my great, great, grandmother, I wish I may be
everlastingly confounded!'

Madame Eugenie Lalande, *quasi* Simpson—formerly
Moissart—was, in sober fact, my great, great, grandmother. In her
youth she had been beautiful, and even at eighty-two, retained the
majestic height, the sculptural contour of head, the fine eyes and
the Grecian nose of her girlhood. By the aid of these, of pearl-
powder, of rouge, of false hair, false teeth, and false tournure, as

well as of the most skilful modistes of Paris, she contrived to hold a respectable footing among the beauties *en peu passées* of the French metropolis. In this respect, indeed, she might have been regarded as little less than the equal of the celebrated Ninon De L'Enclos.

She was immensely wealthy, and being left, for the second time, a widow without children, she bethought herself of my existence in America, and for the purpose of making me her heir, paid a visit to the United States, in company with a distant and exceedingly lovely relative of her second husband's—a Madame Stephanie Lalande.

At the opera, my great, great, grandmother's attention was arrested by my notice; and, upon surveying me through her eyeglass, she was struck with a certain family resemblance to herself. Thus interested, and knowing that the heir she sought was actually in the city, she made inquiries of her party respecting me. The gentleman who attended her knew my person, and told her who I was. The information thus obtained induced her to renew her scrutiny; and this scrutiny it was which so emboldened me that I behaved in the absurd manner already detailed. She returned my bow, however, under the impression that, by some odd accident, I had discovered her identity. When, deceived by my weakness of vision, and the arts of the toilet, in respect to the age and charms of the strange lady, I demanded so enthusiastically of Talbot who she was, he concluded that I meant the younger beauty, as a matter of course, and so informed me, with perfect truth, that she was 'the celebrated widow, Madame Lalande.'

In the street, next morning, my great, great, grandmother encountered Talbot, an old Parisian acquaintance; and the conversation, very naturally turned upon myself. My deficiencies of vision were then explained; for these were notorious, although I was entirely ignorant of their notoriety, and my good old relative discovered, much to her chagrin, that she had been deceived in supposing me aware of her identity, and that I had been merely making a fool of myself in making open love, in a theatre, to an old woman unknown. By way of punishing me for this imprudence, she concocted with Talbot a plot. He purposely kept out of my way to avoid giving me the introduction. My street inquiries about 'the lovely widow, Madame Lalande,' were supposed to refer to the younger lady, of course, and thus the conversation with the three gentlemen whom I encountered shortly after leaving Talbot's hotel will be easily explained, as also their allusion to Ninon De L'Enclos. I had no opportunity of seeing Madame Lalande closely during daylight; and, at her musical soiree, my silly weakness in refusing the aid of glasses effectually prevented me from making a discovery of her age. When 'Madame Lalande' was called upon to sing, the younger lady was intended; and it was she who arose to obey the call; my great, great, grandmother, to further the deception, arising at the same moment and accompanying her to the piano in the main drawing-room. Had I decided upon escorting her thither, it had been her design to suggest the propriety of my remaining where I was; but my own prudential views rendered this unnecessary. The songs which I so much admired, and which so confirmed my impression of the youth of my mistress, were executed by Madame Stephanie Lalande. The eye-glass was presented by way of adding a reproof to the hoax—a sting to the epigram of the deception. Its presentation afforded an opportunity for the lecture upon affectation with which I was so especially edified. It is almost superfluous to add that the glasses of the instrument, as worn by the old lady, had been exchanged by her for a pair better dapted to my years. They suited me, in fact, to a T.

The clergyman, who merely pretended to tie the fatal knot, was a boon companion of Talbot's, and no priest. He was an excellent 'whip', however; and having doffed his cassock to put on a great-coat, he drove the hack which conveyed the 'happy couple' out of town. Talbot took a seat at his side. The two scoundrels were thus 'in at the death', and through a half-open window of the back parlour of the inn, amused themselves in grinning at the *dénouement* of the drama. I believe I shall be forced to call them both out.

Nevertheless, I am not the husband of my great, great, grandmother; and this is a reflection which affords me infinite relief—but I am the husband of Madame Lalande—of Madame Stephanie Lalande—with whom my good old relative, besides making me her sole heir when she dies—if she ever does—has been at the trouble of concocting me a match. In conclusion: I am done forever with billets doux and am never to be met without spectacles.

6

THE FATHER

Guy de Maupassant

Love isn't a feeling; it is a practise.

I

He was a clerk in the Bureau of Public Education and lived at Batignolles. He took the omnibus to Paris every morning and always sat opposite a girl, with whom he fell in love.

She was employed in a shop and went in at the same time every day. She was a little brunette, one of those girls whose eyes are so dark that they look like black spots, on a complexion like ivory. He always saw her coming at the corner of the same street, and she generally had to run to catch the heavy vehicle, and sprang upon the steps before the horses had quite stopped. Then she got inside, out of breath, and, sitting down, looked round her.

The first time that he saw her, Francois Tessier liked the face. One sometimes meets a woman whom one longs to clasp in one's arms without even knowing her. That girl seemed to respond to some chord in his being, to that sort of ideal of love which one cherishes in the depths of the heart, without knowing it.

He looked at her intently, not meaning to be rude, and she became embarrassed and blushed. He noticed it, and tried to turn away his eyes; but he involuntarily fixed them upon her again every moment, although he tried to look in another direction; and, in a few days, they seemed to know each other without having spoken. He gave up his place to her when the omnibus was full, and got outside, though he was very sorry to do it. By this time she had got so far as to greet him with a little smile; and, although she always dropped her eyes under his looks, which she felt were too ardent, yet she did not appear offended at being looked at in such a manner.

They ended by speaking. A kind of rapid friendship had become established between them, a daily freemasonry of half an hour, and that was certainly one of the most charming half hours in his life to him. He thought of her all the rest of the day, saw her image continually during the long office hours. He was haunted and bewitched by that floating and yet tenacious recollection which the form of a beloved woman leaves in us, and it seemed to him that if he could win that little person it would be maddening happiness to him, almost above human realization.

Every morning she now shook hands with him, and he preserved the sense of that touch and the recollection of the gentle pressure of her little fingers until the next day, and he almost fancied that he preserved the imprint on his palm. He anxiously waited for this short omnibus ride, while Sundays seemed to him heartbreaking days. However, there was no doubt that she loved him, for one Saturday, in spring, she promised to go and lunch with him at Maisons-Laffitte the next day.

II

She was at the railway station first, which surprised him, but she said: 'Before going, I want to speak to you. We have twenty minutes, and that is more than I shall take for what I have to say.'

She trembled as she hung on his arm, and looked down, her cheeks pale, as she continued: 'I do not want you to be deceived in me, and I shall not go there with you, unless you promise, unless you swear—not to do—not to do anything—that is at all improper.'

She had suddenly become as red as a poppy, and said no more. He did not know what to reply, for he was happy and disappointed at the same time. He should love her less, certainly, if he knew that her conduct was light, but then it would be so charming, so delicious to have a little flirtation.

As he did not say anything, she began to speak again in an agitated voice and with tears in her eyes. 'If you do not promise to respect me altogether, I shall return home.' And so he squeezed her arm tenderly and replied: 'I promise, you shall only do what you like.' She appeared relieved in mind, and asked, with a smile: 'Do you really mean it?' And he looked into her eyes and replied: 'I swear it!' 'Now you may take the tickets,' she said.

During the journey they could hardly speak, as the carriage was full, and when they reached Maisons-Laffitte they went toward the Seine. The sun, which shone full on the river, on the leaves and the grass, seemed to be reflected in their hearts, and they went, hand in hand, along the bank, looking at the shoals of little fish swimming near the bank, and they walked on, brimming over with happiness, as if they were walking on air.

At last she said: 'How foolish you must think me!'

'Why?' he asked. 'To come out like this, all alone with you.'

'Certainly not; it is quite natural.' 'No, no; it is not natural for me—because I do not wish to commit a fault, and yet this is how girls fall. But if you only knew how wretched it is, every day the same thing, every day in the month and every month in the year. I live quite alone with mamma, and as she has had a great deal of trouble, she is not very cheerful. I do the best I can, and try to laugh in spite of everything, but I do not always succeed. But, all the same, it was wrong in me to come, though you, at any rate, will not be sorry.'

By way of an answer, he kissed her ardently on the ear that was nearest him, but she moved from him with an abrupt movement, and, getting suddenly angry, exclaimed: 'Oh! Monsieur Francois, after what you swore to me!' And they went back to Maisons-Laffitte.

They had lunch at the Petit-Havre, a low house, buried under four enormous poplar trees, by the side of the river. The air, the heat, the weak white wine and the sensation of being so close together made them silent; their faces were flushed and they had a feeling of oppression; but, after the coffee, they regained their high spirits, and, having crossed the Seine, started off along the bank, toward the village of La Frette. Suddenly he asked: 'What is your name?'

'Louise.'

'Louise,' he repeated and said nothing more.

The girl picked daisies and made them into a great bunch, while he sang vigorously, as unrestrained as a colt that has been turned into a meadow. On their left a vine-covered slope followed the river. Francois stopped motionless with astonishment: 'Oh, look there!' he said.

The vines had come to an end, and the whole slope was covered with lilac bushes in flower. It was a purple wood! A kind of great carpet of flowers stretched over the earth, reaching as far as the village, more than two miles off. She also stood, surprised and delighted, and murmured: 'Oh! how pretty!' And, crossing a meadow, they ran toward that curious low hill, which, every year, furnishes all the lilac that is drawn through Paris on the carts of the flower venders.

There was a narrow path beneath the trees, so they took it, and when they came to a small clearing, sat down.

Swarms of flies were buzzing around them and making a continuous, gentle sound, and the sun, the bright sun of a perfectly still day, shone over the bright slopes and from that forest of blossoms a powerful fragrance was borne toward them, a breath of perfume, the breath of the flowers.

A church clock struck in the distance, and they embraced gently, then, without the knowledge of anything but that kiss, lay down on the grass. But she soon came to herself with the feeling of a great misfortune, and began to cry and sob with grief, with her face buried in her hands.

He tried to console her, but she wanted to start to return and to go home immediately; and she kept saying, as she walked along quickly: 'Good heavens! Good heavens!'

He said to her: 'Louise! Louise! Please let us stop here.' But now her cheeks were red and her eyes hollow, and, as soon as they got to the railway station in Paris, she left him without even saying good-by.

III

When he met her in the omnibus, next day, she appeared to him to be changed and thinner, and she said to him: 'I want to speak to you; we will get down at the Boulevard.'

As soon as they were on the pavement, she said:

'We must bid each other good-by; I cannot meet you again.' 'But why?' he asked. 'Because I cannot; I have been culpable, and I will not be so again.'

Then he implored her, tortured by his love, but she replied firmly: 'No, I cannot, I cannot.' He, however, only grew all the more excited and promised to marry her, but she said again: 'No,' and left him.

For a week he did not see her. He could not manage to meet her, and, as he did not know her address, he thought that he had lost her altogether. On the ninth day, however, there was a ring at his bell, and when he opened the door, she was there. She threw herself into his arms and did not resist any longer, and for three months they were close friends. He was beginning to grow tired of her, when she whispered something to him, and then he had one idea and wish—to break with her at any price. As, however, he could not do that, not knowing how to begin, or what to say, full of anxiety through fear of the consequences of his rash indiscretion, he took a decisive step: one night he changed his lodgings and disappeared.

The blow was so heavy that she did not look, for the man who had abandoned her, but threw herself at her mother's knees and confessed her misfortune, and, some months after, gave birth to a boy.

IV

Years passed, and Francois Tessier grew old, without there having been any alteration in his life. He led the dull, monotonous life of an office clerk, without hope and without expectation. Every day he got up at the same time, went through the same streets, went through the same door, past the same porter, went into the same office, sat in the same chair, and did the same work. He was alone in the world, alone during the day in the midst of his different colleagues, and alone at night in his bachelor's lodgings, and he laid by a hundred francs a month against old age.

Every Sunday he went to the Champs-Elysees, to watch the elegant people, the carriages and the pretty women, and the next day he used to say to one of his colleagues: 'The return of the carriages from the Bois du Boulogne was very brilliant yesterday.' One fine Sunday morning, however, he went into the Parc Monceau, where the mothers and nurses, sitting on the sides of the walks, watched the children playing, and suddenly Francois Tessier started. A woman passed by, holding two children by the hand, a little boy of about ten and a little girl of four. It was she!

He walked another hundred yards anti then fell into a chair, choking with emotion. She had not recognized him, and so he came back, wishing to see her again. She was sitting down now, and the boy was standing by her side very quietly, while the little girl was making sand castles. It was she, it was certainly she, but she had the reserved appearance of a lady, was dressed simply, and looked self-possessed and dignified. He looked at her from a distance, for he did not venture to go near; but the little boy raised his head, and Francois Tessier felt himself tremble. It was his own son, there could be no doubt of that. And, as he looked at him, he thought he could recognize himself as he appeared in an old photograph taken years ago. He remained hidden behind a tree, waiting for her to go that he might follow her.

He did not sleep that night. The idea of the child especially tormented him. His son! Oh, if he could only have known, have been sure! But what could he have done? However, he went to the house where she lived and asked about her. He was told that a neighbour, an honourable man of strict morals, had been touched by her distress and had married her; he knew the fault she had committed and had married her, and had even recognized the child, his, Francois Tessier's child, as his own.

He returned to the Parc Monceau every Sunday, for then he always saw her, and each time he was seized with a mad, an irresistible longing to take his son into his arms, to cover him with kisses and to steal him, to carry him off.

He suffered horribly in his wretched isolation as an old bachelor, with nobody to care for him, and he also suffered atrocious mental torture, torn by paternal tenderness springing from remorse, longing and jealousy and from that need of loving one's own children which nature has implanted in all. At last he determined to make a despairing attempt, and, going up to her, as she entered the park, he said, standing in the middle of the path, pale and with trembling lips: 'You do not recognize me.' She raised her eyes, looked at him, uttered an exclamation of horror, of terror, and, taking the two children by the hand, she rushed away, dragging them after her, while he went home and wept inconsolably.

Months passed without his seeing her again, but he suffered, day and night, for he was a prey to his paternal love. He would gladly have died, if he could only have kissed his son; he would have committed murder, performed any task, braved any danger, ventured anything. He wrote to her, but she did not reply, and, after writing her some twenty letters, he saw that there was no hope of altering her determination, and then he formed the desperate resolution of writing to her husband, being quite prepared to receive a bullet from a revolver, if need be. His letter only consisted of a few lines, as follows:

> Monsieur: You must have a perfect horror of my name, but I am so wretched, so overcome by misery that my only hope is in you, and, therefore, I venture to request you to grant me an interview of only five minutes.
>
> I have the honour, etc.

The next day he received the reply:

'Monsieur: I shall expect you to-morrow, Tuesday, at five o'clock.'

As he went up the staircase, Francois Tessier's heart beat so violently that he had to stop several times. There was a dull and violent thumping noise in his breast, as of some animal galloping; and he could breathe only with difficulty, and had to hold on to the banisters, in order not to fall.

He rang the bell on the third floor, and when a maid servant had opened the door, he asked: 'Does Monsieur Flamel live here?' 'Yes, Monsieur. Kindly come in.'

He was shown into the drawing-room; he was alone, and waited, feeling bewildered, as in the midst of a catastrophe, until a door opened, and a man came in. He was tall, serious and rather stout, and wore a black frock coat, and pointed to a chair with his hand. Francois Tessier sat down, and then said, with choking breath: 'Monsieur—monsieur—I do not know whether you know my name—whether you know—'

Monsieur Flamel interrupted him. 'You need not tell it me,

Monsieur, I know it. My wife has spoken to me about you.' He spoke in the dignified tone of voice of a good man who wishes to be severe, and with the commonplace stateliness of an honourable man, and Francois Tessier continued:

'Well, Monsieur, I want to say this: I am dying of grief, of remorse, of shame, and I would like once, only once to kiss the child.'

Monsieur Flamel got up and rang the bell, and when the servant came in, he said: 'Will you bring Louis here?' When she had gone out, they remained face to face, without speaking, as they had nothing more to say to one another, and waited. Then, suddenly, a little boy of ten rushed into the room and ran up to the man whom he believed to be his father, but he stopped when he saw the stranger, and Monsieur Flamel kissed him and said: 'Now, go and kiss that gentleman, my dear.' And the child went up to the stranger and looked at him.

Francois Tessier had risen. He let his hat fall, and was ready to fall himself as he looked at his son, while Monsieur Flamel had turned away, from a feeling of delicacy, and was looking out of the window.

The child waited in surprise; but he picked up the hat and gave it to the stranger. Then Francois, taking the child up in his arms, began to kiss him wildly all over his face; on his eyes, his cheeks, his mouth, his hair; and the youngster, frightened at the shower of kisses, tried to avoid them, turned away his head, and pushed away the man's face with his little hands. But suddenly Francois Tessier put him down and cried: 'Good-by! Good-by!' And he rushed out of the room as if he had been a thief.

7

EVELINE

James Joyce

O let not time deceive you,
You cannot conquer time.

She sat at the window watching the evening invade the avenue. Her head was leaned against the window curtains and in her nostrils was the odour of dusty cretonne. She was tired. Few people passed. The man out of the last house passed on his way home; she heard his footsteps clacking along the concrete pavement and afterwards crunching on the cinder path before the new red houses.

One time there used to be a field there in which they used to play every evening with other people's children. Then a man from Belfast bought the field and built houses in it—not like their little brown houses but bright brick houses with shining roofs. The children of the avenue used to play together in that field—the Devines, the Waters, the Dunns, little Keogh the cripple, she and her brothers and sisters.

Ernest, however, never played: he was too grown up. Her father used often to hunt them in out of the field with his blackthorn stick; but usually little Keogh used to keep nix and call out when he saw her father coming. Still they seemed to have been rather happy then. Her father was not so bad then; and besides, her mother was alive. That was a long time ago; she and her brothers and sisters were all grown up; her mother was dead. Tizzie Dunn was dead, too, and the Waters had gone back to England. Everything changes.

Now she was going to go away like the others, to leave her home. Home! She looked round the room, reviewing all its familiar objects which she had dusted once a week for so many years, wondering where on earth all the dust came from. Perhaps she would never see again those familiar objects from which she had never dreamed of being divided.

And yet during all those years she had never found out the name of the priest whose yellowing photograph hung on the wall above the broken harmonium beside the coloured print of the promises made to Blessed Margaret Mary Alacoque. He had been a school friend of her father. Whenever he showed the photograph to a visitor her father used to pass it with a casual word: 'He is in Melbourne now.'

She had consented to go away, to leave her home. Was that wise? She tried to weigh each side of the question. In her home anyway she had shelter and food; she had those whom she had known all her life about her. Of course she had to work hard, both in the house and at business. What would they say of her in the Stores when they found out that she had run away with a fellow? Say she was a fool, perhaps; and her place would be filled up by advertisement.

Miss Gavan would be glad. She had always had an edge on her, especially whenever there were people listening. 'Miss Hill, don't you see these ladies are waiting?' 'Look lively, Miss Hill, please.' She would not cry many tears at leaving the Stores. But in her new home, in a distant unknown country, it would not be like that. Then she would be married—she, Eveline. People would treat her with respect then. She would not be treated as her mother had been. Even now, though she was over nineteen, she sometimes felt herself in danger of her father's violence. She knew it was that that had given her the palpitations.

When they were growing up he had never gone for her like he used to go for Harry and Ernest, because she was a girl; but latterly he had begun to threaten her and say what he would do to her only for her dead mother's sake. And now she had nobody to protect her. Ernest was dead and Harry, who was in the church decorating business, was nearly always down somewhere in the country. Besides, the invariable squabble for money on Saturday nights had begun to weary her unspeakably. She always gave her entire wages—seven shillings—and Harry always sent up what he could but the trouble was to get any money from her father. He said she used to squander the money, that she had no head, that he wasn't going to give her his hard-earned money to throw about the streets, and much more, for he was usually fairly bad on Saturday night.

In the end he would give her the money and ask her had she any intention of buying Sunday's dinner. Then she had to rush out as quickly as she could and do her marketing, holding her black leather purse tightly in her hand as she elbowed her way through the crowds and returning home late under her load of provisions. She had hard work to keep the house together and to see that the two young children who had been left to her charge went to school regularly and got their meals regularly. It was hard work—a hard life—but now that she was about to leave it she did not find it a wholly undesirable life. She was about to explore another life with Frank.

Frank was very kind, manly, open-hearted. She was to go away with him by the night-boat to be his wife and to live with him in Buenos Ayres where he had a home waiting for her. How well she remembered the first time she had seen him; he was lodging in a house on the main road where she used to visit. It seemed a few weeks ago. He was standing at the gate, his peaked cap pushed back on his head and his hair tumbled forward over a face of bronze. Then they had come to know each other. He used to meet her outside the Stores every evening and see her home. He took her to see *The Bohemian Girl* and she felt elated as she sat in an unaccustomed part of the theatre with him. He was awfully fond of music and sang a little. People knew that they were court-
ing

and, when he sang about the lass that loves a sailor, she always felt pleasantly confused. He used to call her 'Poppens' out of fun.

First of all it had been an excitement for her to have a fellow and then she had begun to like him. He had tales of distant countries. He had started as a deck boy at a pound a month on a ship of the Allan Line going out to Canada. He told her the names of the ships he had been on and the names of the different services. He had sailed through the Straits of Magellan and he told her stories of the terrible Patagonians. He had fallen on his feet in Buenos Ayres, he said, and had come over to the old country just for a holiday.

Of course, her father had found out the affair and had forbidden her to have anything to say to him. 'I know these sailor chaps,' he said. One day he had quarrelled with Frank and after that she had to meet her lover secretly. The evening deepened in the avenue. The white of two letters in her lap grew indistinct. One was to Harry; the other was to her father. Ernest had been her favourite but she liked Harry too.

Her father was becoming old lately, she noticed; he would miss her. Sometimes he could be very nice. Not long before, when she had been laid up for a day, he had read her out a ghost story and made toast for her at the fire. Another day, when their mother was alive, they had all gone for a picnic to the Hill of Howth. She remembered her father putting on her mother's bonnet to make the children laugh.

Her time was running out but she continued to sit by the window, leaning her head against the window curtain, inhaling the odour of dusty cretonne. Down far in the avenue she could hear a street organ playing. She knew the air. Strange that it should come that very night to remind her of the promise to her mother, her promise to keep the home together as long as she could. She remembered the last night of her mother's illness; she was again in the close dark room at the other side of the hall and outside she heard a melancholy air of Italy.

The organ-player had been ordered to go away and given sixpence. She remembered her father strutting back into the sickroom saying: 'Damned Italians! Coming over here!' As she mused the pitiful vision of her mother's life laid its spell on the very quick of her being—that life of commonplace sacrifices closing in final craziness. She trembled as she heard again her mother's voice saying constantly with foolish insistence: 'Derevaun Seraun! Derevaun Seraun!' She stood up in a sudden impulse of terror. Escape! She must escape! Frank would save her. He would give her life, perhaps love, too. But she wanted to live. Why should she be unhappy? She had a right to happiness. Frank would take her in his arms, fold her in his arms. He would save her.

∞

She stood among the swaying crowd in the station at the North Wall. He held her hand and she knew that he was speaking to her, saying something about the passage over and over again. The station was full of soldiers with brown baggages. Through the wide doors of the sheds she caught a glimpse of the black mass of the boat, lying in beside the quay wall, with illumined portholes. She answered nothing. She felt her cheek pale and cold and, out of a maze of distress, she prayed to God to direct her, to show her what was her duty. The boat blew a long mournful whistle into the mist.

If she went, tomorrow she would be on the sea with Frank, steaming towards Buenos Ayres. Their passage had been booked. Could she still draw back after all he had done for her? Her distress awoke a nausea in her body and she kept moving her lips in silent fervent prayer. A bell clanged upon her heart. She felt him seize her hand: 'Come!' All the seas of the world tumbled about her heart. He was drawing her into them: he would drown her. She gripped with both hands at the iron railing.

'Come!'

No! No! No! It was impossible. Her hands clutched the iron in frenzy. Amid the seas she sent a cry of anguish.

'Eveline! Evvy!'

He rushed beyond the barrier and called to her to follow. He was shouted at to go on but he still called to her. She set her white face to him, passive, like a helpless animal. Her eyes gave him no sign of love or farewell or recognition.

8

BY COURIER

O. Henry

Reading lines is important; reading between the lines is much more important. And above all what remains is the remnants of compassion and love.

It was neither the season nor the hour when the Park had frequenters; and it is likely that the young lady, who was seated on one of the benches at the side of the walk, had merely obeyed a sudden impulse to sit for a while and enjoy a foretaste of coming Spring.

She rested there, pensive and still. A certain melancholy that touched her countenance must have been of recent birth, for it had not yet altered the fine and youthful contours of her cheek, nor subdued the arch though resolute curve of her lips.

A tall young man came striding through the park along the path near which she sat. Behind him tagged a boy carrying a suit-case. At sight of the young lady, the man's face changed to red and back to pale again. He watched her countenance as he drew nearer, with hope and anxiety mingled on his own. He passed within a few yards of her, but he saw no evidence that she was aware of his presence or existence.

Some fifty yards further on he suddenly stopped and sat on a bench at one side. The boy dropped the suit-case and stared at him with wondering, shrewd eyes. The young man took out his handkerchief and wiped his brow. It was a good handkerchief, a good brow, and the young man was good to look at. He said to the boy:

'I want you to take a message to that young lady on that bench. Tell her I am on my way to the station, to leave for San Francisco, where I shall join that Alaska moose-hunting expedition. Tell her that, since she has commanded me neither to speak nor to write to her, I take this means of making one last appeal to her sense of justice, for the sake of what has been. Tell her that to condemn and discard one who has not deserved such treatment, without giving him her reasons or a chance to explain is contrary to her nature as I believe it to be. Tell her that I have thus, to a certain degree, disobeyed her injunctions, in the hope that she may yet be inclined to see justice done. Go, and tell her that.'

The young man dropped a half-dollar into the boy's hand. The boy looked at him for a moment with bright, canny eyes out of a dirty, intelligent face, and then set off at a run. He approached the lady on the bench a little doubtfully, but unembarrassed. He touched the brim of the old plaid bicycle cap perched on the back of his head. The lady looked at him coolly, without prejudice or favour.

'Lady,' he said, 'dat gent on de oder bench sent yer a song and dance by me. If yer don't know de guy, and he's tryin' to do de Johnny act, say de word, and I'll call a cop in t'ree minutes. If yer does know him, and he's on de square, w'y I'll spiel yer de bunch of hot air he sent yer.'

The young lady betrayed a faint interest.

'A song and dance!' she said, in a deliberate sweet voice that seemed to clothe her words in a diaphanous garment of impalpable irony. 'A new idea—in the troubadour line, I suppose. I—used to know the gentleman who sent you, so I think it will hardly be necessary to call the police. You may execute your song and dance, but do not sing too loudly. It is a little early yet for open-air vaudeville, and we might attract attention.'

'Awe,' said the boy, with a shrug down the length of him, 'yer know what I mean, lady. 'Tain't a turn, it's wind. He told me to tell yer he's got his collars and cuffs in dat grip for a scoot clean out to 'Frisco. Den he's goin' to shoot snow-birds in de Klondike. He says yer told him not to send 'round no more pink notes nor come hangin' over de garden gate, and he takes dis means of puttin' yer wise. He says yer refereed him out like a has-been, and never give him no chance to kick at de decision. He says yer swiped him, and never said why.'

The slightly awakened interest in the young lady's eyes did not abate. Perhaps it was caused by either the originality or the audacity of the snow-bird hunter, in thus circumventing her express commands against the ordinary modes of communication. She fixed her eye on a statue standing disconsolate in the dishevelled park, and spoke into the transmitter:

'Tell the gentleman that I need not repeat to him a description of my ideals. He knows what they have been and what they still are. So far as they touch on this case, absolute loyalty and truth are the ones paramount. Tell him that I have studied my own heart as well as one can, and I know its weakness as well as I do its needs. That is why I decline to hear his pleas, whatever they may be. I did not condemn him through hearsay or doubtful evidence, and that is why I made no charge. But, since he persists in hearing what he already well knows, you may convey the matter.

'Tell him that I entered the conservatory that evening from the rear, to cut a rose for my mother. Tell him I saw him and Miss Ashburton beneath the pink oleander. The tableau was pretty, but the pose and juxtaposition were too eloquent and evident to require explanation. I left the conservatory, and, at the same time, the rose and my ideal. You may carry that song and dance to your impresario.'

'I'm shy on one word, lady. Jux—jux—put me wise on dat, will yer?'

'Juxtaposition—or you may call it propinquity—or, if you like, being rather too near for one maintaining the position of an ideal.'

The gravel spun from beneath the boy's feet. He stood by the other bench. The man's eyes interrogated him, hungrily. The boy's were shining with the impersonal zeal of the translator.

'De lady says dat she's on to de fact dat gals is dead easy when a feller comes spielin' ghost stories and tryin' to make up, and dat's why she won't listen to no soft-soap. She says she caught yer dead to rights, huggin' a bunch o' calico in de hot-house. She side-stepped in to pull some posies and yer was squeezin' de oder gal to beat de band. She says it looked cute, all right all right, but it made her sick. She says yer better git busy, and make a sneak for de train.'

The young man gave a low whistle and his eyes flashed with a sudden thought. His hand flew to the inside pocket of his coat, and drew out a handful of letters. Selecting one, he handed it to the boy, following it with a silver dollar from his vest-pocket.

'Give that letter to the lady,' he said, 'and ask her to read it. Tell her that it should explain the situation. Tell her that, if she had mingled a little trust with her conception of the ideal, much heartache might have been avoided. Tell her that the loyalty she prizes so much has never wavered. Tell her I am waiting for an answer.'

The messenger stood before the lady.

'De gent says he's had de ski-bunk put on him widout no cause. He says he's no bum guy; and, lady, yer read dat letter, and I'll bet yer he's a white sport, all right.'

The young lady unfolded the letter; somewhat doubtfully, and read it.

Dear Dr. Arnold,

I want to thank you for your most kind and opportune aid to my daughter last Friday evening, when she was overcome by an attack of her old heart-trouble in the conservatory at Mrs Waldron's reception. Had you not been near to catch her as she fell and to render proper attention, we might have lost her. I would be glad if you would call and undertake the treatment of her case.

Gratefully yours,
Robert Ashburton

The young lady refolded the letter, and handed it to the boy.

'De gent wants an answer,' said the messenger. 'Wot's de word?'

The lady's eyes suddenly flashed on him, bright, smiling and wet.

'Tell that guy on the other bench,' she said, with a happy, tremulous laugh, 'that his girl wants him.'

9

THE LADY OR THE TIGER?

Frank R. Stockton

Ambiguity draws a blurred line between unconditional love and jealousy. It is for the reader to decide!

In the very olden time there lived a semi-barbaric king, whose ideas, though somewhat polished and sharpened by the progressiveness of distant Latin neighbours, were still large, florid, and untrammelled, as became the half of him which was barbaric. He was a man of exuberant fancy, and, withal, of an authority so irresistible that, at his will, he turned his varied fancies into facts. He was greatly given to self-communing, and, when he and himself agreed upon anything, the thing was done. When every member of his domestic and political systems moved smoothly in its appointed course, his nature was bland and genial; but, whenever there was a little hitch, and some of his orbs got out of their orbits, he was blander and more genial still, for nothing pleased him so much as to make the crooked straight and crush down uneven places.

Among the borrowed notions by which his barbarism had become semified was that of the public arena, in which, by exhibitions of manly and beastly valour, the minds of his subjects were refined and cultured.

But even here the exuberant and barbaric fancy asserted itself. The arena of the king was built, not to give the people an opportunity of hearing the rhapsodies of dying gladiators, nor to enable them to view the inevitable conclusion of a conflict between religious opinions and hungry jaws, but for purposes far better adapted to widen and develop the mental energies of the people. This vast amphitheatre, with its encircling galleries, its mysterious vaults, and its unseen passages, was an agent of poetic justice, in which crime was punished, or virtue rewarded, by the decrees of an impartial and incorruptible chance.

When a subject was accused of a crime of sufficient importance to interest the king, public notice was given that on an appointed day the fate of the accused person would be decided in the king's arena, a structure which well deserved its name, for, although its form and plan were borrowed from afar, its purpose emanated solely from the brain of this man, who, every barleycorn a king, knew no tradition to which he owed more allegiance than pleased his fancy, and who ingrafted on every adopted form of human thought and action the rich growth of his barbaric idealism.

When all the people had assembled in the galleries, and the king, surrounded by his court, sat high up on his throne of royal state on one side of the arena, he gave a signal, a door beneath him opened, and the accused subject stepped out into the amphitheatre. Directly opposite him, on the other side of the enclosed space, were two doors, exactly alike and side by side. It was the duty and the privilege of the person on trial to walk directly to these doors and open one of them. He could open either door he pleased; he was subject to no guidance or influence but that of the aforementioned impartial and incorruptible chance. If he opened the one, there came out of it a hungry tiger, the fiercest and most cruel that could be procured, which immediately sprang upon him and tore him to pieces as a punishment for his guilt. The moment that the case of the criminal was thus decided, doleful iron bells were clanged, great wails went up from the hired mourners posted on the outer rim of the arena, and the vast audience, with bowed heads and downcast hearts, wended slowly their homeward way, mourning greatly that one so young and fair, or so old and respected, should have merited so dire a fate.

But, if the accused person opened the other door, there came forth from it a lady, the most suitable to his years and station that his majesty could select among his fair subjects, and to this lady he was immediately married, as a reward of his innocence. It mattered not that he might already possess a wife and family, or that his affections might be engaged upon an object of his own selection; the king allowed no such subordinate arrangements to interfere with his great scheme of retribution and reward. The exercises, as in the other instance, took place immediately, and in the arena. Another door opened beneath the king, and a priest, followed by a band of choristers, and dancing maidens blowing joyous airs on golden horns and treading an epithalamic measure, advanced to where the pair stood, side by side, and the wedding was promptly and cheerily solemnized. Then the gay brass bells rang forth their merry peals, the people shouted glad hurrahs, and the innocent man, preceded by children strewing flowers on his path, led his bride to his home.

This was the king's semi-barbaric method of administering justice. Its perfect fairness is obvious. The criminal could not know out of which door would come the lady; he opened either he pleased, without having the slightest idea whether, in the next instant, he was to be devoured or married. On some occasions the tiger came out of one door, and on some out of the other. The decisions of this tribunal were not only fair, they were positively determinate: the accused person was instantly punished if he found himself guilty, and, if innocent, he was rewarded on the spot, whether he liked it or not. There was no escape from the judgments of the king's arena.

The institution was a very popular one. When the people gathered together on one of the great trial days, they never knew whether they were to witness a bloody slaughter or a hilarious wedding. This element of uncertainty lent an interest to the occasion which it could not otherwise have attained. Thus, the masses were entertained and pleased, and the thinking part of the community could bring no charge of unfairness against this plan, for did not the accused person have the whole matter in his own hands?

This semi-barbaric king had a daughter as blooming as his most florid fancies, and with a soul as fervent and imperious as his own. As is usual in such cases, she was the apple of his eye, and was loved by him above all humanity. Among his courtiers was a young man of that fineness of blood and lowness of station common to the conventional heroes of romance who love royal maidens. This royal maiden was well satisfied with her lover, for he was handsome and brave to a degree unsurpassed in all this kingdom, and she loved him with an ardour that had enough of barbarism in it to make it exceedingly warm and strong. This love affair moved on happily for many months, until one day the king happened to discover its existence. He did not hesitate nor waver in regard to his duty in the premises. The youth was immediately cast into prison, and a day was appointed for his trial in the king's arena. This, of course, was an especially important occasion, and his majesty, as well as all the people, was greatly interested in the workings and development of this trial. Never before had such a case occurred; never before had a subject dared to love the daughter of the king. In after years such things became commonplace enough, but then they were in no slight degree novel and startling.

The tiger-cages of the kingdom were searched for the most savage and relentless beasts, from which the fiercest monster might be selected for the arena; and the ranks of maiden youth and beauty throughout the land were carefully surveyed by competent judges in order that the young man might have a fitting bride in case fate did not determine for him a different destiny. Of course, everybody knew that the deed with which the accused was charged had been done. He had loved the princess, and neither he, she, nor any one else, thought of denying the fact; but the king would not think of allowing any fact of this kind to interfere with the workings of the tribunal, in which he took such great delight and satisfaction. No matter how the affair turned out, the youth would be disposed of, and the king would take an aesthetic pleasure in watching the course of events, which would determine whether or not the young man had done wrong in allowing himself to love the princess.

The appointed day arrived. From far and near the people gathered, and thronged the great galleries of the arena, and crowds, unable to gain admittance, massed themselves against its outside walls. The king and his court were in their places, opposite the twin doors, those fateful portals, so terrible in their similarity.

All was ready. The signal was given. A door beneath the royal party opened, and the lover of the princess walked into the arena. Tall, beautiful, fair, his appearance was greeted with a low hum of admiration and anxiety. Half the audience had not known so grand a youth had lived among them. No wonder the princess loved him! What a terrible thing for him to be there!

As the youth advanced into the arena he turned, as the custom was, to bow to the king, but he did not think at all of that royal personage. His eyes were fixed upon the princess, who sat to the right of her father. Had it not been for the moiety of barbarism in her nature it is probable that lady would not have been there, but her intense and fervid soul would not allow her to be absent on an occasion in which she was so terribly interested. From the moment that the decree had gone forth that her lover should decide his fate in the king's arena, she had thought of nothing, night or day, but this great event and the various subjects connected with it. Possessed of more power, influence, and force of character than any one who had ever before been interested in such a case, she had done what no other person had done—she had possessed herself of the secret of the doors. She knew in which of the two rooms, that lay behind those doors, stood the cage of the tiger, with its open front, and in which waited the lady. Through these thick doors, heavily curtained with skins on the inside, it was impossible that any noise or suggestion should come from within to the person who should approach to raise the latch of one of them. But gold, and the power of a woman's will, had brought the secret to the princess.

And not only did she know in which room stood the lady ready to emerge, all blushing and radiant, should her door be opened, but she knew who the lady was. It was one of the fairest and loveliest of the damsels of the court who had been selected as the reward of the accused youth, should he be proved innocent of the crime of aspiring to one so far above him; and the princess hated her. Often had she seen, or imagined that she had seen, this fair creature throwing glances of admiration upon the person of her lover, and sometimes she thought these glances were perceived, and even returned. Now and then she had seen them talking together; it was but for a moment or two, but much can be said in a brief space; it may have been on most unimportant topics, but how could she know that? The girl was lovely, but she had dared to raise her eyes to the loved one of the princess; and, with all the intensity of the savage blood transmitted to her through long lines of wholly barbaric ancestors, she hated the woman who blushed and trembled behind that silent door.

When her lover turned and looked at her, and his eye met hers as she sat there, paler and whiter than any one in the vast ocean of anxious faces about her, he saw, by that power of quick perception which is given to those whose souls are one, that she knew behind which door crouched the tiger, and behind which stood the lady. He had expected her to know it. He understood her nature, and his soul was assured that she would never rest until she had made plain to herself this thing, hidden to all other lookers-on, even to the king. The only hope for the youth in which there was any element of certainty was based upon the success of the princess in discovering this mystery; and the moment he looked upon her, he saw she had succeeded, as in his soul he knew she would succeed.

Then it was that his quick and anxious glance asked the question: 'Which?' It was as plain to her as if he shouted it from where he stood. There was not an instant to be lost. The question was asked in a flash; it must be answered in another.

Her right arm lay on the cushioned parapet before her. She raised her hand, and made a slight, quick movement toward the right. No one but her lover saw her. Every eye but his was fixed on the man in the arena.

He turned, and with a firm and rapid step he walked across the empty space. Every heart stopped beating, every breath was held, every eye was fixed immovably upon that man. Without the slightest hesitation, he went to the door on the right, and opened it.

Now, the point of the story is this: Did the tiger come out of that door, or did the lady?

The more we reflect upon this question, the harder it is to answer. It involves a study of the human heart which leads us through devious mazes of passion, out of which it is difficult to find our way. Think of it, fair reader, not as if the decision of the question depended upon yourself, but upon that hot-blooded, semi-barbaric princess, her soul at a white heat beneath the combined fires of despair and jealousy. She had lost him, but who should have him?

How often, in her waking hours and in her dreams, had she started in wild horror, and covered her face with her hands as she thought of her lover opening the door on the other side of which waited the cruel fangs of the tiger!

But how much oftener had she seen him at the other door! How in her grievous reveries had she gnashed her teeth, and torn her hair, when she saw his start of rapturous delight as he opened the door of the lady! How her soul had burned in agony when she had seen him rush to meet that woman, with her flushing cheek and sparkling eye of triumph; when she had seen him lead her forth, his whole frame kindled with the joy of recovered life; when she had heard the glad shouts from the multitude, and the wild ringing of the happy bells; when she had seen the priest, with his joyous followers, advance to the couple, and make them man and wife before her very eyes; and when she had seen them walk away together upon their path of flowers, followed by the tremendous shouts of the hilarious multitude, in which her one despairing shriek was lost and drowned!

Would it not be better for him to die at once, and go to wait for her in the blessed regions of semi-barbaric futurity?

And yet, that awful tiger, those shrieks, that blood!

Her decision had been indicated in an instant, but it had been made after days and nights of anguished deliberation. She had known she would be asked, she had decided what she would answer, and, without the slightest hesitation, she had moved her hand to the right.

The question of her decision is one not to be lightly considered, and it is not for me to presume to set myself up as the one person able to answer it. And so I leave it with all of you: Which came out of the opened door—the lady, or the tiger?

10

HAPPINESS

Guy de Maupassant

Love goes beyond time and the wrinkles of time. Happiness is a wayside station between 'too much' and 'too little'.

It was tea time, before the lamps were brought in. The villa stood above the sea; the vanished sun had left the sky all rosy with its passing, dusted with a golden powder; and the Mediterranean, without a wave or a ripple, stretching out flat and smooth and shimmering still under the dying day, seemed a vast, polished sheet of metal. To the right, stretching off into the distance, jagged mountains cast their black silhouettes against the fading crimson of the sunset.

They were speaking of love, discussing that old subject, saying again the things that have already been said so many times before. The sweet melancholy of twilight slowed their speech, caused a tender emotion to well up in their souls; and this word 'love', which was heard again and again—now spoken by a strong, manly voice, now by a soft woman's voice—seemed to fill the little salon, fluttering through it like a bird, hovering in it like a spirit.

Can one love continuously for many years?

'Yes,' said some; 'no,' claimed others.

They distinguished cases, established distinctions, cited examples; and everyone, men and women, full of powerful and stirring memories that rose to their lips as examples, seemed touched; and spoke of this banal and sovereign thing, the tender and mysterious accord of two beings, with a profound emotion and ardent interest.

Then all of a sudden someone, staring off into the distance, cried, 'Oh! Look, there! What is that?'

Above the sea, at the edge of the horizon, an enormous, indistinct grey mass was emerging. The women had gotten up and were staring uncomprehendingly at this shocking thing they had never seen before.

Someone said, 'It's Corsica! You can see it two or three times a year like this, under certain unusual atmospheric conditions, when the air becomes perfectly clear and no longer hides it behind the haze that always obscures things in the distance.'

They could vaguely make out the crests of the peaks; some thought they could see snow on the summits. And everyone was surprised, troubled, almost frightened by this sudden appearance of a world, this phantom risen from the sea. Perhaps those who set out, like Columbus, across unexplored oceans, had these strange visions.

Then an elderly gentleman, who had not yet spoken, said, 'Listen, I met on this island—which has appeared before us as if in answer to what we have been saying, and which has reminded me of a singular memory—I met with an admirable example of a constant love, an incredibly happy love. Here it is:

'Five years ago, I took a trip to Corsica. This wild island is more unknown and more distant to us than America, even though you can see it sometimes from the coasts of France, like today.

'Picture a world still in chaos, a tempest of mountains separating narrow ravines with rushing torrents. Not a plain anywhere, but immense crags of granite and giant undulations of earth covered with scrub or high forests of chestnut and pine. Its virgin soil, uncultivated, deserted, even though sometimes you see a village, looking like a pile of rocks at the summit of a mountain. No culture, no industry, no art. You never encounter a piece of worked wood, a bit of sculpted stone, never encounter evidence of an ancestral taste for graceful and beautiful things, however simple. It is precisely this that strikes one the most about this superb and hard land: the hereditary indifference to that search after seductive forms called art.

'Italy—where each palace, full of masterpieces, is itself a masterpiece; where marble, wood, bronze, iron, all metals and stones attest to the genius of man; where the smallest old objects laying around in the old houses reveal this divine care for gracefulness—is for us all the sacred patrimony that we love because it shows us, demonstrates to us, the effort, the grandeur, the power and the triumph of creative intelligence.

'And, just across from Italy, wild Corsica has remained as it was in its first days. Humanity lives there in its crudest house, indifferent to everything that is not immediately relevant to its immediate existence or its family quarrels. And it has retained the faults and qualities of the uncultivated races: violent, hateful, bloody without conscience; but also hospitable, generous, devoted, naïve, opening its door to the passer-by and giving its faithful friendship after the slightest sign of sympathy.

'And so for a month, I had wandered through this magnificent island, with the feeling that I was at the end of the world. No inns, no bars, no roads. By mule paths you reach these tiny villages clinging to the sides of the mountains, and which stand over tortuous abysses from which you hear rising, at night, a continuous noise, the heavy and profound voice of the torrent. You knock on the doors of the houses, you ask for shelter for the night and something to eat to last you till the next day. And you sit at the humble table, and sleep under the humble roof; and in the morning you shake the hand of your host, who has led you to the edge of the village.

'So, one night, after ten hours' walk, I reached a small dwelling all alone at the bottom of a narrow valley that opened onto the sea a little farther on. The two steep slopes of the mountain, covered with brush, broken rock, and giant trees, closed in on this dismally sad ravine like two dark walls. Around the cottage a few vines, a small garden, and farther on, a few large chestnut trees; enough to live by at least, a fortune for this impoverished land.

'The woman who received me was old, severe, and proper without exception. The man, sitting in a cane chair, got up to greet me, then sat down again without saying a word. His companion said to me, "Excuse him; he's deaf now. He's 82 years old."

'She spoke the French of France. I was surprised. I asked her, 'You're not from Corsica?'

'She answered, 'No, we're from the continent. But we have lived here for fifty years now."

'A feeling of anguish and fear seized me at the thought of those fifty years passed in this dark hole, so far from towns where people live. An old sheepdog wandered in, and we sat down to eat the only dinner dish, a thick soup of potatoes, lard, and cabbage.

'When the short meal was finished I went to sit before the door, my heart engulfed by the melancholy of the mournful country, wrapped in that distress which sometimes grips travellers on certain sad evenings, in certain desolate places. It seemed that everything was about to end, existence and the universe. I suddenly saw the terrible misery of life, the isolation of everyone, the nothingness of everything, and the black solitude of the heart, deluding itself with dreams until death.

'The old woman joined me and, tortured by that curiosity that always lives at the bottom of the most resigned souls, asked, "So, you come from France?"

'"Yes, I'm on a pleasure trip."

'"You're from Paris, perhaps?"

'"No, I'm from Nancy."

'It seemed to me that an extraordinary emotion was agitating her. How I saw, or rather sensed this, I don't know.

'She repeated in a slow voice, "You're from Nancy?"

'The man appeared in the doorway, impassive, as deaf people are.

'She said, "Don't pay any attention to him. He can't hear anything." Then, after a few seconds, "So, you know everyone in Nancy?'

'"Of course, almost everyone.'

'"The Sainte-Allaize family?"

'"Yes, very well. They were friends of my father's."

'"What's your name?"

'I told her my name. She stared at me fixedly, then said, in that low voice of awakening memories, "Yes, yes, I remember well. And the Brisemares, what has become of them?"

'"They are all dead."

'"Ah! And the Sirmonts, you know them?"

'"Yes, the last one is a general."

'Then she said, trembling with emotion, with anguish, with I don't know what confused, powerful, and holy sentiments, with I don't know what need to avow, to tell everything, to speak of those things that she had held until then enclosed at the bottom of her heart, to speak of those people whose name shook her soul: "Yes, Henri de Sirmont. I know him well. He is my brother."

'I raised my eyes toward her, bewildered with surprise. And all of a sudden it came back to me.

'A long time ago, it had caused a terrible scandal in noble Lorraine. A young girl, beautiful and rich, Suzanne de Sirmont, had been carried off by a sergeant in the regiment that her father commanded. He was a handsome boy, the son of peasants, but looking good in his dress uniform, this soldier who had seduced the daughter of his colonel. No doubt she had seen him, noticed him, fell in love with him while watching the troops march by. But how had he spoken to her, how had they been able to see each other, to talk? How had she dared to make him understand that she loved him? No one ever knew.

'No one suspected anything. One night, as the soldier had just finished his enlistment, he disappeared with her. They sought for them, but never found them. They never heard from her again, and they considered her dead.

'And I had found her in that sinister valley.

'Then I said, in my turn, "Yes, I remember well. You are Suzanne."

'She shook her head yes. Tears fell from her eyes. Then, with a glance at the old man sitting immobile on the doorstep of the shack, she told me, "It's him."And I understood that she still loved him, that she still saw him with seduced eyes.

'I asked, "Have you been happy, at least?"

'She answered, with a voice that came from the heart, "Oh! Yes, very happy. He has made me very happy. I have never regretted anything."

'I contemplated her, sad, surprised, amazed by the power of love! This rich girl had followed this man, this peasant. She had herself become a peasant. She had lived her life without charms, without luxuries, without delicacies of any sort, she had bent herself to his simple habits. And she loved him still. She had become a rustic, in a bonnet and canvas skirt. She ate on an earthenware plate on a crude wooden table, sitting on a cane seat, a gruel of cabbage and potatoes with lard. She lay on a straw mattress by his side.

'She had never thought of anything, but him! She had missed neither necklaces, nor fineries, nor elegances, nor soft seats, nor the perfumed warmth of rooms enveloped in curtains, nor the sweetness of downy cushions on which to rest one's body. She had never needed anything but him; as long as he was there, she desired nothing.

'She had abandoned life while young, both the world and those who had raised her and loved her. She had come, alone with him, to this wild ravine. And he had been everything for her, everything one desires, everything one dreams of, everything one constantly waits for, everything one endlessly hopes. He had filled her existence with happiness, from one end to the other. She couldn't have been happier.

'And all night, listening to the rough breathing of the old soldier stretched out on his pallet, beside her who had followed him so far, I thought of that strange and simple adventure, of this happiness so complete, made of so little.

'And I left with the rising sun, after having shaken hands with the two old people, man and wife.'

The old man fell silent.

A woman said, 'All the same, she had an ideal that was too easy, needs that were too primitive, and requirements that were too simple. She was just a fool.'

Someone else said in a slow voice, 'What does that matter! She was happy.'

And there, at the farthest edge of the horizon, Corsica disappeared into the night, sank back slowly into the sea, its great shadow fading away, which had appeared as if itself to tell the story of the two humble lovers sheltered on its shores.

11

THE SINGING LESSON

Katherine Mansfield

If music be the food of love, play on.

With despair—cold, sharp despair—buried deep in her heart like a wicked knife, Miss Meadows, in cap and gown and carrying a little baton, trod the cold corridors that led to the music hall. Girls of all ages, rosy from the air, and bubbling over with that gleeful excitement that comes from running to school on a fine autumn morning, hurried, skipped, fluttered by; from the hollow class-rooms came a quick drumming of voices; a bell rang; a voice like a bird cried, 'Muriel'. And then there came from the staircase a tremendous knock-knock-knocking. Some one had dropped her dumbbells.

The Science Mistress stopped Miss Meadows.

'Good mor-ning,' she cried, in her sweet, affected drawl. 'Isn't it cold? It might be win-ter.'

Miss Meadows, hugging the knife, stared in hatred at the Science Mistress. Everything about her was sweet, pale, like honey. You would not have been surprised to see a bee caught in the tangles of that yellow hair.

'It is rather sharp,' said Miss Meadows, grimly.

The other smiled her sugary smile.

'You look frozen,' said she. Her blue eyes opened wide; there came a mocking light in them. (Had she noticed anything?)

'Oh, not quite as bad as that,' said Miss Meadows, and she gave the Science Mistress, in exchange for her smile, a quick grimace and passed on.

Forms Four, Five, and Six were assembled in the music hall. The noise was deafening. On the platform, by the piano, stood Mary Beazley, Miss Meadows' favourite, who played accompaniments. She was turning the music stool. When she saw Miss Meadows she gave a loud, warning 'Sh-sh! Girls!' and Miss Meadows, her hands thrust in her sleeves, the baton under her arm, strode down the centre aisle, mounted the steps, turned sharply, seized the brass music stand, planted it in front of her, and gave two sharp taps with her baton for silence.

'Silence, please! Immediately!' and, looking at nobody, her glance swept over that sea of coloured flannel blouses, with bobbing pink faces and hands, quivering butterfly hair-bows, and music-books outspread. She knew perfectly well what they were thinking. 'Meady is in a wax.' Well, let them think it! Her eyelids quivered; she tossed her head, defying them. What could the thoughts of those creatures matter to some one who stood there bleeding to death, pierced to the heart, to the heart, by such a letter:

> I feel more and more strongly that our marriage would be a mistake. Not that I do not love you. I love you as much as it is possible for me to love any woman, but, truth to tell, I have come to the conclusion that I am not a marrying man, and the idea of settling down fills me with nothing but—

—And the word 'disgust' was scratched out lightly and 'regret' written over the top.

Basil! Miss Meadows stalked over to the piano. And Mary Beazley, who was waiting for this moment, bent forward; her curls fell over her cheeks while she breathed, 'Good morning, Miss Meadows,' and she motioned towards rather than handed to her mistress a beautiful yellow chrysanthemum. This little ritual of the flower had been gone through for ages and ages, quite a term and a half. It was as much part of the lesson as opening the piano. But this morning, instead of taking it up, instead of tucking it into her belt while she leant over Mary and said, 'Thank you, Mary. How very nice! Turn to page thirty-two,' what was Mary's horror when Miss Meadows totally ignored the chrysanthemum, made no reply to her greeting, but said in a voice of ice, 'Page fourteen, please, and mark the accents well.'

Staggering moment! Mary blushed until the tears stood in her eyes, but Miss Meadows was gone back to the music stand; her voice rang through the music hall.

'Page fourteen. We will begin with page fourteen—"A Lament". Now, girls, you ought to know it by this time. We shall take it all together; not in parts, all together. And without expression. Sing it, though, quite simply, beating time with the left hand.'

She raised the baton; she tapped the music stand twice. Down came Mary on the opening chord; down came all those left hands, beating the air, and in chimed those young, mournful voices:

Fast! Ah, too Fast Fade the Ro-o-ses of Pleasure;
Soon Autumn yields unto Wi-i-nter Drear.
Fleetly! Ah, Fleetly Mu-u-sic's Gay Measure
Passes away from the Listening Ear.

Good Heavens, what could be more tragic than that lament! Every note was a sigh, a sob, a groan of awful mournfulness. Miss Meadows lifted her arms in the wide gown and began conducting with both hands. *'...I feel more and more strongly that our marriage would be a mistake...'* she beat. And the voices cried: *Fleetly! Ah, Fleetly.* What could have possessed him to write such a letter! What could have led up to it! It came out of nothing. His last letter had been all about a fumed-oak bookcase he had bought for 'our' books, and a 'natty little hall-stand' he had seen, 'a very neat affair with a carved owl on a bracket, holding three hat-brushes in its claws.' How she had smiled at that! So like a man to think one needed three hat-brushes! *From the Listening Ear*, sang the voices.

'Once again,' said Miss Meadows. 'But this time in parts. Still without expression.' *Fast! Ah, too Fast.* With the gloom of the contraltos added, one could scarcely help shuddering. *Fade the Roses of Pleasure.* Last time he had come to see her, Basil had worn a rose in his buttonhole. How handsome he had looked in that bright blue suit, with that dark red rose! And he knew it, too. He couldn't help knowing it. First he stroked his hair, then his moustache; his teeth gleamed when he smiled.

'The headmaster's wife keeps on asking me to dinner. It's a perfect nuisance. I never get an evening to myself in that place.'

'But can't you refuse?'

'Oh, well, it doesn't do for a man in my position to be unpopular.'

Music's Gay Measure, wailed the voices. The willow trees, outside the high, narrow windows, waved in the wind. They had lost half their leaves. The tiny ones that clung wriggled like fishes caught on a line. *'...I am not a marrying man...'* The voices were silent; the piano waited.

'Quite good,' said Miss Meadows, but still in such a strange, stony tone that the younger girls began to feel positively frightened. 'But now that we know it, we shall take it with expression. As much expression as you can put into it. Think of the words, girls. Use your imaginations. *Fast! Ah, too Fast,*' cried Miss Meadows. 'That ought to break out—a loud, strong *forte*—a lament. And then in the second line, *Winter Drear,* make that *Drear* sound as if a cold wind were blowing through it. *Dre-ear!* said she so awfully that Mary Beazley, on the music stool, wriggled her spine. 'The third line should be one crescendo. *Fleetly! Ah, Fleetly Music's Gay Measure.* Breaking on the first word of the last line, *Passes.* And then on the word, *Away,* you must begin to die...to fade... until *The Listening Ear* is nothing more than a faint whisper... You can slow down as much as you like almost on the last line. Now, please.'

Again the two light taps; she lifted her arms again. *Fast! Ah, too Fast.* **'...and the idea of settling down fills me with nothing but disgust—'** Disgust was what he had written. That was as good as to say their engagement was definitely broken off. Broken off! Their engagement! People had been surprised enough that she had got engaged. The Science Mistress would not believe it at first. But nobody had been as surprised as she. She was thirty. Basil was twenty-five. It had been a miracle, simply a miracle, to hear him say, as they walked home from church that very dark night, 'You know, somehow or other, I've got fond of you.' And he had taken hold of the end of her ostrich feather boa. *Passes away from the Listening Ear.*

'Repeat! Repeat!' said Miss Meadows. 'More expression, girls! Once more!'

Fast! Ah, too Fast. The older girls were crimson; some of the younger ones began to cry. Big spots of rain blew against the windows, and one could hear the willows whispering, **'...not that I do not love you...'**

'But, my darling, if you love me,' thought Miss Meadows, 'I don't mind how much it is. Love me as little as you like.' But she knew he didn't love her. Not to have cared enough to scratch out that word 'disgust', so that she couldn't read it! *Soon Autumn yields unto Winter Drear.* She would have to leave the school, too. She could never face the Science Mistress or the girls after it got known. She would have to disappear somewhere. *Passes away.* The voices began to die, to fade, to whisper...to vanish...

Suddenly the door opened. A little girl in blue walked fussily up the aisle, hanging her head, biting her lips, and twisting the silver bangle on her red little wrist. She came up the steps and stood before Miss Meadows.

'Well, Monica, what is it?'

'Oh, if you please, Miss Meadows,' said the little girl, gasping, 'Miss Wyatt wants to see you in the mistress's room.'

'Very well,' said Miss Meadows. And she called to the girls, 'I shall put you on your honour to talk quietly while I am away.' But they were too subdued to do anything else. Most of them were blowing their noses.

The corridors were silent and cold; they echoed to Miss Meadows' steps. The Head Mistress sat at her desk. For a moment she did not look up. She was as usual disentangling her eyeglasses, which had got caught in her lace tie. 'Sit down, Miss Meadows,' she said very kindly. And then she picked up a pink envelope from the blotting-pad. 'I sent for you just now because this telegram has come for you.'

'A telegram for me, Miss Wyatt?'

Basil! He had committed suicide, decided Miss Meadows. Her hand flew out, but Miss Wyatt held the telegram back a moment. 'I hope it's not bad news,' she said, so more than kindly. And Miss Meadows tore it open.

'Pay no attention to letter, must have been mad, bought hat-stand to-day—Basil,' she read. She couldn't take her eyes off the telegram.

'I do hope it's nothing very serious,' said Miss Wyatt, leaning forward.

'Oh, no, thank you, Miss Wyatt,' blushed Miss Meadows. 'It's nothing bad at all. It's—' and she gave an apologetic little laugh—'it's from my *fiancé* saying that…saying that—' There was a pause. 'I see,' said Miss Wyatt. And another pause. Then—'You've fifteen minutes more of your class, Miss Meadows, haven't you?'

'Yes, Miss Wyatt.' She got up. She half ran towards the door.

'Oh, just one minute, Miss Meadows,' said Miss Wyatt. 'I must say I don't approve of my teachers having telegrams sent to them in school hours, unless in case of very bad news, such as death,' explained Miss Wyatt, 'or a very serious accident, or something to that effect. Good news, Miss Meadows, will always keep, you know.'

On the wings of hope, of love, of joy, Miss Meadows sped back to the music hall, up the aisle, up the steps, over to the piano.

'Page thirty-two, Mary,' she said, 'page thirty-two,' and, picking up the yellow chrysanthemum, she held it to her lips to hide her smile. Then she turned to the girls, rapped with her baton: 'Page thirty-two, girls. Page thirty-two.'

We come here To-day with Flowers o'erladen,
With Baskets of Fruit and Ribbons to boot,
To-oo Congratulate…

'Stop! Stop!' cried Miss Meadows. 'This is awful. This is dreadful.' And she beamed at her girls. 'What's the matter with you all? Think, girls, think of what you're singing. Use your imaginations. *With Flowers o'erladen. Baskets of Fruit and Ribbons to boot.* And *Congratulate.*' Miss Meadows broke off. 'Don't look so doleful, girls. It ought to sound warm, joyful, eager. *Congratulate.* Once more. Quickly. All together. Now then!'

And this time Miss Meadows' voice sounded over all the other voices—full, deep, glowing with expression.

12

MAMMON AND THE ARCHER

O. Henry

If you choose money over love, you will always be poor. Love is fodder for the soul.

Old Anthony Rockwall, retired manufacturer and proprietor of Rockwall's Eureka Soap, looked out the library window of his Fifth Avenue mansion and grinned. His neighbour to the right—the aristocratic clubman, G. Van Schuylight Suffolk-Jones—came out to his waiting motor-car, wrinkling a contumelious nostril, as usual, at the Italian renaissance sculpture of the soap palace's front elevation.

'Stuck-up old statuette of nothing doing!' commented the ex-Soap King. 'The Eden Musee'll get that old frozen Nesselrode yet if he don't watch out. I'll have this house painted red, white, and blue next summer and see if that'll make his Dutch nose turn up any higher.'

And then Anthony Rockwall, who never cared for bells, went to the door of his library and shouted 'Mike!' in the same voice that had once chipped off pieces of the welkin on the Kansas prairies.

'Tell my son,' said Anthony to the answering menial, 'to come in here before he leaves the house.'

When young Rockwall entered the library the old man laid aside his newspaper, looked at him with a kindly grimness on his big, smooth, ruddy countenance, rumpled his mop of white hair with one hand and rattled the keys in his pocket with the other.

'Richard,' said Anthony Rockwail, 'what do you pay for the soap that you use?'

Richard, only six months home from college, was startled a little. He had not yet taken the measure of this sire of his, who was as full of unexpectednesses as a girl at her first party.

'Six dollars a dozen, I think, dad.'

'And your clothes?'

'I suppose about sixty dollars, as a rule.'

'You're a gentleman,' said Anthony, decidedly. 'I've heard of these young bloods spending $24 a dozen for soap, and going over the hundred mark for clothes. You've got as much money to waste as any of 'em, and yet you stick to what's decent and moderate. Now I use the old Eureka—not only for sentiment, but it's the purest soap made. Whenever you pay more than 10 cents a cake for soap you buy bad perfumes and labels. But 50 cents is doing very well for a young man in your generation, position and condition. As I said, you're a gentleman. They say it takes three generations to make one. They're off. Money'll do it as slick as soap grease. It's made you one. By hokey! It's almost made one of me. I'm nearly as impolite and disagreeable and ill-mannered as these two old Knickerbocker gents on each side of me that can't sleep of nights because I bought in between 'em.'

'There are some things that money can't accomplish,' remarked young Rockwall, rather gloomily.

'Now, don't say that,' said old Anthony, shocked. 'I bet my money on money every time. I've been through the encyclopaedia down to Y looking for something you can't buy with it; and I expect to have to take up the appendix next week. I'm for money against the field. Tell me something money won't buy.'

'For one thing,' answered Richard, rankling a little, 'it won't buy one into the exclusive circles of society.' 'Oho! Won't it?' thundered the champion of the root of evil. 'You tell me where your exclusive circles would be if the first Astor hadn't had the money to pay for his steerage passage over?'

Richard sighed.

'And that's what I was coming to,' said the old man, less boisterously. 'That's why I asked you to come in. There's something going wrong with you, boy. I've been noticing it for two weeks. Out with it. I guess I could lay my hands on eleven millions within twenty-four hours, besides the real estate. If it's your liver, there's the Rambler down in the bay, coaled, and ready to steam down to the Bahamas in two days.'

'Not a bad guess, dad; you haven't missed it far.'

'Ah,' said Anthony, keenly; 'what's her name?'

Richard began to walk up and down the library floor. There was enough comradeship and sympathy in this crude old father of his to draw his confidence.

'Why don't you ask her?' demanded old Anthony. 'She'll jump at you. You've got the money and the looks, and you're a decent boy. Your hands are clean. You've got no Eureka soap on 'em. You've been to college, but she'll overlook that.'

'I haven't had a chance,' said Richard.

'Make one,' said Anthony. 'Take her for a walk in the park, or a straw ride, or walk home with her from church Chance! Pshaw!'

'You don't know the social mill, dad. She's part of the stream that turns it. Every hour and minute of her time is arranged for days in advance. I must have that girl, dad, or this town is a blackjack swamp forevermore. And I can't write it—I can't do that.'

'Tut!' said the old man. 'Do you mean to tell me that with all the money I've got you can't get an hour or two of a girl's time for yourself?'

'I've put it off too late. She's going to sail for Europe at noon day after to-morrow for a two years' stay. I'm to see her alone to-morrow evening for a few minutes. She's at Larchmont now at her aunt's. I can't go there. But I'm allowed to meet her with a cab at the Grand Central Station to-morrow evening at the 8.30 train. We drive down Broadway to Wallack's at a gallop, where her mother and a box party will be waiting for us in the lobby.

Do you think she would listen to a declaration from me during that six or eight minutes under those circumstances? No. And what chance would I have in the theatre or afterward? None. No, dad, this is one tangle that your money can't unravel. We can't buy one minute of time with cash; if we could, rich people would live longer. There's no hope of getting a talk with Miss Lantry before she sails.'

'All right, Richard, my boy,' said old Anthony, cheerfully. 'You may run along down to your club now. I'm glad it ain't your liver. But don't forget to burn a few punk sticks in the joss house to the great god Mazuma from time to time. You say money won't buy time? Well, of course, you can't order eternity wrapped up and delivered at your residence for a price, but I've seen Father Time get pretty bad stone bruises on his heels when he walked through the gold diggings.'

That night came Aunt Ellen, gentle, sentimental, wrinkled, sighing, oppressed by wealth, in to Brother Anthony at his evening paper, and began discourse on the subject of lovers' woes.

'He told me all about it,' said brother Anthony, yawning. 'I told him my bank account was at his service. And then he began to knock money. Said money couldn't help. Said the rules of society couldn't be bucked for a yard by a team of ten-millionaires.'

'Oh, Anthony,' sighed Aunt Ellen, 'I wish you would not think so much of money. Wealth is nothing where a true affection is concerned. Love is all-powerful. If he only had spoken earlier! She could not have refused our Richard. But now I fear it is too late. He will have no opportunity to address her. All your gold cannot bring happiness to your son.'

At eight o'clock the next evening Aunt Ellen took a quaint old gold ring from a moth-eaten case and gave it to Richard.

'Wear it to-night, nephew,' she begged. 'Your mother gave it to me. Good luck in love she said it brought. She asked me to give it to you when you had found the one you loved.'

Young Rockwall took the ring reverently and tried it on his smallest finger. It slipped as far as the second joint and stopped. He took it off and stuffed it into his vest pocket, after the manner of man. And then he 'phoned for his cab.

At the station he captured Miss Lantry out of the gadding mob at eight thirty-two.

'We mustn't keep mamma and the others waiting,' said she.

'To Wallack's Theatre as fast as you can drive!' said Richard loyally.

They whirled up Forty-second to Broadway, and then down the white-starred lane that leads from the soft meadows of sunset to the rocky hills of morning.

At Thirty-fourth Street young Richard quickly thrust up the trap and ordered the cabman to stop.

'I've dropped a ring,' he apologized, as he climbed out. 'It was my mother's, and I'd hate to lose it. I won't detain you a minute–I saw where it fell.'

In less than a minute he was back in the cab with the ring.

But within that minute a crosstown car had stopped directly in front of the cab. The cabman tried to pass to the left, but a heavy express wagon cut him off. He tried the right, and had to back away from a furniture van that had no business to be there. He tried to back out, but dropped his reins and swore dutifully. He was blockaded in a tangled mess of vehicles and horses.

One of those street blockades had occurred that sometimes tie up commerce and movement quite suddenly in the big city.

'Why don't you drive on?' said Miss Lantry, impatiently. 'We'll be late.'

Richard stood up in the cab and looked around. He saw a congested flood of wagons, trucks, cabs, vans and street cars filling the vast space where Broadway, Sixth Avenue and Thirty-fourth street cross one another as a twenty-six inch maiden fills her twenty-two inch girdle. And still from all the cross streets they were hurrying and rattling toward the converging point at full speed, and hurling themselves into the struggling mass, locking wheels and adding their drivers' imprecations to the clamour. The entire traffic of Manhattan seemed to have jammed itself around them. The oldest New Yorker among the thousands of spectators that lined the sidewalks had not witnessed a street blockade of the proportions of this one.

'I'm very sorry,' said Richard, as he resumed his seat, 'but it looks as if we are stuck. They won't get this jumble loosened up in an hour. It was my fault. If I hadn't dropped the ring we—'

'Let me see the ring,' said Miss Lantry. 'Now that it can't be helped, I don't care. I think theatres are stupid, anyway.'

At 11 o'clock that night somebody tapped lightly on Anthony Rockwall's door.

'Come in,' shouted Anthony, who was in a red dressing-gown, reading a book of piratical adventures.

Somebody was Aunt Ellen, looking like a grey-haired angel that had been left on earth by mistake.

'They're engaged, Anthony,' she said, softly. 'She has promised to marry our Richard. On their way to the theatre there was a street blockade, and it was two hours before their cab could get out of it.

'And oh, brother Anthony, don't ever boast of the power of money again. A little emblem of true love—a little ring that symbolized unending and unmercenary affection—was the cause of our Richard finding his happiness. He dropped it in the street, and got out to recover it. And before they could continue the blockade occurred. He spoke to his love and won her there while the cab was hemmed in. Money is dross compared with true love, Anthony.'

'All right,' said old Anthony. 'I'm glad the boy has got what he wanted. I told him I wouldn't spare any expense in the matter if—'

'But, brother Anthony, what good could your money have done?'

'Sister,' said Anthony Rockwall. 'I've got my pirate in a devil of a scrape. His ship has just been scuttled, and he's too good a judge of the value of money to let drown. I wish you would let me go on with this chapter.'

The story should end here. I wish it would as heartily as you who read it wish it did. But we must go to the bottom of the well for truth.

The next day a person with red hands and a blue polka-dot necktie, who called himself Kelly, called at Anthony Rockwall's house, and was at once received in the library.

'Well,' said Anthony, reaching for his chequebook, 'it was a good bilin' of soap. Let's see—you had $5,000 in cash.'

'I paid out $3OO more of my own,' said Kelly. 'I had to go a little above the estimate. I got the express wagons and cabs mostly for $5; but the trucks and two-horse teams mostly raised me to $10. The motormen wanted $10, and some of the loaded teams $20. The cops struck me hardest—$50 I paid two, and the rest $20 and $25. But didn't it work beautiful, Mr Rockwall? I'm glad William A. Brady wasn't onto that little outdoor vehicle mob scene. I wouldn't want William to break his heart with jealousy. And never a rehearsal, either! The boys was on time to the fraction of a second. It was two hours before a snake could get below Greeley's statue.'

'Thirteen hundred—there you are, Kelly,' said Anthony, tearing off a cheque. 'Your thousand, and the $300 you were out. You don't despise money, do you, Kelly?'

'Me?' said Kelly. 'I can lick the man that invented poverty.'

Anthony called Kelly when he was at the door.

'You didn't notice,' said he, 'anywhere in the tie-up, a kind of a fat boy without any clothes on shooting arrows around with a bow, did you?'

'Why, no,' said Kelly, mystified. 'I didn't. If he was like you say, maybe the cops pinched him before I got there.'

'I thought the little rascal wouldn't be on hand,' chuckled Anthony. 'Good-by, Kelly.'

13

INDISCRETION

Guy de Maupassant

'In my end is my beginning; in my beginning is my end.'

They had loved each other before marriage with a pure and lofty love. They had first met on the sea-shore. He had thought this young girl charming, as she passed by with her light-coloured parasol and her dainty dress amid the marine landscape against the horizon. He had loved her, blond and slender, in these surroundings of blue ocean and spacious sky. He could not distinguish the tenderness which this budding woman awoke in him from the vague and powerful emotion which the fresh salt air and the grand scenery of surf and sunshine and waves aroused in his soul.

She, on the other hand, had loved him because he courted her, because he was young, rich, kind, and attentive. She had loved him because it is natural for young girls to love men who whisper sweet nothings to them.

So, for three months, they had lived side by side, and hand in hand. The greeting which they exchanged in the morning before the bath, in the freshness of the morning, or in the evening on the sand, under the stars, in the warmth of a calm night, whispered low, very low, already had the flavour of kisses, though their lips had never met.

Each dreamed of the other at night, each thought of the other on awaking, and, without yet having voiced their sentiments, each longing for the other, body and soul.

After marriage their love descended to earth. It was at first a tireless, sensuous passion, then exalted tenderness composed of tangible poetry, more refined caresses, and new and foolish inventions. Every glance and gesture was an expression of passion.

But, little by little, without even noticing it, they began to get tired of each other. Love was still strong, but they had nothing more to reveal to each other, nothing more to learn from each other, no new tale of endearment, no unexpected outburst, no new way of expressing the well-known, oft-repeated verb.

They tried, however, to rekindle the dwindling flame of the first love. Every day they tried some new trick or desperate attempt to bring back to their hearts the uncooled ardour of their first days of married life. They tried moonlight walks under the trees, in the sweet warmth of the summer evenings: the poetry of mist-covered beaches; the excitement of public festivals.

One morning Henriette said to Paul: 'Will you take me to a cafe for dinner?'

'Certainly, dearie.'

'To some well-known cafe?'

'Of course!'

He looked at her with a questioning glance, seeing that she was thinking of something which she did not wish to tell.

She went on:

'You know, one of those cafes—oh, how can I explain myself? A sporty cafe!'

He smiled: 'Of course, I understand—you mean in one of the cafes which are commonly called bohemian.'

'Yes, that's it. But take me to one of the big places, one where you are known, one where you have already supped—no—dined—well, you know—I—I—oh! I will never dare say it!'

'Go ahead, dearie. Little secrets should no longer exist between us.'

'No, I dare not.'

'Go on; don't be prudish. Tell me.'

'Well, I—I—I want to be taken for your sweetheart—there!

And I want the boys, who do not know that you are married, to take me for such; and you too—I want you to think that I am your sweetheart for one hour, in that place which must hold so many memories for you. There! And I will play that I am your sweetheart. It's awful, I know—I am abominably ashamed, I am as red as a peony. Don't look at me!'

He laughed, greatly amused, and answered:

'All right, we will go to-night to a very swell place where I am well known.'

Toward seven o'clock they went up the stairs of one of the big cafes on the Boulevard, he, smiling, with the look of a conqueror, she, timid, veiled, delighted. They were immediately shown to one of the luxurious private dining-rooms, furnished with four large arm-chairs and a red plush couch. The head waiter entered and brought them the menu. Paul handed it to his wife.

'What do you want to eat?'

'I don't care; order whatever is good.'

After handing his coat to the waiter, he ordered dinner and champagne. The waiter looked at the young woman and smiled. He took the order and murmured:

'Will Monsieur Paul have his champagne sweet or dry?'

'Dry, very dry.'

Henriette was pleased to hear that this man knew her husband's name. They sat on the couch, side by side, and began to eat.

Ten candles lighted the room and were reflected in the mirrors all around them, which seemed to increase the brilliancy a thousand-fold. Henriette drank glass after glass in order to keep up her courage, although she felt dizzy after the first few glasses. Paul, excited by the memories which returned to him, kept kissing his wife's hands. His eyes were sparkling.

She was feeling strangely excited in this new place, restless, pleased, a little guilty, but full of life. Two waiters, serious, silent, accustomed to seeing and forgetting everything, to entering the room only when it was necessary and to leaving it when they felt they were intruding, were silently flitting hither and thither.

Toward the middle of the dinner, Henriette was well under the influence of champagne. She was prattling along fearlessly, her cheeks flushed, her eyes glistening.

'Come, Paul; tell me everything.'

'What, sweetheart?'

'I don't dare tell you.'

'Go on!'

'Have you loved many women before me?'

He hesitated, a little perplexed, not knowing whether he should hide his adventures or boast of them.

She continued:

'Oh! please tell me. How many have you loved?'

'A few.'

'How many?'

'I don't know. How do you expect me to know such things?'

'Haven't you counted them?'

'Of course not.'

'Then you must have loved a good many!'

'Perhaps.'

'About how many? Just tell me about how many.'

'But I don't know, dearest. Some years a good many, and some years only a few.'

'How many a year, did you say?'

'Sometimes twenty or thirty, sometimes only four or five.'

'Oh! that makes more than a hundred in all!'

'Yes, just about.'

'Oh! I think that is dreadful!'

'Why dreadful?'

'Because it's dreadful when you think of it—all those women—and always—always the same thing. Oh! it's dreadful, just the same—more than a hundred women!'

He was surprised that she should think that dreadful, and answered, with the air of superiority which men take with women when they wish to make them understand that they have said something foolish:

'That's funny! If it is dreadful to have a hundred women, it's dreadful to have one.'

'Oh, no, not at all!'

'Why not?'

'Because with one woman you have a real bond of love which attaches you to her, while with a hundred women it's not the same at all. There is no real love. I don't understand how a man can associate with such women.'

'But they are all right.'

'No, they can't be!'

'Yes, they are!'

'Oh, stop; you disgust me!'

'But then, why did you ask me how many sweethearts I had had?'

'Because—'

'That's no reason!'

'What were they—actresses, little shop-girls, or society women?'

'A few of each.'

'It must have been rather monotonous toward the last.'

'Oh, no; it's amusing to change.'

She remained thoughtful, staring at her champagne glass. It was full—she drank it in one gulp; then putting it back on the table, she threw her arms around her husband's neck and murmured in his ear:

'Oh! How I love you, sweetheart! How I love you!'

He threw his arms around her in a passionate embrace. A waiter, who was just entering, backed out, closing the door discreetly. In about five minutes the head waiter came back, solemn and dignified, bringing the fruit for dessert. She was once more holding between her fingers a full glass, and gazing into the amber liquid as though seeking unknown things. She murmured in a dreamy voice:

'Yes, it must be fun!'

14

CUPID'S ARROWS

Rudyard Kipling

Falling in love is dying by Cupid's bow, perhaps.

Pit where the buffalo cooled his hide,
By the hot sun emptied, and blistered and dried;
Log in the reh-grass, hidden and alone;
Bund where the earth-rat's mounds are strown:
Cave in the bank where the sly stream steals;
Aloe that stabs at the belly and heels,
Jump if you dare on a steed untried–
Safer it is to go wide–go wide!
Hark, from in front where the best men ride:
'Pull to the off, boys! Wide! Go wide!'

—The Peora Hunt

Once upon a time there lived at Simla a very pretty girl, the daughter of a poor but honest District and Sessions Judge. She was a good girl, but could not help knowing her power and using it. Her Mamma was very anxious about her daughter's future, as all good Mammas should be.

When a man is a Commissioner and a bachelor and has the right of wearing open-work jam-tart jewels in gold and enamel on his clothes, and of going through a door before every one except a Member of Council, a Lieutenant-Governor, or a Viceroy, he is worth marrying. At least, that is what ladies say. There was a Commissioner in Simla, in those days, who was, and wore, and did, all I have said. He was a plain man–an ugly man–the ugliest man in Asia, with two exceptions. His was a face to dream about and try to carve on a pipe-head afterwards. His name was Saggott– Barr-Saggott–Anthony Barr-Saggott and six letters to follow. Departmentally, he was one of the best men the Government of India owned. Socially, he was like a blandishing gorilla.

When he turned his attentions to Miss Beighton, I believe that Mrs Beighton wept with delight at the reward Providence had sent her in her old age.

Mr Beighton held his tongue. He was an easy-going man.

Now a Commissioner is very rich. His pay is beyond the dreams of avarice—is so enormous that he can afford to save and scrape in a way that would almost discredit a Member of Council. Most Commissioners are mean; but Barr-Saggott was an exception. He entertained royally; he horsed himself well; he gave dances; he was a power in the land; and he behaved as such.

Consider that everything I am writing of took place in an almost pre-historic era in the history of British India. Some folk may remember the years before lawn-tennis was born when we all played croquet. There were seasons before that, if you will believe me, when even croquet had not been invented, and archery— which was revived in England in 1844—was as great a pest as lawn-tennis is now. People talked learnedly about 'holding' and 'loosing', 'steles', 'reflexed bows', '56-pound bows', 'backed' or 'self-yew bows', as we talk about 'rallies', 'volleys', 'smashes', 'returns', and '16-ounce rackets'.

Miss Beighton shot divinely over ladies' distance—60 yards, that is—and was acknowledged the best lady archer in Simla. Men called her 'Diana of Tara-Devi'.

Barr-Saggott paid her great attention; and, as I have said, the heart of her mother was uplifted in consequence. Kitty Beighton took matters more calmly. It was pleasant to be singled out by a Commissioner with letters after his name, and to fill the hearts of other girls with bad feelings. But there was no denying the fact that Barr-Saggott was phenomenally ugly; and all his attempts to adorn himself only made him more grotesque. He was not christened 'The Langur'—which means grey ape—for nothing. It was pleasant, Kitty thought, to have him at her feet, but it was better to escape from him and ride with the graceless Cubbon— the man in a Dragoon Regiment at Umballa—the boy with a handsome face, and no prospects. Kitty liked Cubbon more than a little. He never pretended for a moment that he was anything less than head over heels in love with her; for he was an honest boy. So Kitty fled, now and again, from the stately wooings of Barr-Saggott to the company of young Cubbon, and was scolded by her Mamma in consequence. 'But, Mother,' she said, 'Mr Saggot is such–such a–is so *fearfully* ugly, you know!'

'My dear,' said Mrs Beighton, piously, 'we cannot be other than an all-ruling Providence has made us. Besides, you will take precedence of your own Mother, you know! Think of that and be reasonable.'

Then Kitty put up her little chin and said irreverent things about precedence, and Commissioners, and matrimony. Mr Beighton rubbed the top of his head; for he was an easy-going man.

Late in the season, when he judged that the time was ripe, Barr-Saggott developed a plan which did great credit to his administrative powers. He arranged an archery tournament for ladies, with a most sumptuous diamond-studded bracelet as prize. He drew up his terms skilfully, and every one saw that the bracelet was a gift to Miss Beighton; the acceptance carrying with it the hand and the heart of Commissioner Barr-Saggott. The terms were a St. Leonard's Round—thirty-six shots at sixty yards—under the rules of the Simla Toxophilite Society.

All Simla was invited. There were beautifully arranged tea-tables under the deodars at Annandale, where the Grand Stand is now; and, alone in its glory, winking in the sun, sat the diamond bracelet in a blue velvet case. Miss Beighton was anxious—almost too anxious to compete. On the appointed afternoon, all Simla rode down to Annandale to witness the Judgement of Paris turned upside down. Kitty rode with young Cubbon, and it was easy to see that the boy was troubled in his mind. He must be held innocent of everything that followed. Kitty was pale and nervous, and looked long at the bracelet. Barr-Saggott was gorgeously dressed, even more nervous than Kitty, and more hideous than ever.

Mrs Beighton smiled condescendingly, as befitted the mother of a potential Commissioneress, and the shooting began; all the world standing in a semicircle as the ladies came out one after the other.

Nothing is so tedious as an archery competition. They shot, and they shot, and they kept on shooting, till the sun left the valley, and little breezes got up in the deodars, and people waited for Miss Beighton to shoot and win. Cubbon was at one horn of the semicircle round the shooters, and Barr-Saggott at the other. Miss Beighton was last on the list. The scoring had been weak, and the bracelet, *plus* Commissioner Barr-Saggott, was hers to a certainty.

The Commissioner strung her bow with his own sacred hands. She stepped forward, looked at the bracelet, and her first arrow went true to a hair—full into the heart of the 'gold'—counting nine points.

Young Cubbon on the left turned white, and his Devil prompted Barr-Saggott to smile. Now horses used to shy when Barr-Saggott smiled. Kitty saw that smile. She looked to her left-front, gave an almost imperceptible nod to Cubbon, and went on shooting.

I wish I could describe the scene that followed. It was out of the ordinary and most improper. Miss Kitty fitted her arrows with immense deliberation, so that every one might see what she was doing. She was a perfect shot; and her 46-pound bow suited her to a nicety. She pinned the wooden legs of the target with great care four successive times. She pinned the wooden top of the target once, and all the ladies looked at each other. Then she began some fancy shooting at the white, which, if you hit it, counts exactly one point. She put five arrows into the white. It was wonderful archery; but, seeing that her business was to make 'golds' and win the bracelet, Barr-Saggott turned a delicate green like young water-grass. Next, she shot over the target twice, then wide to the left twice—always with the same deliberation—while a chilly hush fell over the company, and Mrs Beighton took out her handkerchief. Then Kitty shot at the ground in front of the target, and split several arrows. Then she made a red—or seven points—just to show what she could do if she liked, and finished up her amazing performance with some more fancy shooting at the target-supports. Here is her score as it was picked off:

	Gold	Red	Blue	Black	White	Total Hits	Total Score
Miss Beighton	1	1	0	0	5	7	21

Barr-Saggott looked as if the last few arrowheads had been driven into his legs instead of the target's, and the deep stillness was broken by a little snubby, mottled, half-grown girl saying in a shrill voice of triumph: 'Then I've won!'

Mrs Beighton did her best to bear up; but she wept in the presence of the people. No training could help her through such a disappointment. Kitty unstrung her bow with a vicious jerk, and went back to her place, while Barr-Saggott was trying to pretend that he enjoyed snapping the bracelet on the snubby girl's raw, red wrist. It was an awkward scene—most awkward. Every one tried to depart in a body and leave Kitty to the mercy of her Mamma.

But Cubbon took her away instead, and—the rest isn't worth printing.

15

THE LAST TEA

Dorothy Parker

The snapping of love is an aspect of frustrated love!

The young man in the chocolate-brown suit sat down at the table, where the girl with the artificial camellia had been sitting for forty minutes.

'Guess I must be late,' he said. 'Sorry you been waiting.'

'Oh, goodness!' she said. 'I just got here myself, just about a second ago. I simply went ahead and ordered because I was dying for a cup of tea. I was late, myself. I haven't been here more than a minute.'

'That's good,' he said. 'Hey, hey, easy on the sugar—one lump is fair enough. And take away those cakes. Terrible! Do I feel terrible!'

'Ah,' she said, 'you do? Ah. Whadda matter?'

'Oh, I'm ruined,' he said. 'I'm in terrible shape.'

'Ah, the poor boy,' she said. 'Was it feelin' mizzable? Ah, and it came way up here to meet me! You shouldn't have done that—I'd have understood. Ah, just think of it coming all the way up here when it's so sick!'

'Oh, that's all right,' he said. 'I might as well be here as any place else. Any place is like any other place, the way I feel today. Oh, I'm all shot.'

'Why, that's just awful,' she said. 'Why, you poor sick thing. Goodness, I hope it isn't influenza. They say there's a lot of it around.'

'Influenza!' he said. 'I wish that was all I had. Oh, I'm poisoned. I'm through. I'm off the stuff for life. Know what time I got to bed? Twenty minutes past five, A. M., this morning. What a night! What an evening!'

'I thought,' she said, 'that you were going to stay at the office and work late. You said you'd be working every night this week.'

'Yeah, I know,' he said. 'But it gave me the jumps, thinking about going down there and sitting at that desk. I went up to May's—she was throwing a party. Say, there was somebody there said they knew you.'

'Honestly?' she said. 'Man or woman?'

'Dame,' he said. 'Name's Carol McCall. Say, why haven't I been told about her before? That's what I call a girl. What a looker she is!'

'Oh, really?' she said. 'That's funny—I never heard of anyone that thought that. I've heard people say she was sort of nice-looking, if she wouldn't make up so much. But I never heard of anyone that thought she was pretty.'

'Pretty is right,' he said. 'What a couple of eyes she's got on her!'

'Really?' she said. 'I never noticed them particularly. But I haven't seen her for a long time—sometimes people change, or something.'

'She says she used to go to school with you,' he said. 'Well, we went to the same school,' she said. 'I simply happened to go to public school because it happened to be right near us, and Mother hated to have me crossing streets. But she was three or four classes ahead of me. She's ages older than I am.'

'She's three or four classes ahead of them all,' he said. 'Dance! Can she step! "Burn your clothes, baby," I kept telling her. I must have been fried pretty.'

'I was out dancing myself, last night,' she said. 'Wally Dillon and I. He's just been pestering me to go out with him. He's the most wonderful dancer. Goodness! I didn't get home till I don't know what time. I must look just simply a wreck. Don't I?'

'You look all right,' he said.

'Wally's crazy,' she said. 'The things he says! For some crazy reason or other, he's got it into his head that I've got beautiful eyes, and, well, he just kept talking about them till I didn't know where to look, I was so embarrassed. I got so red, I thought everybody in the place would be looking at me. I got just as red as a brick. Beautiful eyes! Isn't he crazy?'

'He's all right,' he said. 'Say, this little McCall girl, she's had all kinds of offers to go into moving pictures. "Why don't you go ahead and go?" I told her. But she says she doesn't feel like it.'

'There was a man up at the lake, two summers ago,' she said. 'He was a director or something with one of the big moving-picture people—oh, he had all kinds of influence—and he used to keep insisting and insisting that I ought to be in the movies. Said I ought to be doing sort of Garbo parts. I used to just laugh at him. Imagine!'

'She's had about a million offers,' he said. 'I told her to go ahead and go. She keeps getting these offers all the time.'

'Oh, really?' she said. 'Oh, listen, I knew I had something to ask you. Did you call me up last night, by any chance?'

'Me?' he said. 'No, I didn't call you.'

'While I was out, Mother said this man's voice kept calling up,' she said. 'I thought maybe it might be you, by some chance. I wonder who it could have been. Oh—I guess I know who it was. Yes, that's who it was!'

'No, I didn't call you,' he said. 'I couldn't have seen a telephone, last night. What a head I had on me, this morning! I called Carol up, around ten, and she said she was feeling great. Can that girl hold her liquor!'

'It's a funny thing about me,' she said. 'It just makes me feel sort of sick to see a girl drink. It's just something in me, I guess. I don't mind a man so much, but it makes me feel perfectly terrible to see a girl get intoxicated. It's just the way I am, I suppose.'

'Does she carry it!' he said. 'And then feels great the next day.

There's a girl! Hey, what are you doing there? I don't want any more tea, thanks. I'm not one of these tea boys. And these tea rooms give me the jumps. Look at all those old dames, will you? Enough to give you the jumps.'

'Of course, if you'd rather be some place, drinking, with I don't know what kinds of people,' she said, 'I'm sure I don't see how I can help that. Goodness, there are enough people that are glad enough to take me to tea. I don't know how many people keep calling me up and pestering me to take me to tea. Plenty of people!'

'All right, all right, I'm here, aren't I?' he said. 'Keep your hair on.'

'I could name them all day,' she said.

'All right,' he said. 'What's there to crab about?'

'Goodness, it isn't any of my business what you do,' she said. 'But I hate to see you wasting your time with people that aren't nearly good enough for you. That's all.'

'No need worrying over me,' he said. 'I'll be all right. Listen. You don't have to worry.'

'It's just I don't like to see you wasting your time,' she said, 'staying up all night and then feeling terribly the next day. Ah, I was forgetting he was so sick. Ah, I was mean, wasn't I, scolding him when he was so mizzable. Poor boy. How's he feel now?'

'Oh, I'm all right,' he said. 'I feel fine. You want anything else? How about getting a cheque? I got to make a telephone call before six.'

'Oh, really?' she said. 'Calling up Carol?'

'She said she might be in around now,' he said.

'Seeing her tonight?' she said.

'She's going to let me know when I call up,' he said. 'She's probably got about a million dates. Why?'

'I was just wondering,' she said. 'Goodness, I've got to fly! I'm having dinner with Wally, and he's so crazy, he's probably there now. He's called me up about a hundred times today.'

'Wait till I pay the cheque,' he said, 'and I'll put you on a bus.'

'Oh, don't bother,' she said. 'It's right at the corner. I've got to fly. I suppose you want to stay and call up your friend from here?'

'It's an idea,' he said. 'Sure you'll be all right?'

'Oh, sure,' she said. Busily she gathered her gloves and purse, and left her chair. He rose, not quite fully, as she stopped beside him.

'When'll I see you again?' she said.

'I'll call you up,' he said. 'I'm all tied up, down at the office and everything. Tell you what I'll do. I'll give you a ring.'

'Honestly, I have more dates!' she said. 'It's terrible. I don't know when I'll have a minute. But you call up, will you?'

'I'll do that,' he said. 'Take care of yourself.'

'You take care of yourself,' she said. 'Hope you'll feel all right.'

'Oh, I'm fine,' he said. 'Just beginning to come back to life.'

'Be sure and let me know how you feel,' she said. 'Will you? Sure, now? Well, good-by. Oh, have a good time tonight!'

'Thanks,' he said. 'Hope you have a good time, too.'

'Oh, I will,' she said, 'I expect to. I've got to rush! Oh, I nearly forgot! Thanks ever so much for the tea. It was lovely.'

'Be yourself, will you?' he said.

'It was,' she said 'Well. Now don't forget to call me up, will you? Sure? Well, good-by.'

'So long,' he said.

She walked on down the little line between the blue-painted tables.

16

THE STRANGER

Katherine Mansfield

Even a doorway or a smile may lead to a track in love or much more…

It seemed to the little crowd on the wharf that she was never going to move again. There she lay, immense, motionless on the grey crinkled water, a loop of smoke above her, an immense flock of gulls screaming and diving after the galley droppings at the stern. You could just see little couples parading—little flies walking up and down the dish on the grey crinkled tablecloth. Other flies clustered and swarmed at the edge. Now there was a gleam of white on the lower deck—the cook's apron or the stewardess perhaps. Now a tiny black spider raced up the ladder on to the bridge.

In the front of the crowd a strong-looking, middle-aged man, dressed very well, very snugly in a grey overcoat, grey silk scarf, thick gloves and dark felt hat, marched up and down, twirling his folded umbrella. He seemed to be the leader of the little crowd on the wharf and at the same time to keep them together. He was something between the sheep-dog and the shepherd.

But what a fool—what a fool he had been not to bring any glasses! There wasn't a pair of glasses between the whole lot of them.

'Curious thing, Mr Scott, that none of us thought of glasses. We might have been able to stir 'em up a bit. We might have managed a little signalling. "Don't hesitate to land. Natives harmless." Or: "A welcome awaits you. All is forgiven." What? Eh?'

Mr Hammond's quick, eager glance, so nervous and yet so

friendly and confiding, took in everybody on the wharf, roped in even those old chaps lounging against the gangways. They knew, every man-jack of them, that Mrs Hammond was on that boat, and that he was so tremendously excited it never entered his head not to believe that this marvellous fact meant something to them too. It warmed his heart towards them. They were, he decided, as decent a crowd of people—those old chaps over by the gangways, too—fine, solid old chaps. What chests—by Jove! And he squared his own, plunged his thick-gloved hands into his pockets, rocked from heel to toe.

'Yes, my wife's been in Europe for the last ten months. On a visit to our eldest girl, who was married last year. I brought her up here, as far as Salisbury, myself. So I thought I'd better come and fetch her back. Yes, yes, yes.' The shrewd grey eyes narrowed again and searched anxiously, quickly, the motionless liner. Again his overcoat was unbuttoned. Out came the thin, butter-yellow watch again, and for the twentieth—fiftieth—hundredth time he made the calculation.

'Let me see now. It was two fifteen when the doctor's launch went off. Two fifteen. It is now exactly twenty-eight minutes past four. That is to say, the doctor's been gone two hours and thirteen minutes. Two hours and thirteen minutes! Whee-ooh!' He gave a queer little half-whistle and snapped his watch to again. 'But I think we should have been told if there was anything up—don't you, Mr Gaven?'

'Oh, yes, Mr Hammond! I don't think there's anything to—anything to worry about,' said Mr Gaven, knocking out his pipe against the heel of his shoe. 'At the same time—'

'Quite so! Quite so!' cried Mr Hammond. 'Dashed annoying!' He paced quickly up and down and came back again to his stand between Mr and Mrs Scott and Mr Gaven. 'It's getting quite dark, too,' and he waved his folded umbrella as though the dusk at least might have had the decency to keep off for a bit. But the dusk came slowly, spreading like a slow stain over the water. Little Jean Scott dragged at her mother's hand.

'I wan' my tea, mammy!' she wailed.

'I expect you do,' said Mr Hammond. 'I expect all these ladies want their tea.' And his kind, flushed, almost pitiful glance roped them all in again. He wondered whether Janey was having a final cup of tea in the saloon out there. He hoped so; he thought not. It would be just like her not to leave the deck. In that case perhaps the deck steward would bring her up a cup. If he'd been there he'd have got it for her—somehow. And for a moment he was on deck, standing over her, watching her little hand fold round the cup in the way she had, while she drank the only cup of tea to be got on board. But now he was back here, and the Lord only knew when that cursed Captain would stop hanging about in the stream. He took another turn, up and down, up and down. He walked as far as the cab-stand to make sure his driver hadn't disappeared; back he swerved again to the little flock huddled in the shelter of the banana crates. Little Jean Scott was still wanting her tea. Poor little beggar! He wished he had a bit of chocolate on him.

'Here, Jean!' he said. 'Like a lift up?' And easily, gently, he swung the little girl on to a higher barrel. The movement of holding her, steadying her, relieved him wonderfully, lightened his heart.

'Hold on,' he said, keeping an arm round her.

'Oh, don't worry about Jean, Mr Hammond!' said Mrs Scott.

'That's all right, Mrs Scott. No trouble. It's a pleasure. Jean's a little pal of mine, aren't you, Jean?'

'Yes, Mr Hammond,' said Jean, and she ran her finger down the dent of his felt hat.

But suddenly she caught him by the ear and gave a loud scream. 'Lo-ok, Mr Hammond! She's moving! Look, she's coming in!'

By Jove! So she was. At last! She was slowly, slowly turning round. A bell sounded far over the water and a great spout of steam gushed into the air. The gulls rose; they fluttered away like bits of white paper. And whether that deep throbbing was her engines or his heart Mr Hammond couldn't say. He had to nerve himself to bear it, whatever it was. At that moment old Captain Johnson, the harbour-master, came striding down the wharf, a leather portfolio under his arm.

'Jean'll be all right,' said Mr Scott. 'I'll hold her.' He was just in time. Mr Hammond had forgotten about Jean. He sprang away to greet old Captain Johnson.

'Well, Captain,' the eager, nervous voice rang out again, 'you've taken pity on us at last.'

'It's no good blaming me, Mr Hammond,' wheezed old Captain Johnson, staring at the liner. 'You got Mrs Hammond on board, ain't yer?'

'Yes, yes!' said Hammond, and he kept by the harbour-master's side. 'Mrs Hammond's there. Hul-lo! We shan't be long now!'

With her telephone ring-ringing, the thrum of her screw filling the air, the big liner bore down on them, cutting sharp through the dark water so that big white shavings curled to either side. Hammond and the harbour-master kept in front of the rest. Hammond took off his hat; he raked the decks—they were crammed with passengers; he waved his hat and bawled a loud, strange 'Hul-lo!' across the water; and then turned round and burst out laughing and said something—nothing—to old Captain Johnson.

'Seen her?' asked the harbour-master.

'No, not yet. Steady—wait a bit!' And suddenly, between two great clumsy idiots—'Get out of the way there!' he signed with his umbrella—he saw a hand raised—a white glove shaking a handkerchief. Another moment, and—thank God, thank God!— there she was. There was Janey. There was Mrs Hammond, yes, yes, yes—standing by the rail and smiling and nodding and waving her handkerchief.

'Well that's first class—first class! Well, well, well!' he positively stamped. Like lightning he drew out his cigar-case and offered it to old Captain Johnson. 'Have a cigar, Captain! They're pretty good. Have a couple! Here'—and he pressed all the cigars in the case on the harbour-master—'I've a couple of boxes up at the hotel.'

'Thenks, Mr Hammond!' wheezed old Captain Johnson.

Hammond stuffed the cigar-case back. His hands were shaking, but he'd got hold of himself again. He was able to face Janey. There she was, leaning on the rail, talking to some woman and at the same time watching him, ready for him. It struck him, as the gulf of water closed, how small she looked on that huge ship. His heart was wrung with such a spasm that he could have cried out. How little she looked to have come all that long way and back by herself! Just like her, though. Just like Janey. She had the courage of a—and now the crew had come forward and parted the passengers; they had lowered the rails for the gangways.

The voices on shore and the voices on board flew to greet each other.

'All well?'

'All well.'

'How's mother?'

'Much better.'

'Hullo, Jean!'

'Hillo, Aun' Emily!'

'Had a good voyage?'

'Splendid!'

'Shan't be long now!'

'Not long now.'

The engines stopped. Slowly she edged to the wharf-side.

'Make way there—make way—make way!' And the wharf hands brought the heavy gangways along at a sweeping run. Hammond signed to Janey to stay where she was. The old harbour-master stepped forward; he followed. As to 'ladies first', or any rot like that, it never entered his head.

'After you, Captain!' he cried genially. And, treading on the old man's heels, he strode up the gangway on to the deck in a bee-line to Janey, and Janey was clasped in his arms.

'Well, well, well! Yes, yes! Here we are at last!' he stammered. It was all he could say. And Janey emerged, and her cool little voice—the only voice in the world for him—said,

'Well, darling! Have you been waiting long?'

No; not long. Or, at any rate, it didn't matter. It was over now. But the point was, he had a cab waiting at the end of the wharf. Was she ready to go off. Was her luggage ready? In that case they could cut off sharp with her cabin luggage and let the rest go hang until to-morrow. He bent over her and she looked up with her familiar half-smile. She was just the same. Not a day changed. Just as he'd always known her. She laid her small hand on his sleeve.

'How are the children, John?' she asked.

(Hang the children!) 'Perfectly well. Never better in their lives.'

'Haven't they sent me letters?'

'Yes, yes—of course! I've left them at the hotel for you to digest later on.'

'We can't go quite so fast,' said she. 'I've got people to say good-bye to—and then there's the Captain.' As his face fell she gave his arm a small understanding squeeze. 'If the Captain comes off the bridge I want you to thank him for having looked after your wife so beautifully.' Well, he'd got her. If she wanted another ten minutes—as he gave way she was surrounded. The whole first-class seemed to want to say good-bye to Janey.

'Good-bye, dear Mrs Hammond! And next time you're in Sydney I'll expect you.'

'Darling Mrs Hammond! You won't forget to write to me, will you?'

'Well, Mrs Hammond, what this boat would have been without you!'

It was as plain as a pikestaff that she was by far the most popular woman on board. And she took it all—just as usual. Absolutely composed. Just her little self—just Janey all over; standing there with her veil thrown back. Hammond never noticed what his wife had on. It was all the same to him whatever she wore. But to-day he did notice that she wore a black 'costume'—didn't they call it? With white frills, trimmings he supposed they were, at the neck and sleeves. All this while Janey handed him round.

'John, dear!' And then: 'I want to introduce you to—'

Finally they did escape, and she led the way to her state-room. To follow Janey down the passage that she knew so well—that was so strange to him; to part the green curtains after her and to step into the cabin that had been hers gave him exquisite happiness. But—confound it!—the stewardess was there on the floor, strapping up the rugs.

'That's the last, Mrs Hammond,' said the stewardess, rising and pulling down her cuffs.

He was introduced again, and then Janey and the stewardess disappeared into the passage. He heard whisperings. She was getting the tipping business over, he supposed. He sat down on the striped sofa and took his hat off. There were the rugs she had taken with her; they looked good as new. All her luggage looked fresh, perfect. The labels were written in her beautiful little clear hand—'Mrs John Hammond'.

'Mrs John Hammond!' He gave a long sigh of content and leaned back, crossing his arms. The strain was over. He felt he could have sat there for ever sighing his relief—the relief at being rid of that horrible tug, pull, grip on his heart. The danger was over. That was the feeling. They were on dry land again.

But at that moment Janey's head came round the corner.

'Darling—do you mind? I just want to go and say good-bye to the doctor.'

Hammond started up. 'I'll come with you.'

'No, no!' she said. 'Don't bother. I'd rather not. I'll not be a minute.'

And before he could answer she was gone. He had half a mind to run after her; but instead he sat down again.

Would she really not be long? What was the time now? Out came the watch; he stared at nothing. That was rather queer of Janey, wasn't it? Why couldn't she have told the stewardess to say good-bye for her? Why did she have to go chasing after the ship's doctor? She could have sent a note from the hotel even if the affair had been urgent. Urgent? Did it—could it mean that she had been ill on the voyage—she was keeping something from him? That was it! He seized his hat. He was going off to find that fellow and to wring the truth out of him at all costs. He thought he'd noticed just something. She was just a touch too calm—too steady. From the very first moment—

The curtains rang. Janey was back. He jumped to his feet.

'Janey, have you been ill on this voyage? You have!'

'Ill?' Her airy little voice mocked him. She stepped over the rugs, and came up close, touched his breast, and looked up at him.

'Darling,' she said, 'don't frighten me. Of course I haven't! Whatever makes you think I have? Do I look ill?'

But Hammond didn't see her. He only felt that she was looking at him and that there was no need to worry about anything. She was here to look after things. It was all right. Everything was.

The gentle pressure of her hand was so calming that he put his over hers to hold it there. And she said:

'Stand still. I want to look at you. I haven't seen you yet. You've had your beard beautifully trimmed, and you look—younger, I think, and decidedly thinner! Bachelor life agrees with you.'

'Agrees with me!' He groaned for love and caught her close again. And again, as always, he had the feeling that he was holding something that never was quite his—his. Something too delicate, too precious, that would fly away once he let go.

'For God's sake let's get off to the hotel so that we can be by ourselves!' And he rang the bell hard for some one to look sharp with the luggage.

Walking down the wharf together she took his arm. He had her on his arm again. And the difference it made to get into the cab after Janey—to throw the red-and-yellow striped blanket round them both—to tell the driver to hurry because neither of them had had any tea. No more going without his tea or pouring out his own. She was back. He turned to her, squeezed her hand, and said gently, teasingly, in the 'special' voice he had for her: 'Glad to be home again, dearie?' She smiled; she didn't even bother to answer, but gently she drew his hand away as they came to the brighter streets.

'We've got the best room in the hotel,' he said. 'I wouldn't be put off with another. And I asked the chambermaid to put in a bit of a fire in case you felt chilly. She's a nice, attentive girl. And I thought now we were here we wouldn't bother to go home to-morrow, but spend the day looking round and leave the morning after. Does that suit you? There's no hurry, is there? The children will have you soon enough. I thought a day's sight-seeing might make a nice break in your journey—eh, Janey?'

'Have you taken the tickets for the day after?' she asked.

'I should think I have!' He unbuttoned his overcoat and took out his bulging pocket-book. 'Here we are! I reserved a first-class carriage to Cooktown. There it is—"Mr and Mrs John Hammond". I thought we might as well do ourselves comfortably, and we don't want other people butting in, do we? But if you'd like to stop here a bit longer—?'

'Oh, no!' said Janey quickly. 'Not for the world! The day after to-morrow, then. And the children—'

But they had reached the hotel. The manager was standing in the broad, brilliantly-lighted porch. He came down to greet them. A porter ran from the hall for their boxes.

'Well, Mr Arnold, here's Mrs Hammond at last!'

The manager led them through the hall himself and pressed the elevator-bell. Hammond knew there were business pals of his sitting at the little hall tables having a drink before dinner. But he wasn't going to risk interruption; he looked neither to the right nor the left. They could think what they pleased. If they didn't understand, the more fools they—and he stepped out of the lift, unlocked the door of their room, and shepherded Janey in. The door shut. Now, at last, they were alone together. He turned up the light. The curtains were drawn; the fire blazed. He flung his hat on to the huge bed and went towards her.

But—would you believe it—again they were interrupted. This time it was the porter with the luggage. He made two journeys of it, leaving the door open in between, taking his time, whistling through his teeth in the corridor. Hammond paced up and down the room, tearing off his gloves, tearing off his scarf. Finally he flung his overcoat on to the bedside.

At last the fool was gone. The door clicked. Now they were alone. Said Hammond: 'I feel I'll never have you to myself again. These cursed people! Janey'—and he bent his flushed, eager gaze upon her—'let's have dinner up here. If we go down to the restaurant we'll be interrupted, and then there's the confounded music' (the music he'd praised so highly, applauded so loudly last night!). 'We shan't be able to hear each other speak. Let's have something up here in front of the fire. It's too late for tea. I'll order a little supper, shall I? How does that idea strike you?'

'Do, darling!' said Janey. 'And while you're away—the children's letters—'

'Oh, later on will do!' said Hammond.

'But then we'd get it over,' said Janey. 'And I'd first have time to—'

'Oh, I needn't go down!' explained Hammond. 'I'll just ring and give the order...you don't want to send me away, do you?'

Janey shook her head and smiled.

'But you're thinking of something else. You're worrying about something,' said Hammond. 'What is it? Come and sit here—come and sit on my knee before the fire.'

'I'll just unpin my hat,' said Janey, and she went over to the dressing-table. 'A-ah!' She gave a little cry.

'What is it?'

'Nothing, darling. I've just found the children's letters. That's all right! They will keep. No hurry now!' She turned to him, clasping them. She tucked them into her frilled blouse. She cried quickly, gaily: 'Oh, how typical this dressing-table is of you!'

'Why? What's the matter with it?' said Hammond.

'If it were floating in eternity I should say, John!' laughed Janey, staring at the big bottle of hair tonic, the wicker bottle of eau-de-Cologne, the two hair-brushes, and a dozen new collars tied with pink tape. 'Is this all your luggage?'

'Hang my luggage!' said Hammond; but all the same he liked being laughed at by Janey. 'Let's talk. Let's get down to things. Tell me'—and as Janey perched on his knees he leaned back and drew her into the deep, ugly chair—'tell me you're really glad to be back, Janey.'

'Yes, darling, I am glad,' she said.

But just as when he embraced her he felt she would fly away, so Hammond never knew—never knew for dead certain that she was as glad as he was. How could he know? Would he ever know? Would he always have this craving—this pang like hunger, somehow, to make Janey so much part of him that there wasn't any of her to escape? He wanted to blot out everybody, everything. He wished now he'd turned off the light. That might have brought her nearer. And now those letters from the children rustled in her blouse. He could have chucked them into the fire.

'Janey,' he whispered.

'Yes, dear?' She lay on his breast, but so lightly, so remotely.

Their breathing rose and fell together.

'Janey!'

'What is it?'

'Turn to me,' he whispered. A slow, deep flush flowed into his forehead.

'Kiss me, Janey! You kiss me!'

It seemed to him there was a tiny pause—but long enough for him to suffer torture—before her lips touched his, firmly, lightly— kissing them as she always kissed him, as though the kiss—how could he describe it?—confirmed what they were saying, signed the contract. But that wasn't what he wanted; that wasn't at all what he thirsted for. He felt suddenly, horrible tired.

'If you knew,' he said, opening his eyes, 'what it's been like— waiting to-day. I thought the boat never would come in. There we were, hanging about. What kept you so long?'

She made no answer. She was looking away from him at the fire. The flames hurried—hurried over the coals, flickered, fell.

'Not asleep, are you?' said Hammond, and he jumped her up and down.

'No,' she said. And then: 'Don't do that, dear. No, I was thinking. As a matter of fact,' she said, 'one of the passengers died last night—a man. That's what held us up. We brought him in—I mean, he wasn't buried at sea. So, of course, the ship's doctor and the shore doctor—'

'What was it?' asked Hammond uneasily. He hated to hear of death. He hated this to have happened. It was, in some queer way, as though he and Janey had met a funeral on their way to the hotel.

'Oh, it wasn't anything in the least infectious!' said Janey. She was speaking scarcely above her breath. 'It was heart.' A pause. 'Poor fellow!' she said. 'Quite young.' And she watched the fire flicker and fall. 'He died in my arms,' said Janey.

The blow was so sudden that Hammond thought he would

faint. He couldn't move; he couldn't breathe. He felt all his strength flowing—flowing into the big dark chair, and the big dark chair held him fast, gripped him, forced him to bear it.

'What?' he said dully. 'What's that you say?'

'The end was quite peaceful,' said the small voice. 'He just'— and Hammond saw her lift her gentle hand—'breathed his life away at the end.' And her hand fell.

'Who—else was there?' Hammond managed to ask.

'Nobody. I was alone with him.'

Ah, my God, what was she saying! What was she doing to him! This would kill him! And all the while she spoke:

'I saw the change coming and I sent the steward for the doctor, but the doctor was too late. He couldn't have done anything, anyway.'

'But—why you, why you?' moaned Hammond.

At that Janey turned quickly, quickly searched his face.

'You don't mind, John, do you?' she asked. 'You don't—It's nothing to do with you and me.'

Somehow or other he managed to shake some sort of smile at her. Somehow or other he stammered: 'No—go—on, go on! I want you to tell me.'

'But, John darling—'

'Tell me, Janey!'

'There's nothing to tell,' she said, wondering. 'He was one of the first-class passengers. I saw he was very ill when he came on board. But he seemed to be so much better until yesterday. He had a severe attack in the afternoon—excitement—nervousness, I think, about arriving. And after that he never recovered.'

'But why didn't the stewardess—'

'Oh, my dear—the stewardess!' said Janey. 'What would he have felt? And besides...he might have wanted to leave a message...to—'

'Didn't he?' muttered Hammond. 'Didn't he say anything?'

'No, darling, not a word!' She shook her head softly. 'All the time I was with him he was too weak...he was too weak even to move a finger...'

Janey was silent. But her words, so light, so soft, so chill, seemed to hover in the air, to rain into his breast like snow.

The fire had gone red. Now it fell in with a sharp sound and the room was colder. Cold crept up his arms. The room was huge, immense, glittering. It filled his whole world. There was the great blind bed, with his coat flung across it like some headless man saying his prayers. There was the luggage, ready to be carried away again, anywhere, tossed into trains, carted on to boats.

'He was too weak. He was too weak to move a finger.' And yet he died in Janey's arms. She—who'd never—never once in all these years—never on one single solitary occasion—

No; he mustn't think of it. Madness lay in thinking of it. No, he wouldn't face it. He couldn't stand it. It was too much to bear!

And now Janey touched his tie with her fingers. She pinched the edges of the tie together.

'You're not—sorry I told you, John darling? It hasn't made you sad? It hasn't spoilt our evening—our being alone together?'

But at that he had to hide his face. He put his face into her bosom and his arms enfolded her.

Spoilt their evening! Spoilt their being alone together! They would never be alone together again.

17

LASTING LOVE

Guy de Maupassant

Love has two aspects; giving and taking. Giving is easier; taking is difficult. Let's ponder over this paradox of love.

It was the end of the dinner that opened the shooting season. The Marquis de Bertrans with his guests sat around a brightly lighted table, covered with fruit and flowers. The conversation drifted to love. Immediately there arose an animated discussion, the same eternal discussion as to whether it were possible to love more than once. Examples were given of persons who had loved once; these were offset by those who had loved violently many times. The men agreed that passion, like sickness, may attack the same person several times, unless it strikes to kill. This conclusion seemed quite incontestable. The women, however, who based their opinion on poetry rather than on practical observation, maintained that love, the great passion, may come only once to mortals. It resembles lightning, they said, this love. A heart once touched by it becomes forever such a waste, so ruined, so consumed, that no other strong sentiment can take root there, not even a dream. The Marquis, who had indulged in many love affairs, disputed this belief.

'I tell you it is possible to love several times with all one's heart and soul. You quote examples of persons who have killed themselves for love, to prove the impossibility of a second passion. I wager that if they had not foolishly committed suicide, and so destroyed the possibility of a second experience, they would have found a new love, and still another, and so on till death. It is with love as with drink. He who has once indulged is forever a slave. It is a thing of temperament.'

They chose the old Doctor as umpire. He thought it was as the Marquis had said, a thing of temperament.

'As for me,' he said, 'I once knew of a love which lasted fifty-five years without one day's respite, and which ended only with death.' The wife of the Marquis clasped her hands.

'That is beautiful! Ah, what a dream to be loved in such a way! What bliss to live for fifty-five years enveloped in an intense, unwavering affection! How this happy being must have blessed his life to be so adored!'

The Doctor smiled.

'You are not mistaken, Madame, on this point the loved one was a man. You even know him; it is Monsieur Chouquet, the chemist. As to the woman, you also know her, the old chair-mender, who came every year to the chateau.' The enthusiasm of the women fell. Some expressed their contempt with 'Pouah!' for the loves of common people did not interest them. The Doctor continued: 'Three months ago I was called to the deathbed of the old chair-mender. The priest had preceded me. She wished to make us the executors of her will. In order that we might understand her conduct, she told us the story of her life. It is most singular and touching: Her father and mother were both chair-menders. She had never lived in a house. As a little child she wandered about with them, dirty, unkempt, hungry. They visited many towns, leaving their horse, wagon and dog just outside the limits, where the child played in the grass alone until her parents had repaired all the broken chairs in the place. They seldom spoke, except to cry, 'Chairs! Chairs! Chair-mender!'

'When the little one strayed too far away, she would be called back by the harsh, angry voice of her father. She never heard a word of affection. When she grew older, she fetched and carried the broken chairs. Then it was she made friends with the children in the street, but their parents always called them away and scolded them for speaking to the barefooted child. Often the boys threw stones at her. Once a kind woman gave her a few pennies. She saved them most carefully.

'One day—she was then eleven years old—as she was walking through a country town she met, behind the cemetery, little Chouquet, weeping bitterly, because one of his playmates had stolen two precious liards (mills). The tears of the small bourgeois, one of those much-envied mortals, who, she imagined, never knew trouble, completely upset her. She approached him and, as soon as she learned the cause of his grief, she put into his hands all her savings. He took them without hesitation and dried his eyes. Wild with joy, she kissed him. He was busy counting his money, and did not object. Seeing that she was not repulsed, she threw her arms round him and gave him a hug—then she ran away.

'What was going on in her poor little head? Was it because she had sacrificed all her fortune that she became madly fond of this youngster, or was it because she had given him the first tender kiss? The mystery is alike for children and for those of riper years. For months she dreamed of that corner near the cemetery and of the little chap. She stole a sou here and there from her parents on the chair money or groceries she was sent to buy. When she returned to the spot near the cemetery she had two francs in her pocket, but he was not there. Passing his father's drug store, she caught sight of him behind the counter. He was sitting between a large red globe and a blue one. She only loved him the more, quite carried away at the sight of the brilliant-coloured globes. She cherished the recollection of it forever in her heart. The following year she met him near the school, playing marbles. She rushed up to him, threw her arms round him, and kissed him so passionately that he screamed, in fear. To quiet him, she gave him all her money. Three francs and twenty centimes! A real gold mine, at which he gazed with staring eyes.

'After this he allowed her to kiss him as much as she wished. During the next four years she put into his hands all her savings, which he pocketed conscientiously in exchange for kisses. At one time it was thirty sous, at another two francs. Again, she only had twelve sous. She wept with grief and shame, explaining brokenly that it had been a poor year. The next time she brought five francs, in one whole piece, which made her laugh with joy. She no longer thought of any one but the boy, and he watched for her with impatience; sometimes he would run to meet her. This made her heart thump with joy. Suddenly he disappeared. He had gone to boarding school. She found this out by careful investigation. Then she used great diplomacy to persuade her parents to change their route and pass by this way again during vacation. After a year of scheming she succeeded. She had not seen him for two years, and scarcely recognized him, he was so changed, had grown taller, better looking and was imposing in his uniform, with its brass buttons. He pretended not to see her, and passed by without a glance. She wept for two days and from that time loved and suffered unceasingly.

'Every year he came home and she passed him, not daring to lift her eyes. He never condescended to turn his head toward her. She loved him madly, hopelessly. She said to me:

'"He is the only man whom I have ever seen. I don't even know if another exists." Her parents died. She continued their work.

'One day, on entering the village, where her heart always remained, she saw Chouquet coming out of his pharmacy with a young lady leaning on his arm. She was his wife. That night the chair-mender threw herself into the river. A drunkard passing the spot pulled her out and took her to the drug store. Young Chouquet came down in his dressing gown to revive her. Without seeming to know who she was he undressed her and rubbed her; then he said to her, in a harsh voice:

'"You are mad! People must not do stupid things like that."

His voice brought her to life again. He had spoken to her! She was happy for a long time. He refused remuneration for his trouble, although she insisted.

'All her life passed in this way. She worked, thinking always of him. She began to buy medicines at his pharmacy; this gave her a chance to talk to him and to see him closely. In this way, she was still able to give him money.

'As I said before, she died this spring. When she had closed her pathetic story she entreated me to take her earnings to the man she loved. She had worked only that she might leave him something to remind him of her after her death. I gave the priest fifty francs for her funeral expenses. The next morning I went to see the Chouquets. They were finishing breakfast, sitting opposite each other, fat and red, important and self-satisfied. They welcomed me and offered me some coffee, which I accepted. Then I began my story in a trembling voice, sure that they would be softened, even to tears. As soon as Chouquet understood that he had been loved by "that vagabond, that chair-mender, that wanderer!" he swore with indignation as though his reputation had been sullied, the respect of decent people lost, his personal honour, something precious and dearer to him than life, gone. His exasperated wife kept repeating: "That beggar! That beggar!"

'Seeming unable to find words suitable to the enormity, he stood up and began striding about. He muttered: "Can you understand anything so horrible, doctor? Oh, if I had only known it while she was alive, I should have had her thrown into prison. I promise you she would not have escaped."

'I was dumfounded; I hardly knew what to think or say, but I had to finish my mission. "She commissioned me," I said, "to give you her savings, which amount to three thousand five hundred francs. As what I have just told you seems to be very disagreeable, perhaps you would prefer to give this money to the poor."

'They looked at me, that man and woman, speechless with

amazement. I took the few thousand francs from out of my pocket. Wretched-looking money from every country. Pennies and gold pieces all mixed together. Then I asked:

"'What is your decision?"

'Madame Chouquet spoke first. "Well, since it is the dying woman's wish, it seems to me impossible to refuse it."

'Her husband said, in a shamefaced manner: "We could buy something for our children with it."

'I answered dryly: "As you wish."

'He replied: "Well, give it to us anyhow, since she commissioned you to do so; we will find a way to put it to some good purpose."

'I gave them the money, bowed and left.

'The next day Chouquet came to me and said brusquely:

"'That woman left her wagon here—what have you done with it?"

"'Nothing; take it if you wish."

"'It's just what I wanted," he added, and walked off. I called him back and said:

"'She also left her old horse and two dogs. Don't you need them?"

'He stared at me surprised: "Well, no! Really, what would I do with them?"

"'Dispose of them as you like."

'He laughed and held out his hand to me. I shook it. What could I do? The doctor and the druggist in a country village must not be at enmity. I have kept the dogs. The priest took the old horse. The wagon is useful to Chouquet, and with the money he has bought railroad stock. That is the only deep, sincere love that I have ever known in all my life.'

The Doctor looked up. The Marquis, whose eyes were full of tears, sighed and said:

'There is no denying the fact, only women know how to love.'

18

THE CALIPH, CUPID AND THE CLOCK

O. Henry

Time is a mystery. Time is a fable. Time hangs from clocks and calendars, yet each one has a different time.

Prince Michael, of the Electorate of Valleluna, sat on his favourite bench in the park. The coolness of the September night quickened the life in him like a rare, tonic wine. The benches were not filled; for park loungers, with their stagnant blood, are prompt to detect and fly home from the crispness of early autumn. The moon was just clearing the roofs of the range of dwellings that bounded the quadrangle on the east. Children laughed and played about the fine-sprayed fountain. In the shadowed spots fauns and hamadryads wooed, unconscious of the gaze of mortal eyes. A hand organ—Philomel by the grace of our stage carpenter, Fancy—fluted and droned in a side street. Around the enchanted boundaries of the little park street cars spat and mewed and the stilted trains roared like tigers and lions prowling for a place to enter. And above the trees shone the great, round, shining face of an illuminated clock in the tower of an antique public building.

Prince Michael's shoes were wrecked far beyond the skill of the carefullest cobbler. The ragman would have declined any negotiations concerning his clothes. The two weeks' stubble on his face was grey and brown and red and greenish yellow—as if it had been made up from individual contributions from the chorus of a musical comedy. No man existed who had money enough to wear so bad a hat as his.

Prince Michael sat on his favourite bench and smiled. It was a diverting thought to him that he was wealthy enough to buy every one of those close-ranged, bulky, window-lit mansions that faced him, if he chose. He could have matched gold, equipages, jewels, art treasures, estates and acres with any Croesus in this proud city of Manhattan, and scarcely have entered upon the bulk of his holdings. He could have sat at table with reigning sovereigns. The social world, the world of art, the fellowship of the elect, adulation, imitation, the homage of the fairest, honours from the highest, praise from the wisest, flattery, esteem, credit, pleasure, fame—all the honey of life was waiting in the comb in the hive of the world for Prince Michael, of the Electorate of Valleluna, whenever he might choose to take it. But his choice was to sit in rags and dinginess on a bench in a park. For he had tasted of the fruit of the tree of life, and, finding it bitter in his mouth, had stepped out of Eden for a time to seek distraction close to the unarmoured, beating heart of the world.

These thoughts strayed dreamily through the mind of Prince Michael, as he smiled under the stubble of his polychromatic beard. Lounging thus, clad as the poorest of mendicants in the parks, he loved to study humanity. He found in altruism more pleasure than his riches, his station and all the grosser sweets of life had given him. It was his chief solace and satisfaction to alleviate individual distress, to confer favours upon worthy ones who had need of succour, to dazzle unfortunates by unexpected and bewildering gifts of truly royal magnificence, bestowed, however, with wisdom and judiciousness.

And as Prince Michael's eye rested upon the glowing face of the great clock in the tower, his smile, altruistic as it was, became slightly tinged with contempt. Big thoughts were the Prince's; and it was always with a shake of his head that he considered the subjugation of the world to the arbitrary measures of Time. The comings and goings of people in hurry and dread, controlled by the little metal moving hands of a clock, always made him sad.

By and by came a young man in evening clothes and sat upon the third bench from the Prince. For half an hour he smoked cigars with nervous haste, and then he fell to watching the face of the illuminated clock above the trees. His perturbation was evident, and the Prince noted, in sorrow, that its cause was connected, in some manner, with the slowly moving hands of the timepiece.

His Highness arose and went to the young man's bench.

'I beg your pardon for addressing you,' he said, 'but I perceive that you are disturbed in mind. If it may serve to mitigate the liberty I have taken I will add that I am Prince Michael, heir to the throne of the Electorate of Valleluna. I appear incognito, of course, as you may gather from my appearance. It is a fancy of mine to render aid to others whom I think worthy of it. Perhaps the matter that seems to distress you is one that would more readily yield to our mutual efforts.'

The young man looked up brightly at the Prince. Brightly, but the perpendicular line of perplexity between his brows was not smoothed away. He laughed, and even then it did not. But he accepted the momentary diversion.

'Glad to meet you, Prince,' he said, good humouredly. 'Yes, I'd say you were incog all right. Thanks for your offer of assistance— but I don't see where your butting-in would help things any. It's a kind of private affair, you know—but thanks all the same.'

Prince Michael sat at the young man's side. He was often rebuffed but never offensively. His courteous manner and words forbade that.

'Clocks,' said the Prince, 'are shackles on the feet of mankind. I have observed you looking persistently at that clock. Its face is that of a tyrant, its numbers are false as those on a lottery ticket; its hands are those of a bunco steerer, who makes an appointment with you to your ruin. Let me entreat you to throw off its humiliating bonds and to cease to order your affairs by that insensate monitor of brass and steel.'

'I don't usually,' said the young man. 'I carry a watch except when I've got my radiant rags on.'

'I know human nature as I do the trees and grass,' said the Prince, with earnest dignity. 'I am a master of philosophy, a graduate in art, and I hold the purse of a Fortunatus. There are few mortal misfortunes that I cannot alleviate or overcome. I have read your countenance, and found in it honesty and nobility as well as distress. I beg of you to accept my advice or aid. Do not belie the intelligence I see in your face by judging from my appearance of my ability to defeat your troubles.'

The young man glanced at the clock again and frowned darkly. When his gaze strayed from the glowing horologue of time it rested intently upon a four-story red brick house in the row of dwellings opposite to where he sat. The shades were drawn, and the lights in many rooms shone dimly through them.

'Ten minutes to nine!' exclaimed the young man, with an impatient gesture of despair. He turned his back upon the house and took a rapid step or two in a contrary direction.

'Remain!' commanded Prince Michael, in so potent a voice that the disturbed one wheeled around with a somewhat chagrined laugh.

'I'll give her the ten minutes and then I'm off,' he muttered, and then aloud to the Prince: 'I'll join you in confounding all clocks, my friend, and throw in women, too.'

'Sit down,' said the Prince calmly. 'I do not accept your addition. Women are the natural enemies of clocks, and, therefore, the allies of those who would seek liberation from these monsters that measure our follies and limit our pleasures. If you will so far confide in me I would ask you to relate to me your story.'

The young man threw himself upon the bench with a reckless laugh.

'Your Royal Highness, I will,' he said, in tones of mock deference. 'Do you see yonder house—the one with three upper windows lighted? Well, at 6 o'clock I stood in that house with the young lady I am—that is, I was—engaged to. I had been doing wrong, my dear Prince—I had been a naughty boy, and she had heard of it. I wanted to be forgiven, of course—we are always wanting women to forgive us, aren't we, Prince?

'"I want time to think it over," said she. "There is one thing certain; I will either fully forgive you, or I will never see your face again. There will be no half-way business. At half-past eight," she said, "at exactly half-past eight you may be watching the middle upper window of the top floor. If I decide to forgive I will hang out of that window a white silk scarf. You will know by that that all is as was before, and you may come to me. If you see no scarf you may consider that everything between us is ended forever." That,' concluded the young man bitterly, 'is why I have been watching that clock. The time for the signal to appear has passed twenty-three minutes ago. Do you wonder that I am a little disturbed, my Prince of Rags and Whiskers?'

'Let me repeat to you,' said Prince Michael, in his even, well-modulated tones, 'that women are the natural enemies of clocks. Clocks are an evil, women a blessing. The signal may yet appear.'

'Never, on your principality!' exclaimed the young man, hopelessly. 'You don't know Marian—of course. She's always on time, to the minute. That was the first thing about her that attracted me. I've got the mitten instead of the scarf. I ought to have known at 8.31 that my goose was cooked. I'll go West on the 11.45 to-night with Jack Milburn. The jig's up. I'll try Jack's ranch awhile and top off with the Klondike and whiskey. Good-night...er...er...Prince.'

Prince Michael smiled his enigmatic, gentle, comprehending smile and caught the coat sleeve of the other. The brilliant light in the Prince's eyes was softening to a dreamier, cloudy translucence.

'Wait,' he said solemnly, 'till the clock strikes. I have wealth and power and knowledge above most men, but when the clock strikes I am afraid. Stay by me until then. This woman shall be yours. You have the word of the hereditary Prince of Valleluna. On the day of your marriage I will give you $100,000 and a palace on the Hudson. But there must be no clocks in that palace—they measure our follies and limit our pleasures. Do you agree to that?'

'Of course,' said the young man, cheerfully, 'they're a nuisance, anyway—always ticking and striking and getting you late for dinner.'

He glanced again at the clock in the tower. The hands stood at three minutes to nine.

'I think,' said Prince Michael, 'that I will sleep a little. The day has been fatiguing.'

He stretched himself upon a bench with the manner of one who had slept thus before.

'You will find me in this park on any evening when the weather is suitable,' said the Prince, sleepily. 'Come to me when your marriage day is set and I will give you a cheque for the money.'

'Thanks, Your Highness,' said the young man, seriously. 'It doesn't look as if I would need that palace on the Hudson, but I appreciate your offer, just the same.'

Prince Michael sank into deep slumber. His battered hat rolled from the bench to the ground. The young man lifted it, placed it over the frowsy face and moved one of the grotesquely relaxed limbs into a more comfortable position. 'Poor devil!' he said, as he drew the tattered clothes closer about the Prince's breast.

Sonorous and startling came the stroke of 9 from the clock tower. The young man sighed again, turned his face for one last look at the house of his relinquished hopes—and cried aloud profane words of holy rapture.

From the middle upper window blossomed in the dusk a

waving, snowy, fluttering, wonderful, divine emblem of forgiveness and promised joy.

By came a citizen, rotund, comfortable, home-hurrying, unknowing of the delights of waving silken scarfs on the borders of dimly-lit parks.

'Will you oblige me with the time, sir?' asked the young man; and the citizen, shrewdly conjecturing his watch to be safe, dragged it out and announced:

'Twenty-nine and a half minutes past eight, sir.'

And then, from habit, he glanced at the clock in the tower, and made further oration.

'By George! that clock's half an hour fast! First time in ten years I've known it to be off. This watch of mine never varies a—'

But the citizen was talking to vacancy. He turned and saw his hearer, a fast receding black shadow, flying in the direction of a house with three lighted upper windows.

And in the morning came along two policemen on their way to the beats they owned. The park was deserted save for one dilapidated figure that sprawled, asleep, on a bench. They stopped and gazed upon it.

'It's Dopy Mike,' said one. 'He hits the pipe every night. Park bum for twenty years. On his last legs, I guess.'

The other policeman stooped and looked at something crumpled and crisp in the hand of the sleeper.

'Gee!' he remarked. 'He's doped out a fifty-dollar bill, anyway. Wish I knew the brand of hop that he smokes.'

And then 'Rap, rap, rap!' went the club of realism against the shoe soles of Prince Michael, of the Electorate of Valleluna.

19

FALSE DAWN
Rudyard Kipling

Alas, how easily things can go wrong, a sigh too much, a kiss too long, there comes a mist and a weeping rain, and life is never the same again.

To-night God knows what thing shall tide,
The Earth is racked and faint,
Expectant, sleepless, open-eyed;
And we, who from the Earth were made,
Thrill with our Mother's pain.

—In Durance

No man will ever know the exact truth of this story; though women may sometimes whisper it to one another after a dance, when they are putting up their hair for the night and comparing lists of victims. A man, of course, cannot assist at these functions. So the tale must be told from the outside—in the dark—all wrong.

Never praise a sister to a sister, in the hope of your compliments reaching the proper ears, and so preparing the way for you later on. Sisters are women first, and sisters afterwards; and you will find that you do yourself harm.

Saumarez knew this when he made up his mind to propose to the elder Miss Copleigh. Saumarez was a strange man, with few merits so far as men could see, though he was popular with women, and carried enough conceit to stock a Viceroy's Council and leave a little over for the Commander-in-Chief's Staff. He was a civilian. Very many women took an interest in Saumarez, perhaps, because his manner to them was offensive. If you hit a pony over the nose at the outset of your acquaintance, he may not love you, but he will take a deep interest in your movements ever afterwards. The elder Miss Copleigh was nice, plump, winning, and pretty. The younger was not so pretty, and, from men disregarding the hint set forth above, her style was repellent and unattractive. Both girls had, practically, the same figure, and there was a strong likeness between them in look and voice; though no one could doubt for an instant which was the nicer of the two.

Saumarez made up his mind, as soon as they came into the station from Behar, to marry the elder one. At least, we all made sure that he would, which comes to the same thing. She was two and twenty, and he was thirty-three, with pay and allowances of nearly fourteen hundred rupees a month. So the match, as we arranged it, was in every way a good one. Saumarez was his name, and summary was his nature, as a man once said. Having drafted his Resolution, he formed a Select Committee of One to sit upon it, and resolved to take his time. In our unpleasant slang, the Copleigh girls 'hunted in couples'. That is to say, you could do nothing with one without the other. They were very loving sisters; but their mutual affection was sometimes inconvenient. Saumarez held the balance-hair true between them, and none but himself could have said to which side his heart inclined; though every one guessed. He rode with them a good deal and danced with them, but he never succeeded in detaching them from each other for any length of time.

Women said that the two girls kept together through deep mistrust, each fearing that the other would steal a march on her. But that has nothing to do with a man. Saumarez was silent for good or bad, and as business-likely attentive as he could be, having due regard for his work and his polo. Beyond doubt both girls were fond of him.

As the hot weather drew nearer and Saumarez made no sign, women said that you could see their trouble in the eyes of the girls—that they were looking strained, anxious, and irritable. Men are quite blind in these matters unless they have more of the woman than the man in their composition, in which case it does not matter what they say or think. I maintain it was the hot April days that took the colour out of the Copleigh girls' cheeks. They should have been sent to the Hills early. No one—man or woman—feels an angel when the hot weather is approaching. The younger sister grew more cynical, not to say acid, in her ways; and the winningness of the elder wore thin. There was effort in it.

Noe the Station wherein all these things happened was, though not a little one, off the line of rail, and suffered through want of attention. There were no gardens, or bands or amusements worth speaking of, and it was nearly a day's journey to come into Lahore for a dance. People were grateful for small things to interest them.

About the beginning of May, and just before the final exodus of Hill-goers, when the weather was very hot and there were not more than twenty people in the Station, Saumarez gave a moonlight riding-picnic at an old tomb, six miles away, near the bed of the river. It was a 'Noah's Ark' picnic; and there was to be the usual arrangement of quarter-mile intervals between each couple, on account of the dust. Six couples came altogether, including chaperones. Moonlight picnics are useful just at the very end of the season, before all the girls go away to the Hills. They lead to understandings, and should be encouraged by chaperones; especially those whose girls look sweetish in riding habits. I knew a case once. But that is another story. That picnic was called the 'Great Pop Picnic', because every one knew Saumarez would propose then to the eldest Miss Copleigh; and, besides his affair, there was another which might possibly come to happiness. The social atmosphere was heavily charged and wanted clearing.

We met at the parade-ground at ten: the night was fearfully

hot. The horses sweated even at walking pace, but anything was better than sitting still in our own dark houses. When we moved off under the full moon we were four couples, one triplet, and Me. Saumarez rode with the Copleigh girls, and I loitered at the tail of the procession wondering with whom Saumarez would ride home. Every one was happy and contented; but we all felt that things were going to happen.

We rode slowly; and it was midnight before we reached the old tomb, facing the ruined tank, in the decayed gardens where we were going to eat and drink. I was late in coming up; and, before I went in to the garden, I saw that the horizon to the north carried a faint, dun-coloured feather. But no one would have thanked me for spoiling so well-managed an entertainment as this picnic—and a dust-storm, more or less, does no great harm.

We gathered by the tank. Some one had brought out a banjo—which is a most sentimental instrument—and three or four of us sang. You must not laugh at this.

Our amusements in out-of-the-way Stations are very few indeed. Then we talked in groups or together, lying under the trees, with the sun-baked roses dropping their petals on our feet, until supper was ready. It was a beautiful supper, as cold and as iced as you could wish; and we stayed long over it.

I had felt that the air was growing hotter and hotter; but nobody seemed to notice it until the moon went out and a burning hot wind began lashing the orange trees with a sound like the noise of the sea. Before we knew where we were, the dust-storm was on us and everything was roaring, whirling darkness. The supper table was blown bodily into the tank. We were afraid of staying anywhere near the old tomb for fear it might fall down. So we felt our way to the orange trees where the horses were picketed and waited for the storm to blow over. Then the little remaining light vanished, and you could not see your hand before your face.

The air was heavy with dust and sand from the bed of the

river, that filled boots and pockets and drifted down necks and coated eyebrows and moustaches. We all huddled together close to the trembling horses, with the thunder chattering overhead, and the lightning spurting like water from a sluice, all ways at once. There was no danger, of course, unless the horses broke loose. I was standing with my head downwind and my hands over my mouth, hearing the trees thrashing each other. I could not see who was next me till the flashes came. Then I found that I was packed near Saumarez and the eldest Miss Copleigh, with my own horse just in front of me. I recognized the eldest Miss Copleigh, because she had a pagri round her helmet, and the younger had not. All the electricity in the air had gone into my body and I was quivering and tingling from head to foot—exactly as a corn shoots and tingles before rain. It was a grand storm. The wind seemed to be picking up the earth and pitching it to leeward in great heaps; and the heat beat up from the ground like the heat of the Day of Judgement.

The storm lulled slightly after the first half-hour, and I heard a despairing little voice close to my ear, saying to itself, quietly and softly, as if some lost soul were flying about with the wind, 'O my God!' Then the younger Miss Copleigh stumbled into my arms, saying, 'Where is my horse? Get my horse. I want to go home. I want to go home. Take me home.' I thought that the lightning and the black darkness had frightened her; so I said there was no danger, but she must wait till the storm blew over. She answered, 'It is not that! I want to go home! Oh, take me away from here!' I said that she could not go till the light came; but I felt her brush past me and go away. It was too dark to see where. Then the whole sky was split open with one tremendous flash, as if the end of the world were coming, and all the women shrieked.

Almost directly after this, I felt a man's hand on my shoulder and heard Saumarez bellowing in my ear. Through the rattling of the trees and howling of the wind, I did not catch his words at once, but at last I heard him say, 'I've proposed to the wrong one! What shall I do?' Saumarez had no occasion to make this confidence to me. I was never a friend of his, nor am I now; but I fancy neither of us were ourselves just then. He was shaking as he stood with excitement, and I was feeling queer all over with the electricity. I could not think of anything to say except, 'More fool you for proposing in a dust-storm.' But I did not see how that would improve the mistake.

Then he shouted, 'Where's Edith—Edith Copleigh?' Edith was the younger sister. I answered out of my astonishment, 'What do you want with her?' For the next two minutes, he and I were shouting at each other like maniacs—he vowing that it was the younger sister he had meant to propose to all along, and I telling him till my throat was hoarse that he must have made a mistake! I cannot account for this except, again, by the fact that we were neither of us ourselves. Everything seemed to me like a bad dream—from the stamping of the horses in the darkness to Saumarez telling me the story of his loving Edith Copleigh from the first. He was still clawing my shoulder and begging me to tell him where Edith Copleigh was, when another lull came and brought light with it, and we saw the dust-cloud forming on the plain in front of us. So we knew the worst was over. The moon was low down, and there was just the glimmer of the false dawn that comes about an hour before the real one. But the light was very faint, and the dun cloud roared like a bull. I wondered where Edith Copleigh had gone; and as I was wondering I saw three things together: First, Maud Copleigh's face come smiling out of the darkness and move towards Saumarez who was standing by me. I heard the girl whisper, 'George,' and slide her arm through the arm that was not clawing my shoulder, and I saw that look on her face which only comes once or twice in a lifetime—when a woman is perfectly happy and the air is full of trumpets and gorgeously coloured fire and the Earth turns into cloud because she loves and is loved. At the same time, I saw Saumarez's face as he heard Maud Copleigh's voice, and fifty yards away from the clump of orange trees, I saw a brown holland habit getting upon a horse.

It must have been my state of over-excitement that made me so ready to meddle with what did not concern me. Saumarez was moving off to the habit; but I pushed him back and said, 'Stop here and explain. I'll fetch her back!' And I ran out to get at my own horse. I had a perfectly unnecessary notion that everything must be done decently and in order, and that Saumarez's first care was to wipe the happy look out of Maud Copleigh's face. All the time I was linking up the curb-chain I wondered how he would do it.

I cantered after Edith Copleigh, thinking to bring her back slowly on some pretence or another. But she galloped away as soon as she saw me, and I was forced to ride after her in earnest. She called back over her shoulder—'Go away! I'm going home. Oh, go away!' ;two or three times; but my business was to catch her first, and argue later. The ride fitted in with the rest of the evil dream. The ground was very rough, and now and again we rushed through the whirling, choking 'dust-devils' in the skirts of the flying storm. There was a burning hot wind blowing that brought up a stench of stale brick-kilns with it; and through the half light and through the dust-devils, across that desolate plain, flickered the brown holland habit on the grey horse. She headed for the Station at first. Then she wheeled round and set off for the river through beds of burnt down jungle-grass, bad even to ride pig over. In cold blood I should never have dreamed of going over such a country at night, but it seemed quite right and natural with the lightning crackling overhead, and a reek like the smell of the Pit in my nostrils. I rode and shouted, and she bent forward and lashed her horse, and the aftermath of the dust-storm came up, and caught us both, and drove us downwind like pieces of paper.

I don't know how far we rode; but the drumming of the horse hoofs and the roar of the wind and the race of the faint blood-red moon through the yellow mist seemed to have gone on for years and years, and I was literally drenched with sweat from my helmet to my gaiters when the grey stumbled, recovered himself and pulled up dead lame. My brute was used up altogether.

Edith Copleigh was bareheaded, plastered with dust, and crying bitterly. 'Why can't you let me alone?' she said. 'I only wanted to get away and go home. Oh, please let me go!' 'You have got to come back with me, Miss Copleigh. Saumarez has something to say to you.' It was a foolish way of putting it; but I hardly knew Miss Copleigh, and, though I was playing Providence at the cost of my horse, I could not tell her in as many words what Saumarez had told me. I thought he could do that better himself. All her pretence about being tired and wanting to go home broke down, and she rocked herself to and fro in the saddle as she sobbed, and the hot wind blew her black hair to leeward. I am not going to repeat what she said, because she was utterly unstrung.

This was the cynical Miss Copleigh, and I, almost an utter stranger to her, was trying to tell her that Saumarez loved her and she was to come back to hear him say so. I believe I made myself understood, for she gathered the grey together and made him hobble somehow, and we set off for the tomb, while the storm went thundering down to Umballa and a few big drops of warm rain fell. I found out that she had been standing close to Saumarez when he proposed to her sister, and had wanted to go home to cry in peace, as an English girl should. She dabbed her eyes with her pocket-handkerchief as we went along, and babbled to me out of sheer lightness of heart and hysteria. That was perfectly unnatural; and yet, it seemed all right at the time and in the place. All the world was only the two Copleigh girls, Saumarez and I, ringed in with the lightning and the dark; and the guidance of this misguided world seemed to lie in my hands.

When we returned to the tomb in the deep dead stillness that followed the storm, the dawn was just breaking and nobody had gone away. They were waiting for our return. Saumarez most of all. His face was white and drawn. As Miss Copleigh and I limped up, he came forward to meet us, and, when he helped her down from her saddle, he kissed her before all the picnic. It was like a scene in a theatre, and the likeness was heightened by all the dust white, ghostly looking men and women under the orange trees clapping their hands—as if they were watching a play—at Saumarez's choice. I never knew anything so un-English in my life.

Lastly, Saumarez said we must all go home or the Station would come out to look for us, and would I be good enough to ride home with Maud Copleigh? Nothing would give me greater pleasure, I said.

So we formed up, six couples in all, and went back two by two; Saumarez walking at the side of Edith Copleigh, who was riding his horse. Maud Copleigh did not talk to me at any length.

The air was cleared; and, little by little, as the sun rose, I felt we were all dropping back again into ordinary men and women, and that the 'Great Pop Picnic' was a thing altogether apart and out of the world—never to happen again. It had gone with the dust-storm and the tingle in the hot air.

I felt tired and limp, and a good deal ashamed of myself as I went in for a bath and some sleep.

There is a woman's version of this story, but it will never be written…unless Maud Copleigh cares to try.

20

THE LADY WITH THE DOG

Anton Chekhov

*Love seems to have no frontiers and barriers: it not only contradicts
reason it may also transcend reason.*

I

It was said that a new person had appeared on the sea-front: a
lady with a little dog.

Dmitri Dmitritch Gurov, who had by then been a fortnight at
Yalta, and so was fairly at home there, had begun to take an interest
in new arrivals. Sitting in Verney's pavilion, he saw, walking on
the sea-front, a fair-haired young lady of medium height, wearing
a béret; a white Pomeranian dog was running behind her.

And afterwards he met her in the public gardens and in the
square several times a day. She was walking alone, always wearing
the same béret, and always with the same white dog; no one
knew who she was, and every one called her simply 'the lady
with the dog'.

'If she is here alone without a husband or friends, it wouldn't
be amiss to make her acquaintance,' Gurov reflected.

He was under forty, but he had a daughter already twelve
years old, and two sons at school. He had been married young,
when he was a student in his second year, and by now his wife
seemed half as old again as he. She was a tall, erect woman with
dark eyebrows, staid and dignified, and, as she said of herself,
intellectual. She read a great deal, used phonetic spelling, called
her husband, not Dmitri, but Dimitri, and he secretly considered

her unintelligent, narrow, inelegant, was afraid of her, and did not like to be at home. He had begun being unfaithful to her long ago—had been unfaithful to her often, and, probably on that account, almost always spoke ill of women, and when they were talked about in his presence, used to call them 'the lower race'.

It seemed to him that he had been so schooled by bitter experience that he might call them what he liked, and yet he could not get on for two days together without 'the lower race'. In the society of men he was bored and not himself, with them he was cold and uncommunicative; but when he was in the company of women he felt free, and knew what to say to them and how to behave; and he was at ease with them even when he was silent. In his appearance, in his character, in his whole nature, there was something attractive and elusive which allured women and disposed them in his favour; he knew that, and some force seemed to draw him, too, to them.

Experience often repeated, truly bitter experience, had taught him long ago that with decent people, especially Moscow people— always slow to move and irresolute—every intimacy, which at first so agreeably diversifies life and appears a light and charming adventure, inevitably grows into a regular problem of extreme intricacy, and in the long run the situation becomes unbearable. But at every fresh meeting with an interesting woman this experience seemed to slip out of his memory, and he was eager for life, and everything seemed simple and amusing.

One evening he was dining in the gardens, and the lady in the béret came up slowly to take the next table. Her expression, her gait, her dress, and the way she did her hair told him that she was a lady, that she was married, that she was in Yalta for the first time and alone, and that she was dull there. The stories told of the immorality in such places as Yalta are to a great extent untrue; he despised them, and knew that such stories were for the most part made up by persons who would themselves have been glad to sin if they had been able; but when the lady sat down at the next table three paces from him, he remembered these tales of easy conquests, of trips to the mountains, and the tempting thought of a swift, fleeting love affair, a romance with an unknown woman, whose name he did not know, suddenly took possession of him.

He beckoned coaxingly to the Pomeranian, and when the dog came up to him he shook his finger at it. The Pomeranian growled: Gurov shook his finger at it again.

The lady looked at him and at once dropped her eyes.

'He doesn't bite,' she said, and blushed.

'May I give him a bone?' he asked; and when she nodded he asked courteously, 'Have you been long in Yalta?'

'Five days.'

'And I have already dragged out a fortnight here.'

There was a brief silence.

'Time goes fast, and yet it is so dull here!' she said, not looking at him.

'That's only the fashion to say it is dull here. A provincial will live in Belyov or Zhidra and not be dull, and when he comes here it's "Oh, the dulness! Oh, the dust!" One would think he came from Grenada.'

She laughed. Then both continued eating in silence, like strangers, but after dinner they walked side by side; and there sprang up between them the light jesting conversation of people who are free and satisfied, to whom it does not matter where they go or what they talk about. They walked and talked of the strange light on the sea: the water was of a soft warm lilac hue, and there was a golden streak from the moon upon it. They talked of how sultry it was after a hot day. Gurov told her that he came from Moscow, that he had taken his degree in Arts, but had a post in a bank; that he had trained as an opera-singer, but had given it up, that he owned two houses in Moscow. And from her he learnt that she had grown up in Petersburg, but had lived in S—

since her marriage two years before, that she was staying another month in Yalta, and that her husband, who needed a holiday too, might perhaps come and fetch her. She was not sure whether her husband had a post in a Crown Department or under the Provincial Council—and was amused by her own ignorance. And Gurov learnt, too, that she was called Anna Sergeyevna.

Afterwards he thought about her in his room at the hotel— thought she would certainly meet him next day; it would be sure to happen. As he got into bed he thought how lately she had been a girl at school, doing lessons like his own daughter; he recalled the diffidence, the angularity, that was still manifest in her laugh and her manner of talking with a stranger. This must have been the first time in her life she had been alone in surroundings in which she was followed, looked at, and spoken to merely from a secret motive which she could hardly fail to guess. He recalled her slender, delicate neck, her lovely grey eyes.

'There's something pathetic about her, anyway,' he thought, and fell asleep.

II

A week had passed since they had made acquaintance. It was a holiday. It was sultry indoors, while in the street the wind whirled the dust round and round, and blew people's hats off. It was a thirsty day, and Gurov often went into the pavilion, and pressed Anna Sergeyevna to have syrup and water or an ice. One did not know what to do with oneself.

In the evening when the wind had dropped a little, they went out on the groyne to see the steamer come in. There were a great many people walking about the harbour; they had gathered to welcome some one, bringing bouquets. And two peculiarities of a well-dressed Yalta crowd were very conspicuous: the elderly ladies were dressed like young ones, and there were great numbers of generals.

Owing to the roughness of the sea, the steamer arrived late, after the sun had set, and it was a long time turning about before it reached the groyne. Anna Sergeyevna looked through her lorgnette at the steamer and the passengers as though looking for acquaintances, and when she turned to Gurov her eyes were shining. She talked a great deal and asked disconnected questions, forgetting next moment what she had asked; then she dropped her lorgnette in the crush.

The festive crowd began to disperse; it was too dark to see people's faces. The wind had completely dropped, but Gurov and Anna Sergeyevna still stood as though waiting to see some one else come from the steamer. Anna Sergeyevna was silent now, and sniffed the flowers without looking at Gurov.

'The weather is better this evening,' he said. 'Where shall we go now? Shall we drive somewhere?'

She made no answer.

Then he looked at her intently, and all at once put his arm round her and kissed her on the lips, and breathed in the moisture and the fragrance of the flowers; and he immediately looked round him, anxiously wondering whether any one had seen them.

'Let us go to your hotel,' he said softly. And both walked quickly.

The room was close and smelt of the scent she had bought at the Japanese shop. Gurov looked at her and thought: 'What different people one meets in the world!' From the past he preserved memories of careless, good-natured women, who loved cheerfully and were grateful to him for the happiness he gave them, however brief it might be; and of women like his wife who loved without any genuine feeling, with superfluous phrases, affectedly, hysterically, with an expression that suggested that it was not love nor passion, but something more significant; and of two or three others, very beautiful, cold women, on whose faces he had caught a glimpse of a rapacious expression—an obstinate desire to snatch from life more than it could give, and these were capricious, unreflecting, domineering, unintelligent women not in their first youth, and when Gurov grew cold to them their beauty excited his hatred, and the lace on their linen seemed to him like scales.

But in this case there was still the diffidence, the angularity of inexperienced youth, an awkward feeling; and there was a sense of consternation as though some one had suddenly knocked at the door. The attitude of Anna Sergeyevna—'the lady with the dog'—to what had happened was somehow peculiar, very grave, as though it were her fall—so it seemed, and it was strange and inappropriate. Her face dropped and faded, and on both sides of it her long hair hung down mournfully; she mused in a dejected attitude like 'the woman who was a sinner' in an old-fashioned picture.

'It's wrong,' she said. 'You will be the first to despise me now.'

There was a water-melon on the table. Gurov cut himself a slice and began eating it without haste. There followed at least half an hour of silence.

Anna Sergeyevna was touching; there was about her the purity of a good, simple woman who had seen little of life. The solitary candle burning on the table threw a faint light on her face, yet it was clear that she was very unhappy.

'How could I despise you?' asked Gurov. 'You don't know what you are saying.'

'God forgive me,' she said, and her eyes filled with tears. 'It's awful.'

'You seem to feel you need to be forgiven.'

'Forgiven? No. I am a bad, low woman; I despise myself and don't attempt to justify myself. It's not my husband but myself I have deceived. And not only just now; I have been deceiving myself for a long time. My husband may be a good, honest man, but he is a flunkey! I don't know what he does there, what his work is, but I know he is a flunkey! I was twenty when I was married to him. I have been tormented by curiosity; I wanted something better. "There must be a different sort of life," I said to myself. I wanted to live! To live, to live! I was fired by curiosity—you don't understand it, but, I swear to God, I could not control myself; something happened to me: I could not be restrained. I told my husband I was ill, and came here. And here I have been walking about as though I were dazed, like a mad creature; and now I have become a vulgar, contemptible woman whom any one may despise.'

Gurov felt bored already, listening to her. He was irritated by the naïve tone, by this remorse, so unexpected and inopportune; but for the tears in her eyes, he might have thought she was jesting or playing a part.

'I don't understand,' he said softly. 'What is it you want?'

She hid her face on his breast and pressed close to him.

'Believe me, believe me, I beseech you.' she said. 'I love a pure, honest life, and sin is loathsome to me. I don't know what I am doing. Simple people say: "The Evil One has beguiled me". And I may say of myself now that the Evil One has beguiled me.'

'Hush, hush!' he muttered.

He looked at her fixed, scared eyes, kissed her, talked softly and affectionately, and by degrees she was comforted, and her gaiety returned; they both began laughing.

Afterwards when they went out there was not a soul on the sea-front. The town with its cypresses had quite a deathlike air, but the sea still broke noisily on the shore; a single barge was rocking on the waves, and a lantern was blinking sleepily on it.

They found a cab and drove to Oreanda.

'I found out your surname in the hall just now: it was written on the board—Von Diderits,' said Gurov. 'Is your husband a German?'

'No; I believe his grandfather was a German, but he is an Orthodox Russian himself.'

At Oreanda they sat on a seat not far from the church, looked down at the sea, and were silent. Yalta was hardly visible through the morning mist; white clouds stood motionless on the mountain-tops. The leaves did not stir on the trees, grasshoppers chirruped, and the monotonous hollow sound of the sea rising up from below, spoke of the peace, of the eternal sleep awaiting us. So it must have sounded when there was no Yalta, no Oreanda here; so it sounds now, and it will sound as indifferently and monotonously when we are all no more. And in this constancy, in this complete indifference to the life and death of each of us, there lies hid, perhaps, a pledge of our eternal salvation, of the unceasing movement of life upon earth, of unceasing progress towards perfection. Sitting beside a young woman who in the dawn seemed so lovely, soothed and spellbound in these magical surroundings—the sea, mountains, clouds, the open sky—Gurov thought how in reality everything is beautiful in this world when one reflects: everything except what we think or do ourselves when we forget our human dignity and the higher aims of our existence.

A man walked up to them—probably a keeper—looked at them and walked away. And this detail seemed mysterious and beautiful, too. They saw a steamer come from Theodosia, with its lights out in the glow of dawn.

'There is dew on the grass,' said Anna Sergeyevna, after a silence.

'Yes. It's time to go home.'

They went back to the town.

Then they met every day at twelve o'clock on the sea-front, lunched and dined together, went for walks, admired the sea. She complained that she slept badly, that her heart throbbed violently; asked the same questions, troubled now by jealousy and now by the fear that he did not respect her sufficiently. And often in the square or gardens, when there was no one near them, he suddenly drew her to him and kissed her passionately. Complete idleness, these kisses in broad daylight while he looked round in dread of some one's seeing them, the heat, the smell of the sea, and the continual passing to and fro before him of idle, well-dressed, well-fed people, made a new man of him; he told Anna Sergeyevna how beautiful she was, how fascinating. He was impatiently passionate, he would not move a step away from her, while she was often pensive and continually urged him to confess that he did not respect her, did not love her in the least, and thought of her as nothing but a common woman. Rather late almost every evening they drove somewhere out of town, to Oreanda or to the waterfall; and the expedition was always a success, the scenery invariably impressed them as grand and beautiful.

They were expecting her husband to come, but a letter came from him, saying that there was something wrong with his eyes, and he entreated his wife to come home as quickly as possible. Anna Sergeyevna made haste to go.

'It's a good thing I am going away,' she said to Gurov. 'It's the finger of destiny!'

She went by coach and he went with her. They were driving the whole day. When she had got into a compartment of the express, and when the second bell had rung, she said:

'Let me look at you once more—look at you once again. That's right.'

She did not shed tears, but was so sad that she seemed ill, and her face was quivering.

'I shall remember you—think of you,' she said. 'God be with you; be happy. Don't remember evil against me. We are parting forever—it must be so, for we ought never to have met. Well, God be with you.'

The train moved off rapidly, its lights soon vanished from sight, and a minute later there was no sound of it, as though everything had conspired together to end as quickly as possible that sweet delirium, that madness. Left alone on the platform, and gazing into the dark distance, Gurov listened to the chirrup of the grasshoppers and the hum of the telegraph wires, feeling as though he had only just waked up. And he thought, musing, that there had been another episode or adventure in his life, and it, too, was at an end, and nothing was left of it but a memory. He was moved, sad, and conscious of a slight remorse. This young woman whom he would never meet again had not been happy with him; he was genuinely warm and affectionate with her, but yet in his manner, his tone, and his caresses there had been a shade of light irony, the coarse condescension of a happy man who was, besides, almost twice her age. All the time she had called him kind, exceptional, lofty; obviously he had seemed to her different from what he really was, so he had unintentionally deceived her.

Here at the station was already a scent of autumn; it was a cold evening.

'It's time for me to go north,' thought Gurov as he left the platform. 'High time!'

III

At home in Moscow everything was in its winter routine; the stoves were heated, and in the morning it was still dark when the children were having breakfast and getting ready for school, and the nurse would light the lamp for a short time. The frosts had begun already. When the first snow has fallen, on the first day of sledge-driving it is pleasant to see the white earth, the white roofs, to draw soft, delicious breath, and the season brings back the days of one's youth. The old limes and birches, white with hoar-frost, have a good-natured expression; they are nearer to one's heart than cypresses and palms, and near them one doesn't want to be thinking of the sea and the mountains.

Gurov was Moscow born; he arrived in Moscow on a fine frosty day, and when he put on his fur coat and warm gloves, and walked along Petrovka, and when on Saturday evening he heard the ringing of the bells, his recent trip and the places he had seen lost all charm for him. Little by little he became absorbed in Moscow life, greedily read three newspapers a day, and declared he did not read the Moscow papers on principle! He already felt a longing to go to restaurants, clubs, dinner-parties, anniversary celebrations, and he felt flattered at entertaining distinguished lawyers and artists, and at playing cards with a professor at the doctors' club. He could already eat a whole plateful of salt fish and cabbage.

In another month, he fancied, the image of **Anna Sergeyevna** would be shrouded in a mist in his memory, and only from time to time would visit him in his dreams with a touching smile as others did. But more than a month passed, real winter had come, and everything was still clear in his memory as though he had parted with Anna Sergeyevna only the day before. And his memories glowed more and more vividly. When in the evening stillness he heard from his study the voices of his children, preparing their lessons, or when he listened to a song or the organ at the restaurant, or the storm howled in the chimney, suddenly everything would rise up in his memory: what had happened on the groyne, and the early morning with the mist on the mountains, and the steamer coming from Theodosia, and the kisses. He would pace a long time about his room, remembering it all and smiling; then his memories passed into dreams, and in his fancy the past was mingled with what was to come. Anna Sergeyevna did not visit him in dreams, but followed him about everywhere like a shadow and haunted him. When he shut his eyes he saw her as though she were living before him, and she seemed to him lovelier, younger, tenderer than she was; and he imagined himself finer than he had been in Yalta. In the evenings she peeped out at him from the bookcase, from the fireplace, from the corner—he heard her breathing, the caressing rustle of her dress. In the street he watched the women, looking for some one like her.

He was tormented by an intense desire to confide his memories to some one. But in his home it was impossible to talk of his love, and he had no one outside; he could not talk to his tenants nor to any one at the bank. And what had he to talk of? Had he been in love, then? Had there been anything beautiful, poetical, or edifying or simply interesting in his relations with Anna Sergeyevna? And there was nothing for him but to talk vaguely of love, of woman, and no one guessed what it meant; only his wife twitched her black eyebrows, and said:

'The part of a lady-killer does not suit you at all, Dimitri.'

One evening, coming out of the doctors' club with an official with whom he had been playing cards, he could not resist saying:

'If only you knew what a fascinating woman I made the acquaintance of in Yalta!'

The official got into his sledge and was driving away, but turned suddenly and shouted:

'Dmitri Dmitritch!'

'What?'

'You were right this evening: the sturgeon was a bit too strong!'

These words, so ordinary, for some reason moved Gurov to indignation, and struck him as degrading and unclean. What savage manners, what people! What senseless nights, what uninteresting, uneventful days! The rage for card-playing, the gluttony, the drunkenness, the continual talk always about the same thing. Useless pursuits and conversations always about the same things absorb the better part of one's time, the better part of one's strength, and in the end there is left a life grovelling and curtailed, worthless and trivial, and there is no escaping or getting away from it—just as though one were in a madhouse or a prison.

Gurov did not sleep all night, and was filled with indignation. And he had a headache all next day. And the next night he slept badly; he sat up in bed, thinking, or paced up and down his room. He was sick of his children, sick of the bank; he had no desire to go anywhere or to talk of anything.

In the holidays in December he prepared for a journey, and told his wife he was going to Petersburg to do something in the interests of a young friend—and he set off for S—. What for? He did not very well know himself. He wanted to see Anna Sergeyevna and to talk with her—to arrange a meeting, if possible.

He reached S— in the morning, and took the best room at the hotel, in which the floor was covered with grey army cloth, and on the table was an inkstand, grey with dust and adorned with a figure on horseback, with its hat in its hand and its head broken off. The hotel porter gave him the necessary information; Von Diderits lived in a house of his own in Old Gontcharny Street—it was not far from the hotel: he was rich and lived in good style, and had his own horses; every one in the town knew him. The porter pronounced the name 'Dridirits'.

Gurov went without haste to Old Gontcharny Street and found the house. Just opposite the house stretched a long grey fence adorned with nails.

'One would run away from a fence like that,' thought Gurov, looking from the fence to the windows of the house and back again.

He considered: to-day was a holiday, and the husband would probably be at home. And in any case it would be tactless to go into the house and upset her. If he were to send her a note it might fall into her husband's hands, and then it might ruin everything. The best thing was to trust to chance. And he kept walking up and down the street by the fence, waiting for the chance. He saw a beggar go in at the gate and dogs fly at him; then an hour later he heard a piano, and the sounds were faint and indistinct. Probably it was Anna Sergeyevna playing. The front door suddenly opened, and an old woman came out, followed by the familiar white Pomeranian. Gurov was on the point of calling to the dog, but his heart began beating violently, and in his excitement he could not remember the dog's name.

He walked up and down, and loathed the grey fence more and more, and by now he thought irritably that Anna Sergeyevna had forgotten him, and was perhaps already amusing herself with some one else, and that that was very natural in a young woman who had nothing to look at from morning till night but that confounded fence. He went back to his hotel room and sat for a long while on the sofa, not knowing what to do, then he had dinner and a long nap.

'How stupid and worrying it is!' he thought when he woke and looked at the dark windows: it was already evening. 'Here I've had a good sleep for some reason. What shall I do in the night?'

He sat on the bed, which was covered by a cheap grey blanket, such as one sees in hospitals, and he taunted himself in his vexation:

'So much for the lady with the dog—so much for the adventure—You're in a nice fix.'

That morning at the station a poster in large letters had caught his eye. 'The Geisha' was to be performed for the first time. He thought of this and went to the theatre.

'It's quite possible she may go to the first performance,' he thought.

The theatre was full. As in all provincial theatres, there was a fog above the chandelier, the gallery was noisy and restless; in the front row the local dandies were standing up before the beginning of the performance, with their hands behind them; in the Governor's box the Governor's daughter, wearing a boa, was sitting in the front seat, while the Governor himself lurked modestly behind the curtain with only his hands visible; the orchestra was a long time tuning up; the stage curtain swayed. All the time the audience were coming in and taking their seats Gurov looked at them eagerly.

Anna Sergeyevna, too, came in. She sat down in the third row, and when Gurov looked at her his heart contracted, and he understood clearly that for him there was in the whole world no creature so near, so precious, and so important to him; she, this little woman, in no way remarkable, lost in a provincial crowd, with a vulgar lorgnette in her hand, filled his whole life now, was his sorrow and his joy, the one happiness that he now desired for himself, and to the sounds of the inferior orchestra, of the wretched provincial violins, he thought how lovely she was. He thought and dreamed.

A young man with small side-whiskers, tall and stooping, came in with Anna Sergeyevna and sat down beside her; he bent his head at every step and seemed to be continually bowing. Most likely this was the husband whom at Yalta, in a rush of bitter feeling, she had called a flunkey. And there really was in his long figure, his side-whiskers, and the small bald patch on his head, something of the flunkey's obsequiousness; his smile was sugary, and in his buttonhole there was some badge of distinction like the number on a waiter.

During the first interval the husband went away to smoke; she remained alone in her stall. Gurov, who was sitting in the stalls, too, went up to her and said in a trembling voice, with a forced smile:

'Good-evening.'

She glanced at him and turned pale, then glanced again with horror, unable to believe her eyes, and tightly gripped the fan and the lorgnette in her hands, evidently struggling with herself not to faint. Both were silent. She was sitting, he was standing, frightened by her confusion and not venturing to sit down beside her. The violins and the flute began tuning up. He felt suddenly frightened; it seemed as though all the people in the boxes were looking at them. She got up and went quickly to the door; he followed her, and both walked senselessly along passages, and up and down stairs, and figures in legal, scholastic, and civil service uniforms, all wearing badges, flitted before their eyes. They caught glimpses of ladies, of fur coats hanging on pegs; the draughts blew on them, bringing a smell of stale tobacco. And Gurov, whose heart was beating violently, thought:

'Oh, heavens! Why are these people here and this orchestra!'

And at that instant he recalled how when he had seen Anna Sergeyevna off at the station he had thought that everything was over and they would never meet again. But how far they were still from the end!

On the narrow, gloomy staircase over which was written 'To the Amphitheatre', she stopped.

'How you have frightened me!' she said, breathing hard, still pale and overwhelmed. 'Oh, how you have frightened me! I am half dead. Why have you come? Why?'

'But do understand, Anna, do understand—' he said hastily in a low voice. 'I entreat you to understand—'

She looked at him with dread, with entreaty, with love; she looked at him intently, to keep his features more distinctly in her memory.

'I am so unhappy,' she went on, not heeding him. 'I have thought of nothing but you all the time; I live only in the thought of you. And I wanted to forget, to forget you; but why, oh, why, have you come?'

On the landing above them two schoolboys were smoking and looking down, but that was nothing to Gurov; he drew Anna Sergeyevna to him, and began kissing her face, her cheeks, and her hands.

'What are you doing, what are you doing!' she cried in horror, pushing him away. 'We are mad. Go away to-day; go away at once—I beseech you by all that is sacred, I implore you. There are people coming this way!'

Some one was coming up the stairs.

'You must go away,' Anna Sergeyevna went on in a whisper. 'Do you hear, Dmitri Dmitritch? I will come and see you in Moscow. I have never been happy; I am miserable now, and I never, never shall be happy, never! Don't make me suffer still more! I swear I'll come to Moscow. But now let us part. My precious, good, dear one, we must part!'

She pressed his hand and began rapidly going downstairs, looking round at him, and from her eyes he could see that she really was unhappy. Gurov stood for a little while, listened, then, when all sound had died away, he found his coat and left the theatre.

IV

And Anna Sergeyevna began coming to see him in Moscow. Once in two or three months she left S—, telling her husband that she was going to consult a doctor about an internal complaint—and her husband believed her, and did not believe her. In Moscow she stayed at the Slaviansky Bazaar hotel, and at once sent a man in a red cap to Gurov. Gurov went to see her, and no one in Moscow knew of it.

Once he was going to see her in this way on a winter morning (the messenger had come the evening before when he was out). With him walked his daughter, whom he wanted to take to school: it was on the way. Snow was falling in big wet flakes.

'It's three degrees above freezing-point, and yet it is snowing,' said Gurov to his daughter. 'The thaw is only on the surface of the earth; there is quite a different temperature at a greater height in the atmosphere.'

'And why are there no thunderstorms in the winter, father?'

He explained that, too. He talked, thinking all the while that he was going to see her, and no living soul knew of it, and probably never would know. He had two lives: one, open, seen and known by all who cared to know, full of relative truth and of relative falsehood, exactly like the lives of his friends and acquaintances; and another life running its course in secret. And through some strange, perhaps accidental, conjunction of circumstances, everything that was essential, of interest and of value to him, everything in which he was sincere and did not deceive himself, everything that made the kernel of his life, was hidden from other people; and all that was false in him, the sheath in which he hid himself to conceal the truth—such, for instance, as his work in the bank, his discussions at the club, his 'lower race', his presence with his wife at anniversary festivities—all that was open. And he judged of others by himself, not believing in what he saw, and always believing that every man had his real, most interesting life under the cover of secrecy and under the cover of night. All personal life rested on secrecy, and possibly it was partly on that account that civilized man was so nervously anxious that personal privacy should be respected.

After leaving his daughter at school, Gurov went on to the Slaviansky Bazaar. He took off his fur coat below, went upstairs, and softly knocked at the door. Anna Sergeyevna, wearing his favourite grey dress, exhausted by the journey and the suspense, had been expecting him since the evening before. She was pale; she looked at him, and did not smile, and he had hardly come in when she fell on his breast. Their kiss was slow and prolonged, as though they had not met for two years.

'Well, how are you getting on there?' he asked. 'What news?'

'Wait; I'll tell you directly—I can't talk.'

She could not speak; she was crying. She turned away from him, and pressed her handkerchief to her eyes.

'Let her have her cry out. I'll sit down and wait,' he thought, and he sat down in an arm-chair.

Then he rang and asked for tea to be brought him, and while he drank his tea she remained standing at the window with her back to him. She was crying from emotion, from the miserable consciousness that their life was so hard for them; they could only meet in secret, hiding themselves from people, like thieves! Was not their life shattered?

'Come, do stop!' he said.

It was evident to him that this love of theirs would not soon be over, that he could not see the end of it. Anna Sergeyevna grew more and more attached to him. She adored him, and it was unthinkable to say to her that it was bound to have an end some day; besides, she would not have believed it!

He went up to her and took her by the shoulders to say something affectionate and cheering, and at that moment he saw himself in the looking-glass.

His hair was already beginning to turn grey. And it seemed strange to him that he had grown so much older, so much plainer during the last few years. The shoulders on which his hands rested were warm and quivering. He felt compassion for this life, still so warm and lovely, but probably already not far from beginning to fade and wither like his own. Why did she love him so much? He always seemed to women different from what he was, and they loved in him not himself, but the man created by their imagination, whom they had been eagerly seeking all their lives; and afterwards, when they noticed their mistake, they loved him all the same. And not one of them had been happy with him. Time passed, he had made their acquaintance, got on with them, parted, but he had never once loved; it was anything you like, but not love.

And only now when his head was grey he had fallen properly, really in love, for the first time in his life.

Anna Sergeyevna and he loved each other like people very close and akin, like husband and wife, like tender friends; it seemed to them that fate itself had meant them for one another, and they could not understand why he had a wife and she a husband; and it was as though they were a pair of birds of passage, caught and forced to live in different cages. They forgave each other for what they were ashamed of in their past, they forgave everything in the present, and felt that this love of theirs had changed them both.

In moments of depression in the past he had comforted himself with any arguments that came into his mind, but now he no longer cared for arguments; he felt profound compassion, he wanted to be sincere and tender.

'Don't cry, my darling,' he said. 'You've had your cry; that's enough—let us talk now, let us think of some plan.'

Then they spent a long while taking counsel together, talked of how to avoid the necessity for secrecy, for deception, for living in different towns and not seeing each other for long at a time. How could they be free from this intolerable bondage?

'How? How?' he asked, clutching his head. 'How?'

And it seemed as though in a little while the solution would be found, and then a new and splendid life would begin; and it was clear to both of them that they had still a long, long road before them, and that the most complicated and difficult part of it was only just beginning.

21

THE GIFT OF THE MAGI

O. Henry

Love is built on sacrifice. Give it till it hurts.

One dollar and eighty-seven cents. That was all. And sixty cents of it was in pennies. Pennies saved one and two at a time by bulldozing the grocer and the vegetable man and the butcher until one's cheeks burned with the silent imputation of parsimony that such close dealing implied. Three times Della counted it. One dollar and eighty-seven cents. And the next day would be Christmas.

There was clearly nothing to do but flop down on the shabby little couch and howl. So Della did it. Which instigates the moral reflection that life is made up of sobs, sniffles, and smiles, with sniffles predominating.

While the mistress of the home is gradually subsiding from the first stage to the second, take a look at the home. A furnished flat at $8 per week. It did not exactly beggar description, but it certainly had that word on the lookout for the mendicancy squad.

In the vestibule below was a letter-box into which no letter would go, and an electric button from which no mortal finger could coax a ring. Also appertaining thereunto was a card bearing the name 'Mr James Dillingham Young.' The 'Dillingham' had been flung to the breeze during a former period of prosperity when its possessor was being paid $30 per week. Now, when the income was shrunk to $20, the letters of 'Dillingham' looked blurred, as though they were thinking seriously of contracting to a modest and unassuming D. But whenever Mr James Dillingham Young came home and reached his flat above he was called 'Jim' and greatly hugged by Mrs James Dillingham Young, already introduced to you as Della. Which is all very good.

Della finished her cry and attended to her cheeks with the powder rag. She stood by the window and looked out dully at a grey cat walking a grey fence in a grey backyard. Tomorrow would be Christmas Day, and she had only $1.87 with which to buy Jim a present. She had been saving every penny she could for months, with this result. Twenty dollars a week doesn't go far. Expenses had been greater than she had calculated. They always are. Only $1.87 to buy a present for Jim. Her Jim. Many a happy hour she had spent planning for something nice for him. Something fine and rare and sterling—something just a little bit near to being worthy of the honour of being owned by Jim.

There was a pier-glass between the windows of the room. Perhaps you have seen a pier-glass in an $8 flat. A very thin and very agile person may, by observing his reflection in a rapid sequence of longitudinal strips, obtain a fairly accurate conception of his looks. Della, being slender, had mastered the art.

Suddenly she whirled from the window and stood before the glass. Her eyes were shining brilliantly, but her face had lost its colour within twenty seconds. Rapidly she pulled down her hair and let it fall to its full length.

Now, there were two possessions of the James Dillingham Youngs in which they both took a mighty pride. One was Jim's gold watch that had been his father's and his grandfather's. The other was Della's hair. Had the Queen of Sheba lived in the flat across the airshaft, Della would have let her hair hang out the window some day to dry just to depreciate Her Majesty's jewels and gifts. Had King Solomon been the janitor, with all his treasures piled up in the basement, Jim would have pulled out his watch every time he passed, just to see him pluck at his beard from envy.

So now Della's beautiful hair fell about her, rippling and shining like a cascade of brown waters. It reached below her knee and made itself almost a garment for her. And then she did it up again nervously and quickly. Once she faltered for a minute and stood still while a tear or two splashed on the worn red carpet.

On went her old brown jacket; on went her old brown hat. With a whirl of skirts and with the brilliant sparkle still in her eyes, she fluttered out the door and down the stairs to the street.

Where she stopped, the sign read: 'Mme. Sofronie. Hair Goods of All Kinds.' One flight up Della ran, and collected herself, panting. Madame, large, too white, chilly, hardly looked the 'Sofronie'.

'Will you buy my hair?' asked Della.

'I buy hair,' said Madame. 'Take yer hat off and let's have a sight at the looks of it.'

Down rippled the brown cascade. 'Twenty dollars,' said Madame, lifting the mass with a practiced hand.

'Give it to me quick,' said Della.

Oh, and the next two hours tripped by on rosy wings. Forget the hashed metaphor. She was ransacking the stores for Jim's present.

She found it at last. It surely had been made for Jim and no one else. There was no other like it in any of the stores, and she had turned all of them inside out. It was a platinum fob chain simple and chaste in design, properly proclaiming its value by substance alone and not by meretricious ornamentation—as all good things should do. It was even worthy of The Watch. As soon as she saw it she knew that it must be Jim's. It was like him.

Quietness and value—the description applied to both. Twenty-one dollars they took from her for it, and she hurried home with the 87 cents. With that chain on his watch Jim might be properly anxious about the time in any company. Grand as the watch was, he sometimes looked at it on the sly on account of the old leather strap that he used in place of a chain.

When Della reached home her intoxication gave way a little to prudence and reason. She got out her curling irons and lighted the gas and went to work repairing the ravages made by generosity added to love. Which is always a tremendous task, dear friends—a mammoth task.

Within forty minutes her head was covered with tiny, close-lying curls that made her look wonderfully like a truant schoolboy. She looked at her reflection in the mirror long, carefully, and critically.

'If Jim doesn't kill me,' she said to herself, 'before he takes a second look at me, he'll say I look like a Coney Island chorus girl. But what could I do—oh! What could I do with a dollar and eighty-seven cents?'

At 7 o'clock the coffee was made and the frying-pan was on the back of the stove hot and ready to cook the chops.

Jim was never late. Della doubled the fob chain in her hand and sat on the corner of the table near the door that he always entered. Then she heard his step on the stair away down on the first flight, and she turned white for just a moment. She had a habit for saying little silent prayers about the simplest everyday things, and now she whispered: 'Please God, make him think I am still pretty.'

The door opened and Jim stepped in and closed it. He looked thin and very serious. Poor fellow, he was only twenty-two—and to be burdened with a family! He needed a new overcoat and he was without gloves.

Jim stopped inside the door, as immovable as a setter at the scent of quail. His eyes were fixed upon Della, and there was an expression in them that she could not read, and it terrified her. It was not anger, nor surprise, nor disapproval, nor horror, nor any of the sentiments that she had been prepared for. He simply stared at her fixedly with that peculiar expression on his face.

Della wriggled off the table and went for him.

'Jim, darling,' she cried, 'don't look at me that way. I had my hair cut off and sold it because I couldn't have lived through Christmas without giving you a present. It'll grow out again—you won't mind, will you? I just had to do it. My hair grows awfully fast. Say "Merry Christmas!" Jim, and let's be happy. You don't know what a nice—what a beautiful, nice gift I've got for you.'

'You've cut off your hair?' asked Jim, laboriously, as if he had not arrived at that patent fact yet even after the hardest mental labour.

'Cut it off and sold it,' said Della. 'Don't you like me just as well, anyhow? I'm me without my hair, ain't I?'

Jim looked about the room curiously.

'You say your hair is gone?' he said, with an air almost of idiocy.

'You needn't look for it,' said Della. 'It's sold, I tell you—sold and gone, too. It's Christmas Eve, boy. Be good to me, for it went for you. Maybe the hairs of my head were numbered,' she went on with sudden serious sweetness, 'but nobody could ever count my love for you. Shall I put the chops on, Jim?'

Out of his trance Jim seemed quickly to wake. He enfolded his Della. For ten seconds let us regard with discreet scrutiny some inconsequential object in the other direction. Eight dollars a week or a million a year—what is the difference? A mathematician or a wit would give you the wrong answer. The magi brought valuable gifts, but that was not among them. This dark assertion will be illuminated later on.

Jim drew a package from his overcoat pocket and threw it upon the table.

'Don't make any mistake, Dell,' he said, 'about me. I don't think there's anything in the way of a haircut or a shave or a shampoo that could make me like my girl any less. But if you'll unwrap that package you may see why you had me going a while at first.'

White fingers and nimble tore at the string and paper. And then an ecstatic scream of joy; and then, alas! A quick feminine change to hysterical tears and wails, necessitating the immediate employment of all the comforting powers of the lord of the flat.

For there lay The Combs—the set of combs, side and back, that Della had worshipped long in a Broadway window. Beautiful combs, pure tortoise shell, with jewelled rims—just the shade to wear in the beautiful vanished hair. They were expensive combs, she knew, and her heart had simply craved and yearned over them without the least hope of possession. And now, they were hers, but the tresses that should have adorned the coveted adornments were gone.

But she hugged them to her bosom, and at length she was able to look up with dim eyes and a smile and say: 'My hair grows so fast, Jim!'

And then Della leaped up like a little singed cat and cried, 'Oh, oh!'

Jim had not yet seen his beautiful present. She held it out to him eagerly upon her open palm. The dull precious metal seemed to flash with a reflection of her bright and ardent spirit.

'Isn't it a dandy, Jim? I hunted all over town to find it. You'll have to look at the time a hundred times a day now. Give me your watch. I want to see how it looks on it.'

Instead of obeying, Jim tumbled down on the couch and put his hands under the back of his head and smiled.

'Dell,' said he, 'let's put our Christmas presents away and keep 'em a while. They're too nice to use just at present. I sold the watch to get the money to buy your combs. And now suppose you put the chops on.'

The magi, as you know, were wise men—wonderfully wise men—who brought gifts to the Babe in the manger. They invented the art of giving Christmas presents. Being wise, their gifts were no doubt wise ones, possibly bearing the privilege of exchange in case of duplication. And here I have lamely related to you the uneventful chronicle of two foolish children in a flat who most unwisely sacrificed for each other the greatest treasures of their house. But in a last word to the wise of these days let it be said that of all who give gifts these two were the wisest. Of all who give and receive gifts, such as they are wisest. Everywhere they are wisest. They are the magi.

22

THE GREEN DOOR

O. Henry

Love is the elixir that supports dreams.

Suppose you should be walking down Broadway after dinner, with ten minutes allotted to the consummation of your cigar while you are choosing between a diverting tragedy and something serious in the way of vaudeville. Suddenly a hand is laid upon your arm. You turn to look into the thrilling eyes of a beautiful woman, wonderful in diamonds and Russian sables. She thrusts hurriedly into your hand an extremely hot buttered roll, flashes out a tiny pair of scissors, snips off the second button of your overcoat, meaningly ejaculates the one word, 'parallelogram!' and swiftly flies down a cross street, looking back fearfully over her shoulder.

That would be pure adventure. Would you accept it? Not you. You would flush with embarrassment; you would sheepishly drop the roll and continue down Broadway, fumbling feebly for the missing button. This you would do unless you are one of the blessed few in whom the pure spirit of adventure is not dead.

True adventurers have never been plentiful. They who are set down in print as such have been mostly business men with newly invented methods. They have been out after the things they wanted—golden fleeces, holy grails, lady loves, treasure, crowns and fame. The true adventurer goes forth aimless and uncalculating to meet and greet unknown fate. A fine example was the Prodigal Son—when he started back home.

Half-adventurers—brave and splendid figures—have been

numerous. From the Crusades to the Palisades they have enriched the arts of history and fiction and the trade of historical fiction. But each of them had a prize to win, a goal to kick, an axe to grind, a race to run, a new thrust in tierce to deliver, a name to carve, a crow to pick—so they were not followers of true adventure.

In the big city the twin spirits Romance and Adventure are always abroad seeking worthy wooers. As we roam the streets they slyly peep at us and challenge us in twenty different guises. Without knowing why, we look up suddenly to see in a window a face that seems to belong to our gallery of intimate portraits; in a sleeping thoroughfare we hear a cry of agony and fear coming from an empty and shuttered house; instead of at our familiar curb, a cab-driver deposits us before a strange door, which one, with a smile, opens for us and bids us enter; a slip of paper, written upon, flutters down to our feet from the high lattices of Chance; we exchange glances of instantaneous hate, affection and fear with hurrying strangers in the passing crowds; a sudden douse of rain—and our umbrella may be sheltering the daughter of the Full Moon and first cousin of the Sidereal System; at every corner handkerchiefs drop, fingers beckon, eyes besiege, and the lost, the lonely, the rapturous, the mysterious, the perilous, changing clues of adventure are slipped into our fingers. But few of us are willing to hold and follow them. We are grown stiff with the ramrod of convention down our backs. We pass on; and some day we come, at the end of a very dull life, to reflect that our romance has been a pallid thing of a marriage or two, a satin rosette kept in a safe-deposit drawer, and a lifelong feud with a steam radiator.

Rudolf Steiner was a true adventurer. Few were the evenings on which he did not go forth from his hall bedchamber in search of the unexpected and the egregious. The most interesting thing in life seemed to him to be what might lie just around the next corner. Sometimes his willingness to tempt fate led him into strange paths. Twice he had spent the night in a station-house; again and again he had found himself the dupe of ingenious and mercenary tricksters; his watch and money had been the price of one flattering allurement. But with undiminished ardour he picked up every glove cast before him into the merry lists of adventure.

One evening Rudolf was strolling along a crosstown street in the older central part of the city. Two streams of people filled the sidewalks—the home-hurrying, and that restless contingent that abandons home for the specious welcome of the thousand-candle-power table d'hote.

The young adventurer was of pleasing presence, and moved serenely and watchfully. By daylight he was a salesman in a piano store. He wore his tie drawn through a topaz ring instead of fastened with a stick pin; and once he had written to the editor of a magazine that 'Junie's Love Test' by Miss Libbey, had been the book that had most influenced his life.

During his walk a violent chattering of teeth in a glass case on the sidewalk seemed at first to draw his attention (with a qualm), to a restaurant before which it was set; but a second glance revealed the electric letters of a dentist's sign high above the next door. A giant negro, fantastically dressed in a red embroidered coat, yellow trousers and a military cap, discreetly distributed cards to those of the passing crowd who consented to take them.

This mode of dentistic advertising was a common sight to Rudolf. Usually he passed the dispenser of the dentist's cards without reducing his store; but tonight the African slipped one into his hand so deftly that he retained it there smiling a little at the successful feat.

When he had travelled a few yards further he glanced at the card indifferently. Surprised, he turned it over and looked again with interest. One side of the card was blank; on the other was written in ink three words, 'The Green Door'. And then Rudolf saw, three steps in front of him, a man throw down the card the negro had given him as he passed. Rudolf picked it up. It was printed with the dentist's name and address and the usual schedule of 'plate work' and 'bridge work' and specious promises of 'painless' operations.

The adventurous piano salesman halted at the corner and considered. Then he crossed the street, walked down a block, recrossed and joined the upward current of people again. Without seeming to notice the negro as he passed the second time, he carelessly took the card that was handed him. Ten steps away he inspected it. In the same handwriting that appeared on the first card 'The Green Door' was inscribed upon it. Three or four cards were tossed to the pavement by pedestrians both following and leading him. These fell blank side up. Rudolf turned them over. Every one bore the printed legend of the dental 'parlours'.

Rarely did the arch sprite Adventure need to beckon twice to Rudolf Steiner, his true follower. But twice it had been done, and the quest was on.

Rudolf walked slowly back to where the giant negro stood by the case of rattling teeth. This time as he passed he received no card. In spite of his gaudy and ridiculous garb, the Ethiopian displayed a natural barbaric dignity as he stood, offering the cards suavely to some, allowing others to pass unmolested. Every half minute he chanted a harsh, unintelligible phrase akin to the jabber of car conductors and grand opera. And not only did he withhold a card this time, but it seemed to Rudolf that he received from the shining and massive black countenance a look of cold, almost contemptuous disdain.

The look stung the adventurer. He read in it a silent accusation that he had been found wanting. Whatever the mysterious written words on the cards might mean, the black had selected him twice from the throng for their recipient; and now seemed to have condemned him as deficient in the wit and spirit to engage the enigma.

Standing aside from the rush, the young man made a rapid

estimate of the building in which he conceived that his adventure must lie. Five stories high it rose. A small restaurant occupied the basement.

The first floor, now closed, seemed to house millinery or furs. The second floor, by the winking electric letters, was the dentist's. Above this a polyglot babel of signs struggled to indicate the abodes of palmists, dressmakers, musicians and doctors. Still higher up draped curtains and milk bottles white on the window sills proclaimed the regions of domesticity.

After concluding his survey Rudolf walked briskly up the high flight of stone steps into the house. Up two flights of the carpeted stairway he continued; and at its top paused. The hallway there was dimly lighted by two pale jets of gas one–far to his right, the other nearer–to his left. He looked toward the nearer light and saw, within its wan halo, a green door. For one moment he hesitated; then he seemed to see the contumelious sneer of the African juggler of cards; and then he walked straight to the green door and knocked against it.

Moments like those that passed before his knock was answered measure the quick breath of true adventure. What might not be behind those green panels! Gamesters at play; cunning rogues baiting their traps with subtle skill; beauty in love with courage, and thus planning to be sought by it; danger, death, love, disappointment, ridicule—any of these might respond to that temerarious rap.

A faint rustle was heard inside, and the door slowly opened. A girl not yet twenty stood there, white-faced and tottering. She loosed the knob and swayed weakly, groping with one hand. Rudolf caught her and laid her on a faded couch that stood against the wall. He closed the door and took a swift glance around the room by the light of a flickering gas jet. Neat, but extreme poverty was the story that he read.

The girl lay still, as if in a faint. Rudolf looked around the room excitedly for a barrel. People must be rolled upon a barrel who—no, no; that was for drowned persons. He began to fan her with his hat. That was successful, for he struck her nose with the brim of his derby and she opened her eyes. And then the young man saw that hers, indeed, was the one missing face from his heart's gallery of intimate portraits. The frank, grey eyes, the little nose, turning pertly outward; the chestnut hair, curling like the tendrils of a pea vine, seemed the right end and reward of all his wonderful adventures. But the face was woefully thin and pale.

The girl looked at him calmly, and then smiled.

'Fainted, didn't I?' she asked, weakly. 'Well, who wouldn't? You try going without anything to eat for three days and see!'

'Himmel!' exclaimed Rudolf, jumping up. 'Wait till I come back.'

He dashed out the green door and down the stairs. In twenty minutes he was back again, kicking at the door with his toe for her to open it. With both arms he hugged an array of wares from the grocery and the restaurant. On the table he laid them—bread and butter, cold meats, cakes, pies, pickles, oysters, a roasted chicken, a bottle of milk and one of redhot tea.

'This is ridiculous,' said Rudolf, blusteringly, 'to go without eating. You must quit making election bets of this kind. Supper is ready.' He helped her to a chair at the table and asked: 'Is there a cup for the tea?' 'On the shelf by the window,' she answered. When he turned again with the cup he saw her, with eyes shining rapturously, beginning upon a huge Dill pickle that she had rooted out from the paper bags with a woman's unerring instinct. He took it from her, laughingly, and poured the cup full of milk. 'Drink that first' he ordered, 'and then you shall have some tea, and then a chicken wing. If you are very good you shall have a pickle to-morrow. And now, if you'll allow me to be your guest we'll have supper.'

He drew up the other chair. The tea brightened the girl's

eyes and brought back some of her colour. She began to eat with a sort of dainty ferocity like some starved wild animal. She seemed to regard the young man's presence and the aid he had rendered her as a natural thing—not as though she undervalued the conventions; but as one whose great stress gave her the right to put aside the artificial for the human. But gradually, with the return of strength and comfort, came also a sense of the little conventions that belong; and she began to tell him her little story. It was one of a thousand such as the city yawns at every day—the shop girl's story of insufficient wages, further reduced by 'fines' that go to swell the store's profits; of time lost through illness; and then of lost positions, lost hope, and—the knock of the adventurer upon the green door.

But to Rudolf the history sounded as big as the Iliad or the crisis in 'Junie's Love Test'.

'To think of you going through all that,' he exclaimed.

'It was something fierce,' said the girl, solemnly.

'And you have no relatives or friends in the city?'

'None whatever.'

'I am all alone in the world, too,' said Rudolf, after a pause.

'I am glad of that,' said the girl, promptly; and somehow it pleased the young man to hear that she approved of his bereft condition.

Very suddenly her eyelids dropped and she sighed deeply.

'I'm awfully sleepy,' she said, 'and I feel so good.'

Then Rudolf rose and took his hat. 'I'll say good-night. A long night's sleep will be fine for you.'

He held out his hand, and she took it and said "good-night". But her eyes asked a question so eloquently, so frankly and pathetically that he answered it with words.

'Oh, I'm coming back to-morrow to see how you are getting along. You can't get rid of me so easily.'

Then, at the door, as though the way of his coming had been

so much less important than the fact that he had come, she asked: 'How did you come to knock at my door?'

He looked at her for a moment, remembering the cards, and felt a sudden jealous pain. What if they had fallen into other hands as adventurous as his? Quickly he decided that she must never know the truth. He would never let her know that he was aware of the strange expedient to which she had been driven by her great distress.

'One of our piano tuners lives in this house,' he said. 'I knocked at your door by mistake.'

The last thing he saw in the room before the green door closed was her smile.

At the head of the stairway he paused and looked curiously about him. And then he went along the hallway to its other end; and, coming back, ascended to the floor above and continued his puzzled explorations. Every door that he found in the house was painted green.

Wondering, he descended to the sidewalk. The fantastic African was still there. Rudolf confronted him with his two cards in his hand.

'Will you tell me why you gave me these cards and what they mean?' he asked.

In a broad, good-natured grin the negro exhibited a splendid advertisement of his master's profession.

'Dar it is, boss,' he said, pointing down the street. 'But I 'spect you is a little late for de fust act.'

Looking the way he pointed Rudolf saw above the entrance to a theatre the blazing electric sign of its new play, 'The Green Door'.

'I'm informed dat it's a fust-rate show, sah,' said the negro. 'De agent what represents it pussented me with a dollar, sah, to distribute a few of his cards along with de doctah's. May I offer you one of de doctah's cards, sah?'

At the corner of the block in which he lived Rudolf stopped

for a glass of beer and a cigar. When he had come out with his lighted weed he buttoned his coat, pushed back his hat and said, stoutly, to the lamp post on the corner:

'All the same, I believe it was the hand of Fate that doped out the way for me to find her.'

Which conclusion, under the circumstances, certainly admits Rudolf Steiner to the ranks of the true followers of Romance and Adventure.

23

A WEDDING GIFT

Guy de Maupassant

Some gifts are big; others are small. But the best gifts are those that come from the heart.

For a long time, Jacques Bourdillere had sworn that he would never marry, but he suddenly changed his mind. It happened suddenly, one summer, at the seashore.

One morning as he lay stretched out on the sand, watching the women coming out of the water, a little foot had struck him by its neatness and daintiness. He raised his eyes and was delighted with the whole person, although in fact he could see nothing but the ankles and the head emerging from a flannel bathrobe carefully held closed. He was supposed to be sensual and a fast liver. It was therefore by the mere grace of the form that he was at first captured. Then he was held by the charm of the young girl's sweet mind, so simple and good, as fresh as her cheeks and lips.

He was presented to the family and pleased them. He immediately fell madly in love. When he saw Berthe Lannis in the distance, on the long yellow stretch of sand, he would tingle to the roots of his hair. When he was near her he would become silent, unable to speak or even to think, with a kind of throbbing at his heart, and a buzzing in his ears, and a bewilderment in his mind. Was that love?

He did not know or understand, but he had fully decided to have this child for his wife.

Her parents hesitated for a long time, restrained by the young man's bad reputation. It was said that he had an old sweetheart, one of these binding attachments which one always believes to be broken off and yet which always hold.

Besides, for a shorter or longer period, he loved every woman who came within reach of his lips.

Then he settled down and refused, even once, to see the one with whom he had lived for so long. A friend took care of this woman's pension and assured her an income. Jacques paid, but he did not even wish to hear of her, pretending even to ignore her name. She wrote him letters which he never opened. Every week he would recognize the clumsy writing of the abandoned woman, and every week a greater anger surged within him against her, and he would quickly tear the envelope and the paper, without opening it, without reading one single line, knowing in advance the reproaches and complaints which it contained.

As no one had much faith in his constancy, the test was prolonged through the winter, and Berthe's hand was not granted him until the spring. The wedding took place in Paris at the beginning of May.

The young couple had decided not to take the conventional wedding trip, but after a little dance for the younger cousins, which would not be prolonged after eleven o'clock, in order that this day of lengthy ceremonies might not be too tiresome, the young pair were to spend the first night in the parental home and then, on the following morning, to leave for the beach so dear to their hearts, where they had first known and loved each other.

Night had come, and the dance was going on in the large parlour. The two had retired into a little Japanese boudoir hung with bright silks and dimly lighted by the soft rays of a large coloured lantern hanging from the ceiling like a gigantic egg. Through the open window the fresh air from outside passed over their faces like a caress, for the night was warm and calm, full of the odour of spring.

They were silent, holding each other's hands and from time

to time squeezing them with all their might. She sat there with a dreamy look, feeling a little lost at this great change in her life, but smiling, moved, ready to cry, often also almost ready to faint from joy, believing the whole world to be changed by what had just happened to her, uneasy, she knew not why, and feeling her whole body and soul filled with an indefinable and delicious lassitude.

He was looking at her persistently with a fixed smile. He wished to speak, but found nothing to say, and so sat there, expressing all his ardour by pressures of the hand. From time to time he would murmur: 'Berthe!' And each time she would raise her eyes to him with a look of tenderness; they would look at each other for a second and then her look, pierced and fascinated by his, would fall.

They found no thoughts to exchange. They had been left alone, but occasionally some of the dancers would cast a rapid glance at them, as though they were the discreet and trusty witnesses of a mystery.

A door opened and a servant entered, holding on a tray a letter which a messenger had just brought. Jacques, trembling, took this paper, overwhelmed by a vague and sudden fear, the mysterious terror of swift misfortune.

He looked for a longtime at the envelope, the writing on which he did not know, not daring to open it, not wishing to read it, with a wild desire to put it in his pocket and say to himself: 'I'll leave that till to-morrow, when I'm far away!' But on one corner two big words, underlined, 'Very urgent,' filled him with terror. Saying, 'Please excuse me, my dear,' he tore open the envelope. He read the paper, grew frightfully pale, looked over it again, and, slowly, he seemed to spell it out word for word.

When he raised his head his whole expression showed how upset he was. He stammered: 'My dear, it's—it's from my best friend, who has had, a very great misfortune. He has need of me immediately—for a matter of life or death. Will you excuse me if I leave you for half an hour? I'll be right back.'

Trembling and dazed, she stammered: 'Go, my dear!' not having been his wife long enough to dare to question him, to demand to know. He disappeared. She remained alone, listening to the dancing in the neighbouring parlour.

He had seized the first hat and coat he came to and rushed downstairs three steps at a time. As he was emerging into the street he stopped under the gas-jet of the vestibule and re-read the letter. This is what it said:

> Sir,
>
> A girl by the name of Ravet, an old sweetheart of yours, it seems, has just given birth to a child that she says is yours. The mother is about to die and is begging for you. I take the liberty to write and ask you if you can grant this last request to a woman who seems to be very unhappy and worthy of pity.
>
> Yours truly,
> Dr. Bonnard

When he reached the sick-room the woman was already on the point of death. He did not recognize her at first. The doctor and two nurses were taking care of her. And everywhere on the floor were pails full of ice and rags covered with blood. Water flooded the carpet; two candles were burning on a bureau; behind the bed, in a little wicker crib, the child was crying, and each time it would moan, the mother, in torture, would try to move, shivering under her ice bandages.

She was mortally wounded, killed by this birth. Her life was flowing from her, and, notwithstanding the ice and the care, the merciless haemorrhage continued, hastening her last hour.

She recognized Jacques and wished to raise her arms. They were so weak that she could not do so, but tears coursed down her pallid cheeks. He dropped to his knees beside the bed, seized one of her hands and kissed it frantically. Then, little by little, he drew close to the thin face, which started at the contact. One of the nurses was lighting them with a candle, and the doctor was watching them from the back of the room.

Then she said in a voice which sounded as though it came from a distance: 'I am going to die, dear. Promise to stay to the end. Oh! Don't leave me now. Don't leave me in my last moments!'

He kissed her face and her hair, and, weeping, he murmured: 'Do not be uneasy; I will stay.'

It was several minutes before she could speak again, she was so weak. She continued: 'The little one is yours. I swear it before God and on my soul. I swear it as I am dying! I have never loved another man but you—promise to take care of the child.'

He was trying to take this poor pain-racked body in his arms. Maddened by remorse and sorrow, he stammered: 'I swear to you that I will bring him up and love him. He shall never leave me.'

Then she tried to kiss Jacques. Powerless to lift her head, she held out her white lips in an appeal for a kiss. He approached his lips to respond to this piteous entreaty.

As soon as she felt a little calmer, she murmured: 'Bring him here and let me see if you love him.'

He went and got the child. He placed him gently on the bed between them, and the little one stopped crying. She murmured: 'Don't move any more!' And he was quiet. And he stayed there, holding in his burning hand this other hand shaking in the chill of death, just as, a while ago, he had been holding a hand trembling with love. From time to time he would cast a quick glance at the clock, which marked midnight, then one o'clock, then two.

The physician had returned. The two nurses, after noiselessly moving about the room for a while, were now sleeping on chairs. The child was asleep, and the mother, with eyes shut, appeared also to be resting.

Suddenly, just as pale daylight was creeping in behind the curtains, she stretched out her arms with such a quick and violent motion that she almost threw her baby on the floor. A kind of rattle was heard in her throat, then she lay on her back motionless, dead.

The nurses sprang forward and declared: 'All is over!'

He looked once more at this woman whom he had so loved, then at the clock, which pointed to four, and he ran away, forgetting his overcoat, in the evening dress, with the child in his arms.

After he had left her alone the young wife had waited, calmly enough at first, in the little Japanese boudoir. Then, as she did not see him return, she went back to the parlour with an indifferent and calm appearance, but terribly anxious. When her mother saw her alone she asked: 'Where is your husband?' She answered: 'In his room; he is coming right back.'

After an hour, when everybody had questioned her, she told about the letter, Jacques' upset appearance and her fears of an accident.

Still they waited. The guests left; only the nearest relatives remained. At midnight the bride was put to bed, sobbing bitterly. Her mother and two aunts, sitting around the bed, listened to her crying, silent and in despair. The father had gone to the commissary of police to see if he could obtain some news.

At five o'clock a slight noise was heard in the hall. A door was softly opened and closed. Then suddenly a little cry like the mewing of a cat was heard throughout the silent house.

All the women started forward and Berthe sprang ahead of them all, pushing her way past her aunts, wrapped in a bathrobe.

Jacques stood in the middle of the room, pale and out of breath, holding an infant in his arms. The four women looked at him, astonished; but Berthe, who had suddenly become courageous, rushed forward with anguish in her heart, exclaiming: 'What is it? What's the matter?'

He looked about him wildly and answered shortly:

'I—I have a child and the mother has just died.'

And with his clumsy hands he held out the screaming infant.

Without saying a word, Berthe seized the child, kissed it and hugged it to her. Then she raised her tear-filled eyes to him, asking: 'Did you say that the mother was dead?' He answered: 'Yes—just now—in my arms. I had broken with her since summer. I knew nothing. The physician sent for me.'

Then Berthe murmured: 'Well, we will bring up the little one.'

24

VENUS ANNODOMINI

Rudyard Kipling

Age cannot wither nor customs stale, thy infinite variety.

And the years went on, as the years must do;
But our great Diana was always new—
Fresh, and blooming, and blonde, and fair,
With azure eyes, and with aureate hair;
And all the folk, as they came or went,
Offered her praise to her heart's content.

—Diana of Ephesus

She had nothing to do with Number Eighteen in the Braccio Nuovo of the Vatican, between Visconti's Ceres and the God of the Nile. She was purely an Indian deity—an Anglo-Indian deity, that is to say—and we called her The Venus Annodomini, to distinguish her from other Annodominis of the same everlasting order. There was a legend among the Hills that she had once been young; but no living man was prepared to come forward and say boldly that the legend was true. Men rode up to Simla, and stayed, and went away and made their name and did their life's work, and returned again to find the Venus Annodomini exactly as they had left her. She was as immutable as the Hills. But not quite so green. All that a girl of eighteen could do in the way of riding, walking, dancing, picnicking, and over exertion generally, the Venus Annodomini did, and showed no sign of fatigue or trace of weariness. Besides perpetual youth, she had discovered, men said, the secret of perpetual health; and her fame spread about the land.

From a mere woman, she grew to be an institution, insomuch that no young man could be said to be properly formed, who had not, at some time or another, worshipped at the shrine of the Venus Annodomini. There was no one like her, though there were many imitations. Six years in her eyes were no more than six months to ordinary women; and ten made less visible impression on her than does a week's fever on an ordinary woman. Every one adored her, and in return she was pleasant and courteous to nearly every one. Youth had been a habit of hers for so long, that she could not part with it—never, realized, in fact, the necessity of parting with it—and took for her more chosen associates, young people.

Among the worshippers of the Venus Annodomini was young Gayerson. 'Very Young' Gayerson he was called to distinguish him from his father 'Young' Gayerson, a Bengal Civilian, who affected the customs—as he had the heart—of youth. 'Very Young' Gayerson was not content to worship placidly and for form's sake, as the other young men did, or to accept a ride or a dance, or a talk from the Venus Annodomini in a properly humble and thankful spirit. He was exacting, and, therefore, the Venus Annodomini repressed him. He worried himself nearly sick in a futile sort of way over her; and his devotion and earnestness made him appear either shy or boisterous or rude, as his mood might vary, by the side of the older men who, with him, bowed before the Venus Annodomini. She was sorry for him. He reminded her of a lad who, three-and-twenty years ago, had professed a boundless devotion for her, and for whom in return she had felt something more than a week's weakness. But that lad had fallen away and married another woman less than a year after he had worshipped her; and the Venus Annodomini had almost—not quite—forgotten his name. 'Very Young' Gayerson had the same big blue eyes and the same way of pouting his underlip when he was excited or troubled. But the Venus Annodomini checked him sternly none the less. Too much zeal was a thing that she did not approve of;

preferring instead, a tempered and sober tenderness.

'Very Young' Gayerson was miserable, and took no trouble to conceal his wretchedness. He was in the Army—a Line regiment I think, but am not certain—and, since his face was a looking-glass and his forehead an open book, by reason of his innocence, his brothers-in-arms made his life a burden to him and embittered his naturally sweet disposition. No one except 'Very Young' Gayerson, and he never told his views, knew how old 'Very Young' Gayerson believed the Venus Annodomini to be. Perhaps he thought her five-and-twenty, or perhaps she told him that she was this age. 'Very Young' Gayerson would have forded the Indus in flood to carry her lightest word, and had implicit faith in her. Every one liked him, and every one was sorry when they saw him so bound a slave of the Venus Annodomini. Every one, too, admitted that it was not her fault; for the Venus Annodomini differed from Mrs Hauksbee and Mrs Reiver in this particular, she never moved a finger to attract any one; but, like Ninon de L'Enclos, all men were attracted to her. One could admire and respect Mrs Hauksbee, despise and avoid Mrs Reiver, but one was forced to adore the Venus Annodomini.

'Very Young' Gayerson's papa held a Division, or a Collectorate, or something administrative, in a particularly unpleasant part of Bengal—full of Babus who edited newspapers proving that 'Young' Gayerson was a 'Nero' and a 'Scylla' and a 'Charybdis'; and, in addition to the Babus, there was a good deal of dysentery and cholera abroad for nine months of the year. 'Young' Gayerson—he was about five-and-forty—rather liked Babus, they amused him, but he objected to dysentery, and when he could get away, went to Darjiling for the most part. This particular season he fancied that he would come up to Simla and see his boy. The boy was not altogether pleased. He told the Venus Annodomini that his father was coming up, and she flushed a little and said that she should be delighted to make his acquaintance. Then she looked long and thoughtfully at 'Very Young' Gayerson, because she was very, very sorry for him, and he was a very, very big idiot.

'My daughter is coming out in a fortnight, Mr Gayerson,' she said.

'Your what?' said he.

'Daughter,' said the Venus Annodomini. 'She's been out for a year at Home already, and I want her to see a little of India. She is nineteen and a very sensible nice girl I believe.'

'Very Young' Gayerson, who was a short twenty-two years old, nearly fell out of his chair with astonishment; for he had persisted in believing, against all belief, in the youth of the Venus Annodomini. She, with her back to the curtained window, watched the effect of her sentences and smiled.

'Very Young' Gayerson's papa came up twelve days later, and had not been in Simla four-and-twenty hours before two men, old acquaintances of his, had told him how 'Very Young' Gayerson had been conducting himself.

'Young' Gayerson laughed a good deal, and inquired who the Venus Annodomini might be. Which proves that he had been living in Bengal where nobody knows anything except the rate of Exchange. Then he said boys would be boys, and spoke to his son about the matter. 'Very Young' Gayerson said that he felt wretched and unhappy; and 'Young' Gayerson said that he repented of having helped to bring a fool into the world. He suggested that his son had better cut his leave short and go down to his duties. This led to an unfilial answer, and relations were strained, until 'Young' Gayerson demanded that they should call on the Venus Annodomini. 'Very Young' Gayerson went with his papa, feeling, somehow, uncomfortable and small.

The Venus Annodomini received them graciously, and 'Young' Gayerson said, 'By Jove! It's Kitty!' 'Very Young' Gayerson would have listened for an explanation, if his time had not been taken up with trying to talk to a large, handsome, quiet, well-dressed girl—introduced to him by the Venus Annodomini as her daughter. She was far older in manner, style, and repose than 'Very Young' Gayerson; and, as he realized this thing, he felt sick.

Presently he heard the Venus Annodomini saying, 'Do you know that your son is one of my most devoted admirers?'

'I don't wonder,' said 'Young' Gayerson. Here he raised his voice, 'He follows his father's footsteps. Didn't I worship the ground you trod on, ever so long ago, Kitty—and you haven't changed since then. How strange it all seems!'

'Very Young' Gayerson said nothing. His conversation with the daughter of the Venus Annodomini was, through the rest of the call, fragmentary and disjointed.

'At five to-morrow, then,' said the Venus Annodomini. 'And mind you are punctual.'

'At five punctually,' said 'Young' Gayerson. 'You can lend your old father a horse, I daresay, youngster, can't you? I'm going for a ride tomorrow afternoon.'

'Certainly,' said 'Very Young' Gayerson. 'I am going down to-morrow morning. My ponies are at your service, Sir.'

The Venus Annodomini looked at him across the half-light of the room, and her big grey eyes filled with moisture. She rose and shook hands with him.

'Good-bye, Tom,' whispered the Venus Annodomini.

25

MADEMOISELLE PEARL

Guy de Maupassant

The occasional intoxication of love.

I

What a strange idea it was for me to choose Mademoiselle Pearl for queen that evening!

Every year I celebrate Twelfth Night with my old friend Chantal. My father, who was his most intimate friend, used to take me round there when I was a child. I continued the custom, and I doubtless shall continue it as long as I live and as long as there is a Chantal in this world.

The Chantals lead a peculiar existence; they live in Paris as though they were in Grasse, Evetot, or Pont-a-Mousson.

They have a house with a little garden near the observatory. They live there as though they were in the country. Of Paris, the real Paris, they know nothing at all, they suspect nothing; they are so far, so far away! However, from time to time, they take a trip into it. Mademoiselle Chantal goes to lay in her provisions, as it is called in the family. This is how they go to purchase their provisions:

Mademoiselle Pearl, who has the keys to the kitchen closet (for the linen closets are administered by the mistress herself), Mademoiselle Pearl gives warning that the supply of sugar is low, that the preserves are giving out, that there is not much left in the bottom of the coffee bag. Thus warned against famine, Mademoiselle Chantal passes everything in review, taking notes on a pad. Then she puts down a lot of figures and goes through lengthy calculations and long discussions with Mademoiselle Pearl. At last they manage to agree, and they decide upon the quantity of each thing of which they will lay in a three months' provision; sugar, rice, prunes, coffee, preserves, cans of peas, beans, lobster, salt or smoked fish, etc., etc. After which the day for the purchasing is determined on and they go in a cab with a railing round the top and drive to a large grocery store on the other side of the river in the new sections of the town.

Madame Chantal and Mademoiselle Pearl make this trip together, mysteriously, and only return at dinner time, tired out, although still excited, and shaken up by the cab, the roof of which is covered with bundles and bags, like an express wagon.

For the Chantals all that part of Paris situated on the other side of the Seine constitutes the new quarter, a section inhabited by a strange, noisy population, which cares little for honour, spends its days in dissipation, its nights in revelry, and which throws money out of the windows. From time to time, however, the young girls are taken to the Opera-Comique or the Theatre Francais, when the play is recommended by the paper which is read by M. Chantal.

At present the young ladies are respectively nineteen and seventeen. They are two pretty girls, tall and fresh, very well brought up, in fact, too well brought up, so much so that they pass by unperceived like two pretty dolls. Never would the idea come to me to pay the slightest attention or to pay court to one of the young Chantal ladies; they are so immaculate that one hardly dares speak to them; one almost feels indecent when bowing to them.

As for the father, he is a charming man, well educated, frank, cordial, but he likes calm and quiet above all else, and has thus contributed greatly to the mummifying of his family in order to live as he pleased in stagnant quiescence. He reads a lot, loves to talk and is readily affected. Lack of contact and of elbowing with the world has made his moral skin very tender and sensitive. The slightest thing moves him, excites him, and makes him suffer.

The Chantals have limited connections carefully chosen in the neighbourhood. They also exchange two or three yearly visits with relatives who live in the distance.

As for me, I take dinner with them on the fifteenth of August and on Twelfth Night. That is as much one of my duties as Easter communion is for a Catholic.

On the fifteenth of August a few friends are invited, but on Twelfth Night I am the only stranger.

Well, this year, as every former year, I went to the Chantals' for my Epiphany dinner.

According to my usual custom, I kissed M. Chantal, Madame Chantal and Mademoiselle Pearl, and I made a deep bow to the Misses Louise and Pauline. I was questioned about a thousand and one things, about what had happened on the boulevards, about politics, about how matters stood in Tong-King, and about our representatives in Parliament. Madame Chantal, a fat lady, whose ideas always gave me the impression of being carved out square like building stones, was accustomed to exclaiming at the end of every political discussion: 'All that is seed which does not promise much for the future!' Why have I always imagined that Madame Chantal's ideas are square? I don't know; but everything that she says takes that shape in my head: a big square, with four symmetrical angles. There are other people whose ideas always strike me as being round and rolling like a hoop. As soon as they begin a sentence on any subject it rolls on and on, coming out in ten, twenty, fifty round ideas, large and small, which I see rolling along, one behind the other, to the end of the horizon. Other people have pointed ideas—but enough of this.

We sat down as usual and finished our dinner without anything out of the ordinary being said. At dessert the Twelfth Night cake was brought on. Now, M. Chantal had been king every year. I don't know whether this was the result of continued chance or a family convention, but he unfailingly found the bean in his piece of cake, and he would proclaim Madame Chantal to be queen. Therefore, I was greatly surprised to find something very hard, which almost made me break a tooth, in a mouthful of cake. Gently I took this thing from my mouth and I saw that it was a little porcelain doll, no bigger than a bean. Surprise caused me to exclaim:

'Ah!' All looked at me, and Chantal clapped his hands and cried: 'It's Gaston! It's Gaston! Long live the king! Long live the king!'

All took up the chorus: 'Long live the king!' And I blushed to the tip of my ears, as one often does, without any reason at all, in situations which are a little foolish. I sat there looking at my plate, with this absurd little bit of pottery in my fingers, forcing myself to laugh and not knowing what to do or say, when Chantal once more cried out: 'Now, you must choose a queen!'

Then I was thunderstruck. In a second a thousand thoughts and suppositions flashed through my mind. Did they expect me to pick out one of the young Chantal ladies? Was that a trick to make me say which one I prefer? Was it a gentle, light, direct hint of the parents toward a possible marriage? The idea of marriage roams continually in houses with grown-up girls, and takes every shape and disguise, and employs every subterfuge. A dread of compromising myself took hold of me as well as an extreme timidity before the obstinately correct and reserved attitude of the Misses Louise and Pauline. To choose one of them in preference to the other seemed to me as difficult as choosing between two drops of water; and then the fear of launching myself into an affair which might, in spite of me, lead me gently into matrimonial ties, by means as wary and imperceptible and as calm as this insignificant royalty—the fear of all this haunted me.

Suddenly I had an inspiration, and I held out to Mademoiselle Pearl the symbolical emblem. At first every one was surprised, then they doubtless appreciated my delicacy and discretion, for they applauded furiously. Everybody was crying: 'Long live the queen! Long live the queen!'

As for herself, poor old maid, she was so amazed that she completely lost control of herself; she was trembling and stammering: 'No—no—oh! no—not me—please—not me—I beg of you—'

Then for the first time in my life I looked at Mademoiselle Pearl and wondered what she was.

I was accustomed to seeing her in this house, just as one sees old upholstered armchairs on which one has been sitting since childhood without ever noticing them. One day, with no reason at all, because a ray of sunshine happens to strike the seat, you suddenly think: 'Why, that chair is very curious'; and then you discover that the wood has been worked by a real artist and that the material is remarkable. I had never taken any notice of Mademoiselle Pearl.

She was a part of the Chantal family, that was all. But how? By what right? She was a tall, thin person who tried to remain in the background, but who was by no means insignificant. She was treated in a friendly manner, better than a housekeeper, not so well as a relative. I suddenly observed several shades of distinction which I had never noticed before. Madame Chantal said: 'Pearl.' The young ladies: 'Mademoiselle Pearl,' and Chantal only addressed her as 'Mademoiselle,' with an air of greater respect, perhaps.

I began to observe her. How old could she be? Forty? Yes, forty. She was not old, she made herself old. I was suddenly struck by this fact. She fixed her hair and dressed in a ridiculous manner, and, notwithstanding all that, she was not in the least ridiculous, she had such simple, natural gracefulness, veiled and hidden. Truly, what a strange creature! How was it I had never observed her before? She dressed her hair in a grotesque manner with little old maid curls, most absurd; but beneath this one could see a large, calm brow, cut by two deep lines, two wrinkles of long sadness, then two blue eyes, large and tender, so timid, so bashful, so humble, two beautiful eyes which had kept the expression of naive wonder of a young girl, of youthful sensations, and also of sorrow, which had softened without spoiling them.

Her whole face was refined and discreet, a face the expression of which seemed to have gone out without being used up or faded by the fatigues and great emotions of life.

What a dainty mouth! And such pretty teeth! But one would have thought that she did not dare smile.

Suddenly I compared her to Madame Chantal! Undoubtedly Mademoiselle Pearl was the better of the two, a hundred times better, daintier, prouder, more noble. I was surprised at my observation. They were pouring out champagne. I held my glass up to the queen and, with a well-turned compliment, I drank to her health. I could see that she felt inclined to hide her head in her napkin. Then, as she was dipping her lips in the clear wine, everybody cried: 'The queen drinks! The queen drinks!' She almost turned purple and choked. Everybody was laughing; but I could see that all loved her.

As soon as dinner was over Chantal took me by the arm. It was time for his cigar, a sacred hour. When alone he would smoke it out in the street; when guests came to dinner he would take them to the billiard room and smoke while playing. That evening they had built a fire to celebrate Twelfth Night; my old friend took his cue, a very fine one, and chalked it with great care; then he said:

'You break, my boy!'

He called me 'my boy', although I was twenty-five, but he had known me as a young child.

I started the game and made a few carroms. I missed some others, but as the thought of Mademoiselle Pearl kept returning to my mind, I suddenly asked:

'By the way, Monsieur Chantal, is Mademoiselle Pearl a relative of yours?'

Greatly surprised, he stopped playing and looked at me:

'What! Don't you know? Haven't you heard about Mademoiselle Pearl?'

'No.'

'Didn't your father ever tell you?'

'No.'

'Well, well, that's funny! That certainly is funny! Why, it's a regular romance!'

He paused, and then continued:

'And if you only knew how peculiar it is that you should ask me that to-day, on Twelfth Night!'

'Why?'

'Why? Well, listen. Forty-one years ago to day, the day of the Epiphany, the following events occurred: We were then living at Roily-le-Tors, on the ramparts; but in order that you may understand, I must first explain the house. Roily is built on a hill, or, rather, on a mound which overlooks a great stretch of prairie. We had a house there with a beautiful hanging garden supported by the old battlemented wall; so that the house was in the town on the streets, while the garden overlooked the plain. There was a door leading from the garden to the open country, at the bottom of a secret stairway in the thick wall—the kind you read about in novels. A road passed in front of this door, which was provided with a big bell; for the peasants, in order to avoid the roundabout way, would bring their provisions up this way.

'You now understand the place, don't you? Well, this year, at Epiphany, it had been snowing for a week. One might have thought that the world was coming to an end. When we went to the ramparts to look over the plain, this immense white, frozen country, which shone like varnish, would chill our very souls. One might have thought that the Lord had packed the world in cotton to put it away in the storeroom for old worlds. I can assure you that it was dreary looking.

'We were a very numerous family at that time my father, my mother, my uncle and aunt, my two brothers and four cousins; they were pretty little girls; I married the youngest. Of all that crowd, there are only three of us left: my wife, I, and my sister-in-law, who lives in Marseilles. Zounds! How quickly a family like that dwindles away! I tremble when I think of it! I was fifteen years old then, since I am fifty-six now.

'We were going to celebrate the Epiphany, and we were all happy, very happy! Everybody was in the parlour, awaiting dinner, and my oldest brother, Jacques, said: "There has been a dog howling out in the plain for about ten minutes; the poor beast must be lost."

'He had hardly stopped talking when the garden bell began to ring. It had the deep sound of a church bell, which made one think of death. A shiver ran through everybody. My father called the servant and told him to go outside and look. We waited in complete silence; we were thinking of the snow which covered the ground. When the man returned he declared that he had seen nothing. The dog kept up its ceaseless howling, and always from the same spot.

'We sat down to dinner; but we were all uneasy, especially the young people. Everything went well up to the roast, then the bell began to ring again, three times in succession, three heavy, long strokes which vibrated to the tips of our fingers and which stopped our conversation short. We sat there looking at each other, fork in the air, still listening, and shaken by a kind of supernatural fear.

'At last my mother spoke: "It's surprising that they should have waited so long to come back. Do not go alone, Baptiste; one of these gentlemen will accompany you."

'My Uncle Francois arose. He was a kind of Hercules, very proud of his strength, and feared nothing in the world. My father said to him: "Take a gun. There is no telling what it might be."

'But my uncle only took a cane and went out with the servant.

'We others remained there trembling with fear and

apprehension, without eating or speaking. My father tried to reassure us: "Just wait and see," he said; "it will be some beggar or some traveller lost in the snow. After ringing once, seeing that the door was not immediately opened, he attempted again to find his way, and being unable to, he has returned to our door."

'Our uncle seemed to stay away an hour. At last he came back, furious, swearing: "Nothing at all; it's some practical joker! There is nothing but that damned dog howling away at about a hundred yards from the walls. If I had taken a gun I would have killed him to make him keep quiet."

'We sat down to dinner again, but every one was excited; we felt that all was not over, that something was going to happen, that the bell would soon ring again.

'It rang just as the Twelfth Night cake was being cut. All the men jumped up together. My uncle, Francois, who had been drinking champagne, swore so furiously that he would murder it, whatever it might be, that my mother and my aunt threw themselves on him to prevent his going. My father, although very calm and a little helpless (he limped ever since he had broken his leg when thrown by a horse), declared, in turn, that he wished to find out what was the matter and that he was going. My brothers, aged eighteen and twenty, ran to get their guns; and as no one was paying any attention to me I snatched up a little rifle that was used in the garden and got ready to accompany the expedition.

'It started out immediately. My father and uncle were walking ahead with Baptiste, who was carrying a lantern. My brothers, Jacques and Paul, followed, and I trailed on behind in spite of the prayers of my mother, who stood in front of the house with her sister and my cousins.

'It had been snowing again for the last hour, and the trees were weighted down. The pines were bending under this heavy, white garment, and looked like white pyramids or enormous sugar cones, and through the grey curtains of small hurrying flakes could be seen the lighter bushes which stood out pale in the shadow. The snow was falling so thick that we could hardly see ten feet ahead of us. But the lantern threw a bright light around us. When we began to go down the winding stairway in the wall I really grew frightened. I felt as though some one were walking behind me, were going to grab me by the shoulders and carry me away, and I felt a strong desire to return; but, as I would have had to cross the garden all alone, I did not dare. I heard some one opening the door leading to the plain; my uncle began to swear again, exclaiming: "By—! He has gone again! If I can catch sight of even his shadow, I'll take care not to miss him, the swine!"

'It was a discouraging thing to see this great expanse of plain, or, rather, to feel it before us, for we could not see it; we could only see a thick, endless veil of snow, above, below, opposite us, to the right, to the left, everywhere. My uncle continued: "Listen! There is the dog howling again; I will teach him how I shoot. That will be something gained, anyhow."

'But my father, who was kind-hearted, went on: "It will be much better to go on and get the poor animal, who is crying for hunger. The poor fellow is barking for help; he is calling like a man in distress. Let us go to him."

'So we started out through this mist, through this thick continuous fall of snow, which filled the air, which moved, floated, fell, and chilled the skin with a burning sensation like a sharp, rapid pain as each flake melted. We were sinking in up to our knees in this soft, cold mass, and we had to lift our feet very high in order to walk. As we advanced the dog's voice became clearer and stronger. My uncle cried: "Here he is!" We stopped to observe him as one does when he meets an enemy at night.

'I could see nothing, so I ran up to the others, and I caught sight of him; he was frightful and weird-looking; he was a big black shepherd's dog with long hair and a wolf's head, standing just within the gleam of light cast by our lantern on the snow. He did not move; he was silently watching us.

'My uncle said: "That's peculiar, he is neither advancing nor retreating. I feel like taking a shot at him."

'My father answered in a firm voice: "No, we must capture him."

'Then my brother Jacques added: "But he is not alone. There is something behind him."

'There was indeed something behind him, something grey, impossible to distinguish. We started out again cautiously. When he saw us approaching, the dog sat down. He did not look wicked. Instead, he seemed pleased at having been able to attract the attention of some one.

'My father went straight to him and petted him. The dog licked his hands. We saw that he was tied to the wheel of a little carriage, a sort of toy carriage entirely wrapped up in three or four woollen blankets. We carefully took off these coverings, and as Baptiste approached his lantern to the front of this little vehicle, which looked like a rolling kennel, we saw in it a little baby sleeping peacefully.

'We were so astonished that we couldn't speak.

'My father was the first to collect his wits, and as he had a warm heart and a broad mind, he stretched his hand over the roof of the carriage and said: "Poor little waif, you shall be one of us!" And he ordered my brother Jacques to roll the foundling ahead of us. Thinking out loud, my father continued: "Some child of love whose poor mother rang at my door on this night of Epiphany in memory of the Child of God."

'He once more stopped and called at the top of his lungs through the night to the four corners of the heavens: "We have found it!" Then, putting his hand on his brother's shoulder, he murmured: "What if you had shot the dog, Francois?"

'My uncle did not answer, but in the darkness he crossed

himself, for, notwithstanding his blustering manner, he was very religious.

'The dog, which had been untied, was following us.

'Ah! But you should have seen us when we got to the house! At first we had a lot of trouble in getting the carriage up through the winding stairway; but we succeeded and even rolled it into the vestibule.

'How funny mamma was! How happy and astonished! And my four little cousins (the youngest was only six), they looked like four chickens around a nest. At last we took the child from the carriage. It was still sleeping. It was a girl about six weeks old. In its clothes we found ten thousand francs in gold, yes, my boy, ten thousand francs—which papa saved for her dowry. Therefore, it was not a child of poor people, but, perhaps, the child of some nobleman and a little bourgeoise of the town—or again—we made a thousand suppositions, but we never found out anything–never the slightest clue. The dog himself was recognized by no one. He was a stranger in the country. At any rate, the person who rang three times at our door must have known my parents well, to have chosen them thus.

'That is how, at the age of six weeks, Mademoiselle Pearl entered the Chantal household.

'It was not until later that she was called Mademoiselle Pearl. She was at first baptized "Marie Simonne Claire", Claire being intended, for her family name.

'I can assure you that our return to the diningroom was amusing, with this baby now awake and looking round her at these people and these lights with her vague blue questioning eyes.

'We sat down to dinner again and the cake was cut. I was king, and for queen I took Mademoiselle Pearl, just as you did to-day. On that day she did not appreciate the honour that was being shown her.

'Well, the child was adopted and brought up in the family.

She grew, and the years flew by. She was so gentle and loving and minded so well that every one would have spoiled her abominably had not my mother prevented it.

'My mother was an orderly woman with a great respect for class distinctions. She consented to treat little Claire as she did her own sons, but, nevertheless, she wished the distance which separated us to be well marked, and our positions well established. Therefore, as soon as the child could understand, she acquainted her with her story and gently, even tenderly, impressed on the little one's mind that, for the Chantals, she was an adopted daughter, taken in, but, nevertheless, a stranger. Claire understood the situation with peculiar intelligence and with surprising instinct; she knew how to take the place which was allotted her, and to keep it with so much tact, gracefulness and gentleness that she often brought tears to my father's eyes. My mother herself was often moved by the passionate gratitude and timid devotion of this dainty and loving little creature that she began calling her, "My daughter". At times, when the little one had done something kind and good, my mother would raise her spectacles on her forehead, a thing which always indicated emotion with her, and she would repeat: "This child is a pearl, a perfect pearl!" This name stuck to the little Claire, who became and remained for us Mademoiselle Pearl.'

II

M. Chantal stopped. He was sitting on the edge of the billiard table, his feet hanging, and was playing with a ball with his left hand, while with his right he crumpled a rag which served to rub the chalk marks from the slate. A little red in the face, his voice thick, he was talking away to himself now, lost in his memories, gently drifting through the old scenes and events which awoke in his mind, just as we walk through old family gardens where we were brought up and where each tree, each walk, each hedge reminds us of some occurrence.

I stood opposite him leaning against the wall, my hands resting on my idle cue.

After a slight pause he continued:

'By Jove! She was pretty at eighteen—and graceful—and perfect. Ah! She was so sweet—and good and true—and charming! She had such eyes–blue,transparent,clear—such eyes as I have never seen since!'

He was once more silent. I asked: 'Why did she never marry?'

He answered, not to me, but to the word 'marry' which had caught his ear: 'Why? Why? She never would—she never would! She had a dowry of thirty thousand francs, and she received several offers—but she never would! She seemed sad at that time. That was when I married my cousin, little Charlotte, my wife, to whom I had been engaged for six years.'

I looked at M. Chantal, and it seemed to me that I was looking into his very soul, and I was suddenly witnessing one of those humble and cruel tragedies of honest, straightforward, blameless hearts, one of those secret tragedies known to no one, not even the silent and resigned victims. A rash curiosity suddenly impelled me to exclaim:

'You should have married her, Monsieur Chantal!'

He started, looked at me, and said:

'I? Marry whom?'

'Mademoiselle Pearl.'

'Why?'

'Because you loved her more than your cousin.'

He stared at me with strange, round, bewildered eyes and stammered:

'I loved her—I? How? Who told you that?'

'Why, anyone can see that—and it's even on account of her that you delayed for so long your marriage to your cousin who had been waiting for you for six years.'

He dropped the ball which he was holding in his left hand, and, seizing the chalk rag in both hands, he buried his face in it and began to sob. He was weeping with his eyes, nose and mouth in a heartbreaking yet ridiculous manner, like a sponge which one squeezes. He was coughing, spitting and blowing his nose in the chalk rag, wiping his eyes and sneezing; then the tears would again begin to flow down the wrinkles on his face and he would make a strange gurgling noise in his throat. I felt bewildered, ashamed; I wanted to run away, and I no longer knew what to say, do, or attempt.

Suddenly Madame Chantal's voice sounded on the stairs. 'Haven't you men almost finished smoking your cigars?'

I opened the door and cried: 'Yes, Madame, we are coming right down.'

Then I rushed to her husband, and, seizing him by the shoulders, I cried: 'Monsieur Chantal, my friend Chantal, listen to me; your wife is calling; pull yourself together, we must go downstairs.'

He stammered: 'Yes—yes—I am coming—poor girl! I am coming—tell her that I am coming.'

He began conscientiously to wipe his face on the cloth which, for the last two or three years, had been used for marking off the chalk from the slate; then he appeared, half white and half red, his forehead, nose, cheeks and chin covered with chalk, and his eyes swollen, still full of tears.

I caught him by the hands and dragged him into his bedroom, muttering: 'I beg your pardon, I beg your pardon, Monsieur Chantal, for having caused you such sorrow—but—I did not know—you—you understand.'

He squeezed my hand, saying: 'Yes—yes—there are difficult moments.'

Then he plunged his face into a bowl of water. When he

emerged from it he did not yet seem to me to be presentable; but I thought of a little stratagem. As he was growing worried, looking at himself in the mirror, I said to him: 'All you have to do is to say that a little dust flew into your eye and you can cry before everybody to your heart's content.'

He went downstairs rubbing his eyes with his handkerchief. All were worried; each one wished to look for the speck, which could not be found; and stories were told of similar cases where it had been necessary to call in a physician.

I went over to Mademoiselle Pearl and watched her, tormented by an ardent curiosity, which was turning to positive suffering. She must indeed have been pretty, with her gentle, calm eyes, so large that it looked as though she never closed them like other mortals. Her gown was a little ridiculous, a real old maid's gown, which was unbecoming without appearing clumsy.

It seemed to me as though I were looking into her soul, just as I had into Monsieur Chantal's; that I was looking right from one end to the other of this humble life, so simple and devoted. I felt an irresistible longing to question her, to find out whether she, too, had loved him; whether she also had suffered, as he had, from this long, secret, poignant grief, which one cannot see, know, or guess, but which breaks forth at night in the loneliness of the dark room. I was watching her, and I could observe her heart beating under her waist, and I wondered whether this sweet, candid face had wept on the soft pillow and she had sobbed, her whole body shaken by the violence of her anguish.

I said to her in a low voice, like a child who is breaking a toy to see what is inside: 'If you could have seen Monsieur Chantal crying a while ago it would have moved you.'

She started, asking: 'What? He was weeping?'

'Ah, yes, he was indeed weeping!'

'Why?'

She seemed deeply moved. I answered:

'On your account.'

'On my account?'

'Yes. He was telling me how much he had loved you in the days gone by; and what a pang it had given him to marry his cousin instead of you.'

Her pale face seemed to grow a little longer; her calm eyes, which always remained open, suddenly closed so quickly that they seemed shut forever. She slipped from her chair to the floor, and slowly, gently sank down as would a fallen garment.

I cried: 'Help! Help! Mademoiselle Pearl is ill.'

Madame Chantal and her daughters rushed forward, and while they were looking for towels, water and vinegar, I grabbed my hat and ran away.

I walked away with rapid strides, my heart heavy, my mind full of remorse and regret. And yet sometimes I felt pleased; I felt as though I had done a praiseworthy and necessary act. I was asking myself: 'Did I do wrong or right?' They had that shut up in their hearts, just as some people carry a bullet in a closed wound. Will they not be happier now? It was too late for their torture to begin over again and early enough for them to remember it with tenderness.

And perhaps some evening next spring, moved by the moonlight falling through the branches on the grass at their feet, they will join and press their hands in memory of all this cruel and suppressed suffering; and, perhaps, also this short embrace may infuse in their veins a little of this thrill which they would not have known without it, and will give to those two dead souls, brought to life in a second, the rapid and divine sensation of this intoxication, of this madness which gives to lovers more happiness in an instant than other men can gather during a whole lifetime!

26

THE ROMANCE OF A BUSY BROKER

O. Henry

In the rat race of life, one loses touch of ethereal time and romance.

Pitcher, confidential clerk in the office of Harvey Maxwell, broker, allowed a look of mild interest and surprise to visit his usually expressionless countenance when his employer briskly entered at half past nine in company with his young lady stenographer. With a snappy 'Good-morning, Pitcher,' Maxwell dashed at his desk as though he were intending to leap over it, and then plunged into the great heap of letters and telegrams waiting there for him.

The young lady had been Maxwell's stenographer for a year. She was beautiful in a way that was decidedly unstenographic. She forewent the pomp of the alluring pompadour. She wore no chains, bracelets or lockets. She had not the air of being about to accept an invitation to luncheon. Her dress was grey and plain, but it fitted her figure with fidelity and discretion. In her neat black turban hat was the gold-green wing of a macaw. On this morning she was softly and shyly radiant. Her eyes were dreamily bright, her cheeks genuine peachblow, her expression a happy one, tinged with reminiscence.

Pitcher, still mildly curious, noticed a difference in her ways this morning. Instead of going straight into the adjoining room, where her desk was, she lingered, slightly irresolute, in the outer office. Once she moved over by Maxwell's desk, near enough for him to be aware of her presence.

The machine sitting at that desk was no longer a man; it was a busy New York broker, moved by buzzing wheels and uncoiling springs.

'Well—what is it? Anything?' asked Maxwell sharply. His opened mail lay like a bank of stage snow on his crowded desk. His keen grey eye, impersonal and brusque, flashed upon her half impatiently.

'Nothing,' answered the stenographer, moving away with a little smile.

'Mr Pitcher,' she said to the confidential clerk, 'did Mr Maxwell say anything yesterday about engaging another stenographer?'

'He did,' answered Pitcher. 'He told me to get another one. I notified the agency yesterday afternoon to send over a few samples this morning. It's 9.45 o'clock, and not a single picture hat or piece of pineapple chewing gum has showed up yet.'

'I will do the work as usual, then,' said the young lady, 'until some one comes to fill the place.' And she went to her desk at once and hung the black turban hat with the gold-green macaw wing in its accustomed place.

He who has been denied the spectacle of a busy Manhattan broker during a rush of business is handicapped for the profession of anthropology. The poet sings of the 'crowded hour of glorious life.' The broker's hour is not only crowded, but the minutes and seconds are hanging to all the straps and packing both front and rear platforms.

And this day was Harvey Maxwell's busy day. The ticker began to reel out jerkily its fitful coils of tape, the desk telephone had a chronic attack of buzzing. Men began to throng into the office and call at him over the railing, jovially, sharply, viciously, excitedly. Messenger boys ran in and out with messages and telegrams. The clerks in the office jumped about like sailors during a storm. Even Pitcher's face relaxed into something resembling animation.

On the Exchange there were hurricanes and landslides and snowstorms and glaciers and volcanoes, and those elemental disturbances were reproduced in miniature in the broker's offices. Maxwell shoved his chair against the wall and transacted business after the manner of a toe dancer. He jumped from ticker to phone, from desk to door with the trained agility of a harlequin.

In the midst of this growing and important stress the broker became suddenly aware of a high-rolled fringe of golden hair under a nodding canopy of velvet and ostrich tips, an imitation sealskin sacque and a string of beads as large as hickory nuts, ending near the floor with a silver heart. There was a self-possessed young lady connected with these accessories; and Pitcher was there to construe her.

'Lady from the Stenographer's Agency to see about the position,' said Pitcher.

Maxwell turned half around, with his hands full of papers and ticker tape.

'What position?' he asked, with a frown.

'Position of stenographer,' said Pitcher. 'You told me yesterday to call them up and have one sent over this morning.'

'You are losing your mind, Pitcher,' said Maxwell. 'Why should I have given you any such instructions? Miss Leslie has given perfect satisfaction during the year she has been here. The place is hers as long as she chooses to retain it. There's no place open here, Madam. Countermand that order with the agency, Pitcher, and don't bring any more of 'em in here.'

The silver heart left the office, swinging and banging itself independently against the office furniture as it indignantly departed. Pitcher seized a moment to remark to the bookkeeper that the 'old man' seemed to get more absent-minded and forgetful every day of the world.

The rush and pace of business grew fiercer and faster. On the floor they were pounding half a dozen stocks in which Maxwell's customers were heavy investors. Orders to buy and sell were coming and going as swift as the flight of swallows. Some of his own holdings were imperilled, and the man was working like some high-geared, delicate, strong machine—strung to full tension, going at full speed, accurate, never hesitating, with the proper word and decision and act ready and prompt as clockwork. Stocks and bonds, loans and mortgages, margins and securities—here was a world of finance, and there was no room in it for the human world or the world of nature.

When the luncheon hour drew near there came a slight lull in the uproar.

Maxwell stood by his desk with his hands full of telegrams and memoranda, with a fountain pen over his right ear and his hair hanging in disorderly strings over his forehead. His window was open, for the beloved janitress Spring had turned on a little warmth through the waking registers of the earth.

And through the window came a wandering—perhaps a lost odour—a delicate, sweet odour of lilac that fixed the broker for a moment immovable. For this odour belonged to Miss Leslie; it was her own, and hers only.

The odour brought her vividly, almost tangibly before him. The world of finance dwindled suddenly to a speck. And she was in the next room—twenty steps away.

'By George, I'll do it now,' said Maxwell, half aloud. 'I'll ask her now. I wonder I didn't do it long ago.'

He dashed into the inner office with the haste of a short trying to cover. He charged upon the desk of the stenographer.

She looked up at him with a smile. A soft pink crept over her cheek, and her eyes were kind and frank. Maxwell leaned one elbow on her desk. He still clutched fluttering papers with both hands and the pen was above his ear.

'Miss Leslie,' he began hurriedly, 'I have but a moment to spare. I want to say something in that moment. Will you be my wife? I haven't had time to make love to you in the ordinary way, but I really do love you. Talk quick, please—those fellows are clubbing the stuffing out of Union Pacific.'

'Oh, what are you talking about?' exclaimed the young lady. She rose to her feet and gazed upon him, round-eyed.

'Don't you understand?' said Maxwell, restively. 'I want you to marry me. I love you, Miss Leslie. I wanted to tell you, and I snatched a minute when things had slackened up a bit. They're calling me for the phone now. Tell 'em to wait a minute, Pitcher. Won't you, Miss Leslie?'

The stenographer acted very queerly. At first she seemed overcome with amazement; then tears flowed from her wondering eyes; and then she smiled sunnily through them, and one of her arms slid tenderly about the broker's neck.

'I know now,' she said, softly. 'It's this old business that has driven everything else out of your head for the time. I was frightened at first. Don't you remember, Harvey? We were married last evening at 8 o'clock in the Little Church around the corner.'

27

OCTOBER AND JUNE

O. Henry

Love at times succumbs to the seeds of time.

The Captain gazed gloomily at his sword that hung upon the wall. In the closet near by was stored his faded uniform, stained and worn by weather and service. What a long, long time it seemed since those old days of war's alarms!

And now, veteran that he was of his country's strenuous times, he had been reduced to abject surrender by a woman's soft eyes and smiling lips. As he sat in his quiet room he held in his hand the letter he had just received from her—the letter that had caused him to wear that look of gloom. He re-read the fatal paragraph that had destroyed his hope.

> In declining the honour you have done me in asking me to
> be your wife, I feel that I ought to speak frankly. The reason
> I have for so doing is the great difference between our ages.
> I like you very, very much, but I am sure that our marriage
> would not be a happy one. I am sorry to have to refer to
> this, but I believe that you will appreciate my honesty in
> giving you the true reason.

The Captain sighed, and leaned his head upon his hand. Yes, there were many years between their ages. But he was strong and rugged, he had position and wealth. Would not his love, his tender care, and the advantages he could bestow upon her make her forget the question of age? Besides, he was almost sure that she cared for him.

The Captain was a man of prompt action. In the field he had been distinguished for his decisiveness and energy. He would see her and plead his cause again in person. Age—what was it to come between him and the one he loved?

In two hours he stood ready, in light marching order, for his greatest battle. He took the train for the old Southern town in Tennessee where she lived.

Theodora Deming was on the steps of the handsome, porticoed old mansion, enjoying the summer twilight, when the Captain entered the gate and came up the gravelled walk. She met him with a smile that was free from embarrassment. As the Captain stood on the step below her, the difference in their ages did not appear so great. He was tall and straight and clear-eyed and browned. She was in the bloom of lovely womanhood.

'I wasn't expecting you,' said Theodora, 'but now that you've come you may sit on the step. Didn't you get my letter?'

'I did,' said the Captain, 'and that's why I came. I say, now, Theo, reconsider your answer, won't you?'

Theodora smiled softly upon him. He carried his years well. She was really fond of his strength, his wholesome looks, his manliness—perhaps, if—

'No, no,' she said, shaking her head, positively, 'it's out of the question. I like you a whole lot, but marrying won't do. My age and yours are—but don't make me say it again—I told you in my letter.'

The Captain flushed a little through the bronze on his face. He was silent for a while, gazing sadly into the twilight. Beyond a line of woods that he could see was a field where the boys in blue had once bivouacked on their march toward the sea. How long ago it seemed now! Truly, Fate and Father Time had tricked him sorely. Just a few years interposed between himself and happiness!

Theodora's hand crept down and rested in the clasp of his firm, brown one. She felt, at least, that sentiment that is akin to love.

'Don't take it so hard, please,' she said, gently. 'It's all for the best. I've reasoned it out very wisely all by myself. Some day you'll be glad I didn't marry you. It would be very nice and lovely for a while—but, just think! In only a few short years what different tastes we would have! One of us would want to sit by the fireside and read, and maybe nurse neuralgia or rheumatism of evenings, while the other would be crazy for balls and theatres and late suppers. No, my dear friend. While it isn't exactly January and May, it's a clear case of October and pretty early in June.'

'I'd always do what you wanted me to do, Theo. If you wanted to—'

'No, you wouldn't. You think now that you would, but you wouldn't. Please don't ask me any more.'

The Captain had lost his battle. But he was a gallant warrior, and when he rose to make his final adieu his mouth was grimly set and his shoulders were squared.

He took the train for the North that night. On the next evening he was back in his room, where his sword was hanging against the wall. He was dressing for dinner, tying his white tie into a very careful bow. And at the same time he was indulging in a pensive soliloquy.

''Pon my honour, I believe Theo was right, after all. Nobody can deny that she's a peach, but she must be twenty-eight, at the very kindest calculation.'

For you see, the Captain was only nineteen, and his sword had never been drawn except on the parade ground at Chattanooga, which was as near as he ever got to the Spanish-American War.

28

CLAIR DE LUNE

Guy de Maupassant

Splendid nights are created for love to blossom!

Abbe Marignan's martial name suited him well. He was a tall, thin priest, fanatic, excitable, yet upright. All his beliefs were fixed, never varying. He believed sincerely that he knew his God, understood His plans, desires and intentions.

When he walked with long strides along the garden walk of his little country parsonage, he would sometimes ask himself the question: 'Why has God done this?' And he would dwell on this continually, putting himself in the place of God, and he almost invariably found an answer. He would never have cried out in an outburst of pious humility: 'Thy ways, O Lord, are past finding out.'

He said to himself: 'I am the servant of God; it is right for me to know the reason of His deeds, or to guess it if I do not know it.'

Everything in nature seemed to him to have been created in accordance with an admirable and absolute logic. The 'whys' and 'becauses' always balanced. Dawn was given to make our awakening pleasant, the days to ripen the harvest, the rains to moisten it, the evenings for preparation for slumber, and the dark nights for sleep.

The four seasons corresponded perfectly to the needs of agriculture, and no suspicion had ever come to the priest of the fact that nature has no intentions; that, on the contrary, everything which exists must conform to the hard demands of seasons, climates and matter.

But he hated woman—hated her unconsciously, and despised

her by instinct. He often repeated the words of Christ: 'Woman, what have I to do with thee?' and he would add: 'It seems as though God, Himself, were dissatisfied with this work of His.' She was the tempter who led the first man astray, and who since then had ever been busy with her work of damnation, the feeble creature, dangerous and mysteriously affecting one. And even more than their sinful bodies, he hated their loving hearts.

He had often felt their tenderness directed toward himself, and though he knew that he was invulnerable, he grew angry at this need of love that is always vibrating in them.

According to his belief, God had created woman for the sole purpose of tempting and testing man. One must not approach her without defensive precautions and fear of possible snares. She was, indeed, just like a snare, with her lips open and her arms stretched out to man.

He had no indulgence except for nuns, whom their vows had rendered inoffensive; but he was stern with them, nevertheless, because he felt that at the bottom of their fettered and humble hearts the everlasting tenderness was burning brightly—that tenderness which was shown even to him, a priest.

He felt this cursed tenderness, even in their docility, in the low tones of their voices when speaking to him, in their lowered eyes, and in their resigned tears when he reproved them roughly. And he would shake his cassock on leaving the convent doors, and walk off, lengthening his stride as though flying from danger.

He had a niece who lived with her mother in a little house near him. He was bent upon making a sister of charity of her.

She was a pretty, brainless madcap. When the abbe preached she laughed, and when he was angry with her she would give him a hug, drawing him to her heart, while he sought unconsciously to release himself from this embrace which nevertheless filled him with a sweet pleasure, awakening in his depths the sensation of paternity which slumbers in every man.

Often, when walking by her side, along the country road, he would speak to her of God, of his God. She never listened to him, but looked about her at the sky, the grass and flowers, and one could see the joy of life sparkling in her eyes. Sometimes she would dart forward to catch some flying creature, crying out as she brought it back: 'Look, uncle, how pretty it is! I want to hug it!' And this desire to 'hug' flies or lilac blossoms disquieted, angered, and roused the priest, who saw, even in this, the ineradicable tenderness that is always budding in women's hearts.

Then there came a day when the sexton's wife, who kept house for Abbe Marignan, told him, with caution, that his niece had a lover.

Almost suffocated by the fearful emotion this news roused in him, he stood there, his face covered with soap, for he was in the act of shaving.

When he had sufficiently recovered to think and speak he cried: 'It is not true; you lie, Melanie!'

But the peasant woman put her hand on her heart, saying: 'May our Lord judge me if I lie, Monsieur le Cure! I tell you, she goes there every night when your sister has gone to bed. They meet by the river side; you have only to go there and see, between ten o'clock and midnight.'

He ceased scraping his chin, and began to walk up and down impetuously, as he always did when he was in deep thought. When he began shaving again he cut himself three times from his nose to his ear.

All day long he was silent, full of anger and indignation. To his priestly hatred of this invincible love was added the exasperation of her spiritual father, of her guardian and pastor, deceived and tricked by a child, and the selfish emotion shown by parents when their daughter announces that she has chosen a husband without them, and in spite of them.

After dinner he tried to read a little, but could not, growing

more and, more angry. When ten o'clock struck he seized his
cane, a formidable oak stick, which he was accustomed to carry
in his nocturnal walks when visiting the sick. And he smiled at
the enormous club which he twirled in a threatening manner in
his strong, country fist. Then he raised it suddenly and, gritting
his teeth, brought it down on a chair, the broken back of which
fell over on the floor.

He opened the door to go out, but stopped on the sill, surprised
by the splendid moonlight, of such brilliance as is seldom seen.

And, as he was gifted with an emotional nature, one such as
had all those poetic dreamers, the Fathers of the Church, he felt
suddenly distracted and moved by all the grand and serene beauty
of this pale night.

In his little garden, all bathed in soft light, his fruit trees in
a row cast on the ground the shadow of their slender branches,
scarcely in full leaf, while the giant honeysuckle, clinging to the
wall of his house, exhaled a delicious sweetness, filling the warm
moonlit atmosphere with a kind of perfumed soul.

He began to take long breaths, drinking in the air as drunkards
drink wine, and he walked along slowly, delighted, marvelling,
almost forgetting his niece.

As soon as he was outside of the garden, he stopped to gaze
upon the plain all flooded with the caressing light, bathed in that
tender, languishing charm of serene nights. At each moment was
heard the short, metallic note of the cricket, and distant nightingales
shook out their scattered notes—their light, vibrant music that
sets one dreaming, without thinking, a music made for kisses, for
the seduction of moonlight.

The abbe walked on again, his heart failing, though he knew
not why. He seemed weakened, suddenly exhausted; he wanted
to sit down, to rest there, to think, to admire God in His works.

Down yonder, following the undulations of the little river, a
great line of poplars wound in and out. A fine mist, a white haze

through which the moonbeams passed, silvering it and making it gleam, hung around and above the mountains, covering all the tortuous course of the water with a kind of light and transparent cotton.

The priest stopped once again, his soul filled with a growing and irresistible tenderness.

And a doubt, a vague feeling of disquiet came over him; he was asking one of those questions that he sometimes put to himself.

'Why did God make this? Since the night is destined for sleep, unconsciousness, repose, forgetfulness of everything, why make it more charming than day, softer than dawn or evening? And does why this seductive planet, more poetic than the sun, that seems destined, so discreet is it, to illuminate things too delicate and mysterious for the light of day, make the darkness so transparent?

'Why does not the greatest of feathered songsters sleep like the others? Why does it pour forth its voice in the mysterious night?

'Why this half-veil cast over the world? Why these tremblings of the heart, this emotion of the spirit, this enervation of the body? Why this display of enchantments that human beings do not see, since they are lying in their beds? For whom is destined this sublime spectacle, this abundance of poetry cast from heaven to earth?'

And the abbe could not understand.

But see, out there, on the edge of the meadow, under the arch of trees bathed in a shining mist, two figures are walking side by side.

The man was the taller, and held his arm about his sweetheart's neck and kissed her brow every little while. They imparted life, all at once, to the placid landscape in which they were framed as by a heavenly hand. The two seemed but a single being, the being for whom was destined this calm and silent night, and they came toward the priest as a living answer, the response his Master sent to his questionings.

He stood still, his heart beating, all upset; and it seemed to him that he saw before him some biblical scene, like the loves of Ruth and Boaz, the accomplishment of the will of the Lord, in some of those glorious stories of which the sacred books tell. The verses of the Song of Songs began to ring in his ears, the appeal of passion, all the poetry of this poem replete with tenderness.

And he said unto himself: 'Perhaps God has made such nights as these to idealize the love of men.'

He shrank back from this couple that still advanced with arms intertwined. Yet it was his niece. But he asked himself now if he would not be disobeying God. And does not God permit love, since He surrounds it with such visible splendour?

And he went back musing, almost ashamed, as if he had intruded into a temple where he had, no right to enter.

29

THE LAST LEAF
O. Henry

Love may lead to sacrifice with giving away everything, even one's own life.

In a little district west of Washington Square the streets have run crazy and broken themselves into small strips called 'places'. These 'places' make strange angles and curves. One street crosses itself a time or two. An artist once discovered a valuable possibility in this street. Suppose a collector with a bill for paints, paper and canvas should, in traversing this route, suddenly meet himself coming back, without a cent having been paid on account!

So, to quaint old Greenwich Village the art people soon came prowling, hunting for north windows and eighteenth-century gables and Dutch attics and low rents. Then they imported some pewter mugs and a chafing dish or two from Sixth avenue, and became a 'colony'.

At the top of a squatty, three-story brick Sue and Johnsy had their studio. 'Johnsy' was familiar for Joanna. One was from Maine; the other from California. They had met at the *table d'hôte* of an Eighth street 'Delmonico's', and found their tastes in art, chicory salad and bishop sleeves so congenial that the joint studio resulted.

That was in May. In November a cold, unseen stranger, whom the doctors called Pneumonia, stalked about the colony, touching one here and there with his icy fingers. Over on the east side this ravager strode boldly, smiting his victims by scores, but his feet trod slowly through the maze of the narrow and moss-grown 'places'.

Mr Pneumonia was not what you would call a chivalric old

gentleman. A mite of a little woman with blood thinned by California zephyrs was hardly fair game for the red-fisted, short-breathed old duffer. But Johnsy he smote; and she lay, scarcely moving, on her painted iron bedstead, looking through the small Dutch window-panes at the blank side of the next brick house.

One morning the busy doctor invited Sue into the hallway with a shaggy, grey eyebrow.

'She has one chance in—let us say, ten,' he said, as he shook down the mercury in his clinical thermometer. 'And that chance is for her to want to live. This way people have of lining-up on the side of the undertaker makes the entire pharmacopoeia look silly. Your little lady has made up her mind that she's not going to get well. Has she anything on her mind?'

'She—she wanted to paint the Bay of Naples some day,' said Sue.

'Paint? Bosh! Has she anything on her mind worth thinking about twice—a man, for instance?'

'A man?' said Sue, with a jew's-harp twang in her voice. 'Is a man worth—but, no, doctor; there is nothing of the kind.'

'Well, it is the weakness, then,' said the doctor. 'I will do all that science, so far as it may filter through my efforts, can accomplish. But whenever my patient begins to count the carriages in her funeral procession I subtract 50 per cent from the curative power of medicines. If you will get her to ask one question about the new winter styles in cloak sleeves I will promise you a one-in-five chance for her, instead of one in ten.'

After the doctor had gone Sue went into the workroom and cried a Japanese napkin to a pulp. Then she swaggered into Johnsy's room with her drawing board, whistling ragtime.

Johnsy lay, scarcely making a ripple under the bedclothes, with her face toward the window. Sue stopped whistling, thinking she was asleep.

She arranged her board and began a pen-and-ink drawing to

illustrate a magazine story. Young artists must pave their way to Art by drawing pictures for magazine stories that young authors write to pave their way to Literature.

As Sue was sketching a pair of elegant horseshow riding trousers and a monocle of the figure of the hero, an Idaho cowboy, she heard a low sound, several times repeated. She went quickly to the bedside.

Johnsy's eyes were open wide. She was looking out the window and counting—counting backward.

'Twelve', she said, and a little later 'eleven', and then 'ten', and 'nine', and then 'eight' and 'seven', almost together.

Sue looked solicitously out the window. What was there to count? There was only a bare, dreary yard to be seen, and the blank side of the brick house twenty feet away. An old, old ivy vine, gnarled and decayed at the roots, climbed half way up the brick wall. The cold breath of autumn had stricken its leaves from the vine until its skeleton branches clung, almost bare, to the crumbling bricks.

'What is it, dear?' asked Sue.

'Six,' said Johnsy, in almost a whisper. 'They're falling faster now. Three days ago there were almost a hundred. It made my head ache to count them. But now it's easy. There goes another one. There are only five left now.'

'Five what, dear. Tell your Sudie.'

'Leaves. On the ivy vine. When the last one falls I must go, too. I've known that for three days. Didn't the doctor tell you?'

'Oh, I never heard of such nonsense,' complained Sue, with magnificent scorn. 'What have old ivy leaves to do with your getting well? And you used to love that vine so, you naughty girl. Don't be a goosey. Why, the doctor told me this morning that your chances for getting well real soon were—let's see exactly what he said—he said the chances were ten to one! Why, that's almost as good a chance as we have in New York when we ride on the street cars or walk past a new building. Try to take some broth now, and let Sudie go back to her drawing, so she can sell the editor man with it, and buy port wine for her sick child, and pork chops for her greedy self.'

'You needn't get any more wine,' said Johnsy, keeping her eyes fixed out the window. 'There goes another. No, I don't want any broth. That leaves just four. I want to see the last one fall before it gets dark. Then I'll go, too.'

'Johnsy, dear,' said Sue, bending over her, 'will you promise me to keep your eyes closed, and not look out the window until I am done working? I must hand those drawings in by to-morrow. I need the light, or I would draw the shade down.'

'Couldn't you draw in the other room?' asked Johnsy, coldly.

'I'd rather be here by you,' said Sue. 'Besides I don't want you to keep looking at those silly ivy leaves.'

'Tell me as soon as you have finished,' said Johnsy, closing her eyes, and lying white and still as a fallen statue, 'because I want to see the last one fall. I'm tired of waiting. I'm tired of thinking. I want to turn loose my hold on everything, and go sailing down, down, just like one of those poor, tired leaves.'

'Try to sleep,' said Sue. 'I must call Behrman up to be my model for the old hermit miner. I'll not be gone a minute. Don't try to move 'till I come back.'

Old Behrman was a painter who lived on the ground floor beneath them. He was past sixty and had a Michael Angelo's Moses beard curling down from the head of a satyr along with the body of an imp. Behrman was a failure in art. Forty years he had wielded the brush without getting near enough to touch the hem of his Mistress's robe. He had been always about to paint a masterpiece, but had never yet begun it. For several years he had painted nothing except now and then a daub in the line of commerce or advertising. He earned a little by serving as a model to those young artists in the colony who could not pay the price of a professional. He drank gin to excess, and still talked of his coming masterpiece. For the rest he was a fierce little old man, who scoffed terribly at softness in any one, and who regarded himself as especial mastiff-in-waiting to protect the two young artists in the studio above.

Sue found Behrman smelling strongly of juniper berries in his dimly lighted den below. In one corner was a blank canvas on an easel that had been waiting there for twenty-five years to receive the first line of the masterpiece. She told him of Johnsy's fancy, and how she feared she would, indeed, light and fragile as a leaf herself, float away when her slight hold upon the world grew weaker.

Old Behrman, with his red eyes plainly streaming, shouted his contempt and derision for such idiotic imaginings.

'Vass!' he cried. 'Is dere people in de world mit der foolishness to die because leafs dey drop off from a confounded vine? I haf not heard of such a thing. No, I will not bose as a model for your fool hermit-dunderhead. Vy do you allow dot silly pusiness to come in der brain of her? Ach, dot poor leetle Miss Yohnsy.'

'She is very ill and weak,' said Sue, 'and the fever has left her mind morbid and full of strange fancies. Very well, Mr Behrman, if you do not care to pose for me, you needn't. But I think you are a horrid old—old flibbertigibbet.'

'You are just like a woman!' yelled Behrman. 'Who said I will not bose? Go on. I come mit you. For half an hour I haf peen trying to say dot I am ready to bose. Gott! Dis is not any blace in which one so goot as Miss Yohnsy shall lie sick. Some day I vill baint a masterpiece, and ve shall all go away. Gott! Yes.'

Johnsy was sleeping when they went upstairs. Sue pulled the shade down to the window-sill, and motioned Behrman into the other room. In there they peered out the window fearfully at the ivy vine. Then they looked at each other for a moment without speaking. A persistent, cold rain was falling, mingled with snow.

Behrman, in his old blue shirt, took his seat as the hermit-miner on an upturned kettle for a rock.

When Sue awoke from an hour's sleep the next morning she found Johnsy with dull, wide-open eyes staring at the drawn green shade.

'Pull it up; I want to see,' she ordered, in a whisper.

Wearily Sue obeyed.

But, lo! After the beating rain and fierce gusts of wind that had endured through the livelong night, there yet stood out against the brick wall one ivy leaf. It was the last on the vine. Still dark green near its stem, but with its serrated edges tinted with the yellow of dissolution and decay, it hung bravely from the branch some twenty feet above the ground.

'It is the last one,' said Johnsy. 'I thought it would surely fall during the night. I heard the wind. It will fall to-day, and I shall die at the same time.'

'Dear, dear!' said Sue, leaning her worn face down to the pillow, 'think of me, if you won't think of yourself. What would I do?'

But Johnsy did not answer. The lonesomest thing in all the world is a soul when it is making ready to go on its mysterious, far journey. The fancy seemed to possess her more strongly as one by one the ties that bound her to friendship and to earth were loosed.

The day wore away, and even through the twilight they could see the lone ivy leaf clinging to its stem against the wall. And then, with the coming of the night the north wind was again loosed, while the rain still beat against the windows and pattered down from the low Dutch eaves.

When it was light enough Johnsy, the merciless, commanded that the shade be raised.

The ivy leaf was still there.

Johnsy lay for a long time looking at it. And then she called to Sue, who was stirring her chicken broth over the gas stove.

'I've been a bad girl, Sudie,' said Johnsy. 'Something has made that last leaf stay there to show me how wicked I was. It is a sin to want to die. You may bring me a little broth now, and some milk with a little port in it, and—no; bring me a hand-mirror first, and then pack some pillows about me, and I will sit up and watch you cook.'

An hour later she said.

'Sudie, some day I hope to paint the Bay of Naples.'

The doctor came in the afternoon, and Sue had an excuse to go into the hallway as he left.

'Even chances,' said the doctor, taking Sue's thin, shaking hand in his. 'With good nursing you'll win. And now I must see another case I have downstairs. Behrman, his name is—some kind of an artist, I believe. Pneumonia, too. He is an old, weak man, and the attack is acute. There is no hope for him; but he goes to the hospital to-day to be made more comfortable.'

The next day the doctor said to Sue: 'She's out of danger. You've won. Nutrition and care now—that's all.'

And that afternoon Sue came to the bed where Johnsy lay, contentedly knitting a very blue and very useless woollen shoulder scarf, and put one arm around her, pillows and all.

'I have something to tell you, white mouse,' she said. 'Mr Behrman died of pneumonia to-day in the hospital. He was ill only two days. The janitor found him on the morning of the first day in his room downstairs helpless with pain. His shoes and clothing were wet through and icy cold. They couldn't imagine where he had been on such a dreadful night. And then they found a lantern, still lighted, and a ladder that had been dragged from its place, and some scattered brushes, and a palette with green and yellow colours mixed on it, and—look out the window, dear, at the last ivy leaf on the wall. Didn't you wonder why it never fluttered or moved when the wind blew? Ah, darling, it's Behrman's masterpiece—he painted it there the night that the last leaf fell.'

30

THE KISS

Anton Chekhov

A misconstrued kiss can turn a prince into a frog.

At eight o'clock on the evening of the twentieth of May all the six batteries of the N— Reserve Artillery Brigade halted for the night in the village of Myestetchki on their way to camp. When the general commotion was at its height, while some officers were busily occupied around the guns, while others, gathered together in the square near the church enclosure, were listening to the quartermasters, a man in civilian dress, riding a strange horse, came into sight round the church. The little dun-coloured horse with a good neck and a short tail came, moving not straight forward, but as it were sideways, with a sort of dance step, as though it were being lashed about the legs. When he reached the officers the man on the horse took off his hat and said:

'His Excellency Lieutenant-General von Rabbek invites the gentlemen to drink tea with him this minute.'

The horse turned, danced, and retired sideways; the messenger raised his hat once more, and in an instant disappeared with his strange horse behind the church.

'What the devil does it mean?' grumbled some of the officers, dispersing to their quarters. 'One is sleepy, and here this Von Rabbek with his tea! We know what tea means.'

The officers of all the six batteries remembered vividly an incident of the previous year, when during manoeuvres they, together with the officers of a Cossack regiment, were in the same way invited to tea by a count who had an estate in the neighbourhood and was a retired army officer: the hospitable and genial count made much of them, fed them, and gave them drink, refused to let them go to their quarters in the village and made them stay the night. All that, of course, was very nice—nothing better could be desired, but the worst of it was, the old army officer was so carried away by the pleasure of the young men's company that till sunrise he was telling the officers anecdotes of his glorious past, taking them over the house, showing them expensive pictures, old engravings, rare guns, reading them autograph letters from great people, while the weary and exhausted officers looked and listened, longing for their beds and yawning in their sleeves; when at last their host let them go, it was too late for sleep.

Might not this Von Rabbek be just such another? Whether he were or not, there was no help for it. The officers changed their uniforms, brushed themselves, and went all together in search of the gentleman's house. In the square by the church they were told they could get to His Excellency's by the lower path—going down behind the church to the river, going along the bank to the garden, and there an avenue would taken them to the house; or by the upper way—straight from the church by the road which, half a mile from the village, led right up to His Excellency's granaries. The officers decided to go by the upper way.

'What Von Rabbek is it?' they wondered on the way. 'Surely not the one who was in command of the N— Cavalry Division at Plevna?'

'No, that was not Von Rabbek, but simply Rabbe and no "von."'

'What lovely weather!'

At the first of the granaries the road divided in two: one branch went straight on and vanished in the evening darkness, the other led to the owner's house on the right. The officers turned to the right and began to speak more softly. On both sides of the road stretched stone granaries with red roofs, heavy and sullen-looking, very much like barracks of a district town. Ahead of them gleamed the windows of the manor-house.

'A good omen, gentlemen,' said one of the officers. 'Our setter is the foremost of all; no doubt he scents game ahead of us!'

Lieutenant Lobytko, who was walking in front, a tall and stalwart fellow, though entirely without moustache (he was over five-and-twenty, yet for some reason there was no sign of hair on his round, well-fed face), renowned in the brigade for his peculiar faculty for divining the presence of women at a distance, turned round and said:

'Yes, there must be women here; I feel that by instinct.'

On the threshold the officers were met by Von Rabbek himself, a comely-looking man of sixty in civilian dress. Shaking hands with his guests, he said that he was very glad and happy to see them, but begged them earnestly for God's sake to excuse him for not asking them to stay the night; two sisters with their children, some brothers, and some neighbours, had come on a visit to him, so that he had not one spare room left.

The General shook hands with every one, made his apologies, and smiled, but it was evident by his face that he was by no means so delighted as their last year's count, and that he had invited the officers simply because, in his opinion, it was a social obligation to do so. And the officers themselves, as they walked up the softly carpeted stairs, as they listened to him, felt that they had been invited to this house simply because it would have been awkward not to invite them; and at the sight of the footmen, who hastened to light the lamps in the entrance below and in the anteroom above, they began to feel as though they had brought uneasiness and discomfort into the house with them. In a house in which two sisters and their children, brothers, and neighbours were gathered together, probably on account of some family festivity, or event, how could the presence of nineteen unknown officers possibly be welcome?

At the entrance to the drawing-room the officers were met

by a tall, graceful old lady with black eyebrows and a long face, very much like the Empress Eugénie. Smiling graciously and majestically, she said she was glad and happy to see her guests, and apologized that her husband and she were on this occasion unable to invite *messieurs les officiers* to stay the night. From her beautiful majestic smile, which instantly vanished from her face every time she turned away from her guests, it was evident that she had seen numbers of officers in her day, that she was in no humour for them now, and if she invited them to her house and apologized for not doing more, it was only because her breeding and position in society required it of her.

When the officers went into the big dining-room, there were about a dozen people, men and ladies, young and old, sitting at tea at the end of a long table. A group of men was dimly visible behind their chairs, wrapped in a haze of cigar smoke; and in the midst of them stood a lanky young man with red whiskers, talking loudly, with a lisp, in English. Through a door beyond the group could be seen a light room with pale blue furniture.

'Gentlemen, there are so many of you that it is impossible to introduce you all!' said the General in a loud voice, trying to sound very cheerful. 'Make each other's acquaintance, gentlemen, without any ceremony!'

The officers—some with very serious and even stern faces, others with forced smiles, and all feeling extremely awkward— somehow made their bows and sat down to tea.

The most ill at ease of them all was Ryabovitch—a little officer in spectacles, with sloping shoulders, and whiskers like a lynx's. While some of his comrades assumed a serious expression, while others wore forced smiles, his face, his lynx-like whiskers, and spectacles seemed to say: 'I am the shyest, most modest, and most undistinguished officer in the whole brigade!' At first, on going into the room and sitting down to the table, he could not fix his attention on any one face or object. The faces, the dresses, the cut-glass decanters of brandy, the steam from the glasses, the moulded cornices—all blended in one general impression that inspired in Ryabovitch alarm and a desire to hide his head. Like a lecturer making his first appearance before the public, he saw everything that was before his eyes, but apparently only had a dim understanding of it (among physiologists this condition, when the subject sees but does not understand, is called psychical blindness). After a little while, growing accustomed to his surroundings, Ryabovitch saw clearly and began to observe. As a shy man, unused to society, what struck him first was that in which he had always been deficient— namely, the extraordinary boldness of his new acquaintances. Von Rabbek, his wife, two elderly ladies, a young lady in a lilac dress, and the young man with the red whiskers, who was, it appeared, a younger son of Von Rabbek, very cleverly, as though they had rehearsed it beforehand, took seats between the officers, and at once got up a heated discussion in which the visitors could not help taking part. The lilac young lady hotly asserted that the artillery had a much better time than the cavalry and the infantry, while Von Rabbek and the elderly ladies maintained the opposite. A brisk interchange of talk followed. Ryabovitch watched the lilac young lady who argued so hotly about what was unfamiliar and utterly uninteresting to her, and watched artificial smiles come and go on her face.

Von Rabbek and his family skilfully drew the officers into the discussion, and meanwhile kept a sharp lookout over their glasses and mouths, to see whether all of them were drinking, whether all had enough sugar, why some one was not eating cakes or not drinking brandy. And the longer Ryabovitch watched and listened, the more he was attracted by this insincere but splendidly disciplined family.

After tea the officers went into the drawing-room. Lieutenant Lobytko's instinct had not deceived him. There were a great number of girls and young married ladies. The 'setter' lieutenant was soon standing by a very young, fair girl in a black dress, and, bending down to her jauntily, as though leaning on an unseen sword, smiled and shrugged his shoulders coquettishly. He probably talked very interesting nonsense, for the fair girl looked at his well-fed face condescendingly and asked indifferently, 'Really?' And from that uninterested 'Really?' the setter, had he been intelligent, might have concluded that she would never call him to heel.

The piano struck up; the melancholy strains of a valse floated out of the wide open windows, and every one, for some reason, remembered that it was spring, a May evening. Every one was conscious of the fragrance of roses, of lilac, and of the young leaves of the poplar. Ryabovitch, in whom the brandy he had drunk made itself felt, under the influence of the music stole a glance towards the window, smiled, and began watching the movements of the women, and it seemed to him that the smell of roses, of poplars, and lilac came not from the garden, but from the ladies' faces and dresses.

Von Rabbek's son invited a scraggy-looking young lady to dance, and waltzed round the room twice with her. Lobytko, gliding over the parquet floor, flew up to the lilac young lady and whirled her away. Dancing began! Ryabovitch stood near the door among those who were not dancing and looked on. He had never once danced in his whole life, and he had never once in his life put his arm round the waist of a respectable woman. He was highly delighted that a man should in the sight of all take a girl he did not know round the waist and offer her his shoulder to put her hand on, but he could not imagine himself in the position of such a man. There were times when he envied the boldness and swagger of his companions and was inwardly wretched; the consciousness that he was timid, that he was round-shouldered and uninteresting, that he had a long waist and lynx-like whiskers, had deeply mortified him, but with years he had grown used to this feeling, and now, looking at his comrades dancing or loudly talking, he no longer envied them, but only felt touched and mournful.

When the quadrille began, young Von Rabbek came up to those who were not dancing and invited two officers to have a game at billiards. The officers accepted and went with him out of the drawing-room. Ryabovitch, having nothing to do and wishing to take part in the general movement, slouched after them. From the big drawing-room they went into the little drawing-room, then into a narrow corridor with a glass roof, and thence into a room in which on their entrance three sleepy-looking footmen jumped up quickly from the sofa. At last, after passing through a long succession of rooms, young Von Rabbek and the officers came into a small room where there was a billiard-table. They began to play.

Ryabovitch, who had never played any game but cards, stood near the billiard-table and looked indifferently at the players, while they in unbuttoned coats, with cues in their hands, stepped about, made puns, and kept shouting out unintelligible words.

The players took no notice of him, and only now and then one of them, shoving him with his elbow or accidentally touching him with the end of his cue, would turn round and say 'Pardon'. Before the first game was over he was weary of it, and began to feel he was not wanted and in the way. He felt disposed to return to the drawing-room, and he went out.

On his way back he met with a little adventure. When he had gone half-way he noticed he had taken a wrong turning. He distinctly remembered that he ought to meet three sleepy footmen on his way, but he had passed five or six rooms, and those sleepy figures seemed to have vanished into the earth. Noticing his mistake, he walked back a little way and turned to the right; he found himself in a little dark room which he had not seen on his way to the billiard-room. After standing there a little while, he resolutely opened the first door that met his eyes and walked into an absolutely dark room. Straight in front could be seen the crack in the doorway through which there was a gleam of vivid light; from the other side of the door came the muffled sound of a melancholy mazurka. Here, too, as in the drawing-room, the windows were wide open and there was a smell of poplars, lilac and roses.

Ryabovitch stood still in hesitation. At that moment, to his surprise, he heard hurried footsteps and the rustling of a dress, a breathless feminine voice whispered 'At last!' And two soft, fragrant, unmistakably feminine arms were clasped about his neck; a warm cheek was pressed to his cheek, and simultaneously there was the sound of a kiss. But at once the bestower of the kiss uttered a faint shriek and skipped back from him, as it seemed to Ryabovitch, with aversion. He, too, almost shrieked and rushed towards the gleam of light at the door.

When he went back into the drawing-room his heart was beating and his hands were trembling so noticeably that he made haste to hide them behind his back. At first he was tormented by shame and dread that the whole drawing-room knew that he had just been kissed and embraced by a woman. He shrank into himself and looked uneasily about him, but as he became convinced that people were dancing and talking as calmly as ever, he gave himself up entirely to the new sensation which he had never experienced before in his life. Something strange was happening to him. His neck, round which soft, fragrant arms had so lately been clasped, seemed to him to be anointed with oil; on his left cheek near his moustache where the unknown had kissed him there was a faint chilly tingling sensation as from peppermint drops, and the more he rubbed the place the more distinct was the chilly sensation; all over, from head to foot, he was full of a strange new feeling which grew stronger and stronger. He wanted to dance, to talk, to run into the garden, to laugh aloud. He quite forgot that he was round-shouldered and uninteresting, that he had lynx-like whiskers and an 'undistinguished appearance' (that was how his appearance had been described by some ladies whose conversation he had accidentally overheard). When Von Rabbek's wife happened to pass by him, he gave her such a broad and friendly smile that she stood still and looked at him inquiringly.

'I like your house immensely!' he said, setting his spectacles straight.

The General's wife smiled and said that the house had belonged to her father; then she asked whether his parents were living, whether he had long been in the army, why he was so thin, and so on. After receiving answers to her questions, she went on, and after his conversation with her his smiles were more friendly than ever, and he thought he was surrounded by splendid people.

At supper Ryabovitch ate mechanically everything offered him, drank, and without listening to anything, tried to understand what had just happened to him. The adventure was of a mysterious and romantic character, but it was not difficult to explain it. No doubt some girl or young married lady had arranged a tryst with some one in the dark room; had waited a long time, and being nervous and excited had taken Ryabovitch for her hero; this was the more probable as Ryabovitch had stood still hesitating in the dark room, so that he, too, had seemed like a person expecting something. This was how Ryabovitch explained to himself the kiss he had received.

'And who is she?' he wondered, looking round at the women's faces. 'She must be young, for elderly ladies don't give rendezvous. That she was a lady, one could tell by the rustle of her dress, her perfume, her voice.'

His eyes rested on the lilac young lady, and he thought her very attractive; she had beautiful shoulders and arms, a clever face, and a delightful voice. Ryabovitch, looking at her, hoped that she and no one else was his unknown. But she laughed somehow artificially and wrinkled up her long nose, which seemed to him to make her look old. Then he turned his eyes upon the fair girl in a black dress. She was younger, simpler, and more genuine, had a charming brow, and drank very daintily out of her wineglass. Ryabovitch now hoped that it was she. But soon he began to think her face flat, and fixed his eyes upon the one next her.

'It's difficult to guess,' he thought, musing. 'If one takes the shoulders and arms of the lilac one only, adds the brow of the fair one and the eyes of the one on the left of Lobytko, then—'

He made a combination of these things in his mind and so formed the image of the girl who had kissed him, the image that he wanted her to have, but could not find at the table.

After supper, replete and exhilarated, the officers began to take leave and say thank you. Von Rabbek and his wife began again apologizing that they could not ask them to stay the night.

'Very, very glad to have met you, gentlemen,' said Von Rabbek, and this time sincerely (probably because people are far more sincere and good-humoured at speeding their parting guests than on meeting them). 'Delighted. I hope you will come on your way back! Don't stand on ceremony! Where are you going? Do you want to go by the upper way? No, go across the garden; it's nearer here by the lower way.'

The officers went out into the garden. After the bright light and the noise the garden seemed very dark and quiet. They walked in silence all the way to the gate. They were a little drunk, pleased, and in good spirits, but the darkness and silence made them thoughtful for a minute. Probably the same idea occurred to each one of them as to Ryabovitch: would there ever come a time for them when, like Von Rabbek, they would have a large house, a family, a garden—when they, too, would be able to welcome people, even though insincerely, feed them, make them drunk and contented?

Going out of the garden gate, they all began talking at once and laughing loudly about nothing. They were walking now along the little path that led down to the river, and then ran along the water's edge, winding round the bushes on the bank, the pools, and the willows that overhung the water. The bank and the path

THE KISS • 267

were scarcely visible, and the other bank was entirely plunged in darkness. Stars were reflected here and there on the dark water; they quivered and were broken up on the surface—and from that alone it could be seen that the river was flowing rapidly. It was still. Drowsy curlews cried plaintively on the further bank, and in one of the bushes on the nearest side a nightingale was trilling loudly, taking no notice of the crowd of officers. The officers stood round the bush, touched it, but the nightingale went on singing.

'What a fellow!' they exclaimed approvingly. 'We stand beside him and he takes not a bit of notice! What a rascal!'

At the end of the way the path went uphill, and, skirting the church enclosure, turned into the road. Here the officers, tired with walking uphill, sat down and lighted their cigarettes. On the other side of the river a murky red fire came into sight, and having nothing better to do, they spent a long time in discussing whether it was a camp fire or a light in a window, or something else. Ryabovitch, too, looked at the light, and he fancied that the light looked and winked at him, as though it knew about the kiss.

On reaching his quarters, Ryabovitch undressed as quickly as possible and got into bed. Lobytko and Lieutenant Merzlyakov—a peaceable, silent fellow, who was considered in his own circle a highly educated officer, and was always, whenever it was possible, reading the 'Vyestnik Evropi' which he carried about with him everywhere—were quartered in the same hut with Ryabovitch. Lobytko undressed, walked up and down the room for a long while with the air of a man who has not been satisfied, and sent his orderly for beer. Merzlyakov got into bed, put a candle by his pillow and plunged into reading the 'Vyestnik Evropi'.

'Who was she?' Ryabovitch wondered, looking at the smoky ceiling.

His neck still felt as though he had been anointed with oil, and there was still the chilly sensation near his mouth as though from peppermint drops. The shoulders and arms of the young lady in lilac, the brow and the truthful eyes of the fair girl in black, waists, dresses, and brooches, floated through his imagination. He tried to fix his attention on these images, but they danced about, broke up and flickered. When these images vanished altogether from the broad dark background which every man sees when he closes his eyes, he began to hear hurried footsteps, the rustle of skirts, the sound of a kiss and—an intense groundless joy took possession of him. Abandoning himself to this joy, he heard the orderly return and announce that there was no beer. Lobytko was terribly indignant, and began pacing up and down again.

'Well, isn't he an idiot?' he kept saying, stopping first before Ryabovitch and then before Merzlyakov. 'What a fool and a dummy a man must be not to get hold of any beer! Eh? Isn't he a scoundrel?'

'Of course you can't get beer here,' said Merzlyakov, not removing his eyes from the 'Vyestnik Evropi'.

'Oh! Is that your opinion?' Lobytko persisted. 'Lord have mercy upon us, if you dropped me on the moon I'd find you beer and women directly! I'll go and find some at once. You may call me an impostor if I don't!'

He spent a long time in dressing and pulling on his high boots, then finished smoking his cigarette in silence and went out.

'Rabbek, Grabbek, Labbek,' he muttered, stopping in the outer room. 'I don't care to go alone, damn it all! Ryabovitch, wouldn't you like to go for a walk? Eh?'

Receiving no answer, he returned, slowly undressed and got into bed. Merzlyakov sighed, put the 'Vyestnik Evropi' away, and put out the light.

'H'm!' muttered Lobytko, lighting a cigarette in the dark.

Ryabovitch pulled the bed-clothes over his head, curled himself up in bed, and tried to gather together the floating images in his mind and to combine them into one whole. But nothing came of it. He soon fell asleep, and his last thought was that some one had caressed him and made him happy—that something extraordinary, foolish, but joyful and delightful, had come into his life. The thought did not leave him even in his sleep.

When he woke up the sensations of oil on his neck and the chill of peppermint about his lips had gone, but joy flooded his heart just as the day before. He looked enthusiastically at the window-frames, gilded by the light of the rising sun, and listened to the movement of the passers-by in the street. People were talking loudly close to the window. Lebedetsky, the commander of Ryabovitch's battery, who had only just overtaken the brigade, was talking to his sergeant at the top of his voice, being always accustomed to shout.

'What else?' shouted the commander.

'When they were shoeing yesterday, your high nobility, they drove a nail into Pigeon's hoof. The vet put on clay and vinegar; they are leading him apart now. And also, your honour, Artemyev got drunk yesterday, and the lieutenant ordered him to be put in the limber of a spare gun-carriage.'

The sergeant reported that Karpov had forgotten the new cords for the trumpets and the rings for the tents, and that their honours, the officers, had spent the previous evening visiting General Von Rabbek. In the middle of this conversation the red-bearded face of Lebedetsky appeared in the window. He screwed up his short-sighted eyes, looking at the sleepy faces of the officers, and said good-morning to them.

'Is everything all right?' he asked.

'One of the horses has a sore neck from the new collar,' answered Lobytko, yawning.

The commander sighed, thought a moment, and said in a loud voice:

'I am thinking of going to see Alexandra Yevgrafovna. I must call on her. Well, good-bye. I shall catch you up in the evening.'

A quarter of an hour later the brigade set off on its way. When it was moving along the road by the granaries, Ryabovitch looked at the house on the right. The blinds were down in all the windows. Evidently the household was still asleep. The one who had kissed Ryabovitch the day before was asleep, too. He tried to imagine her asleep. The wide-open windows of the bedroom, the green branches peeping in, the morning freshness, the scent of the poplars, lilac, and roses, the bed, a chair, and on it the skirts that had rustled the day before, the little slippers, the little watch on the table—all this he pictured to himself clearly and distinctly, but the features of the face, the sweet sleepy smile, just what was characteristic and important, slipped through his imagination like quicksilver through the fingers. When he had ridden on half a mile, he looked back: the yellow church, the house, and the river, were all bathed in light; the river with its bright green banks, with the blue sky reflected in it and glints of silver in the sunshine here and there, was very beautiful. Ryabovitch gazed for the last time at Myestetchki, and he felt as sad as though he were parting with something very near and dear to him.

And before him on the road lay nothing but long familiar, uninteresting pictures. To right and to left, fields of young rye and buckwheat with rooks hopping about in them. If one looked ahead, one saw dust and the backs of men's heads; if one looked back, one saw the same dust and faces. Foremost of all marched four men with sabres—this was the vanguard. Next, behind, the crowd of singers, and behind them the trumpeters on horseback. The vanguard and the chorus of singers, like torch-bearers in a funeral procession, often forgot to keep the regulation distance and pushed a long way ahead. Ryabovitch was with the first cannon of the fifth battery. He could see all the four batteries moving in front of him. For any one not a military man this long tedious procession of a moving brigade seems an intricate and unintelligible muddle; one cannot understand why there are so many people round one cannon, and why it is drawn by so many horses in such a strange network of harness, as though it really were so terrible and heavy. To Ryabovitch it was all perfectly comprehensible and therefore uninteresting. He had known for ever so long why at the head of each battery there rode a stalwart bombardier, and why he was called a bombardier; immediately behind this bombardier could be seen the horsemen of the first and then of the middle units. Ryabovitch knew that the horses on which they rode, those on the left, were called one name, while those on the right were called another—it was extremely uninteresting. Behind the horsemen came two shaft-horses. On one of them sat a rider with the dust of yesterday on his back and a clumsy and funny-looking piece of wood on his leg. Ryabovitch knew the object of this piece of wood, and did not think it funny. All the riders waved their whips mechanically and shouted from time to time. The cannon itself was ugly. On the fore part lay sacks of oats covered with canvas, and the cannon itself was hung all over with kettles, soldiers' knapsacks, bags, and looked like some small harmless animal surrounded for some unknown reason by men and horses. To the leeward of it marched six men, the gunners, swinging their arms. After the cannon there came again more bombardiers, riders, shaft-horses, and behind them another cannon, as ugly and unimpressive as the first. After the second followed a third, a fourth; near the fourth an officer, and so on. There were six batteries in all in the brigade, and four cannons in each battery. The procession covered half a mile; it ended in a string of wagons near which an extremely attractive creature—the ass, Magar, brought by a battery commander from Turkey — paced pensively with his long-eared head drooping.

Ryabovitch looked indifferently before and behind, at the backs of heads and at faces; at any other time he would have been half asleep, but now he was entirely absorbed in his new agreeable thoughts. At first when the brigade was setting off on the march he tried to persuade himself that the incident of the kiss could only be interesting as a mysterious little adventure, that it was in reality trivial, and to think of it seriously, to say the least of it, was stupid; but now he bade farewell to logic and gave himself up to dreams. At one moment he imagined himself in Von Rabbek's drawing-room beside a girl who was like the young lady in lilac and the fair girl in black; then he would close his eyes and see himself with another, entirely unknown girl, whose features were very vague. In his imagination he talked, caressed her, leaned on her shoulder, pictured war, separation, then meeting again, supper with his wife, children.

'Brakes on!' the word of command rang out every time they went downhill.

He, too, shouted 'Brakes on!' and was afraid this shout would disturb his reverie and bring him back to reality.

As they passed by some landowner's estate Ryabovitch looked over the fence into the garden. A long avenue, straight as a ruler, strewn with yellow sand and bordered with young birch-trees, met his eyes. With the eagerness of a man given up to dreaming, he pictured to himself little feminine feet tripping along yellow sand, and quite unexpectedly had a clear vision in his imagination of the girl who had kissed him and whom he had succeeded in picturing to himself the evening before at supper. This image remained in his brain and did not desert him again.

At midday there was a shout in the rear near the string of wagons:

'Easy! Eyes to the left! Officers!'

The general of the brigade drove by in a carriage with a pair of white horses. He stopped near the second battery, and shouted something which no one understood. Several officers, among them Ryabovitch, galloped up to them.

'Well?' asked the general, blinking his red eyes. 'Are there any sick?'

Receiving an answer, the general, a little skinny man, chewed, thought for a moment and said, addressing one of the officers:

'One of your drivers of the third cannon has taken off his leg-guard and hung it on the fore part of the cannon, the rascal. Reprimand him.'

He raised his eyes to Ryabovitch and went on:

'It seems to me your front strap is too long.'

Making a few other tedious remarks, the general looked at Lobytko and grinned.

'You look very melancholy today, Lieutenant Lobytko,' he said. 'Are you pining for Madame Lopuhov? Eh? Gentlemen, he is pining for Madame Lopuhov.'

The lady in question was a very stout and tall person who had long passed her fortieth year. The general, who had a predilection for solid ladies, whatever their ages, suspected a similar taste in his officers. The officers smiled respectfully. The general, delighted at having said something very amusing and biting, laughed loudly, touched his coachman's back, and saluted. The carriage rolled on.

'All I am dreaming about now which seems to me so impossible and unearthly is really quite an ordinary thing,' thought Ryabovitch, looking at the clouds of dust racing after the general's carriage. 'It's all very ordinary, and every one goes through it. That general, for instance, has once been in love; now he is married and has children. Captain Vahter, too, is married and beloved, though the nape of his neck is very red and ugly and he has no waist. Salrnanov is coarse and very Tatar, but he has had a love affair that has ended in marriage. I am the same as every one else, and I, too, shall have the same experience as every one else, sooner or later.'

And the thought that he was an ordinary person, and that his life was ordinary, delighted him and gave him courage. He pictured her and his happiness as he pleased, and put no rein on his imagination.

When the brigade reached their halting-place in the evening, and the officers were resting in their tents, Ryabovitch, Merzlyakov, and Lobytko were sitting round a box having supper. Merzlyakov ate without haste, and, as he munched deliberately, read the 'Vyestnik Evropi', which he held on his knees. Lobytko talked incessantly and kept filling up his glass with beer, and Ryabovitch, whose head was confused from dreaming all day long, drank and said nothing. After three glasses he got a little drunk, felt weak, and had an irresistible desire to impart his new sensations to his comrades.

'A strange thing happened to me at those Von Rabbeks',' he began, trying to put an indifferent and ironical tone into his voice. 'You know I went into the billiard-room—'

He began describing very minutely the incident of the kiss, and a moment later relapsed into silence. In the course of that moment he had told everything, and it surprised him dreadfully to find how short a time it took him to tell it. He had imagined that he could have been telling the story of the kiss till next morning. Listening to him, Lobytko, who was a great liar and consequently believed no one, looked at him sceptically and laughed. Merzlyakov twitched his eyebrows and, without removing his eyes from the 'Vyestnik Evropi' said:

'That's an odd thing! How strange! Throws herself on a man's neck, without addressing him by name. She must be some sort of hysterical neurotic.'

'Yes, she must,' Ryabovitch agreed.

'A similar thing once happened to me,' said Lobytko, assuming a scared expression. 'I was going last year to Kovno. I took a second-class ticket. The train was crammed, and it was impossible to sleep. I gave the guard half a rouble; he took my luggage and led me to another compartment. I lay down and covered myself with a rug. It was dark, you understand. Suddenly I felt some one touch me on the shoulder and breathe in my face. I made a movement with my hand and felt somebody's elbow. I opened my eyes and only imagine—a woman. Black eyes, lips red as a prime salmon, nostrils breathing passionately a bosom like a buffer—'

'Excuse me,' Merzlyakov interrupted calmly, 'I understand

about the bosom, but how could you see the lips if it was dark?'

Lobytko began trying to put himself right and laughing at Merzlyakov's unimaginativeness. It made Ryabovitch wince. He walked away from the box, got into bed, and vowed never to confide again.

Camp life began. The days flowed by, one very much like another. All those days Ryabovitch felt, thought, and behaved as though he were in love. Every morning when his orderly handed him water to wash with, and he sluiced his head with cold water, he thought there was something warm and delightful in his life.

In the evenings when his comrades began talking of love and women, he would listen, and draw up closer; and he wore the expression of a soldier when he hears the description of a battle in which he has taken part. And on the evenings when the officers, out on the spree with the setter—Lobytko—at their head, made Don Juan excursions to the 'suburb', and Ryabovitch took part in such excursions, he always was sad, felt profoundly guilty, and inwardly begged her forgiveness. In hours of leisure or on sleepless nights, when he felt moved to recall his childhood, his father and mother—everything near and dear, in fact, he invariably thought of Myestetchki, the strange horse, Von Rabbek, his wife who was like the Empress Eugénie, the dark room, the crack of light at the door.

On the thirty-first of August he went back from the camp, not with the whole brigade, but with only two batteries of it. He was dreaming and excited all the way, as though he were going back to his native place. He had an intense longing to see again the strange horse, the church, the insincere family of the Von Rabbeks, the dark room. The 'inner voice' which so often deceives lovers, whispered to him for some reason that he would be sure to see her—and he was tortured by the questions, How he should meet her? What he would talk to her about? Whether she had forgotten the kiss? If the worst came to the worst, he thought, even if he did not meet her, it would be a pleasure to him merely to go through the dark room and recall the past.

Towards evening there appeared on the horizon the familiar church and white granaries. Ryabovitch's heart beat—he did not hear the officer who was riding beside him and saying something to him, he forgot everything, and looked eagerly at the river shining in the distance, at the roof of the house, at the dovecote round which the pigeons were circling in the light of the setting sun.

When they reached the church and were listening to the billeting orders, he expected every second that a man on horseback would come round the church enclosure and invite the officers to tea, but—the billeting orders were read, the officers were in haste to go on to the village, and the man on horseback did not appear.

'Von Rabbek will hear at once from the peasants that we have come and will send for us,' thought Ryabovitch, as he went into the hut, unable to understand why a comrade was lighting a candle and why the orderlies were hurriedly setting samovars.

A painful uneasiness took possession of him. He lay down, then got up and looked out of the window to see whether the messenger were coming. But there was no sign of him.

He lay down again, but half an hour later he got up, and, unable to restrain his uneasiness, went into the street and strode towards the church. It was dark and deserted in the square near the church. Three soldiers were standing silent in a row where the road began to go downhill. Seeing Ryabovitch, they roused themselves and saluted. He returned the salute and began to go down the familiar path.

On the further side of the river the whole sky was flooded with crimson: the moon was rising; two peasant women, talking loudly, were picking cabbage in the kitchen garden; behind the kitchen garden there were some dark huts. And everything on the near side of the river was just as it had been in May: the path, the bushes, the willows overhanging the water—but there was no sound of the brave nightingale, and no scent of poplar and fresh grass.

Reaching the garden, Ryabovitch looked in at the gate. The garden was dark and still. He could see nothing but the white stems of the nearest birch-trees and a little bit of the avenue; all the rest melted together into a dark blur. Ryabovitch looked and listened eagerly, but after waiting for a quarter of an hour without hearing a sound or catching a glimpse of a light, he trudged back.

He went down to the river. The General's bath-house and the bath-sheets on the rail of the little bridge showed white before him. He went on to the bridge, stood a little, and, quite unnecessarily, touched the sheets. They felt rough and cold. He looked down at the water. The river ran rapidly and with a faintly audible gurgle round the piles of the bath-house. The red moon was reflected near the left bank; little ripples ran over the reflection, stretching it out, breaking it into bits, and seemed trying to carry it away.

'How stupid, how stupid!' thought Ryabovitch, looking at the running water. 'How unintelligent it all is!'

Now that he expected nothing, the incident of the kiss, his impatience, his vague hopes and disappointment, presented themselves in a clear light. It no longer seemed to him strange that he had not seen the General's messenger, and that he would never see the girl who had accidentally kissed him instead of some one else; on the contrary, it would have been strange if he had seen her.

The water was running, he knew not where or why, just as it did in May. In May it had flowed into the great river, from the great river into the sea; then it had risen in vapour, turned into rain, and perhaps the very same water was running now before Ryabovitch's eyes again. What for? Why?

And the whole world, the whole of life, seemed to Ryabovitch an unintelligible, aimless jest. And turning his eyes from the water and looking at the sky, he remembered again how fate in the person of an unknown woman had by chance caressed him, he remembered his summer dreams and fancies, and his life struck him as extraordinarily meagre, poverty-stricken, and colourless.

When he went back to his hut he did not find one of his comrades. The orderly informed him that they had all gone to 'General Von Rabbek's, who had sent a messenger on horseback to invite them.'

For an instant there was a flash of joy in Ryabovitch's heart, but he quenched it at once, got into bed, and in his wrath with his fate, as though to spite it, did not go to the General's.

31

THE FURNISHED ROOM

O. Henry

Let us meet where souls do couch on flowers!

Restless, shifting, fugacious as time itself is a certain vast bulk of the population of the red brick district of the lower West Side. Homeless, they have a hundred homes. They flit from furnished room to furnished room, transients forever—transients in abode, transients in heart and mind. They sing 'Home, Sweet Home' in ragtime; they carry their *lares et penates* in a bandbox; their vine is entwined about a picture hat; a rubber plant is their fig tree.

Hence the houses of this district, having had a thousand dwellers, should have a thousand tales to tell, mostly dull ones, no doubt; but it would be strange if there could not be found a ghost or two in the wake of all these vagrant guests.

One evening after dark a young man prowled among these crumbling red mansions, ringing their bells. At the twelfth he rested his lean hand-baggage upon the step and wiped the dust from his hatband and forehead. The bell sounded faint and far away in some remote, hollow depths.

To the door of this, the twelfth house whose bell he had rung, came a housekeeper who made him think of an unwholesome, surfeited worm that had eaten its nut to a hollow shell and now sought to fill the vacancy with edible lodgers.

He asked if there was a room to let.

'Come in,' said the housekeeper. Her voice came from her throat; her throat seemed lined with fur. 'I have the third floor back, vacant since a week back. Should you wish to look at it?'

The young man followed her up the stairs. A faint light from no particular source mitigated the shadows of the halls. They trod noiselessly upon a stair carpet that its own loom would have forsworn. It seemed to have become vegetable; to have degenerated in that rank, sunless air to lush lichen or spreading moss that grew in patches to the staircase and was viscid under the foot like organic matter. At each turn of the stairs were vacant niches in the wall. Perhaps plants had once been set within them. If so they had died in that foul and tainted air. It may be that statues of the saints had stood there, but it was not difficult to conceive that imps and devils had dragged them forth in the darkness and down to the unholy depths of some furnished pit below.

'This is the room,' said the housekeeper, from her furry throat. 'It's a nice room. It ain't often vacant. I had some most elegant people in it last summer—no trouble at all, and paid in advance to the minute. The water's at the end of the hall. Sprowls and Mooney kept it three months. They done a vaudeville sketch. Miss B'retta Sprowls—you may have heard of her—oh, that was just the stage names—right there over the dresser is where the marriage certificate hung, framed. The gas is here, and you see there is plenty of closet room. It's a room everybody likes. It never stays idle long.'

'Do you have many theatrical people rooming here?' asked the young man.

'They comes and goes. A good proportion of my lodgers is connected with the theatres. Yes, sir, this is the theatrical district. Actor people never stays long anywhere. I get my share. Yes, they comes and they goes.'

He engaged the room, paying for a week in advance. He was tired, he said, and would take possession at once. He counted out the money. The room had been made ready, she said, even to towels and water. As the housekeeper moved away he put, for the thousandth time, the question that he carried at the end of his tongue.

'A young girl—Miss Vashner—Miss Eloise Vashner—do you remember such a one among your lodgers? She would be singing on the stage, most likely. A fair girl, of medium height and slender, with reddish, gold hair and a dark mole near her left eyebrow.'

'No, I don't remember the name. Them stage people has names they change as often as their rooms. They comes and they goes. No, I don't call that one to mind.'

No. Always no. Five months of ceaseless interrogation and the inevitable negative. So much time spent by day in questioning managers, agents, schools and choruses; by night among the audiences of theatres from all-star casts down to music halls so low that he dreaded to find what he most hoped for. He who had loved her best had tried to find her. He was sure that since her disappearance from home this great, water-girt city held her somewhere, but it was like a monstrous quicksand, shifting its particles constantly, with no foundation, its upper granules of to-day buried to-morrow in ooze and slime.

The furnished room received its latest guest with a first glow of pseudo-hospitality, a hectic, haggard, perfunctory welcome like the specious smile of a demirep. The sophistical comfort came in reflected gleams from the decayed furniture, the ragged brocade upholstery of a couch and two chairs, a foot-wide cheap pier-glass between the two windows, from one or two gilt picture frames and a brass bedstead in a corner.

The guest reclined, inert, upon a chair, while the room, confused in speech as though it were an apartment in Babel, tried to discourse to him of its divers tenantry.

A polychromatic rug like some brilliant-flowered rectangular, tropical islet lay surrounded by a billowy sea of soiled matting. Upon the gay-papered wall were those pictures that pursue the homeless one from house to house—The Huguenot Lovers, The First Quarrel, The Wedding Breakfast, Psyche at the Fountain. The mantel's chastely severe outline was ingloriously veiled behind some pert drapery drawn rakishly askew like the sashes of the Amazonian ballet. Upon it was some desolate flotsam cast aside by the room's marooned when a lucky sail had borne them to a fresh port—a trifling vase or two, pictures of actresses, a medicine bottle, some stray cards out of a deck.

One by one, as the characters of a cryptograph become explicit, the little signs left by the furnished room's procession of guests developed a significance. The threadbare space in the rug in front of the dresser told that lovely woman had marched in the throng. Tiny finger prints on the wall spoke of little prisoners trying to feel their way to sun and air. A splattered stain, raying like the shadow of a bursting bomb, witnessed where a hurled glass or bottle had splintered with its contents against the wall. Across the pier-glass had been scrawled with a diamond in staggering letters the name 'Marie'. It seemed that the succession of dwellers in the furnished room had turned in fury—perhaps tempted beyond forbearance by its garish coldness—and wreaked upon it their passions. The furniture was chipped and bruised; the couch, distorted by bursting springs, seemed a horrible monster that had been slain during the stress of some grotesque convulsion. Some more potent upheaval had cloven a great slice from the marble mantel. Each plank in the floor owned its particular cant and shriek as from a separate and individual agony. It seemed incredible that all this malice and injury had been wrought upon the room by those who had called it for a time their home; and yet it may have been the cheated home instinct surviving blindly, the resentful rage at false household gods that had kindled their wrath. A hut that is our own we can sweep and adorn and cherish.

The young tenant in the chair allowed these thoughts to file, soft-shod, through his mind, while there drifted into the room furnished sounds and furnished scents. He heard in one room a tittering and incontinent, slack laughter; in others the monologue of a scold, the rattling of dice, a lullaby, and one crying dully;

above him a banjo tinkled with spirit. Doors banged somewhere; the elevated trains roared intermittently; a cat yowled miserably upon a back fence. And he breathed the breath of the house—a dank savour rather than a smell—a cold, musty effluvium as from underground vaults mingled with the reeking exhalations of linoleum and mildewed and rotten woodwork.

Then, suddenly, as he rested there, the room was filled with the strong, sweet odour of mignonette. It came as upon a single buffet of wind with such sureness and fragrance and emphasis that it almost seemed a living visitant. And the man cried aloud: 'What, dear?' as if he had been called, and sprang up and faced about. The rich odour clung to him and wrapped him around. He reached out his arms for it, all his senses for the time confused and commingled. How could one be peremptorily called by an odour? Surely it must have been a sound. But, was it not the sound that had touched, that had caressed him?

'She has been in this room,' he cried, and he sprang to wrest from it a token, for he knew he would recognize the smallest thing that had belonged to her or that she had touched. This enveloping scent of mignonette, the odour that she had loved and made her own—whence came it?

The room had been but carelessly set in order. Scattered upon the flimsy dresser scarf were half a dozen hairpins—those discreet, indistinguishable friends of womankind, feminine of gender, infinite of mood and uncommunicative of tense. These he ignored, conscious of their triumphant lack of identity. Ransacking the drawers of the dresser he came upon a discarded, tiny, ragged handkerchief. He pressed it to his face. It was racy and insolent with heliotrope; he hurled it to the floor. In another drawer he found odd buttons, a theatre programme, a pawnbroker's card, two lost marshmallows, a book on the divination of dreams. In the last was a woman's black satin hair bow, which halted him, poised between ice and fire. But the black satin hair bow also is femininity's demure, impersonal, common ornament, and tells no tales.

And then he traversed the room like a hound on the scent, skimming the walls, considering the corners of the bulging matting on his hands and knees, rummaging mantel and tables, the curtains and hangings, the drunken cabinet in the corner, for a visible sign, unable to perceive that she was there beside, around, against, within, above him, clinging to him, wooing him, calling him so poignantly through the finer senses that even his grosser ones became cognizant of the call. Once again he answered loudly: 'Yes, dear!' and turned, wild-eyed, to gaze on vacancy, for he could not yet discern form and colour and love and outstretched arms in the odour of mignonette. Oh, God! whence that odour, and since when have odours had a voice to call? Thus he groped.

He burrowed in crevices and corners, and found corks and cigarettes. These he passed in passive contempt. But once he found in a fold of the matting a half-smoked cigar, and this he ground beneath his heel with a green and trenchant oath. He sifted the room from end to end. He found dreary and ignoble small records of many a peripatetic tenant; but of her whom he sought, and who may have lodged there, and whose spirit seemed to hover there, he found no trace.

And then he thought of the housekeeper.

He ran from the haunted room downstairs and to a door that showed a crack of light. She came out to his knock. He smothered his excitement as best he could.

'Will you tell me, madam,' he besought her, 'who occupied the room I have before I came?'

'Yes, sir. I can tell you again. 'Twas Sprowls and Mooney, as I said. Miss B'retta Sprowls it was in the theatres, but Missis Mooney she was. My house is well known for respectability. The marriage certificate hung, framed, on a nail over—'

'What kind of a lady was Miss Sprowls—in looks, I mean?'

'Why, black-haired, sir, short, and stout, with a comical face. They left a week ago Tuesday.'

'And before they occupied it?'

'Why, there was a single gentleman connected with the draying business. He left owing me a week. Before him was Missis Crowder and her two children, that stayed four months; and back of them was old Mr Doyle, whose sons paid for him. He kept the room six months. That goes back a year, sir, and further I do not remember.'

He thanked her and crept back to his room. The room was dead. The essence that had vivified it was gone. The perfume of mignonette had departed. In its place was the old, stale odour of mouldy house furniture, of atmosphere in storage.

The ebbing of his hope drained his faith. He sat staring at the yellow, singing gaslight. Soon he walked to the bed and began to tear the sheets into strips. With the blade of his knife he drove them tightly into every crevice around windows and door. When all was snug and taut, he turned out the light, turned the gas full on again and laid himself gratefully upon the bed.

∾

It was Mrs McCool's night to go with the can for beer. So she fetched it and sat with Mrs Purdy in one of those subterranean retreats where housekeepers foregather and the worm dieth seldom.

'I rented out my third floor, back, this evening,' said Mrs Purdy, across a fine circle of foam. 'A young man took it. He went up to bed two hours ago.'

'Now, did ye, Mrs Purdy, ma'am?' said Mrs McCool, with intense admiration. 'You do be a wonder for rentin' rooms of that kind. And did ye tell him, then?' she concluded in a husky whisper, laden with mystery.

'Rooms,' said Mrs Purdy, in her furriest tones, 'are furnished for to rent. I did not tell him, Mrs McCool.'

''Tis right ye are, ma'am; 'tis by renting rooms we kape alive.

Ye have the rale sense for business, ma'am. There be many people will rayjict the rentin' of a room if they be tould a suicide has been after dyin' in the bed of it.'

'As you say, we has our living to be making,' remarked Mrs Purdy.

'Yis, ma'am; 'tis true. 'Tis just one wake ago this day I helped ye lay out the third floor, back. A pretty slip of a colleen she was to be killin' herself wid the gas—a swate little face she had, Mrs Purdy, ma'am.'

'She'd a-been called handsome, as you say,' said Mrs Purdy, assenting but critical, 'but for that mole she had a-growin' by her left eyebrow. Do fill up your glass again, Mrs McCool.'

32

FAREWELL!

Guy de Maupassant

Love is a speck of time that may disillusion one as time takes its toll.

The two friends were getting near the end of their dinner. Through the café windows they could see the Boulevard, crowded with people. They could feel the gentle breezes which are wafted over Paris on warm summer evenings and make you feel like going out somewhere, you care not where, under the trees, and make you dream of moonlit rivers, of fireflies and of larks.

One of the two, Henri Simon, heaved a deep sigh and said: 'Ah! I am growing old. It's sad. Formerly, on evenings like this, I felt full of life. Now, I only feel regrets. Life is short!'

He was perhaps forty-five years old, very bald and already growing stout.

The other, Pierre Carnier, a trifle older, but thin and lively, answered:

'Well, my boy, I have grown old without noticing it in the least. I have always been merry, healthy, vigorous and all the rest. As one sees oneself in the mirror every day, one does not realize the work of age, for it is slow, regular, and it modifies the countenance so gently that the changes are unnoticeable. It is for this reason alone that we do not die of sorrow after two or three years of excitement. For we cannot understand the alterations which time produces. In order to appreciate them one would have to remain six months without seeing one's own face— then, oh, what a shock!

'And the women, my friend, how I pity the poor beings! All

their joy, all their power, all their life, lies in their beauty, which lasts ten years.

'As I said, I aged without noticing it; I thought myself practically a youth, when I was almost fifty years old. Not feeling the slightest infirmity, I went about, happy and peaceful.

'The revelation of my decline came to me in a simple and terrible manner, which overwhelmed me for almost six months— then I became resigned.

'Like all men, I have often been in love, but most especially once.

'I met her at the seashore, at Etretat, about twelve years ago, shortly after the war. There is nothing prettier than this beach during the morning bathing hour. It is small, shaped like a horseshoe, framed by high white cliffs, which are pierced by strange holes called the 'Portes', one stretching out into the ocean like the leg of a giant, the other short and dumpy. The women gather on the narrow strip of sand in this frame of high rocks, which they make into a gorgeous garden of beautiful gowns. The sun beats down on the shores, on the multicoloured parasols, on the blue-green sea; and all is gay, delightful, smiling. You sit down at the edge of the water and you watch the bathers. The women come down, wrapped in long bath robes, which they throw off daintily when they reach the foamy edge of the rippling waves; and they run into the water with a rapid little step, stopping from time to time for a delightful little thrill from the cold water, a short gasp.

'Very few stand the test of the bath. It is there that they can be judged, from the ankle to the throat. Especially on leaving the water are the defects revealed, although water is a powerful aid to flabby skin.

'The first time that I saw this young woman in the water, I was delighted, entranced. She stood the test well. There are faces whose charms appeal to you at first glance and delight you instantly. You seem to have found the woman whom you were born to love. I had that feeling and that shock.

'I was introduced, and was soon smitten worse than I had ever been before. My heart longed for her. It is a terrible yet delightful thing thus to be dominated by a young woman. It is almost torture, and yet infinite delight. Her look, her smile, her hair fluttering in the wind, the little lines of her face, the slightest movement of her features, delighted me, upset me, entranced me. She had captured me, body and soul, by her gestures, her manners, even by her clothes, which seemed to take on a peculiar charm as soon as she wore them. I grew tender at the sight of her veil on some piece of furniture, her gloves thrown on a chair. Her gowns seemed to me inimitable. Nobody had hats like hers.

'She was married, but her husband came only on Saturday, and left on Monday. I didn't concern myself about him, anyhow. I wasn't jealous of him, I don't know why; never did a creature seem to me to be of less importance in life, to attract my attention less than this man.

'But she! How I loved her! How beautiful, graceful and young she was! She was youth, elegance, freshness itself! Never before had I felt so strongly what a pretty, distinguished, delicate, charming, graceful being woman is. Never before had I appreciated the seductive beauty to be found in the curve of a cheek, the movement of a lip, the pinkness of an ear, the shape of that foolish organ called the nose.

'This lasted three months; then I left for America, overwhelmed with sadness. But her memory remained in me, persistent, triumphant. From far away I was as much hers as I had been when she was near me. Years passed by, and I did not forget her. The charming image of her person was ever before my eyes and in my heart. And my love remained true to her, a quiet tenderness now, something like the beloved memory of the most beautiful and the most enchanting thing I had ever met in my life.

'Twelve years are not much in a lifetime! One does not feel them slip by. The years follow each other gently and quickly, slowly yet rapidly, each one is long and yet so soon over! They add up so rapidly, they leave so few traces behind them, they disappear so completely, that, when one turns round to look back over bygone years, one sees nothing and yet one does not understand how one happens to be so old. It seemed to me, really, that hardly a few months separated me from that charming season on the sands of Etretat.

'Last spring I went to dine with some friends at Maisons-Laffitte.

'Just as the train was leaving, a big, fat lady, escorted by four little girls, got into my car. I hardly looked at this mother hen, very big, very round, with a face as full as the moon framed in an enormous, beribboned hat.

'She was puffing, out of breath from having been forced to walk quickly. The children began to chatter. I unfolded my paper and began to read.

'We had just passed Asnieres, when my neighbour suddenly turned to me and said:

'"Excuse me, sir, but are you not Monsieur Carnier?"

'"Yes, Madame."

'Then she began to laugh, the pleased laugh of a good woman; and yet it was sad.

'"You do not seem to recognize me."

'I hesitated. It seemed to me that I had seen that face somewhere; but where? When? I answered:

'"Yes—and no. I certainly know you, and yet I cannot recall your name."

'She blushed a little:

'"Madame Julie Lefevre."

'Never had I received such a shock. In a second it seemed to me as though it were all over with me! I felt that a veil had been torn from my eyes and that I was going to make a horrible and heart-rending discovery.

'So that was she! That big, fat, common woman, she! She had become the mother of these four girls since I had last seen her. And these little beings surprised me as much as their mother. They were part of her; they were big girls, and already had a place in life. Whereas she no longer counted, she, that marvel of dainty and charming gracefulness. It seemed to me that I had seen her but yesterday, and this is how I found her again! Was it possible? A poignant grief seized my heart; and also a revolt against nature herself, an unreasoning indignation against this brutal, injurious act of destruction.

'I looked at her, bewildered. Then I took her hand in mine, and tears came to my eyes. I wept for her lost youth. For I did not know this fat lady.

'She was also excited, and stammered: "I am greatly changed, am I not? What can you expect—everything has its time! You see, I have become a mother, nothing but a good mother. Farewell to the rest, that is over. Oh! I never expected you to recognize me if we met. You, too, have changed. It took me quite a while to be sure that I was not mistaken. Your hair is all white. Just think! Twelve years ago! Twelve years! My oldest girl is already ten."

'I looked at the child. And I recognized in her something of her mother's old charm, but something as yet unformed, something which promised for the future. And life seemed to me as swift as a passing train.

'We had reached Maisons-Laffitte. I kissed my old friend's hand. I had found nothing to utter but the most commonplace remarks. I was too much upset to talk.

'At night, alone, at home, I stood in front of the mirror for a long time, a very long time. And I finally remembered what I had been, finally saw in my mind's eye my brown mustache, my black hair and the youthful expression of my face. Now I was old. Farewell!'

33

HOW TO AVOID GETTING MARRIED

Stephen Leacock

Sometimes a man falls in love with the dimples of a woman but makes the mistake of marrying the whole woman!

Some years ago, when I was the Editor of a Correspondence Column, I used to receive heart-broken letters from young men asking for advice and sympathy. They found themselves the object of marked attentions from girls which they scarcely knew how to deal with. They did not wish to give pain or to seem indifferent to a love which they felt was as ardent as it was disinterested, and yet they felt that they could not bestow their hands where their hearts had not spoken.

They wrote to me fully and frankly, and as one soul might write to another for relief. I accepted their confidences as under the pledge of a secrecy, never divulging their disclosures beyond the circulation of my newspapers, or giving any hint of their identity other than printing their names and addresses and their letters in full. But I may perhaps without dishonour reproduce one of these letters, and my answer to it, inasmuch as the date is now months ago, and the softening hand of Time has woven its roses—how shall I put it?; the mellow haze of reminiscences has—what I mean is that the young man has gone back to work and is all right again.

Here then is a letter from a young man whose name I must not reveal, but whom I will designate as D. F., and whose address I must not divulge, but will simply indicate as Q. Street, West.

Dear Mr Leacock,

For some time past I have been the recipient of very marked attentions from a young lady. She has been calling at the house almost every evening, and has taken me out in her motor, and invited me to concerts and the theatre. On these latter occasions I have insisted on her taking my father with me, and have tried as far as possible to prevent her saying anything to me which would be unfit for father to hear. But my position has become a very difficult one. I do not think it right to accept her presents when I cannot feel that my heart is hers.

Yesterday she sent to my house a beautiful bouquet of American Beauty roses addressed to me, and a magnificent bunch of Timothy Hay for father. I do not know what to say. Would it be right for father to keep all this valuable hay? I have confided fully in father, and we have discussed the question of presents. He thinks that there are some that we can keep with propriety, and others that a sense of delicacy forbids us to retain. He himself is going to sort out the presents into the two classes. He thinks that as far as he can see, the Hay is in class B. Meantime I write to you, as I understand that Miss Laura Jean Libby and Miss Beatrix Fairfax are on their vacation, and in any case a friend of mine who follows their writings closely tells me that they are always full.

I enclose a dollar, because I do not think it right to ask you to give all your valuable time and your best thought without giving you back what it is worth.

On receipt of this I wrote back at once a private and confidential letter which I printed in the following edition of the paper.

My dear, dear Boy,

Your letter has touched me. As soon as I opened it and saw

the green and blue tint of the dollar bill which you had so daintily and prettily folded within the pages of your sweet letter, I knew that the note was from someone that I could learn to love, if our correspondence were to continue as it had begun. I took the dollar from your letter and kissed and fondled it a dozen times. Dear unknown boy! I shall always keep that dollar! No matter how much I may need it, or how many necessaries, yes, absolute necessities, of life I may be wanting, I shall always keep that dollar. Do you understand, dear? I shall keep it. I shall not spend it. As far as the use of it goes, it will be just as if you had not sent it. Even if you were to send me another dollar, I should still keep the first one, so that no matter how many you sent, the recollection of one first friendship would not be contaminated with mercenary considerations. When I say dollar, darling, of course an express order, or a postal note, or even stamps would be all the same. But in that case do not address me in care of this office, as I should not like to think of your pretty little letters lying round where others might handle them.

But now I must stop chatting about myself, for I know that you cannot be interested in a simple old fogey such as I am. Let me talk to you about your letter and about the difficult question it raises for all marriageable young men.

In the first place, let me tell you how glad I am that you confide in your father. Whatever happens, go at once to your father, put your arms about his neck, and have a good cry together. And you are right, too, about presents. It needs a wiser head than my poor perplexed boy to deal with them. Take them to your father to be sorted, or, if you feel that you must not overtax his love, address them to me in your own pretty hand.

And now let us talk, dear, as one heart to another.

Remember always that if a girl is to have your heart she must be worthy of you. When you look at your own bright innocent face in the mirror, resolve that you will give your hand to no girl who is not just as innocent as you are and no brighter than yourself. So that you must first find out how innocent she is. Ask her quietly and frankly—remember, dear, that the days of false modesty are passing away—whether she has ever been in jail. If she has not (and if you have not), then you know that you are dealing with a dear confiding girl who will make you a life mate. Then you must know, too, that her mind is worthy of your own. So many men to-day are led astray by the merely superficial graces and attractions of girls who in reality possess no mental equipment at all. Many a man is bitterly disillusioned after marriage when he realizes that his wife cannot solve a quadratic equation, and that he is compelled to spend all his days with a woman who does not know that *x-squared* plus *2xy* plus *y-squared* is the same thing, or, I think nearly the same thing, as *x* plus *y* squared.

Nor should the simple domestic virtues be neglected. If a girl desires to woo you, before allowing her to press her suit, ask her if she knows how to press yours. If she can, let her woo; if not, tell her to whoa. But I see I have written quite as much as I need for this column. Won't you write again, just as before, dear boy?

—Stephen Leacock

34

THE PENDULUM

O. Henry

Only when one loses someone does appreciation happen, rather late.

'Eighty-first street—let 'em out, please,' yelled the shepherd in blue.

A flock of citizen sheep scrambled out and another flock scrambled aboard. Ding-ding! The cattle cars of the Manhattan Elevated rattled away, and John Perkins drifted down the stairway of the station with the released flock.

John walked slowly toward his flat. Slowly, because in the lexicon of his daily life there was no such word as 'perhaps'. There are no surprises awaiting a man who has been married two years and lives in a flat. As he walked John Perkins prophesied to himself with gloomy and downtrodden cynicism the foregone conclusions of the monotonous day.

Katy would meet him at the door with a kiss flavoured with cold cream and butter-scotch. He would remove his coat, sit upon a macadamized lounge and read, in the evening paper, of Russians and Japs slaughtered by the deadly linotype. For dinner there would be pot roast, a salad flavoured with a dressing warranted not to crack or injure the leather, stewed rhubarb and the bottle of strawberry marmalade blushing at the certificate of chemical purity on its label. After dinner Katy would show him the new patch in her crazy quilt that the iceman had cut for her off the end of his four-in-hand. At half-past seven they would spread newspapers over the furniture to catch the pieces of plastering that fell when the fat man in the flat overhead began to take his physical culture exercises. Exactly at eight, Hickey & Mooney, of the vaudeville team (unbooked) in the flat across the hall, would yield to the gentle influence of delirium tremens and begin to overturn chairs under the delusion that Hammerstein was pursuing them with a five-hundred-dollar-a-week contract. Then the gent at the window across the air-shaft would get out his flute; the nightly gas leak would steal forth to frolic in the highways; the dumbwaiter would slip off its trolley; the janitor would drive Mrs Zanowitski's five children once more across the Yalu, the lady with the champagne shoes and the Skye terrier would trip downstairs and paste her Thursday name over her bell and letter-box—and the evening routine of the Frogmore flats would be under way.

John Perkins knew these things would happen. And he knew that at a quarter past eight he would summon his nerve and reach for his hat, and that his wife would deliver this speech in a querulous tone:

'Now, where are you going, I'd like to know, John Perkins?'

'Thought I'd drop up to McCloskey's,' he would answer, 'and play a game or two of pool with the fellows.'

Of late such had been John Perkins's habit. At ten or eleven he would return. Sometimes Katy would be asleep; sometimes waiting up, ready to melt in the crucible of her ire a little more gold plating from the wrought steel chains of matrimony. For these things Cupid will have to answer when he stands at the bar of justice with his victims from the Frogmore flats.

To-night John Perkins encountered a tremendous upheaval of the commonplace when he reached his door. No Katy was there with her affectionate, confectionate kiss. The three rooms seemed in portentous disorder. All about lay her things in confusion. Shoes in the middle of the floor, curling tongs, hair bows, kimonos, powder box, jumbled together on dresser and chairs—this was not Katy's way. With a sinking heart John saw the comb with a curling cloud of her brown hair among its teeth. Some unusual hurry and perturbation must have possessed her, for she always carefully placed these combings in the little blue vase on the mantel to be some day formed into the coveted feminine 'rat'.

Hanging conspicuously to the gas jet by a string was a folded paper. John seized it. It was a note from his wife running thus:

Dear John,

I just had a telegram saying mother is very sick. I am going to take the 4.30 train. Brother Sam is going to meet me at the depot there. There is cold mutton in the ice box. I hope it isn't her quinzy again. Pay the milkman 50 cents. She had it bad last spring. Don't forget to write to the company about the gas meter, and your good socks are in the top drawer. I will write to-morrow.

Hastily, Katy

Never during their two years of matrimony had he and Katy been separated for a night. John read the note over and over in a dumbfounded way. Here was a break in a routine that had never varied, and it left him dazed.

There on the back of a chair hung, pathetically empty and formless, the red wrapper with black dots that she always wore while getting the meals. Her week-day clothes had been tossed here and there in her haste. A little paper bag of her favourite butterscotch lay with its string yet unwound. A daily paper sprawled on the floor, gaping rectangularly where a railroad time-table had been clipped from it. Everything in the room spoke of a loss, of an essence gone, of its soul and life departed. John Perkins stood among the dead remains with a queer feeling of desolation in his heart.

He began to set the rooms tidy as well as he could. When he touched her clothes a thrill of something like terror went through him. He had never thought what existence would be without

Katy. She had become so thoroughly annealed into his life that she was like the air he breathed—necessary but scarcely noticed. Now, without warning, she was gone, vanished, as completely absent as if she had never existed. Of course it would be only for a few days, or at most a week or two, but it seemed to him as if the very hand of death had pointed a finger at his secure and uneventful home.

John dragged the cold mutton from the ice-box, made coffee and sat down to a lonely meal face to face with the strawberry marmalade's shameless certificate of purity. Bright among withdrawn blessings now appeared to him the ghosts of pot roasts and the salad with tan polish dressing. His home was dismantled. A quinzied mother-in-law had knocked his lares and penates sky-high. After his solitary meal John sat at a front window.

He did not care to smoke. Outside the city roared to him to come join in its dance of folly and pleasure. The night was his. He might go forth unquestioned and thrum the strings of jollity as free as any gay bachelor there. He might carouse and wander and have his fling until dawn if he liked; and there would be no wrathful Katy waiting for him, bearing the chalice that held the dregs of his joy. He might play pool at McCloskey's with his roistering friends until Aurora dimmed the electric bulbs if he chose. The hymeneal strings that had curbed him always when the Frogmore flats had palled upon him were loosened. Katy was gone.

John Perkins was not accustomed to analyzing his emotions. But as he sat in his Katy-bereft 10×12 parlour he hit unerringly upon the keynote of his discomfort. He knew now that Katy was necessary to his happiness. His feeling for her, lulled into unconsciousness by the dull round of domesticity, had been sharply stirred by the loss of her presence. Has it not been dinned into us by proverb and sermon and fable that we never prize the music till the sweet-voiced bird has flown—or in other no less florid and true utterances?

'I'm a double-dyed dub,' mused John Perkins, 'the way I've been treating Katy. Off every night playing pool and bumming with the boys instead of staying home with her. The poor girl here all alone with nothing to amuse her, and me acting that way! John Perkins, you're the worst kind of a shine. I'm going to make it up for the little girl. I'll take her out and let her see some amusement. And I'll cut out the McCloskey gang right from this minute.'

Yes, there was the city roaring outside for John Perkins to come dance in the train of Momus. And at McCloskey's the boys were knocking the balls idly into the pockets against the hour for the nightly game. But no primrose way nor clicking cue could woo the remorseful soul of Perkins the bereft. The thing that was his, lightly held and half scorned, had been taken away from him, and he wanted it. Backward to a certain man named Adam, whom the cherubim bounced from the orchard, could Perkins, the remorseful, trace his descent.

Near the right hand of John Perkins stood a chair. On the back of it stood Katy's blue shirtwaist. It still retained something of her contour. Midway of the sleeves were fine, individual wrinkles made by the movements of her arms in working for his comfort and pleasure. A delicate but impelling odour of bluebells came from it. John took it and looked long and soberly at the unresponsive grenadine. Katy had never been unresponsive. Tears—yes, tears—came into John Perkins's eyes. When she came back things would be different. He would make up for all his neglect. What was life without her?

The door opened. Katy walked in carrying a little hand satchel. John stared at her stupidly.

'My! I'm glad to get back,' said Katy. 'Ma wasn't sick to amount to anything. Sam was at the depot, and said she just had a little spell, and got all right soon after they telegraphed. So I took the next train back. I'm just dying for a cup of coffee.'

Nobody heard the click and rattle of the cog-wheels as the

third-floor front of the Frogmore flats buzzed its machinery back into the Order of Things. A band slipped, a spring was touched, the gear was adjusted and the wheels revolve in their old orbit.

John Perkins looked at the clock. It was 8.15. He reached for his hat and walked to the door.

'Now, where are you going, I'd like to know, John Perkins?' asked Katy, in a querulous tone.

'Thought I'd drop up to McCloskey's,' said John, 'and play a game or two of pool with the fellows.'

35

THE LAGOON

Joseph Conrad

*Infatuation, loyalty, betrayal, remorse and guilt all lie in the fringe
of relationships...a lagoon of sorts.*

The white man, leaning with both arms over the roof of the
little house in the stern of the boat, said to the steersman—
'We will pass the night in Arsat's clearing. It is late.'

The Malay only grunted, and went on looking fixedly at the
river. The white man rested his chin on his crossed arms and gazed
at the wake of the boat. At the end of the straight avenue of forests
cut by the intense glitter of the river, the sun appeared unclouded
and dazzling, poised low over the water that shone smoothly like
a band of metal. The forests, sombre and dull, stood motionless
and silent on each side of the broad stream. At the foot of big,
towering trees, trunkless nipa palms rose from the mud of the bank,
in bunches of leaves enormous and heavy, that hung unstirring
over the brown swirl of eddies. In the stillness of the air every tree,
every leaf, every bough, every tendril of creeper and every petal of
minute blossoms seemed to have been bewitched into an immobility
perfect and final. Nothing moved on the river but the eight paddles
that rose flashing regularly, dipped together with a single splash;
while the steersman swept right and left with a periodic and sudden
flourish of his blade describing a glinting semicircle above his head.
The churned-up water frothed alongside with a confused murmur.
And the white man's canoe, advancing upstream in the short-lived
disturbance of its own making, seemed to enter the portals of a
land from which the very memory of motion had forever departed.

The white man, turning his back upon the setting sun, looked along the empty and broad expanse of the sea-reach. For the last three miles of its course the wandering, hesitating river, as if enticed irresistibly by the freedom of an open horizon, flows straight into the sea, flows straight to the east—to the east that harbours both light and darkness. Astern of the boat the repeated call of some bird, a cry discordant and feeble, skipped along over the smooth water and lost itself, before it could reach the other shore, in the breathless silence of the world.

The steersman dug his paddle into the stream, and held hard with stiffened arms, his body thrown forward. The water gurgled aloud; and suddenly the long straight reach seemed to pivot on its centre, the forests swung in a semicircle, and the slanting beams of sunset touched the broadside of the canoe with a fiery glow, throwing the slender and distorted shadows of its crew upon the streaked glitter of the river. The white man turned to look ahead. The course of the boat had been altered at right-angles to the stream, and the carved dragon-head of its prow was pointing now at a gap in the fringing bushes of the bank. It glided through, brushing the overhanging twigs, and disappeared from the river like some slim and amphibious creature leaving the water for its lair in the forests.

The narrow creek was like a ditch: tortuous, fabulously deep; filled with gloom under the thin strip of pure and shining blue of the heaven. Immense trees soared up, invisible behind the festooned draperies of creepers. Here and there, near the glistening blackness of the water, a twisted root of some tall tree showed amongst the tracery of small ferns, black and dull, writhing and motionless, like an arrested snake. The short words of the paddlers reverberated loudly between the thick and sombre walls of vegetation. Darkness oozed out from between the trees, through the tangled maze of the creepers, from behind the great fantastic and unstirring leaves; the darkness, mysterious and invincible; the darkness scented and poisonous of impenetrable forests.

The men poled in the shoaling water. The creek broadened, opening out into a wide sweep of a stagnant lagoon. The forests receded from the marshy bank, leaving a level strip of bright green, reedy grass to frame the reflected blueness of the sky. A fleecy pink cloud drifted high above, trailing the delicate colouring of its image under the floating leaves and the silvery blossoms of the lotus. A little house, perched on high piles, appeared black in the distance. Near it, two tall nibong palms, that seemed to have come out of the forests in the background, leaned slightly over the ragged roof, with a suggestion of sad tenderness and care in the droop of their leafy and soaring heads.

The steersman, pointing with his paddle, said, 'Arsat is there. I see his canoe fast between the piles.'

The polers ran along the sides of the boat glancing over their shoulders at the end of the day's journey. They would have preferred to spend the night somewhere else than on this lagoon of weird aspect and ghostly reputation. Moreover, they disliked Arsat, first as a stranger, and also because he who repairs a ruined house, and dwells in it, proclaims that he is not afraid to live amongst the spirits that haunt the places abandoned by mankind. Such a man can disturb the course of fate by glances or words; while his familiar ghosts are not easy to propitiate by casual wayfarers upon whom they long to wreak the malice of their human master. White men care not for such things, being unbelievers and in league with the Father of Evil, who leads them unharmed through the invisible dangers of this world. To the warnings of the righteous they oppose an offensive pretence of disbelief. What is there to be done?

So they thought, throwing their weight on the end of their long poles. The big canoe glided on swiftly, noiselessly and smoothly, towards Arsat's clearing, till, in a great rattling of poles thrown down, and the loud murmurs of 'Allah be praised!' it came with a gentle knock against the crooked piles below the house.

The boatmen with uplifted faces shouted discordantly, 'Arsat! O Arsat!' Nobody came. The white man began to climb the rude ladder giving access to the bamboo platform before the house. The juragan of the boat said sulkily, 'We will cook in the sampan, and sleep on the water.'

'Pass my blankets and the basket,' said the white man curtly.

He knelt on the edge of the platform to receive the bundle. Then the boat shoved off, and the white man, standing up, confronted Arsat, who had come out through the low door of his hut. He was a man young, powerful, with a broad chest and muscular arms. He had nothing on but his sarong. His head was bare. His big, soft eyes stared eagerly at the white man, but his voice and demeanour were composed as he asked, without any words of greeting—

'Have you medicine, Tuan?'

'No,' said the visitor in a startled tone. 'No. Why? Is there sickness in the house?'

'Enter and see,' replied Arsat, in the same calm manner, and turning short round, passed again through the small doorway. The white man, dropping his bundles, followed.

In the dim light of the dwelling he made out on a couch of bamboos a woman stretched on her back under a broad sheet of red cotton cloth. She lay still, as if dead; but her big eyes, wide open, glittered in the gloom, staring upwards at the slender rafters, motionless and unseeing. She was in a high fever, and evidently unconscious. Her cheeks were sunk slightly, her lips were partly open, and on the young face there was the ominous and fixed expression—the absorbed, contemplating expression of the unconscious who are going to die. The two men stood looking down at her in silence.

'Has she been long ill?' asked the traveller.

'I have not slept for five nights,' answered the Malay, in a deliberate tone. 'At first she heard voices calling her from the water and struggled against me who held her. But since the sun of to-day rose she hears nothing—she hears not me. She sees nothing. She sees not me—me!'

He remained silent for a minute, then asked softly—

'Tuan, will she die?'

'I fear so,' said the white man sorrowfully. He had known Arsat years ago, in a far country in times of trouble and danger, when no friendship is to be despised. And since his Malay friend had come unexpectedly to dwell in the hut on the lagoon with a strange woman, he had slept many times there, in his journeys up or down the river. He liked the man who knew how to keep faith in council and how to fight without fear by the side of his white friend. He liked him—not so much perhaps as a man likes his favourite dog—but still he liked him well enough to help and ask no questions, to think sometimes vaguely and hazily in the midst of his own pursuits, about the lonely man and the long-haired woman with audacious face and triumphant eyes, who lived together hidden by the forests—alone and feared.

The white man came out of the hut in time to see the enormous conflagration of sunset put out by the swift and stealthy shadows that, rising like a black and impalpable vapour above the tree-tops, spread over the heaven, extinguishing the crimson glow of floating clouds and the red brilliance of departing daylight. In a few moments all the stars came out above the intense blackness of the earth, and the great lagoon gleaming suddenly with reflected lights resembled an oval patch of night sky flung down into the hopeless and abysmal night of the wilderness. The white man had some supper out of the basket, then collecting a few sticks that lay about the platform, made up a small fire, not for warmth, but for the sake of the smoke, which would keep off the mosquitoes. He wrapped himself in his blankets and sat with his back against the reed wall of the house, smoking thoughtfully.

Arsat came through the doorway with noiseless steps and squatted down by the fire. The white man moved his outstretched legs a little.

'She breathes,' said Arsat in a low voice, anticipating the expected question. 'She breathes and burns as if with a great fire. She speaks not; she hears not—and burns!'

He paused for a moment, then asked in a quiet, incurious tone—

'Tuan, will she die?'

The white man moved his shoulders uneasily, and muttered in a hesitating manner—

'If such is her fate.'

'No, Tuan,' said Arsat calmly. 'If such is my fate. I hear, I see, I wait. I remember. Tuan, do you remember the old days? Do you remember my brother?'

'Yes,' said the white man. The Malay rose suddenly and went in. The other, sitting still outside, could hear the voice in the hut. Arsat said: 'Hear me! Speak!' His words were succeeded by a complete silence. 'O! Diamelen!' he cried suddenly. After that cry there was a deep sigh. Arsat came out and sank down again in his old place.

They sat in silence before the fire. There was no sound within the house, there was no sound near them; but far away on the lagoon they could hear the voices of the boatmen ringing fitful and distinct on the calm water. The fire in the bows of the sampan shone faintly in the distance with a hazy red glow. Then it died out. The voices ceased. The land and the water slept invisible, unstirring and mute. It was as though there had been nothing left in the world but the glitter of stars streaming, ceaseless and vain, through the black stillness of the night.

The white man gazed straight before him into the darkness with wide-open eyes. The fear and fascination, the inspiration and the wonder of death—of death near, unavoidable and unseen, soothed the unrest of his race and stirred the most indistinct, the most intimate of his thoughts. The ever-ready suspicion of evil, the gnawing suspicion that lurks in our hearts, flowed out into the stillness round him—into the stillness profound and dumb, and made it appear untrustworthy and infamous, like the placid and impenetrable mask of an unjustifiable violence. In that fleeting and powerful disturbance of his being the earth enfolded in the starlight peace became a shadowy country of inhuman strife, a battle-field of phantoms terrible and charming, august or ignoble, struggling ardently for the possession of our helpless hearts. An unquiet and mysterious country of inextinguishable desires and fears.

A plaintive murmur rose in the night; a murmur saddening and startling, as if the great solitudes of surrounding woods had tried to whisper into his ear the wisdom of their immense and lofty indifference. Sounds hesitating and vague floated in the air round him, shaped themselves slowly into words; and at last flowed on gently in a murmuring stream of soft and monotonous sentences. He stirred like a man waking up and changed his position slightly. Arsat, motionless and shadowy, sitting with bowed head under the stars, was speaking in a low and dreamy tone:

> '...for where can we lay down the heaviness of our trouble but in a friend's heart? A man must speak of war and of love. You, Tuan, know what war is, and you have seen me in time of danger seek death as other men seek life! A writing may be lost; a lie may be written; but what the eye has seen is truth and remains in the mind!'

'I remember,' said the white man quietly. Arsat went on with mournful composure.

'Therefore I shall speak to you of love. Speak in the night. Speak before both night and love are gone—and the eye of day looks upon my sorrow and my shame; upon my blackened face; upon my burnt-up heart.'

A sigh, short and faint, marked an almost imperceptible pause, and then his words flowed on, without a stir, without a gesture.

'After the time of trouble and war was over and you went away from my country in the pursuit of your desires, which we, men of the islands, cannot understand, I and my brother became again, as we had been before, the sword-bearers of the Ruler. You know we were men of family, belonging to a ruling race, and more fit than any to carry on our right shoulder the emblem of power. And in the time of prosperity Si Dendring showed us favour, as we, in time of sorrow, had showed to him the faithfulness of our courage. It was a time of peace. A time of deer-hunts and cock-fights; of idle talks and foolish squabbles between men whose bellies are full and weapons are rusty. But the sower watched the young rice-shoots grow up without fear, and the traders came and went, departed lean and returned fat into the river of peace. They brought news too. Brought lies and truth mixed together, so that no man knew when to rejoice and when to be sorry. We heard from them about you also. They had seen you here and had seen you there. And I was glad to hear, for I remembered the stirring times, and I always remembered you, Tuan, till the time came when my eyes could see nothing in the past, because they had looked upon the one who is dying there—in the house.'

He stopped to exclaim in an intense whisper, 'O Mara bahia! O Calamity!' then went on speaking a little louder.

'There's no worse enemy and no better friend than a brother, Tuan, for one brother knows another, and in perfect knowledge is strength for good or evil. I loved my brother. I went to him and told him that I could see nothing but one face, hear nothing but one voice. He told me: "Open your heart so that she can see what is in it—and wait. Patience is wisdom. Inchi Midah may die or our Ruler may throw off his fear of a woman!" I waited! You remember the lady with the veiled face, Tuan, and the fear of our Ruler before her cunning and temper. And if she wanted her servant, what could I do? But I fed the hunger of my heart on short glances and stealthy words. I loitered on the path to the bath-houses in the daytime, and when the sun had fallen behind the forest I crept along the jasmine hedges of the women's courtyard. Unseeing, we spoke to one another through the scent of flowers, through the veil of leaves, through the blades of long grass that stood still before our lips: so great was our prudence, so faint was the murmur of our great longing. The time passed swiftly…and there were whispers amongst women—and our enemies watched— my brother was gloomy, and I began to think of killing and of a fierce death…

'We are of a people who take what they want—like you whites. There is a time when a man should forget loyalty and respect. Might and authority are given to rulers, but to all men is given love and strength and courage. My brother said, "You shall take her from their midst. We are two who are like one." And I answered, "Let it be soon, for I find no warmth in sunlight that does not shine upon her." Our time came when the Ruler and all the great people went to the mouth of the river to fish by torchlight. There were hundreds of boats, and on the white sand, between the water and the forests, dwellings of leaves were built for the households of the Rajahs. The smoke of cooking-fires was like a blue mist of the evening, and many voices rang in it joyfully.

'While they were making the boats ready to beat up the fish, my brother came to me and said, "To-night!" I made ready my weapons, and when the time came our canoe took its place in the circle of boats carrying the torches. The lights blazed on the water, but behind the boats there was darkness. When the shouting began and the excitement made them like mad we dropped out. The water swallowed our fire, and we floated back to the shore that was dark with only here and there the glimmer of embers. We could hear the talk of slavegirls amongst the sheds. Then we found a place deserted and silent. We waited there. She came. She came running along the shore, rapid and leaving no trace, like a leaf driven by the wind into the sea. My brother said gloomily, "Go and take her; carry her into our boat." I lifted her in my arms. She panted. Her heart was beating against my breast. I said, "I take you from those people. You came to the cry of my heart, but my arms take you into my boat against the will of the great!" "It is right," said my brother. "We are men who take what we want and can hold it against many. We should have taken her in daylight." I said, "Let us be off," for since she was in my boat I began to think of our Ruler's many men. "Yes. Let us be off," said my brother. "We are cast out and this boat is our country now—and the sea is our refuge."

'He lingered with his foot on the shore, and I entreated him to hasten, for I remembered the strokes of her heart against my breast and thought that two men cannot withstand a hundred. We left, paddling downstream close to the bank; and as we passed by the creek where they were fishing, the great shouting had ceased, but the murmur of voices was loud like the humming of insects flying at noonday. The boats floated, clustered together, in the red light of torches, under a black roof of smoke; and men talked of their sport. Men that boasted, and praised, and jeered—men that would have been our friends in the morning, but on that night were already our enemies. We paddled swiftly past. We had no more friends in the country of our birth. She sat in the middle of the canoe with covered face; silent as she is now; unseeing as she is now—and I had no regret at what I was leaving because I could hear her breathing close to me—as I can hear her now.'

He paused, listened with his ear turned to the doorway, then shook his head and went on.

'My brother wanted to shout the cry of challenge—one cry only—to let the people know we were freeborn robbers that trusted our arms and the great sea. And again I begged him in the name of our love to be silent. Could I not hear her breathing close to me? I knew the pursuit would come quick enough. My brother loved me. He dipped his paddle without a splash. He only said, "There is half a man in you now—the other half is in that woman. I can wait. When you are a whole man again, you will come back with me here to shout defiance. We are sons of the same mother." I made no answer. All my strength and all my spirit were in my hands that held the paddle—for I longed to be with her in a safe place beyond the reach of men's anger and of women's spite.

'My love was so great, that I thought it could guide me to a country where death was unknown, if I could only escape from Inchi Midah's spite and from our Ruler's sword. We paddled with fury, breathing through our teeth. The blades bit deep into the smooth water. We passed out of the river; we flew in clear channels amongst the shallows. We skirted the black coast; we skirted the sand beaches where the sea speaks in whispers to the land; and the gleam of white sand flashed back past our boat, so swiftly she ran upon the water. We spoke not. Only once I said, "Sleep, Diamelen, for soon you may want all your strength." I heard the sweetness of her voice, but I never turned my head. The sun rose and still we went on. Water fell from my face like rain from a cloud. We flew in the light and heat. I never looked back, but I knew that my brother's eyes, behind me, were looking steadily ahead, for the boat went as straight as a bushman's dart, when it leaves the end of the sumpitan. There was no better paddler, no better steersman than my brother. Many times, together, we had won races in that canoe. But we never had put out our strength as we did then—then, when for the last time we paddled together! There was no braver or stronger man in our country than my brother. I could not spare the strength to turn my head and look at him, but every moment I heard the hiss of his breath getting louder behind me. Still he did not speak. The sun was high. The heat clung to my back like a flame of fire. My ribs were ready to burst, but I could no longer get enough air into my chest.

And then I felt I must cry out with my last breath, "Let us rest!" "Good!" he answered; and his voice was firm. He was strong. He was brave. He knew not fear and no fatigue...my brother!'

A rumour powerful and gentle, a rumour vast and faint; the rumour of trembling leaves, of stirring boughs, ran through the tangled depths of the forests, ran over the starry smoothness of the lagoon, and the water between the piles lapped the slimy timber once with a sudden splash. A breath of warm air touched the two men's faces and passed on with a mournful sound—a breath loud and short like an uneasy sigh of the dreaming earth.

Arsat went on in an even, low voice.

'We ran our canoe on the white beach of a little bay close to a long tongue of land that seemed to bar our road; a long wooded cape going far into the sea. My brother knew that place. Beyond the cape a river has its entrance. Through the jungle of that land there is a narrow path. We made a fire and cooked rice. Then we slept on the soft sand in the shade of our canoe, while she watched. No sooner had I closed my eyes than I heard her cry of alarm. We leaped up. The sun was halfway down the sky already, and coming in sight in the opening of the bay we saw a prau manned by many paddlers. We knew it at once; it was one of our Rajah's praus. They were watching the shore, and saw us. They beat the gong, and turned the head of the prau into the bay. I felt my heart become weak within my breast. Diamelen sat on the sand and covered her face. There was no escape by sea. My brother laughed. He had the gun you had given him, Tuan, before you went away, but there was only a handful of powder.

'He spoke to me quickly: "Run with her along the path. I shall keep them back, for they have no firearms, and landing in the face of a man with a gun is certain death for some. Run with her. On the other side of that wood there is a fisherman's house— and a canoe. When I have fired all the shots I will follow. I am a great runner, and before they can come up we shall be gone. I will hold out as long as I can, for she is but a woman—that can neither run nor fight, but she has your heart in her weak hands." He dropped behind the canoe. The prau was coming.

'She and I ran, and as we rushed along the path I heard shots. My brother fired—once—twice—and the booming of the gong ceased. There was silence behind us. That neck of land is narrow. Before I heard my brother fire the third shot I saw the shelving shore, and I saw the water again: the mouth of a broad river. We crossed a grassy glade. We ran down to the water. I saw a low hut above the black mud, and a small canoe hauled up. I heard another shot behind me. I thought, "That is his last charge." We rushed down to the canoe; a man came running from the hut, but I leaped on him, and we rolled together in the mud. Then I got up, and he lay still at my feet. I don't know whether I had killed him or not. I and Diamelen pushed the canoe afloat. I heard yells behind me, and I saw my brother run across the glade. Many men were bounding after him. I took her in my arms and threw her into the boat, then leaped in myself. When I looked back I saw that my brother had fallen. He fell and was up again, but the men were closing round him. He shouted, "I am coming!" The men were close to him. I looked. Many men. Then I looked at her. Tuan, I pushed the canoe! I pushed it into deep water. She was kneeling forward looking at me, and I said, "Take your paddle," while I struck the water with mine.

'Tuan, I heard him cry. I heard him cry my name twice; and I heard voices shouting, "Kill! Strike!" I never turned back. I heard him calling my name again with a great shriek, as when life is going out together with the voice—and I never turned my head. My own name! My brother! Three times he called—but I was not afraid of life. Was she not there in that canoe? And could I not with her find a country where death is forgotten—where death is unknown?'

The white man sat up. Arsat rose and stood, an indistinct and silent figure above the dying embers of the fire. Over the lagoon a mist drifting and low had crept, erasing slowly the glittering images of the stars. And now a great expanse of white vapour covered the land: flowed cold and grey in the darkness, eddied in noiseless whirls round the tree-trunks and about the platform of the house, which seemed to float upon a restless and impalpable illusion of a sea; seemed the only thing surviving the destruction of the world by that undulating and voiceless phantom of a flood. Only far away the tops of the trees stood outlined on the twinkle of heaven, like a somber and forbidding shore—a coast deceptive, pitiless and black.

Arsat's voice vibrated loudly in the profound peace.

'I had her there! I had her! To get her I would have faced all mankind. But I had her—and—'

His words went out ringing into the empty distances. He paused, and seemed to listen to them dying away very far—beyond help and beyond recall. Then he said quietly—

'Tuan, I loved my brother.'

A breath of wind made him shiver. High above his head, high above the silent sea of mist the drooping leaves of the palms rattled together with a mournful and expiring sound. The white man stretched his legs. His chin rested on his chest, and he murmured sadly without lifting his head—

'We all love our brothers.'

Arsat burst out with an intense whispering violence—

'What did I care who died? I wanted peace in my own heart.'

He seemed to hear a stir in the house–listened–then stepped in noiselessly. The white man stood up. A breeze was coming in fitful puffs. The stars shone paler as if they had retreated into the frozen depths of immense space. After a chill gust of wind there were a few seconds of perfect calm and absolute silence. Then from behind the black and wavy line of the forests a column of golden light shot up into the heavens and spread over the semicircle of the eastern horizon. The sun had risen. The mist lifted, broke into drifting patches, vanished into thin flying wreaths; and the unveiled lagoon lay, polished and black, in the heavy shadows at the foot of the wall of trees. A white eagle rose over it with a slanting and ponderous flight, reached the clear sunshine and appeared dazzlingly brilliant for a moment, then soaring higher, became a dark and motionless speck before it vanished into the blue as if it had left the earth for ever. The white man, standing gazing upwards before the doorway, heard in the hut a confused and broken murmur of distracted words ending with a loud groan. Suddenly Arsat stumbled out with outstretched hands, shivered, and stood still for some time with fixed eyes. Then he said—

'She burns no more.'

Before his face the sun showed its edge above the tree-tops, rising steadily. The breeze freshened; a great brilliance burst upon the lagoon, sparkled on the rippling water. The forests came out of the clear shadows of the morning, became distinct, as if they had rushed nearer—to stop short in a great stir of leaves, of nodding boughs, of swaying branches. In the merciless sunshine the whisper of unconscious life grew louder, speaking in an incomprehensible voice round the dumb darkness of that human sorrow. Arsat's eyes wandered slowly, then stared at the rising sun.

'I can see nothing,' he said half aloud to himself.

'There is nothing,' said the white man, moving to the edge of the platform and waving his hand to his boat. A shout came faintly over the lagoon and the sampan began to glide towards the abode of the friend of ghosts.

'If you want to come with me, I will wait all the morning,' said the white man, looking away upon the water.

'No, Tuan,' said Arsat softly. 'I shall not eat or sleep in this house, but I must first see my road. Now I can see nothing—see nothing! There is no light and no peace in the world; but there is death—death for many. We were sons of the same mother—and d her. 'Twenty-eight guineas, Madame.'

ht guineas.' Rosemary gave no sign. She laid the
; she buttoned her gloves again. Twenty-eight
one is rich—she looked vague. She stared at a
like a plump hen above the shopman's head, and
eamy as she answered: 'Well, keep it for me—will

man had already bowed as though keeping it for
uman being could ask. He would be willing, of
for her for ever.

door shut with a click. She was outside on the
e winter afternoon. Rain was falling, and with
the dark came too, spinning down like ashes.
itter taste in the air, and the new-lighted lamps
ere the lights in the houses opposite. Dimly they
ting something. And people hurried by, hidden
umbrellas. Rosemary felt a strange pang. She
o her breast; she wished she had the little box,
f course, the car was there. She'd only to cross
still she waited. There are moments, horrible
hen _____ _____ shelter and looks out.

I left him in the midst of enemies; but I am going back now.'

He drew a long breath and went on in a dreamy tone.

'In a little while I shall see clear enough to strike—to strike.
But she has died, and...now...darkness.'

He flung his arms wide open, let them fall along his body, then
stood still with unmoved face and stony eyes, staring at the sun.
The white man got down into his canoe. The polers ran smartly
along the sides of the boat, looking over their shoulders at the
beginning of a weary journey. High in the stern, his head muffled
up in white rags, the juragan sat moody, letting his paddle trail in
the water. The white man, leaning with both arms over the grass
roof of the little cabin, looked back at the shining ripple of the
boat's wake. Before the sampan passed out of the lagoon into the
creek he lifted his eyes. Arsat had not moved. In the searching
clearness of crude sunshine he was still standing before the house,
he was still looking through the great light of a cloudless day into
the hopeless darkness of the world.

36

A CUP OF TEA

Katherine Mansfield

Vulgarity in a certain class suddenly snaps at the sight of envy.

Rosemary Fell was not exactly beautiful. No, you couldn't have called her beautiful. Pretty? Well, if you took her to pieces. But why be so cruel as to take anyone to pieces? She was young, brilliant, extremely modern, exquisitely well dressed, amazingly well read in the newest of the new books, and her parties were the most delicious mixture of the really important people and artists—quaint creatures, discoveries of hers, some of them too terrifying for words, but others quite presentable and amusing.

Rosemary had been married two years. She had a duck of a boy. No, not Peter—Michael. And her husband absolutely adored her. They were rich, really rich, not just comfortably well off, which is odious and stuffy and sounds like one's grandparents. But if Rosemary wanted to shop she would go to Paris as you and I would go to Bond Street. If she wanted to buy flowers, the car pulled up at that perfect shop in Regent Street, and Rosemary inside the shop just gazed in her dazzled, rather exotic way, and said: 'I want those and those and those. Give me four bunches of those. And that jar of roses. Yes, I'll have all the roses in the jar. No, no lilac. I hate lilac. It's got no shape.' The attendant bowed and put the lilac out of sight, as though this was only too true; lilac was dreadfully shapeless. 'Give me those stumpy little tulips. Those red and white ones.' And she was followed to the car by a thin shopgirl staggering under an immense white paper armful that looked like a baby in long clothes.

One winter afternoo[n]
little antique shop in C
For one thing, one usua
who kept it was ridicu
whenever she came in.
he could scarcely speak
was something.

'You see, Madam,'
tones, 'I love my thing
sell them to someone
not that fine feeling
unrolled a tiny square
counter with his pale

Today it was a li[ttle]
had shown it to nobo
a glaze so fine it loo
On the lid a minut[e]
more minute creatu
hat, really no bigge[r]
it had green ribbon
cherub floating abo[ut]

Rosemary took
took off her gloves
[m]uch. She loved i
[...]g the cream
[...] how cha
[...]an, in

murmur reache[d]
'Twenty-eig[ht]
little box dow[n]
guineas. Even i[f]
plump tea-kettle
her voice was dr[e]
you? I'll—'

But the shop
her was all any
course, to keep i

The discreet
step, gazing at th
the rain it seeme[d]
There was a cold
looked sad. Sad w
burned as if regre[t]
under their hatefu[l]
pressed her muff
too, to cling to. O
the pavement. Bu[t]
moments in life,
and it's awful. On[e]
go home and hav[e]
of thinking that, a
she come from?—
like a sigh, almost
to you a moment?'

'Speak to me?'
creature with enorm
herself, who clutche[d]
shivered as though
'M-madame,' st[a]
the price of a cup o[f]

'A cup of tea?' There was something simple, sincere in that voice; it wasn't in the least the voice of a beggar. 'Then have you no money at all?' asked Rosemary.

'None, Madam,' came the answer.

'How extraordinary!' Rosemary peered through the dusk, and the girl gazed back at her. How more than extraordinary! And suddenly it seemed to Rosemary such an adventure. It was like something out of a novel by Dostoevsky, this meeting in the dusk. Supposing she took the girl home? Supposing she did do one of those things she was always reading about or seeing on the stage, what would happen? It would be thrilling. And she heard herself saying afterwards to the amazement of her friends: 'I simply took her home with me,' as she stepped forward and said to that dim person beside her: 'Come home to tea with me.'

The girl drew back startled. She even stopped shivering for a moment. Rosemary put out a hand and touched her arm. 'I mean it,' she said, smiling. And she felt how simple and kind her smile was. 'Why won't you? Do. Come home with me now in my car and have tea.'

'You—you don't mean it, Madam,' said the girl, and there was pain in her voice.

'But I do,' cried Rosemary. 'I want you to. To please me. Come along.'

The girl put her fingers to her lips and her eyes devoured Rosemary. 'You're—you're not taking me to the police station?' she stammered.

'The police station!' Rosemary laughed out. 'Why should I be so cruel? No, I only want to make you warm and to hear—anything you care to tell me.'

Hungry people are easily led. The footman held the door of the car open, and a moment later they were skimming through the dusk.

'There!' said Rosemary. She had a feeling of triumph as she

slipped her hand through the velvet strap. She could have said, 'Now I've got you,' as she gazed at the little captive she had netted. But of course she meant it kindly. Oh, more than kindly. She was going to prove to this girl that—wonderful things did happen in life, that—fairy godmothers were real, that—rich people had hearts, and that women were sisters. She turned impulsively, saying: 'Don't be frightened. After all, why shouldn't you come back with me? We're both women. If I'm the more fortunate, you ought to expect—'

But happily at that moment, for she didn't know how the sentence was going to end, the car stopped. The bell was rung, the door opened, and with a charming, protecting, almost embracing movement, Rosemary drew the other into the hall. Warmth, softness, light, a sweet scent, all those things so familiar to her she never even thought about them, she watched that other receive. It was fascinating. She was like the little rich girl in her nursery with all the cupboards to open, all the boxes to unpack.

'Come, come upstairs,' said Rosemary, longing to begin to be generous. 'Come up to my room.' And, besides, she wanted to spare this poor little thing from being stared at by the servants; she decided as they mounted the stairs she would not even ring for Jeanne, but take off her things by herself. The great thing was to be natural!

And 'There!' cried Rosemary again, as they reached her beautiful big bedroom with the curtains drawn, the fire leaping on her wonderful lacquer furniture, her gold cushions and the primrose and blue rugs.

The girl stood just inside the door; she seemed dazed. But Rosemary didn't mind that.

'Come and sit down,' she cried, dragging her big chair up to the fire, 'in this comfy chair. Come and get warm. You look so dreadfully cold.'

'I daren't, Madam,' said the girl, and she edged backwards.

'Oh, please,'—Rosemary ran forward—'you mustn't be

frightened, you mustn't, really. Sit down, and when I've taken off my things we shall go into the next room and have tea and be cozy. Why are you afraid?' And gently she half pushed the thin figure into its deep cradle.

But there was no answer. The girl stayed just as she had been put, with her hands by her sides and her mouth slightly open. To be quite sincere, she looked rather stupid. But Rosemary wouldn't acknowledge it. She leant over her, saying: 'Won't you take off your hat? Your pretty hair is all wet. And one is so much more comfortable without a hat, isn't one?'

There was a whisper that sounded like 'Very good, Madam,' and the crushed hat was taken off.

'Let me help you off with your coat, too,' said Rosemary.

The girl stood up. But she held on to the chair with one hand and let Rosemary pull. It was quite an effort. The other scarcely helped her at all. She seemed to stagger like a child, and the thought came and went through Rosemary's mind, that if people wanted helping they must respond a little, just a little, otherwise it became very difficult indeed. And what was she to do with the coat now? She left it on the floor, and the hat too. She was just going to take a cigarette off the mantel-piece when the girl said quickly, but so lightly and strangely: 'I'm very sorry, Madam, but I'm going to faint. I shall go off, Madam, if I don't have something.'

'Good heavens, how thoughtless I am!' Rosemary rushed to the bell.

'Tea! Tea at once! And some brandy immediately!'

The maid was gone again, but the girl almost cried out. 'No, I don't want no brandy. I never drink brandy. It's a cup of tea I want, madam.' And she burst into tears.

It was a terrible and fascinating moment. Rosemary knelt beside her chair.

'Don't cry, poor little thing,' she said. 'Don't cry.' And she gave the other her lace handkerchief. She really was touched beyond words. She put her arm round those thin, bird-like shoulders.

Now at last the other forgot to be shy, forgot everything except that they were both women, and gasped out: 'I can't go on no longer like this. I can't bear it. I shall do away with myself. I can't bear no more.'

'You shan't have to. I'll look after you. Don't cry any more. Don't you see what a good thing it was that you met me? We'll have tea and you'll tell me everything. And I shall arrange something. I promise. Do stop crying. It's so exhausting. Please!'

The other did stop just in time for Rosemary to get up before the tea came. She had the table placed between them. She plied the poor little creature with everything, all the sandwiches, all the bread and butter, and every time her cup was empty she filled it with tea, cream and sugar. People always said sugar was so nourishing. As for herself she didn't eat; she smoked and looked away tactfully so that the other should not be shy.

And really the effect of that slight meal was marvellous. When the tea-table was carried away a new being, a light, frail creature with tangled hair, dark lips, deep, lighted eyes, lay back in the big chair in a kind of sweet langour, looking at the blaze. Rosemary lit a fresh cigarette; it was time to begin.

'And when did you have your last meal?' she asked softly.

But at that moment the door-handle turned.

'Rosemary, may I come in?' It was Philip.

'Of course.'

He came in. 'Oh, I'm so sorry,' he said, and stopped and stared.

'It's quite all right,' said Rosemary smiling. 'This is my friend, Miss—'

'Smith, Madam,' said the languid figure, who was strangely still and unafraid.

'Smith,' said Rosemary. 'We are going to have a little talk.'

'Oh, yes,' said Philip. 'Quite,' and his eye caught sight of the coat and hat on the floor. He came over to the fire and turned his back to it. 'It's a beastly afternoon,' he said curiously, still looking at that listless figure, looking at its hands and boots, and then at Rosemary again.

'Yes, isn't it?' said Rosemary enthusiastically. 'Vile.'

Philip smiled his charming smile. 'As a matter of fact,' said he, 'I wanted you to come into the library for a moment. Would you? Will Miss Smith excuse us?'

The big eyes were raised to him, but Rosemary answered for her. 'Of course she will.' And they went out of the room together.

'I say,' said Philip, when they were alone. 'Explain. Who is she? What does it all mean?'

Rosemary, laughing, leaned against the door and said: 'I picked her up in Curzon Street. Really. She's a real pick-up. She asked me for the price of a cup of tea, and I brought her home with me.'

'But what on earth are you going to do with her?' cried Philip.

'Be nice to her,' said Rosemary quickly. 'Be frightfully nice to her. Look after her. I don't know how. We haven't talked yet. But show her—treat her—make her feel—'

'My darling girl,' said Philip, 'you're quite mad, you know. It simply can't be done.'

'I knew you'd say that,' retorted Rosemary. 'Why not? I want to. Isn't that a reason? And besides, one's always reading about these things. I decided—'

'But,' said Philip slowly, and he cut the end of a cigar, 'she's so astonishingly pretty.'

'Pretty?' Rosemary was so surprised that she blushed. 'Do you think so? I—I hadn't thought about it.'

'Good Lord!' Philip struck a match. 'She's absolutely lovely. Look again, my child. I was bowled over when I came into your room just now. However ... I think you're making a ghastly mistake. Sorry, darling, if I'm crude and all that. But let me know if Miss Smith is going to dine with us in time for me to look up *The Milliner's Gazette*.'

'You absurd creature!' said Rosemary, and she went out of the library, but not back to her bedroom. She went to her writing-room and sat down at her desk. Pretty! Absolutely lovely! Bowled over! Her heart beat like a heavy bell. Pretty! Lovely! She drew her cheque book towards her. But no, cheques would be no use, of course. She opened a drawer and took out five pound notes, looked at them, put two back, and holding the three squeezed in her hand, she went back to her bedroom.

Half an hour later Philip was still in the library, when Rosemary came in.

'I only wanted to tell you,' said she, and she leaned against the door again and looked at him with her dazzled exotic gaze, 'Miss Smith won't dine with us tonight.'

Philip put down the paper. 'Oh, what's happened? Previous engagement?'

Rosemary came over and sat down on his knee. 'She insisted on going,' said she, 'so I gave the poor little thing a present of money. I couldn't keep her against her will, could I?' she added softly.

Rosemary had just done her hair, darkened her eyes a little, and put on her pearls. She put up her hands and touched Philip's cheeks.

'Do you like me?' said she, and her tone, sweet, husky, troubled him.

'I like you awfully,' he said, and he held her tighter. 'Kiss me.'

There was a pause.

Then Rosemary said dreamily, 'I saw a fascinating little box today. It cost twenty-eight guineas. May I have it?'

Philip jumped her on his knee. 'You may, little wasteful one,' said he.

But that was not really what Rosemary wanted to say.

'Philip,' she whispered, and she pressed his head against her bosom, 'am I *pretty*?'

37

SECOND BEST

D.H. Lawrence

Feelings and even moments which at times seems not to be love may also metaphorically be connected with love.

'Oh, I'm tired!' Frances exclaimed petulantly, and in the same instant she dropped down on the turf, near the hedge-bottom. Anne stood a moment surprised, then, accustomed to the vagaries of her beloved Frances, said:

'Well, and aren't you always likely to be tired, after travelling that blessed long way from Liverpool yesterday?' and she plumped down beside her sister. Anne was a wise young body of fourteen, very buxom, brimming with common sense. Frances was much older, about twenty-three, and whimsical, spasmodic. She was the beauty and the clever child of the family. She plucked the goose-grass buttons from her dress in a nervous, desperate fashion. Her beautiful profile, looped above with black hair, warm with the dusky-and-scarlet complexion of a pear, was calm as a mask, her thin brown hand plucked nervously.

'It's not the journey,' she said, objecting to Anne's obtuseness. Anne looked inquiringly at her darling. The young girl, in her self-confident, practical way, proceeded to reckon up this whimsical creature. But suddenly she found herself full in the eyes of Frances; felt two dark, hectic eyes flaring challenge at her, and she shrank away. Frances was peculiar for these great, exposed looks, which disconcerted people by their violence and their suddenness.

'What's a matter, poor old duck?' asked Anne, as she folded the slight, wilful form of her sister in her arms. Frances laughed shakily, and nestled down for comfort on the budding breasts of the strong girl.

'Oh, I'm only a bit tired,' she murmured, on the point of tears.

'Well, of course you are, what do you expect?' soothed Anne. It was a joke to Frances that Anne should play elder, almost mother to her. But then, Anne was in her unvexed teens; men were like big dogs to her: while Frances, at twenty-three, suffered a good deal.

The country was intensely morning-still. On the common everything shone beside its shadow, and the hillside gave off heat in silence. The brown turf seemed in a low state of combustion, the leaves of the oaks were scorched brown. Among the blackish foliage in the distance shone the small red and orange of the village.

The willows in the brook-course at the foot of the common suddenly shook with a dazzling effect like diamonds. It was a puff of wind. Anne resumed her normal position. She spread her knees, and put in her lap a handful of hazel nuts, whity-green leafy things, whose one cheek was tanned between brown and pink. These she began to crack and eat. Frances, with bowed head, mused bitterly.

'Eh, you know Tom Smedley?' began the young girl, as she pulled a tight kernel out of its shell.

'I suppose so,' replied Frances sarcastically.

'Well, he gave me a wild rabbit what he'd caught, to keep with my tame one—and it's living.'

'That's a good thing,' said Frances, very detached and ironic.

'Well, it is! He reckoned he'd take me to Ollerton Feast, but he never did. Look here, he took a servant from the rectory; I saw him.'

'So he ought,' said Frances.

'No, he oughtn't! and I told him so. And I told him I should tell you—an' I have done.'

Click and snap went a nut between her teeth. She sorted out the kernel, and chewed complacently.

'It doesn't make much difference,' said Frances.

'Well, 'appen it doesn't; but I was mad with him all the same.'

'Why?'

'Because I was; he's no right to go with a servant.'

'He's a perfect right,' persisted Frances, very just and cold.

'No, he hasn't, when he'd said he'd take me.'

Frances burst into a laugh of amusement and relief.

'Oh, no; I'd forgot that,' she said, adding, 'And what did he say when you promised to tell me?'

'He laughed and said, "she won't fret her fat over that".'

'And she won't,' sniffed Frances.

There was silence. The common, with its sere, blonde-headed thistles, its heaps of silent bramble, its brown-husked gorse in the glare of sunshine, seemed visionary. Across the brook began the immense pattern of agriculture, white chequering of barley stubble, brown squares of wheat, khaki patches of pasture, red stripes of fallow, with the woodland and the tiny village dark like ornaments, leading away to the distance, right to the hills, where the check-pattern grew smaller and smaller, till, in the blackish haze of heat, far off, only the tiny white squares of barley stubble showed distinct.

'Eh, I say, here's a rabbit hole!' cried Anne suddenly. 'Should we watch if one comes out? You won't have to fidget, you know.'

The two girls sat perfectly still. Frances watched certain objects in her surroundings: they had a peculiar, unfriendly look about them: the weight of greenish elderberries on their purpling stalks; the twinkling of the yellowing crab-apples that clustered high up in the hedge, against the sky: the exhausted, limp leaves of the primroses lying flat in the hedge-bottom: all looked strange to her. Then her eyes caught a movement. A mole was moving silently over the warm, red soil, nosing, shuffling hither and thither, flat, and dark as a shadow, shifting about, and as suddenly brisk, and as silent, like a very ghost of *joie de vivre*. Frances started, from habit was about to call on Anne to kill the little pest. But, to-day, her lethargy of unhappiness was too much for her. She watched the little brute paddling, snuffing, touching things to discover them, running in blindness, delighted to ecstasy by the sunlight and the hot, strange things that caressed its belly and its nose. She felt a keen pity for the little creature.

'Eh, our Fran, look there! It's a mole.'

Anne was on her feet, standing watching the dark, unconscious beast. Frances frowned with anxiety.

'It doesn't run off, does it?' said the young girl softly. Then she stealthily approached the creature. The mole paddled fumblingly away. In an instant Anne put her foot upon it, not too heavily. Frances could see the struggling, swimming movement of the little pink hands of the brute, the twisting and twitching of its pointed nose, as it wrestled under the sole of the boot.

'It does wriggle!' said the bonny girl, knitting her brows in a frown at the eerie sensation. Then she bent down to look at her trap. Frances could now see, beyond the edge of the boot-sole, the heaving of the velvet shoulders, the pitiful turning of the sightless face, the frantic rowing of the flat, pink hands.

'Kill the thing,' she said, turning away her face.

'Oh—I'm not,' laughed Anne, shrinking. 'You can, if you like.'

'I don't like,' said Frances, with quiet intensity.

After several dabbling attempts, Anne succeeded in picking up the little animal by the scruff of its neck. It threw back its head, flung its long blind snout from side to side, the mouth open in a peculiar oblong, with tiny pinkish teeth at the edge. The blind, frantic mouth gaped and writhed. The body, heavy and clumsy, hung scarcely moving.

'Isn't it a snappy little thing,' observed Anne twisting to avoid the teeth.

'What are you going to do with it?' asked Frances sharply.

'It's got to be killed—look at the damage they do. I s'll take it home and let dadda or somebody kill it. I'm not going to let it go.'

She swaddled the creature clumsily in her pocket-handkerchief and sat down beside her sister. There was an interval of silence, during which Anne combated the efforts of the mole.

'You've not had much to say about Jimmy this time. Did you see him often in Liverpool?' Anne asked suddenly.

'Once or twice,' replied Frances, giving no sign of how the question troubled her.

'And aren't you sweet on him any more, then?'

'I should think I'm not, seeing that he's engaged.'

'Engaged? Jimmy Barrass! Well, of all things! I never thought he'd get engaged.'

'Why not, he's as much right as anybody else?' snapped Frances.

Anne was fumbling with the mole.

''Appen so,' she said at length; 'but I never thought Jimmy would, though.'

'Why not?' snapped Frances.

'I don't know—this blessed mole, it'll not keep still!—who's he got engaged to?'

'How should I know?'

'I thought you'd ask him; you've known him long enough. I s'd think he thought he'd get engaged now he's a Doctor of Chemistry.'

Frances laughed in spite of herself.

'What's that got to do with it?' she asked.

'I'm sure it's got a lot. He'll want to feel somebody now, so he's got engaged. Hey, stop it; go in!'

But at this juncture the mole almost succeeded in wriggling clear. It wrestled and twisted frantically, waved its pointed blind head, its mouth standing open like a little shaft, its big, wrinkled hands spread out.

'Go in with you!' urged Anne, poking the little creature with her forefinger, trying to get it back into the handkerchief.

Suddenly the mouth turned like a spark on her finger.

'Oh!' she cried, 'he's bit me.'

She dropped him to the floor. Dazed, the blind creature fumbled round. Frances felt like shrieking. She expected him to dart away in a flash, like a mouse, and there he remained groping; she wanted to cry to him to be gone. Anne, in a sudden decision of wrath, caught up her sister's walking-cane. With one blow the mole was dead. Frances was startled and shocked. One moment the little wretch was fussing in the heat, and the next it lay like a little bag, inert and black—not a struggle, scarce a quiver.

'It is dead!' Frances said breathlessly. Anne took her finger from her mouth, looked at the tiny pinpricks, and said:

'Yes, he is, and I'm glad. They're vicious little nuisances, moles are.'

With which her wrath vanished. She picked up the dead animal.

'Hasn't it got a beautiful skin,' she mused, stroking the fur with her forefinger, then with her cheek.

'Mind,' said Frances sharply. 'You'll have the blood on your skirt!'

One ruby drop of blood hung on the small snout, ready to fall. Anne shook it off on to some harebells. Frances suddenly became calm; in that moment, grown-up.

'I suppose they have to be killed,' she said, and a certain rather dreary indifference succeeded to her grief. The twinkling crab-apples, the glitter of brilliant willows now seemed to her trifling, scarcely worth the notice. Something had died in her, so that things lost their poignancy. She was calm, indifference overlying her quiet sadness. Rising, she walked down to the brook course.

'Here, wait for me,' cried Anne, coming tumbling after.

Frances stood on the bridge, looking at the red mud trodden into pockets by the feet of cattle. There was not a drain of water left, but everything smelled green, succulent. Why did she care so little for Anne, who was so fond of her? she asked herself. Why did she care so little for anyone? She did not know, but she felt a rather stubborn pride in her isolation and indifference.

They entered a field where stooks of barley stood in rows, the straight, blonde tresses of the corn streaming on to the ground. The stubble was bleached by the intense summer, so that the expanse glared white. The next field was sweet and soft with a second crop of seeds; thin, straggling clover whose little pink knobs rested prettily in the dark green. The scent was faint and sickly. The girls came up in single file, Frances leading.

Near the gate a young man was mowing with the scythe some fodder for the afternoon feed of the cattle. As he saw the girls he left off working and waited in an aimless kind of way. Frances was dressed in white muslin, and she walked with dignity, detached and forgetful. Her lack of agitation, her simple, unheeding advance made him nervous. She had loved the far-off Jimmy for five years, having had in return his half-measures. This man only affected her slightly.

Tom was of medium stature, energetic in build. His smooth, fair-skinned face was burned red, not brown, by the sun, and this ruddiness enhanced his appearance of good humour and easiness. Being a year older than Frances, he would have courted her long ago had she been so inclined. As it was, he had gone his uneventful way amiably, chatting with many a girl, but remaining unattached, free of trouble for the most part. Only he knew he wanted a woman. He hitched his trousers just a trifle self-consciously as the girls approached. Frances was a rare, delicate kind of being, whom he realized with a queer and delicious stimulation in his veins. She gave him a slight sense of suffocation. Somehow, this morning, she affected him more than usual. She was dressed in white. He, however, being matter-of-fact in his mind, did not realize. His feeling had never become conscious, purposive.

Frances knew what she was about. Tom was ready to love her as soon as she would show him. Now that she could not have Jimmy, she did not poignantly care. Still, she would have something. If she could not have the best—Jimmy, whom she knew to be something of a snob—she would have the second best, Tom. She advanced rather indifferently.

'You are back, then!' said Tom. She marked the touch of uncertainty in his voice.

'No,' she laughed, 'I'm still in Liverpool,' and the undertone of intimacy made him burn.

'This isn't you, then?' he asked.

Her heart leapt up in approval. She looked in his eyes, and for a second was with him.

'Why, what do you think?' she laughed.

He lifted his hat from his head with a distracted little gesture. She liked him, his quaint ways, his humour, his ignorance, and his slow masculinity.

'Here, look here, Tom Smedley,' broke in Anne.

'A moudiwarp! Did you find it dead?' he asked.

'No, it bit me,' said Anne.

'Oh, aye! An' that got your rag out, did it?'

'No, it didn't!' Anne scolded sharply. 'Such language!'

'Oh, what's up wi' it?'

'I can't bear you to talk broad.'

'Can't you?'

He glanced at Frances.

'It isn't nice,' Frances said. She did not care, really. The vulgar speech jarred on her as a rule; Jimmy was a gentleman. But Tom's manner of speech did not matter to her.

'I like you to talk nicely,' she added.

'Do you,' he replied, tilting his hat, stirred.

'And generally you do, you know,' she smiled.

'I s'll have to have a try,' he said, rather tensely gallant.

'What?' she asked brightly.

'To talk nice to you,' he said. Frances coloured furiously, bent her head for a moment, then laughed gaily, as if she liked this clumsy hint.

'Eh now, you mind what you're saying,' cried Anne, giving the young man an admonitory pat.

'You wouldn't have to give yon mole many knocks like that,' he teased, relieved to get on safe ground, rubbing his arm.

'No indeed, it died in one blow,' said Frances, with a flippancy that was hateful to her.

'You're not so good at knockin' 'em?' he said, turning to her.

'I don't know, if I'm cross,' she said decisively.

'No?' he replied, with alert attentiveness.

'I could,' she added, harder, 'if it was necessary.'

He was slow to feel her difference.

'And don't you consider it is necessary?' he asked, with misgiving.

'W—ell—is it?' she said, looking at him steadily, coldly.

'I reckon it is,' he replied, looking away, but standing stubborn.

She laughed quickly.

'But it isn't necessary for me,' she said, with slight contempt.

'Yes, that's quite true,' he answered.

She laughed in a shaky fashion.

'I know it is,' she said; and there was an awkward pause.

'Why, would you like me to kill moles then?' she asked tentatively, after a while.

'They do us a lot of damage,' he said, standing firm on his own ground, angered.

'Well, I'll see the next time I come across one,' she promised, defiantly. Their eyes met, and she sank before him, her pride troubled. He felt uneasy and triumphant and baffled, as if fate had gripped him. She smiled as she departed.

'Well,' said Anne, as the sisters went through the wheat stubble; 'I don't know what you two's been jawing about, I'm sure.'

'Don't you?' laughed Frances significantly.

'No, I don't. But, at any rate, Tom Smedley's a good deal better to my thinking.'

'Perhaps he is,' said Frances coldly.

And the next day, after a secret, persistent hunt, she found another mole playing in the heat. She killed it, and in the evening, when Tom came to the gate to smoke his pipe after supper, she took him the dead creature.

'Here you are then!' she said.

'Did you catch it?' he replied, taking the velvet corpse into his fingers and examining it minutely. This was to hide his trepidation.

'Did you think I couldn't?' she asked, her face very near his.

'Nay, I didn't know.'

She laughed in his face, a strange little laugh that caught her breath, all agitation, and tears, and recklessness of desire. He looked frightened and upset. She put her hand to his arm.

'Shall you go out wi' me?' he asked, in a difficult, troubled tone.

She turned her face away, with a shaky laugh. The blood came up in him, strong, overmastering. He resisted it. But it drove him down, and he was carried away. Seeing the winsome, frail nape of her neck, fierce love came upon him for her, and tenderness.

'We s'll 'ave to tell your mother,' he said. And he stood, suffering, resisting his passion for her.

'Yes,' she replied, in a dead voice. But there was a thrill of pleasure in this death.

38

ARABY

James Joyce

Puppy Love sometimes is at the brink of obsessions.

North Richmond Street, being blind, was a quiet street except at the hour when the Christian Brothers' School set the boys free. An uninhabited house of two storeys stood at the blind end, detached from its neighbours in a square ground. The other houses of the street, conscious of decent lives within them, gazed at one another with brown imperturbable faces.

The former tenant of our house, a priest, had died in the back drawing-room. Air, musty from having been long enclosed, hung in all the rooms, and the waste room behind the kitchen was littered with old useless papers. Among these I found a few paper-covered books, the pages of which were curled and damp: *The Abbot*, by Walter Scott, *The Devout Communicant* and *The Memoirs of Vidocq*. I liked the last best because its leaves were yellow. The wild garden behind the house contained a central apple-tree and a few straggling bushes under one of which I found the late tenant's rusty bicycle-pump. He had been a very charitable priest; in his will he had left all his money to institutions and the furniture of his house to his sister.

When the short days of winter came dusk fell before we had well eaten our dinners. When we met in the street the houses had grown sombre. The space of sky above us was the colour of ever-changing violet and towards it the lamps of the street lifted their feeble lanterns. The cold air stung us and we played till our bodies glowed. Our shouts echoed in the silent street. The career of our play brought us through the dark muddy lanes behind the houses where we ran the gauntlet of the rough tribes from the cottages, to the back doors of the dark dripping gardens where odours arose from the ashpits, to the dark odorous stables where a coachman smoothed and combed the horse or shook music from the buckled harness. When we returned to the street light from the kitchen windows had filled the areas. If my uncle was seen turning the corner we hid in the shadow until we had seen him safely housed. Or if Mangan's sister came out on the doorstep to call her brother in to his tea we watched her from our shadow peer up and down the street. We waited to see whether she would remain or go in and, if she remained, we left our shadow and walked up to Mangan's steps resignedly. She was waiting for us, her figure defined by the light from the half-opened door. Her brother always teased her before he obeyed and I stood by the railings looking at her. Her dress swung as she moved her body and the soft rope of her hair tossed from side to side.

Every morning I lay on the floor in the front parlour watching her door. The blind was pulled down to within an inch of the sash so that I could not be seen. When she came out on the doorstep my heart leaped. I ran to the hall, seized my books and followed her. I kept her brown figure always in my eye and, when we came near the point at which our ways diverged, I quickened my pace and passed her. This happened morning after morning. I had never spoken to her, except for a few casual words, and yet her name was like a summons to all my foolish blood.

Her image accompanied me even in places the most hostile to romance. On Saturday evenings when my aunt went marketing I had to go to carry some of the parcels. We walked through the flaring streets, jostled by drunken men and bargaining women, amid the curses of labourers, the shrill litanies of shop-boys who stood on guard by the barrels of pigs' cheeks, the nasal chanting of street-singers, who sang a come-all-you about O'Donovan Rossa, or a ballad about the troubles in our native land. These noises converged in a single sensation of life for me: I imagined that I bore my chalice safely through a throng of foes. Her name sprang to my lips at moments in strange prayers and praises which I myself did not understand. My eyes were often full of tears (I could not tell why) and at times a flood from my heart seemed to pour itself out into my bosom. I thought little of the future. I did not know whether I would ever speak to her or not or, if I spoke to her, how I could tell her of my confused adoration. But my body was like a harp and her words and gestures were like fingers running upon the wires.

One Evening I went into the back drawing-room in which the priest had died. It was a dark rainy evening and there was no sound in the house. Through one of the broken panes I heard the rain impinge upon the earth, the fine incessant needles of water playing in the sodden beds. Some distant lamp or lighted window gleamed below me. I was thankful that I could see so little. All my senses seemed to desire to veil themselves and, feeling that I was about to slip from them, I pressed the palms of my hands together until they trembled, murmuring: 'O love! O love!' many times.

At last she spoke to me. When she addressed the first words to me I was so confused that I did not know what to answer. She asked me was I going to Araby. I forgot whether I answered yes or no. It would be a splendid bazaar; she said she would love to go.

'And why can't you?' I asked.

While she spoke she turned a silver bracelet round and round her wrist. She could not go, she said, because there would be a retreat that week in her convent. Her brother and two other boys were fighting for their caps and I was alone at the railings. She held one of the spikes, bowing her head towards me. The light from the lamp opposite our door caught the white curve of her neck, lit up her hair that rested there and, falling, lit up the hand upon the railing. It fell over one side of her dress and caught the white border of a petticoat, just visible as she stood at ease.

'It's well for you,' she said.

'If I go,' I said, 'I will bring you something.'

What innumerable follies laid waste my waking and sleeping thoughts after that evening! I wished to annihilate the tedious intervening days. I chafed against the work of school. At night in my bedroom and by day in the classroom her image came between me and the page I strove to read. The syllables of the word Araby were called to me through the silence in which my soul luxuriated and cast an Eastern enchantment over me. I asked for leave to go to the bazaar on Saturday night. My aunt was surprised and hoped it was not some Freemason affair. I answered few questions in class. I watched my master's face pass from amiability to sternness; he hoped I was not beginning to idle. I could not call my wandering thoughts together. I had hardly any patience with the serious work of life which, now that it stood between me and my desire, seemed to me child's play, ugly monotonous child's play.

On Saturday morning I reminded my uncle that I wished to go to the bazaar in the evening. He was fussing at the hallstand, looking for the hat-brush, and answered me curtly:

'Yes, boy, I know.'

As he was in the hall I could not go into the front parlour and lie at the window. I left the house in bad humour and walked slowly towards the school. The air was pitilessly raw and already my heart misgave me.

When I came home to dinner my uncle had not yet been home. Still it was early. I sat staring at the clock for some time, and when its ticking began to irritate me, I left the room. I mounted the staircase and gained the upper part of the house. The high cold empty gloomy rooms liberated me and I went from room to room singing. From the front window I saw my companions playing below in the street. Their cries reached me weakened and indistinct and, leaning my forehead against the cool glass, I looked over at the dark house where she lived. I may have stood there for an hour, seeing nothing but the brown-clad figure cast by my imagination, touched discreetly by the lamplight at the curved neck, at the hand upon the railings and at the border below the dress.

When I came downstairs again I found Mrs Mercer sitting at the fire. She was an old garrulous woman, a pawnbroker's widow, who collected used stamps for some pious purpose. I had to endure the gossip of the tea-table. The meal was prolonged beyond an hour and still my uncle did not come. Mrs Mercer stood up to go: she was sorry she couldn't wait any longer, but it was after eight o'clock and she did not like to be out late as the night air was bad for her. When she had gone I began to walk up and down the room, clenching my fists. My aunt said:

'I'm afraid you may put off your bazaar for this night of Our Lord.'

At nine o'clock I heard my uncle's latchkey in the halldoor. I heard him talking to himself and heard the hallstand rocking when it had received the weight of his overcoat. I could interpret these signs. When he was midway through his dinner I asked him to give me the money to go to the bazaar. He had forgotten.

'The people are in bed and after their first sleep now,' he said.

I did not smile. My aunt said to him energetically:

'Can't you give him the money and let him go? You've kept him late enough as it is.'

My uncle said he was very sorry he had forgotten. He said he believed in the old saying: 'All work and no play makes Jack a dull boy.' He asked me where I was going and, when I had told him a second time he asked me did I know *The Arab's Farewell to his Steed*. When I left the kitchen he was about to recite the opening lines of the piece to my aunt.

I held a florin tightly in my hand as I strode down Buckingham Street towards the station. The sight of the streets thronged with buyers and glaring with gas recalled to me the purpose of my journey. I took my seat in a third-class carriage of a deserted train. After an intolerable delay the train moved out of the station slowly. It crept onward among ruinous houses and over the twinkling river. At Westland Row Station a crowd of people pressed to the carriage doors; but the porters moved them back, saying that it was a special train for the bazaar. I remained alone in the bare carriage. In a few minutes the train drew up beside an improvised wooden platform. I passed out on to the road and saw by the lighted dial of a clock that it was ten minutes to ten. In front of me was a large building which displayed the magical name.

I could not find any sixpenny entrance and, fearing that the bazaar would be closed, I passed in quickly through a turnstile, handing a shilling to a weary-looking man. I found myself in a big hall girdled at half its height by a gallery. Nearly all the stalls were closed and the greater part of the hall was in darkness. I recognized a silence like that which pervades a church after a service. I walked into the centre of the bazaar timidly. A few people were gathered about the stalls which were still open. Before a curtain, over which the words *Café Chantant* were written in coloured lamps, two men were counting money on a salver. I listened to the fall of the coins.

Remembering with difficulty why I had come I went over to one of the stalls and examined porcelain vases and flowered tea-sets. At the door of the stall a young lady was talking and laughing with two young gentlemen. I remarked their English accents and listened vaguely to their conversation.

'O, I never said such a thing!'

'O, but you did!'

'O, but I didn't!'

'Didn't she say that?'

'Yes. I heard her.'

'O, there's a...fib!'

Observing me the young lady came over and asked me did I

wish to buy anything. The tone of her voice was not encouraging; she seemed to have spoken to me out of a sense of duty. I looked humbly at the great jars that stood like eastern guards at either side of the dark entrance to the stall and murmured:

'No, thank you.'

The young lady changed the position of one of the vases and went back to the two young men. They began to talk of the same subject. Once or twice the young lady glanced at me over her shoulder.

I lingered before her stall, though I knew my stay was useless, to make my interest in her wares seem the more real. Then I turned away slowly and walked down the middle of the bazaar. I allowed the two pennies to fall against the sixpence in my pocket. I heard a voice call from one end of the gallery that the light was out. The upper part of the hall was now completely dark.

Gazing up into the darkness I saw myself as a creature driven and derided by vanity; and my eyes burned with anguish and anger.

39

SALVATORE

W. Somerset Maugham

Love and affection do go side by side.

I wonder if I can do it.

I knew Salvatore first when he was a boy of fifteen with a pleasant face, a laughing mouth and care-free eyes. He used to spend the morning lying about the beach with next to nothing on and his brown body was as thin as a rail. He was full of grace. He was in and out of the sea all the time swimming with the clumsy, effortless stroke common to the fisher boat.

Scrambling up the jagged rocks on his hard feet, for except on Sundays never wore shoes, he would throw himself into the deep water with a scream of delight. His father was a fisherman who owned his own little vineyard and Salvatore acted as nursemaid to his two younger brothers. He shouted to them to come inshore when they ventured out too far and made them dress when it was time to climb the hot, vineclad hill for the frugal midday meal.

But boys in those Southern parts grow apace and in a little while he was madly in love with a pretty girl who lived on the Grande Marina. She had eyes like forest pools and held herself like a daughter of the Caesars. They were affianced, but they could not marry till Salvatore had done his military service, and when he left the island which he had never left in his life before, to become a sailor in the navy of King Victor Emmanuel, he wept like a child. It was hard for one who had never been less free than the birds to be at the beck and call of others, it was harder still to live in a battleship with strangers instead of in a little white cottage among the vines; and when he was ashore, to walk in noisy, friendless cities with streets so crowded that he was frightened to cross them, when he had been used to silent paths and the mountains and the sea. I suppose it had never struck him that Ischia, which he looked at every evening (it was like a fairy island in the sunset) to see what the weather would be like next day, or Vesuvius, pearly in the dawn, had anything to do with him at all; but when he ceased to have them before his eyes he realized in some dim fashion that they were as much part of him as his hands and his feet. He was dreadfully homesick. But it was hardest of all to be parted from the girl he loved with all his passionate young heart. He wrote to her (in his childlike handwriting) long, ill-spelt letters in which he told her how constantly he thought of her and how much he longed to be back. He was sent here and there, to Spezzia, to Venice, to Ban and finally to China. Here he fell ill of some mysterious ailment that kept him in hospital for months. He bore it with the mute and uncomprehending patience of a dog. When he learnt that it was a form of rheumatism that made him unfit for further service his heart exulted, for he could go home; and he did not bother, in fact he scarcely listened, when the doctors told him that he would never again be quite well. What did he care when he was going back to the little island he loved so well and the girl who was waiting for him?

When he got into the rowing-boat that met the steamer from Naples and was rowed ashore he saw his father and mother standing on the jetty and his two brothers, big boys now, and he waved to them. His eyes searched among the crowd that waited there, for the girl. He could not see her. There was a great deal of kissing when he jumped up the steps and they all, emotional creatures, cried a little when they exchanged their greetings. He asked where the girl was. His mother told him that she did not know; they had not seen her for two or three weeks; so in the evening when the moon was shining over the placid sea and the lights of Naples twinkled in the distance he walked down to the Grande Marina to her house. She was sitting on the doorstep with her mother. He was a little shy because he had not seen her for so long. He asked her if she had not received the letter that he had written to her to say that he was coming home. Yes, they had received a letter, and they had been told by another of the island boys that he was ill. Yes, that was why he was back; was it not a piece of luck? Oh, but they had heard that he would never be quite well again. The doctor talked a lot of nonsense, but he knew very well that now he was home again he would recover. They were silent for a little, and then the mother nudged the girl. She did not try to soften the blow. She told him straight out, with the blunt directness of her race that she could not marry a man who would never be strong enough to work like a man. They had made up their minds, her mother and father and she, and her father would never give consent.

When Salvatore went home he found that they all knew. The girl's father had been to tell them what they had decided, but they had lacked the courage to tell him themselves. He wept on his mother's bosom. He was terribly unhappy, but he did not blame the girl. A fisherman's life is hard and it needs strength and endurance. He knew very well that a girl could not afford to marry a man who might not be able to support her. His smile was very sad and his eyes had the look of a dog that has been beaten, but he did not complain, and he never said a hard word of the girl he had loved so well.

Then, a few months later, when he had settled down to the common round, working in his father's vineyard and fishing, his mother told him that there was a young woman in the village who was willing to marry him. Her name was Assunta.

'She's as ugly as the devil,' he said.

She was older than he, twenty-four or twenty-five, and she had been engaged to a man who, while doing his military service, had been killed in Africa. She had a little money of her own and if Salvatore married her she could buy him a boat of his own and they could take a vineyard that by happy chance happened at that moment to be without a tenant. His mother told him that Assunta had seen him at the festa and had fallen in love with him. Salvatore smiled his sweet smile and said he would think about it. On the following Sunday, dressed in the stiff black clothes in which he looked so much less well than in the ragged shirt and trousers of every day, he went up to High Mass at the parish church and placed himself so that he could have a good look at the young woman. When he came down again he told his mother that he was willing.

Well, they were married and they settled down in a tiny white-washed house in the middle of a handsome vineyard. Salvatore was now a great, big husky fellow, tall and broad, but still with that ingenuous smile and those trusting, kindly eyes that he had as a boy. He had the most beautiful manners I have ever seen in my life. Assunta was a grim-visaged female, with decided features, and she looked old for her years. But she had a good heart and she was no fool. I used to be amused by the little smile of devotion that she gave her husband when he was being very masculine and masterful; she never ceased to be touched by his gentle sweetness. But she could not bear the girl who had thrown him over, and notwithstanding Salvatore's smiling expostulations she had nothing but harsh words for her. Presently children were born to them.

It was a hard enough life. All through the fishing season towards evening he set out in his boat with one of his brothers for the fishing grounds. It was a long pull of six or seven miles, and he spent the night catching the profitable cuttlefish. Then there was the long row back again in order to sell the catch in time for it to go on the early boat to Naples. At other times he was working in his vineyard from dawn till the heat drove him to rest and then again, when it was a trifle cooler, till dusk. Often his rheumatism prevented him from doing anything at all and then he would lie about the beach, smoking cigarettes, with a pleasant word for everyone notwithstanding the pain that racked his limbs. The foreigners who came down to bathe and saw him there said that these Italian fishermen were lazy devils.

Sometimes he used to bring his children down to give them a bath. They were both boys and at this time the elder was three and the younger less than two. They sprawled about at the water's edge stark naked and Salvatore standing on a rock would dip them in the water. The elder one bore it with stoicism, but the baby screamed lustily. Salvatore had enormous hands, like legs of mutton, coarse and hard from constant toil, but when he bathed his children, holding them so tenderly, drying them with delicate care; upon my word they were like flowers. He would seat the naked baby on the palm of his hand and hold him up, laughing a little at his smallness, and his laugh was like the laughter of an angel. His eyes then were as candid as his child's.

I started by saying that I wondered if I could do it and now I must tell you what it is that I have tried to do. I wanted to see whether I could hold your attention for a few pages while I drew for you the portrait of a man, just an ordinary fisherman who possessed nothing in the world except a quality which is the rarest, the most precious and the loveliest that anyone can have. Heaven only knows why he should so strangely and unexpectedly have possessed it. All I know is that it shone in him with a radiance that, if it had not been unconscious and so humble, would have been to the common run of men hardly bearable. And in case you have not guessed what the quality was, I will tell you. Goodness—just goodness.

40

AN ANGEL IN DISGUISE

T.S. Arthur

*Love can conquer anything in the world be it the innocence of
a child...the pristine.*

Idleness, vice, and intemperance had done their miserable work,
and the dead mother lay cold and still amid her wretched
children. She had fallen upon the threshold of her own door in
a drunken fit, and died in the presence of her frightened little ones.

Death touches the spring of our common humanity. This
woman had been despised, scoffed at, and angrily denounced by
nearly every man, woman, and child in the village; but now,
as the fact of her death was passed from lip to lip, in subdued
tones, pity took the place of anger, and sorrow of denunciation.
Neighbours went hastily to the old tumble-down hut, in which she
had secured little more than a place of shelter from summer heats
and winter cold: some with grave-clothes for a decent interment
of the body; and some with food for the half-starving children,
three in number. Of these, John, the oldest, a boy of twelve, was
a stout lad, able to earn his living with any farmer. Kate, between
ten and eleven, was bright, active girl, out of whom something
clever might be made, if in good hands; but poor little Maggie,
the youngest, was hopelessly diseased. Two years before a fall from
a window had injured her spine, and she had not been able to
leave her bed since, except when lifted in the arms of her mother.

'What is to be done with the children?' That was the chief
question now. The dead mother would go underground, and be
forever beyond all care or concern of the villagers. But the children

must not be left to starve. After considering the matter, and talking it over with his wife, farmer Jones said that he would take John, and do well by him, now that his mother was out of the way; and Mrs Ellis, who had been looking out for a bound girl, concluded that it would be charitable in her to make choice of Kate, even though she was too young to be of much use for several years.

'I could do much better, I know,' said Mrs Ellis; 'but as no one seems inclined to take her, I must act from a sense of duty expect to have trouble with the child; for she's an undisciplined thing—used to having her own way.'

But no one said 'I'll take Maggie'. Pitying glances were cast on her wan and wasted form and thoughts were troubled on her account. Mothers brought cast-off garments and, removing her soiled and ragged clothes, dressed her in clean attire. The sad eyes and patient face of the little one touched many hearts, and even knocked at them for entrance. But none opened to take her in. Who wanted a bed-ridden child?

'Take her to the poorhouse,' said a rough man, of whom the question 'What's to be done with Maggie?' was asked. 'Nobody's going to be bothered with her.'

'The poorhouse is a sad place for a sick and helpless child,' answered one.

'For your child or mine,' said the other, lightly speaking; 'but for tis brat it will prove a blessed change, she will be kept clean, have healthy food, and be doctored, which is more than can be said of her past condition.'

There was reason in that, but still it didn't satisfy. The day following the day of death was made the day of burial. A few neighbours were at the miserable hovel, but none followed dead cart as it bore the unhonoured remains to its pauper grave. Farmer Jones, after the coffin was taken out, placed John in his wagon and drove away, satisfied that he had done his part. Mrs Ellis spoke to Kate with a hurried air, 'Bid your sister good by,' and drew the tearful children apart ere scarcely their lips had touched in a sobbing farewell. Hastily others went out, some glancing at Maggie, and some resolutely refraining from a look, until all had gone. She was alone! Just beyond the threshold Joe Thompson, the wheelwright, paused, and said to the blacksmith's wife, who was hastening off with the rest—

'It's a cruel thing to leave her so.'

'Then take her to the poorhouse: she'll have to go there,' answered the blacksmith's wife, springing away, and leaving Joe behind.

For a little while the man stood with a puzzled air; then he turned back, and went into the hovel again. Maggie with painful effort, had raised herself to an upright position and was sitting on the bed, straining her eyes upon the door out of which all had just departed, a vague terror had come into her thin white face.

'O, Mr Thompson!' she cried out, catching her suspended breath, 'don't leave me here all alone!'

Though rough in exterior, Joe Thompson, the wheelwright, had a heart, and it was very tender in some places. He liked children, and was pleased to have them come to his shop, where sleds and wagons were made or mended for the village lads without a draft on their hoarded sixpences.

'No, dear,' he answered, in a kind voice, going to the bed, and stooping down over the child, 'You sha'n't be left here alone.' Then he wrapped her with the gentleness almost of a woman, in the clean bedclothes which some neighbour had brought; and, lifting her in his strong arms, bore her out into the air and across the field that lay between the hovel and his home.

Now, Joe Thompson's wife, who happened to be childless, was not a woman of saintly temper, nor much given to self-denial for others' good, and Joe had well-grounded doubts touching the manner of greeting he should receive on his arrival. Mrs Thompson saw him approaching from the window, and with ruffling feathers met him a few paces from the door, as he opened the garden gate, and came in. He bore a precious burden, and he felt it to be so. As his arms held the sick child to his breast, a sphere of tenderness went out from her, and penetrated his feelings. A bond had already corded itself around them both, and love was springing into life.

'What have you there?' sharply questioned Mrs Thompson.

Joe, felt the child start and shrink against him. He did not reply, except by a look that was pleading and cautionary, that said, 'Wait a moment for explanations, and be gentle,' and, passing in, carried Maggie to the small chamber on the first floor, and laid her on a bed. Then, stepping back, he shut the door, and stood face to face with his vinegar-tempered wife in the passage-way outside.

'You haven't brought home that sick brat!' anger and astonishment were in the tones of Mrs Joe Thompson; her face was in a flame.

'I think women's hearts are sometimes very hard,' said Joe. Usually Joe Thompson got out of his wife's way, or kept rigidly silent and non-combative when she fired up on any subject; it was with some surprise, therefore, that she now encountered a firmly-set countenance and a resolute pair of eyes.

'Women's hearts are not half so hard as men's!'

Joe saw, by a quick intuition, that his resolute bearing had impressed his wife and he answered quickly, and with real indignation, 'Be that as it may, every woman at the funeral turned her eyes steadily from the sick child's face, and when the cart went off with her dead mother, hurried away, and left her alone in that old hut, with the sun not an hour in the sky.'

'Where were John and Kate?' asked Mrs Thompson.

'Farmer Jones tossed John into his wagon, and drove off. Kate went home with Mrs Ellis; but nobody wanted the poor sick one. "Send her to the poorhouse," was the cry.'

'Why didn't you let her go, then. What did you bring her here for?'

'She can't walk to the poorhouse,' said Joe; 'somebody's arms must carry her, and mine are strong enough for that task.'

'Then why didn't you keep on? Why did you stop here?' demanded the wife.

'Because I'm not apt to go on fools' errands. The Guardians must first be seen, and a permit obtained.'

There was no gainsaying this.

'When will you see the Guardians?' was asked, with irrepressible impatience.

'To-morrow.'

'Why put it off till to-morrow? Go at once for the permit, and get the whole thing off of your hands to-night.'

'Jane,' said the wheelwright, with an impressiveness of tone that greatly subdued his wife, 'I read in the Bible sometimes, and find much said about little children. How the Saviour rebuked the disciples who would not receive them; how he took them up in his arms, and blessed them; and how he said that 'whosoever gave them even a cup of cold water should not go unrewarded'. Now, it is a small thing for us to keep this poor motherless little one for a single night; to be kind to her for a single night; to make her life comfortable for a single night.'

The voice of the strong, rough man shook, and he turned his head away, so that the moisture in his eyes might not be seen. Mrs Thompson did not answer, but a soft feeling crept into her heart.

'Look at her kindly, Jane; speak to her kindly,' said Joe. 'Think of her dead mother, and the loneliness, the pain, the sorrow that must be on all her coming life.' The softness of his heart gave unwonted eloquence to his lips.

Mrs Thompson did not reply, but presently turned towards the little chamber where her husband had deposited Maggie; and, pushing open the door, went quietly in. Joe did not follow; he saw that, her state had changed, and felt that it would be best to leave her alone with the child. So he went to his shop, which stood near the house, and worked until dusky evening released him from labour. A light shining through the little chamber windows was the first object that attracted Joe's attention on turning towards the house: it was a good omen. The path led him by this windows and, when opposite, he could not help pausing to look in. It was now dark enough outside to screen him from observation. Maggie lay, a little raised on the pillow with the lamp shining full upon her face. Mrs Thompson was sitting by the bed, talking to the child; but her back was towards the window, so that her countenance was not seen. From Maggie's face, therefore, Joe must read the character of their intercourse. He saw that her eyes were intently fixed upon his wife; that now and then a few words came, as if in answers from her lips; that her expression was sad and tender; but he saw nothing of bitterness or pain. A deep-drawn breath was followed by one of relief, as a weight lifted itself from his heart.

On entering, Joe did not go immediately to the little chamber. His heavy tread about the kitchen brought his wife somewhat hurriedly from the room where she had been with Maggie. Joe thought it best not to refer to the child, nor to manifest any concern in regard to her.

'How soon will supper be ready?' he asked.

'Right soon,' answered Mrs Thompson, beginning to bustle about. There was no asperity in her voice.

After washing from his hands and face the dust and soil of work, Joe left the kitchen, and went to the little bedroom. A pair of large bright eyes looked up at him from the snowy bed; looked at him tenderly, gratefully, pleadingly. How his heart swelled in his bosom! With what a quicker motion came the heart-beats! Joe sat down, and now, for the first time, examining the thin frame carefully under the lamp light, saw that it was an attractive face, and full of a childish sweetness which suffering had not been able to obliterate.

'Your name is Maggie?' he said, as he sat down and took her soft little hand in his.

'Yes, sir.' Her voice struck a chord that quivered in a low strain of music.

'Have you been sick long?'

'Yes, sir.' What a sweet patience was in her tone!

'Has the doctor been to see you?'

'He used to come.'

'But not lately?'

'No, sir.'

'Have you any pain?'

'Sometimes, but not now.'

'When had you pain?'

'This morning my side ached, and my back hurt when you carried me.'

'It hurts you to be lifted or moved about?'

'Yes, sir.'

'Your side doesn't ache now?'

'No, sir.'

'Does it ache a great deal?'

'Yes, sir; but it hasn't ached any since I've been on this soft bed.'

'The soft bed feels good.'

'O, yes, sir—so good!' What a satisfaction, mingled with gratitude, was in her voice!

'Supper is ready,' said Mrs Thompson, looking into the room a little while afterwards.

Joe glanced from his wife's face to that of Maggie; she understood him, and answered,—

'She can wait until we are done; then I will bring her somethings to eat.' There was an effort at indifference on the part of Mrs Thompson, but her husband had seen her through the window, and understood that the coldness was assumed. Joe waited, after sitting down to the table, for his wife to introduce the subject uppermost in both of their thoughts; but she kept silent on that theme, for many minutes, and he maintained a like reserve. At last she said, abruptly—

'What are you going to do with that child?'

'I thought you understood me that she was to go to the poorhouse,' replied Joe, as if surprised at her question.

Mrs Thompson looked rather strangely at her husband for sonic moments, and then dropped her eyes. The subject was not again referred to during the meal. At its close, Mrs Thompson toasted a slice of bread, and softened it with milk and butter; adding to this a cup of tea, she took them into Maggie, and held the small waiter, on which she had placed them, while the hungry child ate with every sign of pleasure.

'Is it good?' asked Mrs Thompson, seeing with what a keen relish the food was taken.

The child paused with the cup in her hand, and answered with a look of gratitude that awoke to new life old human feelings which had been slumbering in her heart for half a score of years.

'We'll keep her a day or two longer; she is so weak and helpless,' said Mrs Joe Thompson, in answer to her husband's remark, at breakfast-time on the next morning, that he must step down and see the Guardians of the Poor about Maggie.

'She'll be so much in your way,' said Joe.

'I sha'n't mind that for a day or two. Poor thing!'

Joe did not see the Guardians of the Poor on that day, on the next, nor on the day following. In fact, he never saw them at all on Maggie's account, for in less than a week Mrs Joe Thompson would as soon leave thought of taking up her own abode in the almshouse as sending Maggie there.

What light and blessing did that sick and helpless child bring to the home of Joe Thompson, the poor wheelwright! It had been dark, and cold, and miserable there for a long time just because his wife had nothing to love and care for out of herself, and so became sore, irritable, ill-tempered, and self-afflicting in the desolation of her woman's nature. Now the sweetness of that sick child, looking ever to her in love, patience, and gratitude, was as honey to her soul, and she carried her in her heart as well as in her arms, a precious burden. As for Joe Thompson, there was not a man in all the neighbourhood who drank daily of a more precious wine of life than he. An angel had come into his house, disguised as a sick, helpless, and miserable child, and filled all its dreary chambers with the sunshine of love.

41

A BLUNDER

Anton Chekhov

Marriage and tradition: aspirations and desperation all wrapped into one.

Ilya Sergeitch Peplov and his wife Kleopatra Petrovna were standing at the door, listening greedily. On the other side in the little drawing-room a love scene was apparently taking place between two persons: their daughter Natashenka and a teacher of the district school, called Shchupkin.

'He's rising!' whispered Peplov, quivering with impatience and rubbing his hands. 'Now, Kleopatra, mind; as soon as they begin talking of their feelings, take down the ikon from the wall and we'll go in and bless them. We'll catch him. A blessing with an ikon is sacred and binding. He couldn't get out of it, if he brought it into court.'

On the other side of the door this was the conversation:

'Don't go on like that!' said Shchupkin, striking a match against his checked trousers. 'I never wrote you any letters!'

'I like that! As though I didn't know your writing!' giggled the girl with an affected shriek, continually peeping at herself in the glass. 'I knew it at once! And what a queer man you are! You are a writing master, and you write like a spider! How can you teach writing if you write so badly yourself?'

'H'm...that means nothing. The great thing in writing lessons is not the hand one writes, but keeping the boys in order. You hit one on the head with a ruler, make another kneel down. Besides, there's nothing in handwriting! Nekrassov was an author, but his handwriting's a disgrace, there's a specimen of it in his collected works.'

'You are not Nekrassov.' (A sigh) 'I should love to marry an author. He'd always be writing poems to me.'

'I can write you a poem, too, if you like.'

'What can you write about?'

'Love—passion—your eyes. You'll be crazy when you read it. It would draw a tear from a stone! And if I write you a real poem, will you let me kiss your hand?'

'That's nothing much! You can kiss it now if you like.'

Shchupkin jumped up, and making sheepish eyes, bent over the fat little hand that smelt of egg soap.

'Take down the ikon,' Peplov whispered in a fluster, pale with excitement, and buttoning his coat as he prodded his wife with his elbow. 'Come along, now!'

And without a second's delay Peplov flung open the door.

'Children,' he muttered, lifting up his arms and blinking tearfully, 'the Lord bless you, my children. May you live—be fruitful—and multiply.'

'And—and I bless you, too,' the mamma brought out, crying with happiness. 'May you be happy, my dear ones! Oh, you are taking from me my only treasure!' she said to Shchupkin. 'Love my girl, be good to her.'

Shchupkin's mouth fell open with amazement and alarm. The parents' attack was so bold and unexpected that he could not utter a single word.

I'm in for it! I'm spliced! he thought, going limp with horror. *It's all over with you now, my boy! There's no escape!*

And he bowed his head submissively, as though to say, 'Take me, I'm vanquished.'

'Ble—blessings on you,' the papa went on, and he, too, shed tears. 'Natashenka, my daughter, stand by his side. Kleopatra, give me the ikon.'

But at this point the father suddenly left off weeping, and his face was contorted with anger.

'You ninny!' he said angrily to his wife. 'You are an idiot! Is that the ikon?'

'Ach, saints alive!'

What had happened? The writing master raised himself and saw that he was saved; in her flutter the mamma had snatched from the wall the portrait of Lazhetchnikov, the author, in mistake for the ikon. Old Peplov and his wife stood disconcerted in the middle of the room, holding the portrait aloft, not knowing what to do or what to say. The writing master took advantage of the general confusion and slipped away.

42

THE LOCKET

Kate Chopin

Love and war may become the two facets of life.

I

One night in autumn a few men were gathered about a fire on the slope of a hill. They belonged to a small detachment of Confederate forces and were awaiting orders to march. Their grey uniforms were worn beyond the point of shabbiness. One of the men was heating something in a tin cup over the embers. Two were lying at full length a little distance away, while a fourth was trying to decipher a letter and had drawn close to the light. He had unfastened his collar and a good bit of his flannel shirt front.

'What's that you got around your neck, Ned?' asked one of the men lying in the obscurity.

Ned—or Edmond—mechanically fastened another button of his shirt and did not reply. He went on reading his letter.

'Is it your sweet heart's picture?'

''Taint no gal's picture,' offered the man at the fire. He had removed his tin cup and was engaged in stirring its grimy contents with a small stick. 'That's a charm; some kind of hoodoo business that one o' them priests gave him to keep him out o' trouble. I know them Cath'lics. That's how come Frenchy got permoted an never got a scratch sence he's been in the ranks. Hey, French! Aint I right?' Edmond looked up absently from his letter.

'What is it?' he asked.

'Aint that a charm you got round your neck?'

'It must be, Nick,' returned Edmond with a smile. 'I don't know how I could have gone through this year and a half without it.'

The letter had made Edmond heart sick and home sick. He stretched himself on his back and looked straight up at the blinking stars. But he was not thinking of them nor of anything but a certain spring day when the bees were humming in the clematis; when a girl was saying good bye to him. He could see her as she unclasped from her neck the locket which she fastened about his own. It was an old fashioned golden locket bearing miniatures of her father and mother with their names and the date of their marriage. It was her most precious earthly possession. Edmond could feel again the folds of the girl's soft white gown, and see the droop of the angel-sleeves as she circled her fair arms about his neck. Her sweet face, appealing, pathetic, tormented by the pain of parting, appeared before him as vividly as life. He turned over, burying his face in his arm and there he lay, still and motionless.

The profound and treacherous night with its silence and semblance of peace settled upon the camp. He dreamed that the fair Octavie brought him a letter. He had no chair to offer her and was pained and embarrassed at the condition of his garments. He was ashamed of the poor food which comprised the dinner at which he begged her to join them.

He dreamt of a serpent coiling around his throat, and when he strove to grasp it the slimy thing glided away from his clutch. Then his dream was clamour.

'Git your duds! You! Frenchy!' Nick was bellowing in his face. There was what appeared to be a scramble and a rush rather than any regulated movement. The hill side was alive with clatter and motion; with sudden up-springing lights among the pines. In the east the dawn was unfolding out of the darkness. Its glimmer was yet dim in the plain below.

'What's it all about?' wondered a big black bird perched in

the top of the tallest tree. He was an old solitary and a wise one, yet he was not wise enough to guess what it was all about. So all day long he kept blinking and wondering.

The noise reached far out over the plain and across the hills and awoke the little babes that were sleeping in their cradles. The smoke curled up toward the sun and shadowed the plain so that the stupid birds thought it was going to rain; but the wise one knew better.

'They are children playing a game,' thought he. 'I shall know more about it if I watch long enough.'

At the approach of night they had all vanished away with their din and smoke. Then the old bird plumed his feathers. At last he had understood! With a flap of his great, black wings he shot downward, circling toward the plain.

A man was picking his way across the plain. He was dressed in the garb of a clergyman. His mission was to administer the consolations of religion to any of the prostrate figures in whom there might yet linger a spark of life. A negro accompanied him, bearing a bucket of water and a flask of wine.

There were no wounded here; they had been borne away. But the retreat had been hurried and the vultures and the good Samaritans would have to look to the dead.

There was a soldier—a mere boy—lying with his face to the sky. His hands were clutching the sward on either side and his finger nails were stuffed with earth and bits of grass that he had gathered in his despairing grasp upon life. His musket was gone; he was hatless and his face and clothing were begrimed. Around his neck hung a gold chain and locket. The priest, bending over him, unclasped the chain and removed it from the dead soldier's neck. He had grown used to the terrors of war and could face them unflinchingly; but its pathos, someway, always brought the tears to his old, dim eyes.

The angelus was ringing half a mile away. The priest and the negro knelt and murmured together the evening benediction and a prayer for the dead.

II

The peace and beauty of a spring day had descended upon the earth like a benediction. Along the leafy road which skirted a narrow, tortuous stream in central Louisiana, rumbled an old fashioned cabriolet, much the worse for hard and rough usage over country roads and lanes. The fat, black horses went in a slow, measured trot, notwithstanding constant urging on the part of the fat, black coachman. Within the vehicle were seated the fair Octavie and her old friend and neighbour, Judge Pillier, who had come to take her for a morning drive.

Octavie wore a plain black dress, severe in its simplicity. A narrow belt held it at the waist and the sleeves were gathered into close fitting wristbands. She had discarded her hoopskirt and appeared not unlike a nun. Beneath the folds of her bodice nestled the old locket. She never displayed it now. It had returned to her sanctified in her eyes; made precious as material things sometimes are by being forever identified with a significant moment of one's existence.

A hundred times she had read over the letter with which the locket had come back to her. No later than that morning she had again pored over it. As she sat beside the window, smoothing the letter out upon her knee, heavy and spiced odours stole in to her with the songs of birds and the humming of insects in the air.

She was so young and the world was so beautiful that there came over her a sense of unreality as she read again and again the priest's letter. He told of that autumn day drawing to its close, with the gold and the red fading out of the west, and the night gathering its shadows to cover the faces of the dead. Oh! She could not believe that one of those dead was her own! With visage uplifted to the grey sky in an agony of supplication. A spasm of resistance and rebellion seized and swept over her. Why was the spring here with its flowers and its seductive breath if he was dead? Why was she here? What further had she to do with life and the living?

Octavie had experienced many such moments of despair, but a blessed resignation had never failed to follow, and it fell then upon her like a mantle and enveloped her.

'I shall grow old and quiet and sad like poor Aunt Tavie,' she murmured to herself as she folded the letter and replaced it in the secretary. Already she gave herself a little demure air like her Aunt Tavie. She walked with a slow glide in unconscious imitation of Mademoiselle Tavie whom some youthful affliction had robbed of earthly compensation while leaving her in possession of youth's illusions.

As she sat in the old cabriolet beside the father of her dead lover, again there came to Octavie the terrible sense of loss which had assailed her so often before. The soul of her youth clamoured for its rights; for a share in the world's glory and exultation. She leaned back and drew her veil a little closer about her face. It was an old black veil of her Aunt Tavie's. A whiff of dust from the road had blown in and she wiped her cheeks and her eyes with her soft, white handkerchief, a homemade handkerchief, fabricated from one of her old fine muslin petticoats.

'Will you do me the favour, Octavie,' requested the judge in the courteous tone which he never abandoned, 'to remove that veil which you wear. It seems out of harmony, someway, with the beauty and promise of the day.'

The young girl obediently yielded to her old companion's wish and unpinning the cumbersome, sombre drapery from her bonnet, folded it neatly and laid it upon the seat in front of her.

'Ah! that is better; far better!' he said in a tone expressing unbounded relief. 'Never put it on again, dear.' Octavie felt a little hurt; as if he wished to debar her from share and parcel in the burden of affliction which had been placed upon all of them. Again she drew forth the old muslin handkerchief.

They had left the big road and turned into a level plain which had formerly been an old meadow. There were clumps of thorn trees here and there, gorgeous in their spring radiance. Some cattle were grazing off in the distance in spots where the grass was tall and luscious. At the far end of the meadow was the towering lilac hedge, skirting the lane that led to Judge Pillier's house, and the scent of its heavy blossoms met them like a soft and tender embrace of welcome.

As they neared the house the old gentleman placed an arm around the girl's shoulders and turning her face up to him he said: 'Do you not think that on a day like this, miracles might happen? When the whole earth is vibrant with life, does it not seem to you, Octavie, that heaven might for once relent and give us back our dead?' He spoke very low, advisedly, and impressively. In his voice was an old quaver which was not habitual and there was agitation in every line of his visage. She gazed at him with eyes that were full of supplication and a certain terror of joy.

They had been driving through the lane with the towering hedge on one side and the open meadow on the other. The horses had somewhat quickened their lazy pace. As they turned into the avenue leading to the house, a whole choir of feathered songsters fluted a sudden torrent of melodious greeting from their leafy hiding places.

Octavie felt as if she had passed into a stage of existence which was like a dream, more poignant and real than life. There was the old grey house with its sloping eaves. Amid the blur of green, and dimly, she saw familiar faces and heard voices as if they came from far across the fields, and Edmond was holding her. Her dead Edmond; her living Edmond, and she felt the beating of his heart against her and the agonizing rapture of his kisses striving to awake her. It was as if the spirit of life and the awakening spring had given back the soul to her youth and bade her rejoice.

It was many hours later that Octavie drew the locket from her bosom and looked at Edmond with a questioning appeal in her glance.

'It was the night before an engagement,' he said. 'In the hurry of the encounter, and the retreat next day, I never missed it till the fight was over. I thought of course I had lost it in the heat of the struggle, but it was stolen.'

'Stolen,' she shuddered, and thought of the dead soldier with his face uplifted to the sky in an agony of supplication.

Edmond said nothing; but he thought of his messmate; the one who had lain far back in the shadow; the one who had said nothing.

43

THE DARLING

Anton Chekhov

Life can be a love affair in continuum.

Olenka, the daughter of the retired collegiate assessor, Plemyanniakov, was sitting in her back porch, lost in thought. It was hot, the flies were persistent and teasing, and it was pleasant to reflect that it would soon be evening. Dark rainclouds were gathering from the east, and bringing from time to time a breath of moisture in the air.

Kukin, who was the manager of an open-air theatre called the Tivoli, and who lived in the lodge, was standing in the middle of the garden looking at the sky.

'Again!' he observed despairingly. 'It's going to rain again! Rain every day, as though to spite me. I might as well hang myself! It's ruin! Fearful losses every day.'

He flung up his hands, and went on, addressing Olenka:

'There! That's the life we lead, Olga Semyonovna. It's enough to make one cry. One works and does one's utmost, one wears oneself out, getting no sleep at night, and racks one's brain what to do for the best. And then what happens? To begin with, one's public is ignorant, boorish. I give them the very best operetta, a dainty masque, first rate music-hall artists. But do you suppose that's what they want! They don't understand anything of that sort. They want a clown; what they ask for is vulgarity. And then look at the weather! Almost every evening it rains. It started on the tenth of May, and it's kept it up all May and June. It's simply awful! The public doesn't come, but I've to pay the rent just the same, and pay the artists.'

The next evening the clouds would gather again, and Kukin would say with a hysterical laugh:

'Well, rain away, then! Flood the garden, drown me! Damn my luck in this world and the next! Let the artists have me up! Send me to prison! To Siberia! The scaffold! Ha, ha, ha!'

And next day the same thing.

Olenka listened to Kukin with silent gravity, and sometimes tears came into her eyes. In the end his misfortunes touched her; she grew to love him. He was a small thin man, with a yellow face, and curls combed forward on his forehead. He spoke in a thin tenor; as he talked his mouth worked on one side, and there was always an expression of despair on his face; yet he aroused a deep and genuine affection in her. She was always fond of some one, and could not exist without loving. In earlier days she had loved her papa, who now sat in a darkened room, breathing with difficulty; she had loved her aunt who used to come every other year from Bryansk; and before that, when she was at school, she had loved her French master. She was a gentle, soft-hearted, compassionate girl, with mild, tender eyes and very good health. At the sight of her full rosy cheeks, her soft white neck with a little dark mole on it, and the kind, naïve smile, which came into her face when she listened to anything pleasant, men thought, 'Yes, not half bad,' and smiled too, while lady visitors could not refrain from seizing her hand in the middle of a conversation, exclaiming in a gush of delight—'You darling!'

The house in which she had lived from her birth upwards, and which was left her in her father's will, was at the extreme end of the town, not far from the Tivoli. In the evenings and at night she could hear the band playing, and the crackling and banging of fireworks, and it seemed to her that it was Kukin struggling with his destiny, storming the entrenchments of his chief foe, the indifferent public; there was a sweet thrill at her heart, she had no desire to sleep, and when he returned home at day-break, she tapped softly at her bedroom window, and showing him only her face and one shoulder through the curtain, she gave him a friendly smile.

He proposed to her, and they were married. And when he had a closer view of her neck and her plump, fine shoulders, he threw up his hands, and said:

'You darling!'

He was happy, but as it rained on the day and night of his wedding, his face still retained an expression of despair.

They got on very well together. She used to sit in his office, to look after things in the Tivoli, to put down the accounts and pay the wages. And her rosy cheeks, her sweet, naïve, radiant smile, were to be seen now at the office window, now in the refreshment bar or behind the scenes of the theatre. And already she used to say to her acquaintances that the theatre was the chief and most important thing in life and that it was only through the drama that one could derive true enjoyment and become cultivated and humane.

'But do you suppose the public understands that?' she used to say. 'What they want is a clown. Yesterday we gave "Faust Inside Out" and almost all the boxes were empty; but if Vanitchka and I had been producing some vulgar thing, I assure you the theatre would have been packed. Tomorrow Vanitchka and I are doing "Orpheus in Hell". Do come.'

And what Kukin said about the theatre and the actors she repeated. Like him she despised the public for their ignorance and their indifference to art; she took part in the rehearsals, she corrected the actors, she kept an eye on the behaviour of the musicians, and when there was an unfavourable notice in the local paper, she shed tears, and then went to the editor's office to set things right.

The actors were fond of her and used to call her 'Vanitchka and I', and 'the darling'; she was sorry for them and used to lend them small sums of money, and if they deceived her, she used to shed a few tears in private, but did not complain to her husband.

They got on well in the winter too. They took the theatre in the town for the whole winter, and let it for short terms to a Little Russian company, or to a conjurer, or to a local dramatic society. Olenka grew stouter, and was always beaming with satisfaction, while Kukin grew thinner and yellower, and continually complained of their terrible losses, although he had not done badly all the winter. He used to cough at night, and she used to give him hot raspberry tea or lime-flower water, to rub him with eau-de-Cologne and to wrap him in her warm shawls.

'You're such a sweet pet!' she used to say with perfect sincerity, stroking his hair. 'You're such a pretty dear!'

Towards Lent he went to Moscow to collect a new troupe, and without him she could not sleep, but sat all night at her window, looking at the stars, and she compared herself with the hens, who are awake all night and uneasy when the cock is not in the hen-house. Kukin was detained in Moscow, and wrote that he would be back at Easter, adding some instructions about the Tivoli. But on the Sunday before Easter, late in the evening, came a sudden ominous knock at the gate; some one was hammering on the gate as though on a barrel—*boom, boom, boom!* The drowsy cook went flopping with her bare feet through the puddles, as she ran to open the gate.

'Please open,' said some one outside in a thick bass. 'There is a telegram for you.'

Olenka had received telegrams from her husband before, but this time for some reason she felt numb with terror. With shaking hands she opened the telegram and read as follows:

'Ivan Petrovitch died suddenly to-day. Awaiting immate instructions fufuneral tuesday.'

That was how it was written in the telegram—'fufuneral' and the utterly incomprehensible word 'immate'. It was signed by the stage manager of the operatic company.

'My darling!' sobbed Olenka. 'Vanka, my precious, my darling! Why did I ever meet you! Why did I know you and love you! Your poor heart-broken Olenka is alone without you!'

Kukin's funeral took place on Tuesday in Moscow, Olenka returned home on Wednesday, and as soon as she got indoors, she threw herself on her bed and sobbed so loudly that it could be heard next door, and in the street.

'Poor darling!' the neighbours said, as they crossed themselves. 'Olga Semyonovna, poor darling! How she does take on!'

Three months later Olenka was coming home from mass, melancholy and in deep mourning. It happened that one of her neighbours, Vassily Andreitch Pustovalov, returning home from church, walked back beside her. He was the manager at Babakayev's, the timber merchant's. He wore a straw hat, a white waistcoat, and a gold watch-chain, and looked more a country gentleman than a man in trade.

'Everything happens as it is ordained, Olga Semyonovna,' he said gravely, with a sympathetic note in his voice; 'and if any of our dear ones die, it must be because it is the will of God, so we ought have fortitude and bear it submissively.'

After seeing Olenka to her gate, he said good-bye and went on. All day afterwards she heard his sedately dignified voice, and whenever she shut her eyes she saw his dark beard. She liked him very much. And apparently she had made an impression on him too, for not long afterwards an elderly lady, with whom she was only slightly acquainted, came to drink coffee with her, and as soon as she was seated at table began to talk about Pustovalov, saying that he was an excellent man whom one could thoroughly depend upon, and that any girl would be glad to marry him. Three days later Pustovalov came himself. He did not stay long, only about ten minutes, and he did not say much, but when he left, Olenka loved him—loved him so much that she lay awake all night in a perfect fever, and in the morning she sent for the elderly lady. The match was quickly arranged, and then came the wedding.

Pustovalov and Olenka got on very well together when they were married.

Usually he sat in the office till dinner-time, then he went out on business, while Olenka took his place, and sat in the office till evening, making up accounts and booking orders.

'Timber gets dearer every year; the price rises twenty per cent,' she would say to her customers and friends. 'Only fancy we used to sell local timber, and now Vassitchka always has to go for wood to the Mogilev district. And the freight!' she would add, covering her cheeks with her hands in horror. 'The freight!'

It seemed to her that she had been in the timber trade for ages and ages, and that the most important and necessary thing in life was timber; and there was something intimate and touching to her in the very sound of words such as 'baulk', 'post', 'beam', 'pole', 'scantling', 'batten', 'lath', 'plank', etc.

At night when she was asleep she dreamed of perfect mountains of planks and boards, and long strings of wagons, carting timber somewhere far away. She dreamed that a whole regiment of six-inch beams forty feet high, standing on end, was marching upon the timber-yard; that logs, beams, and boards knocked together with the resounding crash of dry wood, kept falling and getting up again, piling themselves on each other. Olenka cried out in her sleep, and Pustovalov said to her tenderly: 'Olenka, what's the matter, darling? Cross yourself!'

Her husband's ideas were hers. If he thought the room was too hot, or that business was slack, she thought the same. Her husband did not care for entertainments, and on holidays he stayed at home. She did likewise.

'You are always at home or in the office,' her friends said to her. 'You should go to the theatre, darling, or to the circus.'

'Vassitchka and I have no time to go to theatres,' she would answer sedately. 'We have no time for nonsense. What's the use of these theatres?'

On Saturdays Pustovalov and she used to go to the evening service; on holidays to early mass, and they walked side by side with softened faces as they came home from church. There was a pleasant fragrance about them both, and her silk dress rustled agreeably. At home they drank tea, with fancy bread and jams of various kinds, and afterwards they ate pie. Every day at twelve o'clock there was a savoury smell of beet-root soup and of mutton or duck in their yard, and on fast-days of fish, and no one could pass the gate without feeling hungry. In the office the samovar was always boiling, and customers were regaled with tea and cracknels. Once a week the couple went to the baths and returned side by side, both red in the face.

'Yes, we have nothing to complain of, thank God,' Olenka used to say to her acquaintances. 'I wish every one were as well off as Vassitchka and I.'

When Pustovalov went away to buy wood in the Mogilev district, she missed him dreadfully, lay awake and cried. A young veterinary surgeon in the army, called Smirnin, to whom they had let their lodge, used sometimes to come in in the evening. He used to talk to her and play cards with her, and this entertained her in her husband's absence. She was particularly interested in what he told her of his home life. He was married and had a little boy, but was separated from his wife because she had been unfaithful to him, and now he hated her and used to send her forty roubles a month for the maintenance of their son. And hearing of all this, Olenka sighed and shook her head. She was sorry for him.

'Well, God keep you,' she used to say to him at parting, as she lighted him down the stairs with a candle. 'Thank you for coming to cheer me up, and may the Mother of God give you health.'

And she always expressed herself with the same sedateness and dignity, the same reasonableness, in imitation of her husband. As the veterinary surgeon was disappearing behind the door below, she would say:

'You know, Vladimir Platonitch, you'd better make it up with your wife. You should forgive her for the sake of your son. You may be sure the little fellow understands.'

And when Pustovalov came back, she told him in a low voice about the veterinary surgeon and his unhappy home life, and both sighed and shook their heads and talked about the boy, who, no doubt, missed his father, and by some strange connection of ideas, they went up to the holy ikons, bowed to the ground before them and prayed that God would give them children.

And so the Pustovalovs lived for six years quietly and peaceably in love and complete harmony.

But behold! One winter day after drinking hot tea in the office, Vassily Andreitch went out into the yard without his cap on to see about sending off some timber, caught cold and was taken ill. He had the best doctors, but he grew worse and died after four months' illness. And Olenka was a widow once more.

'I've nobody, now you've left me, my darling,' she sobbed, after her husband's funeral. 'How can I live without you, in wretchedness and misery! Pity me, good people, all alone in the world!'

She went about dressed in black with long 'weepers', and gave up wearing hat and gloves for good. She hardly ever went out, except to church, or to her husband's grave, and led the life of a nun. It was not till six months later that she took off the weepers and opened the shutters of the windows. She was sometimes seen in the mornings, going with her cook to market for provisions, but what went on in her house and how she lived now could only be surmised. People guessed, from seeing her drinking tea in her garden with the veterinary surgeon, who read the newspaper aloud to her, and from the fact that, meeting a lady she knew at the post-office, she said to her:

'There is no proper veterinary inspection in our town, and

that's the cause of all sorts of epidemics. One is always hearing of people's getting infection from the milk supply, or catching diseases from horses and cows. The health of domestic animals ought to be as well cared for as the health of human beings.'

She repeated the veterinary surgeon's words, and was of the same opinion as he about everything. It was evident that she could not live a year without some attachment, and had found new happiness in the lodge. In any one else this would have been censured, but no one could think ill of Olenka; everything she did was so natural. Neither she nor the veterinary surgeon said anything to other people of the change in their relations, and tried, indeed, to conceal it, but without success, for Olenka could not keep a secret. When he had visitors, men serving in his regiment, and she poured out tea or served the supper, she would begin talking of the cattle plague, of the foot and mouth disease, and of the municipal slaughterhouses. He was dreadfully embarrassed, and when the guests had gone, he would seize her by the hand and hiss angrily:

'I've asked you before not to talk about what you don't understand. When we veterinary surgeons are talking among ourselves, please don't put your word in. It's really annoying.'

And she would look at him with astonishment and dismay, and ask him in alarm: 'But, Voloditchka, what am I to talk about?'

And with tears in her eyes she would embrace him, begging him not to be angry, and they were both happy.

But this happiness did not last long. The veterinary surgeon departed, departed for ever with his regiment, when it was transferred to a distant place—to Siberia, it may be. And Olenka was left alone.

Now she was absolutely alone. Her father had long been dead, and his armchair lay in the attic, covered with dust and lame of one leg. She got thinner and plainer, and when people met her in the street they did not look at her as they used to, and did not smile to her; evidently her best years were over and left behind, and now a new sort of life had begun for her, which did not bear thinking about. In the evening Olenka sat in the porch, and heard the band playing and the fireworks popping in the Tivoli, but now the sound stirred no response. She looked into her yard without interest, thought of nothing, wished for nothing, and afterwards, when night came on she went to bed and dreamed of her empty yard. She ate and drank as it were unwillingly.

And what was worst of all, she had no opinions of any sort. She saw the objects about her and understood what she saw, but could not form any opinion about them, and did not know what to talk about. And how awful it is not to have any opinions! One sees a bottle, for instance, or the rain, or a peasant driving in his cart, but what the bottle is for, or the rain, or the peasant, and what is the meaning of it, one can't say, and could not even for a thousand roubles. When she had Kukin, or Pustovalov, or the veterinary surgeon, Olenka could explain everything, and give her opinion about anything you like, but now there was the same emptiness in her brain and in her heart as there was in her yard outside. And it was as harsh and as bitter as wormwood in the mouth.

Little by little the town grew in all directions. The road became a street, and where the Tivoli and the timber-yard had been, there were new turnings and houses. How rapidly time passes! Olenka's house grew dingy, the roof got rusty, the shed sank on one side, and the whole yard was overgrown with docks and stinging-nettles. Olenka herself had grown plain and elderly; in summer she sat in the porch, and her soul, as before, was empty and dreary and full of bitterness. In winter she sat at her window and looked at the snow. When she caught the scent of spring, or heard the chime of the church bells, a sudden rush of memories from the past came over her, there was a tender ache in her heart, and her eyes brimmed over with tears; but this was only for a minute, and then came emptiness again and the sense of the futility of life. The black kitten, Briska, rubbed against her and purred softly, but Olenka was not touched by these feline caresses. That was not what she needed. She wanted a love that would absorb her whole being, her whole soul and reason—that would give her ideas and an object in life, and would warm her old blood. And she would shake the kitten off her skirt and say with vexation:

'Get along; I don't want you!'

And so it was, day after day and year after year, and no joy, and no opinions. Whatever Mavra, the cook, said she accepted.

One hot July day, towards evening, just as the cattle were being driven away, and the whole yard was full of dust, some one suddenly knocked at the gate. Olenka went to open it herself and was dumbfounded when she looked out: she saw Smirnin, the veterinary surgeon, grey-headed, and dressed as a civilian. She suddenly remembered everything. She could not help crying and letting her head fall on his breast without uttering a word, and in the violence of her feeling she did not notice how they both walked into the house and sat down to tea.

'My dear Vladimir Platonitch! What fate has brought you?' she muttered, trembling with joy.

'I want to settle here for good, Olga Semyonovna,' he told her. 'I have resigned my post, and have come to settle down and try my luck on my own account. Besides, it's time for my boy to go to school. He's a big boy. I am reconciled with my wife, you know.'

'Where is she?' asked Olenka.

'She's at the hotel with the boy, and I'm looking for lodgings.'

'Good gracious, my dear soul! Lodgings? Why not have my house? Why shouldn't that suit you? Why, my goodness, I wouldn't take any rent!' cried Olenka in a flutter, beginning to cry again. 'You live here, and the lodge will do nicely for me. Oh dear! How glad I am!'

Next day the roof was painted and the walls were whitewashed, and Olenka, with her arms akimbo walked about the yard giving directions. Her face was beaming with her old smile, and she was brisk and alert as though she had waked from a long sleep. The veterinary's wife arrived—a thin, plain lady, with short hair and a peevish expression. With her was her little Sasha, a boy of ten, small for his age, blue-eyed, chubby, with dimples in his cheeks. And scarcely had the boy walked into the yard when he ran after the cat, and at once there was the sound of his gay, joyous laugh.

'Is that your puss, auntie?' he asked Olenka. 'When she has little ones, do give us a kitten. Mamma is awfully afraid of mice.'

Olenka talked to him, and gave him tea. Her heart warmed and there was a sweet ache in her bosom, as though the boy had been her own child. And when he sat at the table in the evening, going over his lessons, she looked at him with deep tenderness and pity as she murmured to herself:

'You pretty pet! My precious! Such a fair little thing, and so clever.'

'An island is a piece of land which is entirely surrounded by water,' he read aloud.

'An island is a piece of land,' she repeated, and this was the first opinion to which she gave utterance with positive conviction after so many years of silence and dearth of ideas.

Now she had opinions of her own, and at supper she talked to Sasha's parents, saying how difficult the lessons were at the high schools, but that yet the high school was better than a commercial one, since with a high-school education all careers were open to one, such as being a doctor or an engineer.

Sasha began going to the high school. His mother departed to Harkov to her sister's and did not return; his father used to go off every day to inspect cattle, and would often be away from home for three days together, and it seemed to Olenka as though Sasha was entirely abandoned, that he was not wanted at home, that he was being starved, and she carried him off to her lodge and gave him a little room there.

And for six months Sasha had lived in the lodge with her. Every morning Olenka came into his bedroom and found him fast asleep, sleeping noiselessly with his hand under his cheek. She was sorry to wake him.

'Sashenka,' she would say mournfully, 'get up, darling. It's time for school.'

He would get up, dress and say his prayers, and then sit down to breakfast, drink three glasses of tea, and eat two large cracknels and a half a buttered roll. All this time he was hardly awake and a little ill-humoured in consequence.

'You don't quite know your fable, Sashenka,' Olenka would say, looking at him as though he were about to set off on a long journey. 'What a lot of trouble I have with you! You must work and do your best, darling, and obey your teachers.'

'Oh, do leave me alone!' Sasha would say.

Then he would go down the street to school, a little figure, wearing a big cap and carrying a satchel on his shoulder. Olenka would follow him noiselessly.

'Sashenka!' she would call after him, and she would pop into his hand a date or a caramel. When he reached the street where the school was, he would feel ashamed of being followed by a tall, stout woman, he would turn round and say:

'You'd better go home, auntie. I can go the rest of the way alone.'

She would stand still and look after him fixedly till he had disappeared at the school-gate.

Ah, how she loved him! Of her former attachments not one had been so deep; never had her soul surrendered to any feeling so spontaneously, so disinterestedly, and so joyously as now that her maternal instincts were aroused. For this little boy with the dimple in his cheek and the big school cap, she would have given her whole life, she would have given it with joy and tears of tenderness. Why? Who can tell why?

When she had seen the last of Sasha, she returned home, contented and serene, brimming over with love; her face, which had grown younger during the last six months, smiled and beamed; people meeting her looked at her with pleasure.

'Good-morning, Olga Semyonovna, darling. How are you, darling?'

'The lessons at the high school are very difficult now,' she would relate at the market. 'It's too much; in the first class yesterday they gave him a fable to learn by heart, and a Latin translation and a problem. You know it's too much for a little chap.'

And she would begin talking about the teachers, the lessons, and the school books, saying just what Sasha said.

At three o'clock they had dinner together: in the evening they learned their lessons together and cried. When she put him to bed, she would stay a long time making the Cross over him and murmuring a prayer; then she would go to bed and dream of that far-away misty future when Sasha would finish his studies and become a doctor or an engineer, would have a big house of his own with horses and a carriage, would get married and have children. She would fall asleep still thinking of the same thing, and tears would run down her cheeks from her closed eyes, while the black cat lay purring beside her: 'Mrr, mrr, mrr.'

Suddenly there would come a loud knock at the gate.

Olenka would wake up breathless with alarm, her heart throbbing. Half a minute later would come another knock.

'It must be a telegram from Harkov,' she would think, beginning to tremble from head to foot. 'Sasha's mother is sending for him from Harkov. Oh, mercy on us!'

She was in despair. Her head, her hands, and her feet would turn chill, and she would feel that she was the most unhappy woman in the world. But another minute would pass, voices would be heard: it would turn out to be the veterinary surgeon coming home from the club.

'Well, thank God!' she would think.

And gradually the load in her heart would pass off, and she would feel at ease. She would go back to bed thinking of Sasha, who lay sound asleep in the next room, sometimes crying out in his sleep:

'I'll give it you! Get away! Shut up!'

44

THE NIGHTINGALE AND THE ROSE
Oscar Wilde

Alas! Love invokes risks and sacrifices and does not always triumph.

'She said that she would dance with me if I brought her red roses,' cried the young Student; 'but in all my garden there is no red rose.'

From her nest in the holm-oak tree the Nightingale heard him, and she looked out through the leaves, and wondered.

'No red rose in all my garden!' he cried, and his beautiful eyes filled with tears. 'Ah, on what little things does happiness depend! I have read all that the wise men have written, and all the secrets of philosophy are mine, yet for want of a red rose is my life made wretched.'

'Here at last is a true lover,' said the Nightingale. 'Night after night have I sung of him, though I knew him not: night after night have I told his story to the stars, and now I see him. His hair is dark as the hyacinth-blossom, and his lips are red as the rose of his desire; but passion has made his lace like pale Ivory, and sorrow has set her seal upon his brow.'

'The Prince gives a ball to-morrow night,' murmured the young Student, 'and my love will be of the company. If I bring her a red rose she will dance with me till dawn. If I bring her a red rose, I shall hold her in my arms, and she will lean her head upon my shoulder, and her hand will be clasped in mine. But there is no red rose in my garden, so I shall sit lonely, and she will pass me by. She will have no heed of me, and my heart will break.'

'Here indeed is the true lover,' said the Nightingale. 'What

I sing of he suffers: what is joy to me, to him is pain. Surely Love is a wonderful thing. It is more precious than emeralds, and dearer than fine opals. Pearls and pomegranates cannot buy it, nor is it set forth in the market-place. It may not be purchased of the merchants, or can it be weighed out in the balance for gold.'

'The musicians will sit in their gallery,' said the young Student, 'and play upon their stringed instruments, and my love will dance to the sound of the harp and the violin. She will dance so lightly that her feet will not touch the floor, and the courtiers in their gay dresses will throng round her. But with me she will not dance, for I have no red rose to give her,' and he flung himself down on the grass, and buried his face in his hands, and wept.

'Why is he weeping?' asked a little green Lizard, as he ran past him with his tail in the air.

'Why, indeed?' said a Butterfly, who was fluttering about after a sunbeam.

'Why, indeed?' whispered a Daisy to his neighbour, in a soft, low voice.

'He is weeping for a red rose,' said the Nightingale.

'For a red rose!' they cried, 'How very ridiculous!' and the little Lizard, who was something of a cynic, laughed outright.

But the Nightingale understood the secret of the Student's sorrow, and she sat silent in the oak-tree, and thought about the mystery of Love.

Suddenly she spread her brown wings for flight, and soared into the air. She passed through the grove like a shadow, and like a shadow she sailed across the garden.

In the centre of the grass-plot was standing a beautiful Rose-tree, and when she saw it, she flew over to it, and lit upon a spray.

'Give me a red rose,' she cried, 'and I will sing you my sweetest song.'

But the Tree shook its head.

'My roses are white,' it answered; 'as white as the foam of the sea, and whiter than the snow upon the mountain. But go to my brother who grows round the old sun-dial, and perhaps he will give you what you want.'

So the Nightingale flew over to the Rose-tree that was growing round the old sun-dial.

'Give me a red rose,' she cried, 'and I will sing you my sweetest song.'

But the Tree shook its head.

'My roses are yellow,' it answered; 'as yellow as the hair of the mermaiden who sits upon an amber throne, and yellower than the daffodil that blooms in the meadow before the mower comes with his scythe. But go to my brother who grows beneath the Student's window, and perhaps he will give you what you want.'

So the Nightingale flew over to the Rose-tree that was growing beneath the Student's window.

'Give me a red rose,' she cried, 'and I will sing you my sweetest song.'

But the Tree shook its head.

'My roses are red,' it answered, 'as red as the feet of the dove, and redder than the great fans of coral that wave and wave in the ocean-cavern. But the winter has chilled my veins, and the frost has nipped my buds, and the storm has broken my branches, and I shall have no roses at all this year.'

'One red rose is all I want,' cried the Nightingale, 'only one red rose! Is there no way by which I can get it?'

'There is a way,' answered the Tree; 'but it is so terrible that I dare not tell it to you.'

'Tell it to me,' said the Nightingale, 'I am not afraid.'

'If you want a red rose,' said the Tree, 'you must build it out of music by moonlight, and stain it with your own heart's blood. You must sing to me with your breast against a thorn. All night long you must sing to me, and the thorn must pierce your heart, and your life-blood must flow into my veins, and become mine.'

'Death is a great price to pay for a red rose,' cried the Nightingale, 'and Life is very dear to all. It is pleasant to sit in the green wood, and to watch the Sun in his chariot of gold, and the Moon in her chariot of pearl. Sweet is the scent of the hawthorn, and sweet are the bluebells that hide in the valley, and the heather that blows on the hill. Yet Love is better than Life, and what is the heart of a bird compared to the heart of a man?'

So she spread her brown wings for flight, and soared into the air. She swept over the garden like a shadow, and like a shadow she sailed through the grove.

The young Student was still lying on the grass, where she had left him, and the tears were not yet dry in his beautiful eyes.

'Be happy,' cried the Nightingale, 'be happy; you shall have your red rose. I will build it out of music by moonlight, and stain it with my own heart's blood. All that I ask of you in return is that you will be a true lover, for Love is wiser than Philosophy, though she is wise, and mightier than Power, though he is mighty. Flame-coloured are his wings, and coloured like flame is his body. His lips are sweet as honey, and his breath is like frankincense.'

The Student looked up from the grass, and listened, but he could not understand what the Nightingale was saying to him, for he only knew the things that are written down in books.

But the Oak-tree understood, and felt sad, for he was very fond of the little Nightingale who had built her nest in his branches.

'Sing me one last song,' he whispered; 'I shall feel very lonely when you are gone.'

So the Nightingale sang to the Oak-tree, and her voice was like water bubbling from a silver jar.

When she had finished her song the Student got lip, and pulled a note-book and a lead-pencil out of his pocket.

'She has form,' he said to himself, as he walked away through the grove, 'that cannot be denied to her; but has she got feeling? I am afraid not. In fact, she is like most artists; she is all style, without any sincerity. She would not sacrifice herself for others. She thinks merely of music, and everybody knows that the arts are selfish. Still, it must be admitted that she has some beautiful notes in her voice. What a pity it is that they do not mean anything, or do any practical good.' And he went into his room, and lay down on his little pallet-bed, and began to think of his love; and, after a time, he fell asleep.

And when the Moon shone in the heavens the Nightingale flew to the Rose-tree, and set her breast against the thorn. All night long she sang with her breast against the thorn, and the cold crystal Moon leaned down and listened. All night long she sang, and the thorn went deeper and deeper into her breast, and her life-blood ebbed away from her.

She sang first of the birth of love in the heart of a boy and a girl. And on the topmost spray of the Rose-tree there blossomed a marvellous rose, petal following petal, as song followed song. Pale was it, at first, as the mist that hangs over the river—pale as the feet of the morning, and silver as the wings of the dawn. As the shadow of a rose in a mirror of silver, as the shadow of a rose in a water-pool, so was the rose that blossomed on the topmost spray of the Tree.

But the Tree cried to the Nightingale to press closer against the thorn. 'Press closer, little Nightingale,' cried the Tree, 'or the Day will come before the rose is finished.'

So the Nightingale pressed closer against the thorn, and louder and louder grew her song, for she sang of the birth of passion in the soul of a man and a maid.

And a delicate flush of pink came into the leaves of the rose, like the flush in the face of the bridegroom when he kisses the lips of the bride. But the thorn had not yet reached her heart, so the rose's heart remained white, for only a Nightingale's heart's-blood can crimson the heart of a rose.

And the Tree cried to the Nightingale to press closer against the thorn. 'Press closer, little Nightingale,' cried the Tree, 'or the Day will come before the rose is finished.'

So the Nightingale pressed closer against the thorn, and the thorn touched her heart, and a fierce pang of pain shot through her. Bitter, bitter was the pain, and wilder and wilder grew her song, for she sang of the Love that is perfected by Death, of the Love that dies not in the tomb.

And the marvellous rose became crimson, like the rose of the eastern sky. Crimson was the girdle of petals, and crimson as a ruby was the heart.

But the Nightingale's voice grew fainter, and her little wings began to beat, and a film came over her eyes. Fainter and fainter grew her song, and she felt something choking her in her throat.

Then she gave one last burst of music. The white Moon heard it, and she forgot the dawn, and lingered on in the sky. The red rose heard it, and it trembled all over with ecstasy, and opened its petals to the cold morning air. Echo bore it to her purple cavern in the hills, and woke the sleeping shepherds from their dreams. It floated through the reeds of the river, and they carried its message to the sea.

'Look, look!' cried the Tree, 'the rose is finished now,' but the Nightingale made no answer, for she was lying dead in the long grass, with the thorn in her heart.

And at noon the Student opened his window and looked out.

'Why, what a wonderful piece of luck!' he cried; 'here is a red rose! I have never seen any rose like it in all my life. It is so beautiful that I am sure it has a long Latin name,' and he leaned down and plucked it.

Then he put on his hat, and ran up to the Professor's house with the rose in his hand.

The daughter of the Professor was sitting in the doorway winding blue silk on a reel, and her little dog was lying at her feet.

'You said that you would dance with me if I brought you a

red rose,' cried the Student. Here is the reddest rose in all the world. You will wear it to-night next your heart, and as we dance together it will tell you how I love you.'

But the girl frowned.

'I am afraid it will not go with my dress,' she answered; 'and, besides, the Chamberlain's nephew has sent me some real jewels, and everybody knows that jewels cost far more than flowers.'

'Well, upon my word, you are very ungrateful,' said the Student angrily; and he threw the rose into the street, where it fell into the gutter, and a cart-wheel went over it.

'Ungrateful!' said the girl. 'I tell you what, you are very rude; and, after all, who are you? Only a Student. Why, I don't believe you have even got silver buckles to your shoes as the Chamberlain's nephew has,' and she got up from her chair and went into the house.

'What a silly thing Love is,' said the Student as he walked away. 'It is not half as useful as Logic, for it does not prove anything, and it is always telling one of things that are not going to happen, and making one believe things that are not true. In fact, it is quite unpractical, and, as in this age to be practical is everything, I shall go back to Philosophy and study Metaphysics.'

So he returned to his room and pulled out a great dusty book, and began to read.

45

ON THE GULL'S ROAD

Willa Cather

Requiem of love: sadness, pain, loneliness, happiness and unattainable love.

I

It often happens that one or another of my friends stops before a red chalk drawing in my study and asks me where I ever found so lovely a creature. I have never told the story of that picture to any one, and the beautiful woman on the wall, until yesterday, in all these twenty years has spoken to no one but me. Yesterday a young painter, a countryman of mine, came to consult me on a matter of business, and upon seeing my drawing of Alexandra Ebbling, straightway forgot his errand. He examined the date upon the sketch and asked me, very earnestly, if I could tell him whether the lady were still living. When I answered him, he stepped back from the picture and said slowly:

'So long ago? She must have been very young. She was happy?'

'As to that, who can say—about any one of us?' I replied. 'Out of all that is supposed to make for happiness, she had very little.'

We returned to the object of his visit, but when he bade me goodbye at the door his troubled gaze again went back to the drawing, and it was only by turning sharply about that he took his eyes away from her.

I went back to my study fire, and as the rain kept away less impetuous visitors, I had a long time in which to think of Mrs Ebbling. I even got out the little box she gave me, which I had not opened for years, and when Mrs Hemway brought my tea I had barely time to close the lid and defeat her disapproving gaze.

My young countryman's perplexity, as he looked at Mrs Ebbling, had recalled to me the delight and pain she gave me when I was of his years. I sat looking at her face and trying to see it through his eyes—freshly, as I saw it first upon the deck of the Germania, twenty years ago. Was it her loveliness, I often ask myself, or her loneliness, or her simplicity, or was it merely my own youth? Was her mystery only that of the mysterious North out of which she came? I still feel that she was very different from all the beautiful and brilliant women I have known; as the night is different from the day, or as the sea is different from the land. But this is our story, as it comes back to me.

For two years I had been studying Italian and working in the capacity of clerk to the American legation at Rome, and I was going home to secure my first consular appointment. Upon boarding my steamer at Genoa, I saw my luggage into my cabin and then started for a rapid circuit of the deck. Everything promised well. The boat was thinly peopled, even for a July crossing; the decks were roomy; the day was fine; the sea was blue; I was sure of my appointment, and, best of all, I was coming back to Italy. All these things were in my mind when I stopped sharply before a chaise longue placed sidewise near the stern. Its occupant was a woman, apparently ill, who lay with her eyes closed, and in her open arm was a chubby little red-haired girl, asleep. I can still remember that first glance at Mrs Ebbling, and how I stopped as a wheel does when the band slips. Her splendid, vigorous body lay still and relaxed under the loose folds of her clothing, her white throat and arms and red-gold hair were drenched with sunlight. Such hair as it was: wayward as some kind of gleaming seaweed that curls and undulates with the tide. A moment gave me her face; the high cheek-bones, the thin cheeks, the gentle chin, arching back to a girlish throat, and the singular loveliness of the mouth.

Even then it flashed through me that the mouth gave the whole face its peculiar beauty and distinction. It was proud and sad and tender, and strangely calm. The curve of the lips could not have been cut more cleanly with the most delicate instrument, and whatever shade of feeling passed over them seemed to partake of their exquisiteness.

But I am anticipating. While I stood stupidly staring (as if, at twenty-five, I had never before beheld a beautiful woman) the whistles broke into a hoarse scream, and the deck under us began to vibrate. The woman opened her eyes, and the little girl struggled into a sitting position, rolled out of her mother's arm, and ran to the deck rail. After putting my chair near the stern, I went forward to see the gang-plank up and did not return until we were dragging out to sea at the end of a long tow-line.

The woman in the chaise longue was still alone. She lay there all day, looking at the sea. The little girl, Carin, played noisily about the deck. Occasionally she returned and struggled up into the chair, plunged her head, round and red as a little pumpkin, against her mother's shoulder in an impetuous embrace, and then struggled down again with a lively flourishing of arms and legs. Her mother took such opportunities to pull up the child's socks or to smooth the fiery little braids; her beautiful hands, rather large and very white, played about the riotous little girl with a quieting tenderness. Carin chattered away in Italian and kept asking for her father, only to be told that he was busy.

When any of the ship's officers passed, they stopped for a word with my neighbour, and I heard the first mate address her as Mrs Ebbling. When they spoke to her, she smiled appreciatively and answered in low, faltering Italian, but I fancied that she was glad when they passed on and left her to her fixed contemplation of the sea. Her eyes seemed to drink the colour of it all day long, and after every interruption they went back to it. There was a kind of pleasure in watching her satisfaction, a kind of excitement in wondering what the water made her remember or forget. She seemed not to wish to talk to any one, but I knew I should like to hear whatever she might be thinking. One could catch some hint of her thoughts, I imagined, from the shadows that came and went across her lips, like the reflection of light clouds. She had a pile of books beside her, but she did not read, and neither could I. I gave up trying at last, and watched the sea, very conscious of her presence, almost of her thoughts. When the sun dropped low and shone in her face, I rose and asked if she would like me to move her chair. She smiled and thanked me, but said the sun was good for her. Her yellow-hazel eyes followed me for a moment and then went back to the sea.

After the first bugle sounded for dinner, a heavy man in uniform came up the deck and stood beside the chaise longue, looking down at its two occupants with a smile of satisfied possession. The breast of his trim coat was hidden by waves of soft blond beard, as long and heavy as a woman's hair, which blew about his face in glittering profusion. He wore a large turquoise ring upon the thick hand that he rubbed good-humouredly over the little girl's head. To her he spoke Italian, but he and his wife conversed in some Scandinavian tongue. He stood stroking his fine beard until the second bugle blew, then bent stiffly from his hips, like a soldier, and patted his wife's hand as it lay on the arm of her chair. He hurried down the deck, taking stock of the passengers as he went, and stopped before a thin girl with frizzed hair and a lace coat, asking her a facetious question in thick English. They began to talk about Chicago and went below. Later I saw him at the head of his table in the dining room, the befrizzed Chicago lady on his left. They must have got a famous start at luncheon, for by the end of the dinner Ebbling was peeling figs for her and presenting them on the end of a fork.

The Doctor confided to me that Ebbling was the chief engineer and the dandy of the boat; but this time he would have to behave

394 • 50 GREATEST LOVE STORIES

himself, for he had brought his sick wife along for the voyage. She had a bad heart valve, he added, and was in a serious way.

After dinner Ebbling disappeared, presumably to his engines, and at ten o'clock, when the stewardess came to put Mrs Ebbling to bed, I helped her to rise from her chair, and the second mate ran up and supported her down to her cabin. About midnight I found the engineer in the card room, playing with the Doctor, an Italian naval officer, and the commodore of a Long Island yacht club. His face was even pinker than it had been at dinner, and his fine beard was full of smoke. I thought a long while about Ebbling and his wife before I went to sleep.

The next morning we tied up at Naples to take on our cargo, and I went on shore for the day. I did not, however, entirely escape the ubiquitous engineer, whom I saw lunching with the Long Island commodore at a hotel in the Santa Lucia. When I returned to the boat in the early evening, the passengers had gone down to dinner, and I found Mrs Ebbling quite alone upon the deserted deck. I approached her and asked whether she had had a dull day. She looked up smiling and shook her head, as if her Italian had quite failed her. I saw that she was flushed with excitement, and her yellow eyes were shining like two clear topazes.

'Dull? Oh, no! I love to watch Naples from the sea, in this white heat. She has just lain there on her hillside among the vines and laughed for me all day long. I have been able to pick out many of the places I like best.'

I felt that she was really going to talk to me at last. She had turned to me frankly, as to an old acquaintance, and seemed not to be hiding from me anything of what she felt. I sat down in a glow of pleasure and excitement and asked her if she knew Naples well.

'Oh, yes! I lived there for a year after I was first married. My husband has a great many friends in Naples. But he was at sea most of the time, so I went about alone. Nothing helps one to know a city like that. I came first by sea, like this. Directly to Naples from Finmark, and I had never been South before.' Mrs Ebbling stopped and looked over my shoulder. Then, with a quick, eager glance at me, she said abruptly: 'It was like a baptism of fire. Nothing has ever been quite the same since. Imagine how this bay looked to a Finmark girl. It seemed like the overture to Italy.'

I laughed. 'And then one goes up the country—song by song and wine by wine.'

Mrs Ebbling sighed. 'Ah, yes. It must be fine to follow it. I have never been away from the seaports myself. We live now in Genoa.'

The deck steward brought her tray, and I moved forward a little and stood by the rail. When I looked back, she smiled and nodded to let me know that she was not missing anything. I could feel her intentness as keenly as if she were standing beside me.

The sun had disappeared over the high ridge behind the city, and the stone pines stood black and flat against the fires of the afterglow. The lilac haze that hung over the long, lazy slopes of Vesuvius warmed with golden light, and films of blue vapour began to float down toward Baiae. The sky, the sea, and the city between them turned a shimmering violet, fading greyer as the lights began to glow like luminous pearls along the water-front—the necklace of an irreclaimable queen. Behind me I heard a low exclamation; a slight, stifled sound, but it seemed the perfect vocalization of that weariness with which we at last let go of beauty, after we have held it until the senses are darkened. When I turned to her again, she seemed to have fallen asleep.

That night, as we were moving out to sea and the tail lights of Naples were winking across the widening stretch of black water, I helped Mrs Ebbling to the foot of the stairway. She drew herself up from her chair with effort and leaned on me wearily. I could have carried her all night without fatigue.

'May I come and talk to you to-morrow?' I asked. She did

not reply at once. 'Like an old friend?' I added. She gave me her languid hand, and her mouth, set with the exertion of walking, softened altogether. 'Grazia,' she murmured.

I returned to the deck and joined a group of my countrywomen, who, primed with inexhaustible information, were discussing the baseness of Renaissance art. They were intelligent and alert, and as they leaned forward in their deck chairs under the circle of light, their faces recalled to me Rembrandt's picture of a clinical lecture. I heard them through, against my will, and then went to the stern to smoke and to see the last of the island lights. The sky had clouded over, and a soft, melancholy wind was rushing over the sea. I could not help thinking how disappointed I would be if rain should keep Mrs Ebbling in her cabin to-morrow. My mind played constantly with her image. At one moment she was very clear and directly in front of me; the next she was far away. Whatever else I thought about, some part of my consciousness was busy with Mrs Ebbling; hunting for her, finding her, losing her, then groping again. How was it that I was so conscious of whatever she might be feeling? That when she sat still behind me and watched the evening sky, I had had a sense of speed and change, almost of danger; and when she was tired and sighed, I had wished for night and loneliness.

II

Though when we are young we seldom think much about it, there is now and again a golden day when we feel a sudden, arrogant pride in our youth; in the lightness of our feet and the strength of our arms, in the warm fluid that courses so surely within us; when we are conscious of something powerful and mercurial in our breasts, which comes up wave after wave and leaves us irresponsible and free. All the next morning I felt this flow of life, which continually impelled me toward Mrs Ebbling. After the merest greeting, however, I kept away. I found it pleasant to thwart myself, to measure myself against a current that was sure to carry me with it in the end. I was content to let her watch the sea—the sea that seemed now to have come into me, warm and soft, still and strong. I played shuffleboard with the Commodore, who was anxious to keep down his figure, and ran about the deck with the stout legs of the little pumpkin-coloured Carin about my neck. It was not until the child was having her afternoon nap below that I at last came up and stood beside her mother.

'You are better to-day,' I exclaimed, looking down at her white gown. She coloured unreasonably, and I laughed with a familiarity which she must have accepted as the mere foolish noise of happiness, or it would have seemed impertinent.

We talked at first of a hundred trivial things, and we watched the sea. The coast of Sardinia had lain to our port for some hours and would lie there for hours to come, now advancing in rocky promontories, now retreating behind blue bays. It was the naked south coast of the island, and though our course held very near the shore, not a village or habitation was visible; there was not even a goat-herd's hut hidden away among the low pinkish sand hills. Pinkish sand hills and yellow head-lands; with dull-coloured scrubby bushes massed about their bases and following the dried water-courses. A narrow strip of beach glistened like white paint between the purple sea and the umber rocks, and the whole island lay gleaming in the yellow sunshine and translucent air. Not a wave broke on that fringe of white sand, not the shadow of a cloud played across the bare hills. In the air about us, there was no sound but that of a vessel moving rapidly through absolutely still water. She seemed like some great sea-animal, swimming silently, her head well up. The sea before us was so rich and heavy and opaque that it might have been lapis lazuli. It was the blue of legend, simply; the colour that satisfies the soul like sleep.

And it was of the sea we talked, for it was the substance of Mrs Ebbling's story. She seemed always to have been swept along by ocean streams, warm or cold, and to have hovered about the edge of great waters. She was born and had grown up in a little fishing town on the Arctic ocean. Her father was a doctor, a widower, who lived with his daughter and who divided his time between his books and his fishing rod. Her uncle was skipper on a coasting vessel, and with him she had made many trips along the Norwegian coast. But she was always reading and thinking about the blue seas of the South.

'There was a curious old woman in our village, Dame Ericson, who had been in Italy in her youth. She had gone to Rome to study art, and had copied a great many pictures there. She was well connected, but had little money, and as she grew older and poorer she sold her pictures one by one, until there was scarcely a well-to-do family in our district that did not own one of Dame Ericson's paintings. But she brought home many other strange things; a little orange-tree which she cherished until the day of her death, and bits of coloured marble, and sea shells and pieces of coral, and a thin flask full of water from the Mediterranean. When I was a little girl she used to show me her things and tell me about the South; about the coral fishers, and the pink islands, and the smoking mountains, and the old, underground Naples. I suppose the water in her flask was like any other, but it never seemed so to me. It looked so elastic and alive, that I used to think if one unsealed the bottle something penetrating and fruitful might leap out and work an enchantment over Finmark.'

Lars Ebbling, I learned, was one of her father's friends. She could remember him from the time when she was a little girl and he a dashing young man who used to come home from the sea and make a stir in the village. After he got his promotion to an Atlantic liner and went South, she did not see him until the summer she was twenty, when he came home to marry her.

That was five years ago. The little girl, Carin, was three. From her talk, one might have supposed that Ebbling was proprietor of the Mediterranean and its adjacent lands, and could have kept her away at his pleasure. Her own rights in him she seemed not to consider.

But we wasted very little time on Lars Ebbling. We talked, like two very young persons, of arms and men, of the sea beneath us and the shores it washed. We were carried a little beyond ourselves, for we were in the presence of the things of youth that never change; fleeing past them. To-morrow they would be gone, and no effort of will or memory could bring them back again. All about us was the sea of great adventure, and below us, caught somewhere in its gleaming meshes, were the bones of nations and navies…nations and navies that gave youth its hope and made life something more than a hunger of the bowels. The unpeopled Sardinian coast unfolded gently before us, like something left over out of a world that was gone; a place that might well have had no later news since the corn ships brought the tidings of Actium.

'I shall never go to Sardinia,' said Mrs Ebbling. 'It could not possibly be as beautiful as this.'

'Neither shall I,' I replied.

As I was going down to dinner that evening, I was stopped by Lars Ebbling, freshly brushed and scented, wearing a white uniform, and polished and glistening as one of his own engines. He smiled at me with his own kind of geniality. 'You have been very kind to talk to my wife,' he explained. 'It is very bad for her this trip that she speaks no English. I am indebted to you.'

I told him curtly that he was mistaken, but my acrimony made no impression upon his blandness. I felt that I should certainly strike the fellow if he stood there much longer, running his blue ring up and down his beard. I should probably have hated any man who was Mrs Ebbling's husband, but Ebbling made me sick.

III

The next day I began my drawing of Mrs Ebbling. She seemed pleased and a little puzzled when I asked her to sit for me. It occurred to me that she had always been among dull people who took her looks as a matter of course, and that she was not at all sure that she was really beautiful. I can see now her quick, confused look of pleasure. I thought very little about the drawing then, except that the making of it gave me an opportunity to study her face; to look as long as I pleased into her yellow eyes, at the noble lines of her mouth, at her splendid, vigorous hair.

'We have a yellow vine at home,' I told her, 'that is very like your hair. It seems to be growing while one looks at it, and it twines and tangles about itself and throws out little tendrils in the wind.'

'Has it any name?'

'We call it love vine.'

How little a thing could disconcert her!

As for me, nothing disconcerted me. I awoke every morning with a sense of speed and joy. At night I loved to hear the swish of the water rushing by. As fast as the pistons could carry us, as fast as the water could bear us, we were going forward to something delightful; to something together. When Mrs Ebbling told me that she and her husband would be five days in the docks in New York and then return to Genoa, I was not disturbed, for I did not believe her. I came and went, and she sat still all day, watching the water. I heard an American lady say that she watched it like one who is going to die, but even that did not frighten me: I somehow felt that she had promised me to live.

All those long blue days when I sat beside her talking about Finmark and the sea, she must have known that I loved her. I sat with my hands idle on my knees and let the tide come up in me. It carried me so swiftly that, across the narrow space of deck between us, it must have swayed her, too, a little. I had no wish to disturb or distress her. If a little, a very little of it reached her, I was satisfied. If it drew her softly, but drew her, I wanted no more. Sometimes I could see that even the light pressure of my thoughts made her paler. One still evening, after a long talk, she whispered to me, 'You must go and walk now, and—don't think about me.' She had been held too long and too closely in my thoughts, and she begged me to release her for a little while. I went out into the bow and put her far away, at the sky line, with the faintest star, and thought of her gently across the water. When I went back to her, she was asleep.

But even in those first days I had my hours of misery. Why, for instance, should she have been born in Finmark, and why should Lars Ebbling have been her only door of escape? Why should she be silently taking leave of the world at the age when I was just beginning it, having had nothing, nothing of whatever is worth while?

She never talked about taking leave of things, and yet I sometimes felt that she was counting the sunsets. One yellow afternoon, when we were gliding between the shores of Spain and Africa, she spoke of her illness for the first time. I had got some magnolias at Gibraltar, and she wore a bunch of them in her girdle and the rest lay on her lap. She held the cool leaves against her cheek and fingered the white petals. 'I can never,' she remarked, 'get enough of the flowers of the South. They make me breathless, just as they did at first. Because of them I should like to live a long while—almost forever.'

I leaned forward and looked at her. 'We could live almost forever if we had enough courage. It's of our lives that we die. If we had the courage to change it all, to run away to some blue coast like that over there, we could live on and on, until we were tired.'

She smiled tolerantly and looked southward through half shut eyes. 'I am afraid I should never have courage enough to go behind that mountain, at least. Look at it, it looks as if it hid horrible things.'

A sea mist, blown in from the Atlantic, began to mask the impassive African coast, and above the fog, the grey mountain peak took on the angry red of the sunset. It burned sullen and threatening until the dark land drew the night about her and settled back into the sea. We watched it sink, while under us, slowly but ever increasing, we felt the throb of the Atlantic come and go, the thrill of the vast, untamed waters of that lugubrious and passionate sea. I drew Mrs Ebbling's wraps about her and shut the magnolias under her cloak. When I left her, she slipped me one warm, white flower.

IV

From the Straits of Gibraltar we dropped into the abyss, and by morning we were rolling in the trough of a sea that drew us down and held us deep, shaking us gently back and forth until the timbers creaked, and then shooting us out on the crest of a swelling mountain. The water was bright and blue, but so cold that the breath of it penetrated one's bones, as if the chill of the deep under-fathoms of the sea were being loosed upon us. There were not more than a dozen people upon the deck that morning, and Mrs Ebbling was sheltered behind the stern, muffled in a sea jacket, with drops of moisture upon her long lashes and on her hair. When a shower of icy spray beat back over the deck rail, she took it gleefully.

'After all,' she insisted, 'this is my own kind of water; the kind I was born in. This is first cousin to the Pole waters, and the sea we have left is only a kind of fairy tale. It's like the burnt out volcanoes; its day is over. This is the real sea now, where the doings of the world go on.'

'It is not our reality, at any rate,' I answered.

'Oh, yes, it is! These are the waters that carry men to their work, and they will carry you to yours.'

I sat down and watched her hair grow more alive and iridescent in the moisture. 'You are pleased to take an attitude,' I complained.

'No, I don't love realities any more than another, but I admit them, all the same.'

'And who are you and I to define the realities?'

'Our minds define them clearly enough, yours and mine, everybody's. Those are the lines we never cross, though we flee from the equator to the Pole. I have never really got out of Finmark, of course. I shall live and die in a fishing town on the Arctic ocean, and the blue seas and the pink islands are as much a dream as they ever were. All the same, I shall continue to dream them.'

The Gulf Stream gave us warm blue days again, but pale, like sad memories. The water had faded, and the thin, tepid sunshine made something tighten about one's heart. The stars watched us coldly, and seemed always to be asking me what I was going to do. The advancing line on the chart, which at first had been mere foolishness, began to mean something, and the wind from the west brought disturbing fears and forebodings. I slept lightly, and all day I was restless and uncertain except when I was with Mrs Ebbling. She quieted me as she did little Carin, and soothed me without saying anything, as she had done that evening at Naples when we watched the sunset. It seemed to me that every day her eyes grew more tender and her lips more calm. A kind of fortitude seemed to be gathering about her mouth, and I dreaded it. Yet when, in an involuntary glance, I put to her the question that tortured me, her eyes always met mine steadily, deep and gentle and full of reassurance. That I had my word at last, happened almost by accident.

On the second night out from shore there was the concert for the Sailors' Orphanage, and Mrs Ebbling dressed and went down to dinner for the first time, and sat on her husband's right. I was not the only one who was glad to see her. Even the women were pleased. She wore a pale green gown, and she came up out of it regally white and gold. I was so proud that I blushed when any one spoke of her. After dinner she was standing by her deck-chair talking to her husband when people began to go below for the concert. She took up a long cloak and attempted to put it on. The wind blew the light thing about, and Ebbling chatted and smiled his public smile while she struggled with it. Suddenly his roving eye caught sight of the Chicago girl, who was having a similar difficulty with her draperies, and he pranced half the length of the deck to assist her. I had been watching from the rail, and when she was left alone I threw my cigar away and wrapped Mrs Ebbling up roughly.

'Don't go down,' I begged. 'Stay up here. I want to talk to you.'

She hesitated a moment and looked at me thoughtfully. Then, with a sigh, she sat down. Every one hurried down to the saloon, and we were absolutely alone at last, behind the shelter of the stern, with the thick darkness all about us and a warm east wind rushing over the sea. I was too sore and angry to think. I leaned toward her, holding the arm of her chair with both hands, and began anywhere.

'You remember those two blue coasts out of Gibraltar? It shall be either one you choose, if you will come with me. I have not much money, but we shall get on somehow. There has got to be an end of this. We are neither one of us cowards, and this is humiliating, intolerable.'

She sat looking down at her hands, and I pulled her chair impatiently toward me.

'I felt,' she said at last, 'that you were going to say something like this. You are sorry for me, and I don't wish to be pitied. You think Ebbling neglects me, but you are mistaken. He has had his disappointments, too. He wants children and a gay, hospitable house, and he is tied to a sick woman who can not get on with people. He has more to complain of than I have, and yet he bears with me. I am grateful to him, and there is no more to be said.'

'Oh, isn't there?' I cried, 'and I?'

She laid her hand entreatingly upon my arm. 'Ah, you! You! Don't ask me to talk about that. You—' Her fingers slipped down my coat sleeve to my hand and pressed it. I caught her two hands and held them, telling her I would never let them go.

'And you meant to leave me day after tomorrow, to say goodbye to me as you will to the other people on this boat? You meant to cut me adrift like this, with my heart on fire and all my life unspent in me?'

She sighed despondently. 'I am willing to suffer—whatever I must suffer—to have had you,' she answered simply. 'I was ill—and so lonely—and it came so quickly and quietly. Ah, don't begrudge it to me! Do not leave me in bitterness. If I have been wrong, forgive me.' She bowed her head and pressed my fingers entreatingly. A warm tear splashed on my hand. It occurred to me that she bore my anger as she bore little Carin's importunities, as she bore Ebbling. What a circle of pettiness she had about her! I fell back in my chair and my hands dropped at my side. I felt like a creature with its back broken. I asked her what she wished me to do.

'Don't ask me,' she whispered. 'There is nothing that we can do. I thought you knew that. You forget that—that I am too ill to begin my life over. Even if there were nothing else in the way, that would be enough. And that is what has made it all possible, our loving each other, I mean. If I were well, we couldn't have had even this much. Don't reproach me. Hasn't it been at all pleasant to you to find me waiting for you every morning, to feel me thinking of you when you went to sleep? Every night I have watched the sea for you, as if it were mine and I had made it, and I have listened to the water rushing by you, full of sleep and youth and hope. And everything you had done or said during the day came back to me, and when I went to sleep it was only to feel you more. You see there was never any one else; I have never thought of any one in the dark but you.' She spoke pleadingly, and her voice had sunk so low that I could scarcely hear her.

'And yet you will do nothing,' I groaned. 'You will dare nothing. You will give me nothing.'

'Don't say that. When I leave you day after tomorrow, I shall have given you all my life. I can't tell you how, but it is true. There is something in each of us that does not belong to the family or to society, not even to ourselves. Sometimes it is given in marriage, and sometimes it is given in love, but oftener it is never given at all. We have nothing to do with giving or withholding it. It is a wild thing that sings in us once and flies away and never comes back, and mine has flown to you. When one loves like that, it is enough, somehow. The other things can go if they must. That is why I can live without you, and die without you.'

I caught her hands and looked into her eyes that shone warm in the darkness. She shivered and whispered in a tone so different from any I ever heard from her before or afterward: 'Do you grudge it to me? You are so young and strong, and you have everything before you. I shall have only a little while to want you in and I could want you forever and not weary.' I kissed her hair, her cheeks, her lips, until her head fell forward on my shoulder and she put my face away with her soft, trembling fingers. She took my hand and held it close to her, in both her own. We sat silent, and the moments came and went, bringing us closer and closer, and the wind and water rushed by us, obliterating our tomorrows and all our yesterdays.

The next day Mrs Ebbling kept her cabin, and I sat stupidly by her chair until dark, with the rugged little girl to keep me company, and an occasional nod from the engineer.

I saw Mrs Ebbling again only for a few moments, when we were coming into the New York harbour. She wore a street dress and a hat, and these alone would have made her seem far away from me. She was very pale, and looked down when she spoke to me, as if she had been guilty of a wrong toward me. I have never been able to remember that interview without heartache and shame, but then I was too desperate to care about anything. I stood like a wooden post and let her approach me, let her speak to me, let her leave me. She came up to me as if it were a hard thing to do, and held out a little package, timidly, and her gloved hand shook as if she were afraid of me.

'I want to give you something,' she said. 'You will not want it now, so I shall ask you to keep it until you hear from me. You gave me your address a long time ago, when you were making that drawing. Some day I shall write to you and ask you to open this. You must not come to tell me goodbye this morning, but I shall be watching you when you go ashore. Please don't forget that.'

I took the little box mechanically and thanked her. I think my eyes must have filled, for she uttered an exclamation of pity, touched my sleeve quickly, and left me. It was one of those strange, low, musical exclamations which meant everything and nothing, like the one that had thrilled me that night at Naples, and it was the last sound I ever heard from her lips.

An hour later I went on shore, one of those who crowded over the gang-plank the moment it was lowered. But the next afternoon I wandered back to the docks and went on board the Germania. I asked for the engineer, and he came up in his shirt sleeves from the engine room. He was red and dishevelled, angry and voluble; his bright eye had a hard glint, and I did not once see his masterful smile. When he heard my inquiry he became profane. Mrs Ebbling had sailed for Bremen on the Hobenstauffen that morning at eleven o'clock. She had decided to return by the northern route and pay a visit to her father in Finmark. She was in no condition to travel alone, he said. He evidently smarted under her extravagance. But who, he asked, with a blow of his fist on the rail, could stand between a woman and her whim? She had always been a wilful girl, and she had a doting father behind her. When she set her head with the wind, there was no holding her; she ought to have married the Arctic Ocean. I think Ebbling was still talking when I walked away.

I spent that winter in New York. My consular appointment hung fire (indeed, I did not pursue it with much enthusiasm), and I had a good many idle hours in which to think of Mrs Ebbling. She had never mentioned the name of her father's village, and somehow I could never quite bring myself to go to the docks when Ebbling's boat was in and ask for news of her. More than once I made up my mind definitely to go to Finmark and take my chance at finding her; the shipping people would know where Ebbling came from. But I never went. I have often wondered why. When my resolve was made and my courage high, when I could almost feel myself approaching her, suddenly everything crumbled under me, and I fell back as I had done that night when I dropped her hands, after telling her, only a moment before, that I would never let them go.

In the twilight of a wet March day, when the gutters were running black outside and the Square was liquefying under crusts of dirty snow, the housekeeper brought me a damp letter which bore a blurred foreign postmark. It was from Niels Nannestad, who wrote that it was his sad duty to inform me that his daughter, Alexandra Ebbling, had died on the second day of February, in the twenty-sixth year of her age. Complying with her request, he inclosed a letter which she had written some days before her death.

I at last brought myself to break the seal of the second letter. It read thus:

My Friend,

You may open now the little package I gave you. May I ask you to keep it? I gave it to you because there is no one else who would care about it in just that way. Ever since I left you I have been thinking what it would be like to live a lifetime caring and being cared for like that. It was not the life I was meant to live, and yet, in a way, I have been living it ever since I first knew you.

Of course, you understand now why I could not go with you. I would have spoiled your life for you. Besides that, I was ill—and I was too proud to give you the shadow of myself. I had much to give you, if you had come earlier. As it was, I was ashamed. Vanity sometimes saves us when nothing else will, and mine saved you. Thank you for everything. I hold this to my heart, where I once held your hand.

Alexandra

The dusk had thickened into night long before I got up from my chair and took the little box from its place in my desk drawer. I opened it and lifted out a thick coil, cut from where her hair grew thickest and brightest. It was tied firmly at one end, and when it fell over my arm it curled and clung about my sleeve like a living thing set free. How it gleamed, how it still gleams in the firelight! It was warm and softly scented under my lips, and stirred under my breath like seaweed in the tide. This, and a withered magnolia flower, and two pink sea shells; nothing more. And it was all twenty years ago!

46

THE STORM

Kate Chopin

Romantic love with rebellion and conformity seems a conundrum.

I

The leaves were so still that even Bibi thought it was going to rain. Bobint, who was accustomed to converse on terms of perfect equality with his little son, called the child's attention to certain sombre clouds that were rolling with sinister intention from the west, accompanied by a sullen, threatening roar. They were at Friedheimer's store and decided to remain there till the storm had passed. They sat within the door on two empty kegs. Bibi was four years old and looked very wise.

'Mama'll be 'fraid, yes,' he suggested with blinking eyes.

'She'll shut the house. Maybe she got Sylvie helpin' her this evenin',' Bobint responded reassuringly.

'No; she ent got Sylvie. Sylvie was helpin' her yistiday,' piped Bibi.

Bobint arose and going across to the counter purchased a can of shrimps, of which Calixta was very fond. Then he retumed to his perch on the keg and sat stolidly holding the can of shrimps while the storm burst. It shook the wooden store and seemed to be ripping great furrows in the distant field. Bibi laid his little hand on his father's knee and was not afraid.

II

Calixta, at home, felt no uneasiness for their safety. She sat at a side window sewing furiously on a sewing machine. She was greatly occupied and did not notice the approaching storm. But she felt very warm and often stopped to mop her face on which the perspiration gathered in beads. She unfastened her white sacque at the throat. It began to grow dark, and suddenly realizing the situation she got up hurriedly and went about closing windows and doors.

Out on the small front gallery she had hung Bobint's Sunday clothes to dry and she hastened out to gather them before the rain fell. As she stepped outside, Alce Laballire rode in at the gate. She had not seen him very often since her marriage, and never alone. She stood there with Bobint's coat in her hands, and the big rain drops began to fall. Alce rode his horse under the shelter of a side projection where the chickens had huddled and there were plows and a harrow piled up in the corner.

'May I come and wait on your gallery till the storm is over, Calixta?' he asked.

'Come 'long in, M'sieur Alce.'

His voice and her own startled her as if from a trance, and she seized Bobint's vest. Alce, mounting to the porch, grabbed the trousers and snatched Bibi's braided jacket that was about to be carried away by a sudden gust of wind. He expressed an intention to remain outside, but it was soon apparent that he might as well have been out in the open: the water beat in upon the boards in driving sheets, and he went inside, closing the door after him. It was even necessary to put something beneath the door to keep the water out.

'My! What a rain! It's good two years sence it rain' like that,' exclaimed Calixta as she rolled up a piece of bagging and Alce helped her to thrust it beneath the crack.

She was a little fuller of figure than five years before when she married; but she had lost nothing of her vivacity. Her blue eyes still retained their melting quality; and her yellow hair, dishevelled by the wind and rain, kinked more stubbornly than ever about her ears and temples.

The rain beat upon the low, shingled roof with a force and clatter that threatened to break an entrance and deluge them there. They were in the dining room, the sitting room, the general utility room. Adjoining was her bed room, with Bibi's couch along side her own. The door stood open, and the room with its white, monumental bed, its closed shutters, looked dim and mysterious.

Alce flung himself into a rocker and Calixta nervously began to gather up from the floor the lengths of a cotton sheet which she had been sewing.

'If this keeps up, Dieu sait if the levees goin' to stan it!' she exclaimed.

'What have you got to do with the levees?'

'I got enough to do! An' there's Bobint with Bibi out in that storm if he only didn' left Friedheimer's!'

'Let us hope, Calixta, that Bobint's got sense enough to come in out of a cyclone.'

She went and stood at the window with a greatly disturbed look on her face. She wiped the frame that was clouded with moisture. It was stiflingly hot. Alce got up and joined her at the window, looking over her shoulder. The rain was coming down in sheets obscuring the view of far-off cabins and enveloping the distant wood in a grey mist. The playing of the lightning was incessant. A bolt struck a tall chinaberry tree at the edge of the field. It filled all visible space with a blinding glare and the crash seemed to invade the very boards they stood upon.

Calixta put her hands to her eyes, and with a cry, staggered backward. Alce's arm encircled her, and for an instant he drew her close and spasmodically to him.

'Bont!' she cried, releasing herself from his encircling arm and retreating from the window, 'the house'll go next! If I only knew w'ere Bibi was!' She would not compose herself; she would not be seated. Alce clasped her shoulders and looked into her face. The contact of her warm, palpitating body when he had unthinkingly drawn her into his arms, had aroused all the old-time infatuation and desire for her flesh.

'Calixta,' he said, 'don't be frightened. Nothing can happen. The house is too low to be struck, with so many tall trees standing about. There! Aren't you going to be quiet? Say, aren't you?' He pushed her hair back from her face that was warm and steaming. Her lips were as red and moist as pomegranate seed. Her white neck and a glimpse of her full, firm bosom disturbed him powerfully. As she glanced up at him the fear in her liquid blue eyes had given place to a drowsy gleam that unconsciously betrayed a sensuous desire. He looked down into her eyes and there was nothing for him to do but to gather her lips in a kiss. It reminded him of Assumption.

'Do you remember Assumption, Calixta?' he asked in a low voice broken by passion. Oh! she remembered; for in Assumption he had kissed her and kissed and kissed her; until his senses would well nigh fail, and to save her he would resort to a desperate flight. If she was not an immaculate dove in those days, she was still inviolate; a passionate creature whose very defenselessness had made her defense, against which his honour forbade him to prevail. Now well, now her lips seemed in a manner free to be tasted, as well as her round, white throat and her whiter breasts.

They did not heed the crashing torrents, and the roar of the elements made her laugh as she lay in his arms. She was a revelation in that dim, mysterious chamber; as white as the couch she lay upon. Her firm, elastic flesh that was knowing for the first time its birthright, was like a creamy lily that the sun invites to contribute its breath and perfume to the undying life of the world.

The generous abundance of her passion, without guile or trickery, was like a white flame which penetrated and found response in depths of his own sensuous nature that had never yet been reached.

When he touched her breasts they gave themselves up in quivering ecstasy, inviting his lips. Her mouth was a fountain of delight. And when he possessed her, they seemed to swoon together at the very borderland of life's mystery.

He stayed cushioned upon her, breathless, dazed, enervated, with his heart beating like a hammer upon her. With one hand she clasped his head, her lips lightly touching his forehead. The other hand stroked with a soothing rhythm his muscular shoulders.

The growl of the thunder was distant and passing away. The rain beat softly upon the shingles, inviting them to drowsiness and sleep. But they dared not yield.

III

The rain was over; and the sun was turning the glistening green world into a palace of gems. Calixta, on the gallery, watched Alce ride away. He turned and smiled at her with a beaming face; and she lifted her pretty chin in the air and laughed aloud.

Bobint and Bibi, trudging home, stopped without at the cistern to make themselves presentable.

'My! Bibi, w'at will yo' mama say! You ought to be ashame'. You oughta' put on those good pants. Look at 'em! An' that mud on yo' collar! How you got that mud on yo' collar, Bibi? I never saw such a boy!' Bibi was the picture of pathetic resignation. Bobint was the embodiment of serious solicitude as he strove to remove from his own person and his son's the signs of their tramp over heavy roads and through wet fields. He scraped the mud off Bibi's bare legs and feet with a stick and carefully removed all traces from his heavy brogans. Then, prepared for the worst, the meeting with an over-scrupulous housewife, they entered cautiously at the back door.

Calixta was preparing supper. She had set the table and was dripping coffee at the hearth. She sprang up as they came in.

'Oh, Bobint! You back! My! But I was uneasy. W'ere you been during the rain? An' Bibi? He ain't wet? He ain't hurt?' She had clasped Bibi and was kissing him effusively. Bobint's explanations and apologies which he had been composing all along the way, died on his lips as Calixta felt him to see if he were dry, and seemed to express nothing but satisfaction at their safe return.

'I brought you some shrimps, Calixta,' offered Bobint, hauling the can from his ample side pocket and laying it on the table.

'Shrimps! Oh, Bobint! You too good fo' anything!' and she gave him a smacking kiss on the cheek that resounded, 'J'vous rponds, we'll have a feas' to-night! Umph-umph!'

Bobint and Bibi began to relax and enjoy themselves, and when the three seated themselves at table they laughed much and so loud that anyone might have heard them as far away as Laballire's.

IV

Alce Laballire wrote to his wife, Clarisse, that night. It was a loving letter, full of tender solicitude. He told her not to hurry back, but if she and the babies liked it at Biloxi, to stay a month longer. He was getting on nicely; and though he missed them, he was willing to bear the separation a while longer realizing that their health and pleasure were the first things to be considered.

V

As for Clarisse, she was charmed upon receiving her husband's letter. She and the babies were doing well. The society was agreeable; many of her old friends and acquaintances were at the bay. And the first free breath since her marriage seemed to restore the pleasant liberty of her maiden days. Devoted as she was to her husband, their intimate conjugal life was something which she was more than willing to forego for a while.

So the storm passed and every one was happy.

47

A LOVE PASSAGE

W.W. Jacobs

Love is like travelling. The journey is better than the destination.

The mate was leaning against the side of the schooner, idly watching a few red-coated linesmen lounging on the Tower Quay. Careful mariners were getting out their side-lights, and careless lightermen were progressing by easy bumps from craft to craft on their way up the river. A tug, half burying itself in its own swell, rushed panting by, and a faint scream came from aboard an approaching skiff as it tossed in the wash.

'JESSICA ahoy!' bawled a voice from the skiff as she came rapidly alongside.

The mate, roused from his reverie, mechanically caught the line and made it fast, moving with alacrity as he saw that the captain's daughter was one of the occupants. Before he had got over his surprise she was on deck with her boxes, and the captain was paying off the watermen.

'You've seen my daughter Hetty afore, haven't you?' said the skipper. 'She's coming with us this trip. You'd better go down and make up her bed, Jack, in that spare bunk.'

'Ay, ay,' said the mate dutifully, moving off.

'Thank you, I'll do it myself,' said the scandalized Hetty, stepping forward hastily.

'As you please,' said the skipper, leading the way below. 'Let's have a light on, Jack.'

The mate struck a match on his boot, and lit the lamp.

'There's a few things in there'll want moving,' said the skipper,

as he opened the door. 'I don't know where we're to keep the
onions now, Jack.'

'We'll find a place for 'em,' said the mate confidently, as he
drew out a sack and placed it on the table.

'I'm not going to sleep in there,' said the visitor decidedly, as
she peered in. 'Ugh! There's a beetle. Ugh!'

'It's quite dead,' said the mate reassuringly. 'I've never seen a
live beetle on this ship.'

'I want to go home,' said the girl. 'You've no business to make
me come when I don't want to.'

'You should behave yourself then,' said her father magisterially.
'What about sheets, Jack; and pillers?'

The mate sat on the table, and, grasping his chin, pondered.
Then as his gaze fell upon the pretty, indignant face of the passenger,
he lost the thread of his ideas.

'She'll have to have some o' my things for the present,' said
the skipper.

'Why not,' said the mate, looking up again—'why not let her
have your state-room?'

'Cos I want it myself,' replied the other calmly.

The mate blushed for him, and, the girl leaving them to
arrange matters as they pleased, the two men, by borrowing here
and contriving there, made up the bunk. The girl was standing
by the galley when they went on deck again, an object of curious
and respectful admiration to the crew, who had come on board
in the meantime. She stayed on deck until the air began to blow
fresher in the wider reaches, and then, with a brief good-night to
her father, retired below.

'She made up her mind to come with us rather suddenly,
didn't she?' inquired the mate after she had gone.

'She didn't make up her mind at all,' said the skipper; 'we did
it for her, me an' the missus. It's a plan on our part.'

'Wants strengthening?' said the mate suggestively.

'Well, the fact is,' said the skipper, 'it's like this, Jack; there's a friend o' mine, a provision dealer in a large way o' business, wants to marry my girl, and me an' the missus want him to marry her, so, o' course, she wants to marry someone else. Me an' 'er mother we put our 'eads together and decided for her to come away. When she's at 'ome, instead o' being out with Towson, direckly her mother's back's turned she's out with that young sprig of a clerk.'

'Nice-looking young feller, I s'pose?' said the mate somewhat anxiously.

'Not a bit of it,' said the other firmly. 'Looks as though he had never had a good meal in his life. Now my friend Towson, he's all right; he's a man of about my own figger.'

'She'll marry the clerk,' said the mate, with conviction.

'I'll bet you she don't,' said the skipper. 'I'm an artful man, Jack, an' I, generally speaking, get my own way. I couldn't live with my missus peaceable if it wasn't for management.'

The mate smiled safely in the darkness, the skipper's management consisting chiefly of slavish obedience.

'I've got a cabinet fortygraph of him for the cabin mantel-piece, Jack,' continued the wily father. 'He gave it to me o' purpose. She'll see that when she won't see the clerk, an' by-and-bye she'll fall into our way of thinking. Anyway, she's going to stay here till she does.'

'You know your way about, cap'n,' said the mate, in pretended admiration.

The skipper laid his finger on his nose, and winked at the mainmast. 'There's few can show me the way, Jack,' he answered softly; 'very few. Now I want you to help me too; I want you to talk to her a great deal.'

'Ay, ay,' said the mate, winking at the mast in his turn.

'Admire the fortygraph on the mantel-piece,' said the skipper.

'I will,' said the other.

'Tell her about a lot o' young girls you know as married young middle-aged men, an' loved 'em more an' more every day of their lives,' continued the skipper.

'Not another word,' said the mate. 'I know just what you want. She shan't marry the clerk if I can help it.'

The other turned and gripped him warmly by the hand. 'If ever you are a father your elf, Jack,' he said with emotion, 'I hope as how somebody'll stand by you as you're standing by me.'

The mate was relieved the next day when he saw the portrait of Towson. He stroked his moustache, and felt that he gained in good looks every time he glanced at it.

Breakfast finished, the skipper, who had been on deck all night, retired to his bunk. The mate went on deck and took charge, watching with great interest the movements of the passenger as she peered into the galley and hotly assailed the cook's method of washing up.

'Don't you like the sea?' he inquired politely, as she came and sat on the cabin skylight.

Miss Alsen shook her head dismally. 'I've got to it,' she remarked.

'Your father was saying something to me about it,' said the mate guardedly.

'Did he tell the cook and the cabin boy too?' inquired Miss Alsen, flushing somewhat. 'What did he tell you?'

'Told me about a man named Towson,' said the mate, becoming intent on the sails, 'and—another fellow.'

'I took a little notice of him just to spoil the other,' said the girl, 'not that I cared for him. I can't understand a girl caring for any man. Great, clumsy, ugly things.'

'You don't like him then?' said the mate.

'Of course not,' said the girl, tossing her head.

'And yet they've sent you to sea to get out of his way,' said the mate meditatively. 'Well, the best thing you can do—'His hardihood failed him at the pitch.

'Go on,' said the girl.

'Well, it's this way,' said the mate, coughing; 'they've sent you to sea to get you out of this fellow's way, so if you fall in love with somebody on the ship they'll send you home again.'

'So they will,' said the girl eagerly. 'I'll pretend to fall in love with that nice-looking sailor you call Harry. What a lark!'

'I shouldn't do that,' said the mate gravely.

'Why not?' said the girl.

"'Tisn't discipline,' said the mate very firmly; 'it wouldn't do at all. He's before the mast.'

'Oh, I see,' remarked Miss Alsen, smiling scornfully.

'I only mean pretend, of course,' said the mate, colouring. 'Just to oblige you.'

'Of course,' said the girl calmly. 'Well, how are we to be in love?'

The mate flushed darkly. 'I don't know much about such things,' he said at length; 'but we'll have to look at each other, and all that sort of thing, you know.'

'I don't mind that,' said the girl.

'Then we'll get on by degrees,' said the other. 'I expect we shall both find it come easier after a time.'

'Anything to get home again,' said the girl, rising and walking slowly away.

The mate began his part of the love-making at once, and, fixing a gaze of concentrated love on the object of his regard, nearly ran down a smack. As he had prognosticated, it came easy to him, and other well-marked symptoms, such as loss of appetite and a partiality for bright colours, developed during the day. Between breakfast and tea he washed five times, and raised the ire of the skipper to a dangerous pitch by using the ship's butter to remove tar from his fingers.

By ten o'clock that night he was far advanced in a profound melancholy. All the looking had been on his side, and, as he stood at the wheel keeping the schooner to her course, he felt a fellow-feeling for the hapless Towson. His meditations were interrupted by a slight figure which emerged from the companion, and, after a moment's hesitation, came and took its old seat on the skylight.

'Calm and peaceful up here, isn't it?' said he, after waiting some time for her to speak. 'Stars are very bright to-night.'

'Don't talk to me,' said Miss Alsen snappishly.

'Why doesn't this nasty little ship keep still? I believe it's you making her jump about like this.'

'Me?' said the mate in amazement.

'Yes, with that wheel.'

'I can assure you—' began the mate.

'Yes, I knew you'd say so,' said the girl.

'Come and steer yourself,' said the mate; 'then you'll see.'

Much to his surprise she came, and, leaning limply against the wheel, put her little hands on the spokes, while the mate explained the mysteries of the compass. As he warmed with his subject he ventured to put his hands on the same spokes, and, gradually becoming more venturesome, boldly supported her with his arm every time the schooner gave a lurch.

'Thank you,' said Miss Alsen, coldly extricating herself, as the male fancied another lurch was coming. 'Good-night.'

She retired to the cabin as a dark figure, which was manfully knuckling the last remnant of sleep from its eyelids, stood before the mate, chuckling softly.

'Clear night,' said the seaman, as he took the wheel in his great paws.

'Beastly,' said the mate absently, and, stifling a sigh, went below and turned in.

He lay awake for a few minutes, and then, well satisfied with the day's proceedings, turned over and fell asleep. He was pleased to discover, when he awoke, that the slight roll of the night before had disappeared, and that there was hardly any motion on the schooner. The passenger herself was already at the breakfast-table.

'Cap'n's on deck, I s'pose?' said the mate, preparing to resume negotiations where they were broken off the night before. 'I hope you feel better than you did last night.'

'Yes, thank you,' said she.

'You'll make a good sailor in time,' said the mate.

'I hope not,' said Miss Alsen, who thought it time to quell a gleam of peculiar tenderness plainly apparent in the mate's eyes. 'I shouldn't like to be a sailor even if I were a man.'

'Why not?' inquired the other.

'I don't know,' said the girl meditatively; 'but sailors are generally such scrubby little men, aren't they?'

'Scrubby?' repeated the mate, in a dazed voice.

'I'd sooner be a soldier,' she continued; 'I like soldiers—they're so manly. I wish there was one here now.'

'What for?' inquired the mate, in the manner of a sulky schoolboy.

'If there was a man like that here now,' said Miss Alsen thoughtfully, 'I'd dare him to mustard old Towson's nose.'

'Do what?' inquired the astonished mate.

'Mustard old Towson's nose,' said Miss Alsen, glancing lightly from the cruet-stand to the portrait.

The infatuated man hesitated a moment, and then, reaching over to the cruet, took out the spoon, and with a pale, determined face, indignantly daubed the classic features of the provision dealer. His indignation was not lessened by the behaviour of the temptress, who, instead of fawning upon him for his bravery, crammed her handkerchief to her mouth and giggled foolishly.

'Where's father,' she said suddenly, as a step sounded above. 'Oh, you will get it!'

She rose from her seat, and, standing aside to let her father pass, went on deck. The skipper sank on to a locker, and, raising the tea-pot, poured himself out a cup of tea, which he afterwards decanted into a saucer. He had just raised it to his lips, when he saw something over the rim of it which made him put it down again untasted, and stare blankly at the mantel-piece.

'Who the—what the—who the devil's done this?' he inquired in a strangulated voice, as he rose and regarded the portrait.

'I did,' said the mate.

'You did?' roared the other. 'You? What for?'

'I don't know,' said the mate awkwardly. 'Something seemed to come over me all of a sudden, and I felt as though I must do it.'

'But what for? Where's the sense of it?' said the skipper.

The mate shook his head sheepishly.

'But what did you want to do such a monkey-trick for?' roared the skipper.

'I don't know,' said the mate doggedly; 'but it's done, ain't it? And it's no good talking about it.'

The skipper looked at him in wrathful perplexity. 'You'd better have advice when we get to port, Jack,' he said at length; 'the last few weeks I've noticed you've been a bit strange in your manner. You go an' show that 'ed of yours to a doctor.'

The mate grunted, and went on deck for sympathy, but, finding Miss Alsen in a mood far removed from sentiment, and not at all grateful, drew off whistling. Matters were in this state when the skipper appeared, wiping his mouth.

'I've put another portrait on the mantel-piece, Jack,' he said menacingly; 'it's the only other one I've got, an' I wish you to understand that if that only smells mustard, there'll be such a row in this 'ere ship that you won't be able to 'ear yourself speak for the noise.'

He moved off with dignity as his daughter, who had overheard the remark, came sidling up to the mate and smiled on him agreeably.

'He's put another portrait there,' she said softly.

'You'll find the mustard-pot in the cruet,' said the mate coldly.

Miss Alsen turned and watched her father as he went forward, and then, to the mate's surprise, went below without another word. A prey to curiosity, but too proud to make any overture, he compromised matters by going and standing near the companion.

'Mate!' said a stealthy whisper at the foot of the ladder.

The mate gazed calmly out to sea.

'Jack!' said the girl again, in a lower whisper than before.

The mate went hot all over, and at once descended. He found Miss Alsen, her eyes sparkling, with the mustard-pot in her left hand and the spoon in her right, executing a war-dance in front of the second portrait.

'Don't do it,' said the mate, in alarm.

'Why not?' she inquired, going within an inch of it.

'He'll think it's me,' said the mate.

'That's why I called you down here,' said she; 'you don't think I wanted you, do you?'

'You put that spoon down,' said the mate, who was by no means desirous of another interview with the skipper.

'Shan't!' said Miss Alsen.

The mate sprang at her, but she dodged round the table. He leaned over, and, catching her by the left arm, drew her towards him; then, with her flushed, laughing face close to his, he forgot everything else, and kissed her.

'Oh!' said Hetty indignantly.

'Will you give it to me now?' said the mate, trembling at his boldness.

'Take it,' said she. She leaned across the table, and, as the mate advanced, dabbed viciously at him with the spoon. Then she suddenly dropped both articles on the table and moved away, as the mate, startled by a footstep at the door, turned a flushed visage, ornamented with three streaks of mustard, on to the dumbfounded skipper.

'Sakes alive!' said that astonished mariner, as soon as he could speak; 'if he ain't a-mustarding his own face now—I never 'card of such a thing in all my life. Don't go near 'im, Hetty. Jack!'

'Well,' said the mate, wiping his smarting face with his handkerchief.

'You've never been took like this before?' queried the skipper anxiously.

'O'course not,' said the mortified mate.

'Don't you say o'course not to me,' said the other warmly, 'after behaving like this. A straight weskit's what you want. I'll go an' see old Ben about it. He's got an uncle in a 'sylum. You come up too, my girl.'

He went in search of Ben, oblivious of the fact that his daughter, instead of following him, came no farther than the door, where she stood and regarded her victim compassionately.

'I'm so sorry,' she said 'Does it smart?'

'A little,' said the mate; 'don't you trouble about me.'

'You see what you get for behaving badly,' said Miss Alsen judicially.

'It's worth it,' said the mate, brightening.

'I'm afraid it'll blister,' said she. She crossed over to him, and putting her head on one side, eyed the traces wisely. 'Three marks,' she said.

'I only had one,' suggested the mate.

'One what?' enquired Hetty.

'Those,' said the mate.

In full view of the horrified skipper, who was cautiously peeping at the supposed lunatic through the skylight, he kissed her again.

'You can go away, Ben,' said the skipper huskily to the expert. 'D'ye hear, you can go away, and not a word about this, mind.'

The expert went away grumbling, and the father, after another glance, which showed him his daughter nestling comfortably on the mate's right shoulder, stole away and brooded darkly over this crowning complication. An ordinary man would have run down and interrupted them; the master of the Jessica thought he could attain his ends more certainly by diplomacy, and so careful was his demeanour that the couple in the cabin had no idea that they had been observed—the mate listening calmly to a lecture on incipient idiocy which the skipper thought it advisable to bestow.

Until the mid-day meal on the day following he made no sign. If anything he was even more affable than usual, though his wrath rose at the glances which were being exchanged across the table.

'By the way, Jack,' he said at length, 'what's become of Kitty Loney?'

'Who?' inquired the mate. 'Who's Kitty Loney?'

It was now the skipper's turn to stare, and he did it admirably.

'Kitty Loney,' he said in surprise, 'the little girl you are going to marry.'

'Who are you getting at?' said the mate, going scarlet as he met the gaze opposite.

'I don't know what you mean,' said the skipper with dignity. 'I'm allooding to Kitty Loney, the little girl in the red hat and white feathers you introduced to me as your future.'

The mate sank back in his seat, and regarded him with openmouthed, horrified astonishment.

'You don't mean to say you've chucked 'er,' pursued the heartless skipper, 'after getting an advance from me to buy the ring with, too? Didn't you buy the ring with the money?'

'No,' said the mate, 'I—oh, no—of course—what on earth are you talking about?'

The skipper rose from his seat and regarded him sorrowfully but severely. 'I'm sorry, Jack,' he said stiffly, 'if I've said anything to annoy you, or anyway hurt your feelings. O' course it's your business, not mine. P'raps you'll say you never heard o' Kitty Loney?'

'I do say so,' said the bewildered mate; 'I do say so.'

The skipper eyed him sternly, and without another word left the cabin. 'If she's like her mother,' he said to himself, chuckling as he went up the companion-ladder, 'I think that'll do.'

There was an awkward pause after his departure. 'I'm sure I don't know what you must think of me,' said the mate at length, 'but I don't know what your father's talking about.'

'I don't think anything,' said Hetty calmly. 'Pass the potatoes, please.'

'I suppose it's a joke of his,' said the mate, complying.

'And the salt,' said she; 'thank you.'

'But you don't believe it?' said the mate pathetically.

'Oh, don't be silly,' said the girl calmly. 'What does it matter whether I do or not?'

'It matters a great deal,' said the mate gloomily. 'It's life or death to me.'

'Oh, nonsense,' said Hetty. 'She won't know of your foolishness. I won't tell her.'

'I tell you,' said the mate desperately, 'there never was a Kitty Loney. What do you think of that?'

'I think you are very mean,' said the girl scornfully; 'don't talk to me any more, please.'

'Just as you like,' said the mate, beginning to lose his temper.

He pushed his plate from him and departed, while the girl, angry and resentful, put the potatoes back as being too floury for consumption in the circumstances.

For the remainder of the passage she treated him with a politeness and good humour through which he strove in vain to break. To her surprise her father made no objection, at the end of the voyage, when she coaxingly suggested going back by train; and the mate, as they sat at dummy-whist on the evening before her departure, tried in vain to discuss the journey in an unconcerned fashion.

'It'll be a long journey,' said Hetty, who still liked him well enough to make him smart a bit, 'What's trumps?'

'You'll be all right,' said her father. 'Spades.'

He won for the third time that evening, and, feeling wonderfully well satisfied with the way in which he had played his cards generally, could not resist another gibe at the crestfallen mate.

'You'll have to give up playing cards and all that sort o' thing when you're married, Jack,' said he.

'Ay, ay,' said the mate recklessly, 'Kitty don't like cards.'

'I thought there was no Kitty,' said the girl, looking up, scornfully.

'She don't like cards,' repeated the mate. 'Lord, what a spree we had. Cap'n, when we went to the Crystal Palace with her that night.'

'Ay, that we did,' said the skipper.

'Remember the roundabouts?' said the mate.

'I do,' said the skipper merrily. 'I'll never forget 'em.'

'You and that friend of hers, Bessie Watson, lord how you did go on!' continued the mate, in a sort of ecstasy. The skipper stiffened suddenly in his chair. 'What on earth are you talking about?' he inquired gruffly.

'Bessie Watson,' said the mate, in tones of innocent surprise. 'Little girl in a blue hat with white feathers, and a blue frock, that came with us.'

'You're drunk,' said the skipper, grinding his teeth, as he saw the trap into which he had walked.

'Don't you remember when you two got lost, an' me and Kitty were looking all over the place for you?' demanded the mate, still in the same tones of pleasant reminiscence.

He caught Hetty's eye, and noticed with a thrill that it beamed with soft and respectful admiration.

'You've been drinking,' repeated the skipper, breathing hard. 'How dare you talk like that afore my daughter?'

'It's only right I should know,' said Hetty, drawing herself up. 'I wonder what mother'll say to it all?'

'You say anything to your mother if you dare,' said the now maddened skipper. 'You know what she is. It's all the mate's nonsense.'

'I'm very sorry, cap'n,' said the mate, 'if I've said anything to annoy you, or anyway hurt your feelings. O' course it's your business, not mine. Perhaps you'll say you never heard o' Bessie Watson?'

'Mother shall hear of her,' said Hetty, while her helpless sire was struggling for breath.

'Perhaps you'll tell us who this Bessie Watson is, and where she lives?' he said at length.

'She lives with Kitty Loney,' said the mate simply.

The skipper rose, and his demeanour was so alarming that Hetty shrank instinctively to the mate for protection. In full view of his captain, the mate placed his arm about her waist, and in this position they confronted each other for some time in silence. Then Hetty looked up and spoke.

'I'm going home by water,' she said briefly.

48

THE MODEL MILLIONAIRE

Oscar Wilde

Love and compassion can be exemplified.

Unless one is wealthy there is no use in being a charming fellow. Romance is the privilege of the rich, not the profession of the unemployed. The poor should be practical and prosaic. It is better to have a permanent income than to be fascinating. These are the great truths of modern life which Hughie Erskine never realized. Poor Hughie! Intellectually, we must admit, he was not of much importance. He never said a brilliant or even an ill-natured thing in his life. But then he was wonderfully good-looking, with his crisp brown hair, his clear-cut profile, and his grey eyes. He was as popular with men as he was with women, and he had every accomplishment except that of making money. His father had bequeathed him his cavalry sword, and a History of the Peninsular War in fifteen volumes. Hughie hung the first over his looking-glass, put the second on a shelf between Ruff's Guide and Bailey's Magazine, and lived on two hundred a year that an old aunt allowed him. He had tried everything. He had gone on the Stock Exchange for six months; but what was a butterfly to do among bulls and bears? He had been a tea-merchant for a little longer, but had soon tired of pekoe and souchong. Then he had tried selling dry sherry. That did not answer; the sherry was a little too dry. Ultimately he became nothing, a delightful, ineffectual young man with a perfect profile and no profession.

To make matters worse, he was in love. The girl he loved was Laura Merton, the daughter of a retired Colonel who had lost his temper and his digestion in India, and had never found either of them again. Laura adored him, and he was ready to kiss her shoe-strings. They were the handsomest couple in London, and had not a penny-piece between them. The Colonel was very fond of Hughie, but would not hear of any engagement.

'Come to me, my boy, when you have got ten thousand pounds of your own, and we will see about it,' he used to say; and Hughie looked very glum on those days, and had to go to Laura for consolation.

One morning, as he was on his way to Holland Park, where the Mertons lived, he dropped in to see a great friend of his, Alan Trevor. Trevor was a painter. Indeed, few people escape that nowadays. But he was also an artist, and artists are rather rare. Personally he was a strange rough fellow, with a freckled face and a red ragged beard. However, when he took up the brush he was a real master, and his pictures were eagerly sought after. He had been very much attracted by Hughie at first, it must be acknowledged, entirely on account of his personal charm. 'The only people a painter should know,' he used to say, 'are people who are *bête* and beautiful, people who are an artistic pleasure to look at and an intellectual repose to talk to. Men who are dandies and women who are darlings rule the world, at least they should do so.' However, after he got to know Hughie better, he liked him quite as much for his bright buoyant spirits and his generous reckless nature, and had given him the permanent entrée to his studio.

When Hughie came in he found Trevor putting the finishing touches to a wonderful life-size picture of a beggar-man. The beggar himself was standing on a raised platform in a corner of the studio. He was a wizened old man, with a face like wrinkled parchment, and a most piteous expression. Over his shoulders was flung a coarse brown cloak, all tears and tatters; his thick boots were patched and cobbled, and with one hand he leant on a rough stick, while with the other he held out his battered hat for alms.

'What an amazing model!' whispered Hughie, as he shook hands with his friend.

'An amazing model?' shouted Trevor at the top of his voice; 'I should think so! Such beggars as he are not to be met with every day. A *trouvaille, mon cher*; a living Velasquez! My stars! What an etching Rembrandt would have made of him!'

'Poor old chap!' said Hughie, 'how miserable he looks! But I suppose, to you painters, his face is his fortune?'

'Certainly,' replied Trevor, 'you don't want a beggar to look happy, do you?'

'How much does a model get for sitting?' asked Hughie, as he found himself a comfortable seat on a divan.

'A shilling an hour.'

'And how much do you get for your picture, Alan?'

'Oh, for this I get two thousand!'

'Pounds?'

'Guineas. Painters, poets, and physicians always get guineas.'

'Well, I think the model should have a percentage,' cried Hughie, laughing; 'they work quite as hard as you do.'

'Nonsense, nonsense! Why, look at the trouble of laying on the paint alone, and standing all day long at one's easel! It's all very well, Hughie, for you to talk, but I assure you that there are moments when Art almost attains to the dignity of manual labour. But you mustn't chatter; I'm very busy. Smoke a cigarette, and keep quiet.'

After some time the servant came in, and told Trevor that the frame-maker wanted to speak to him.

'Don't run away, Hughie,' he said, as he went out, 'I will be back in a moment.'

The old beggar-man took advantage of Trevor's absence to rest for a moment on a wooden bench that was behind him. He looked so forlorn and wretched that Hughie could not help pitying him, and felt in his pockets to see what money he had. All he could find was a sovereign and some coppers. 'Poor old fellow,' he thought to himself, 'he wants it more than I do, but it means no hansoms for a fortnight'; and he walked across the studio and slipped the sovereign into the beggar's hand.

The old man started, and a faint smile flitted across his withered lips. 'Thank you, sir,' he said, 'thank you.'

Then Trevor arrived, and Hughie took his leave, blushing a little at what he had done. He spent the day with Laura, got a charming scolding for his extravagance, and had to walk home.

That night he strolled into the Palette Club about eleven o'clock, and found Trevor sitting by himself in the smoking-room drinking hock and seltzer.

'Well, Alan, did you get the picture finished all right?' he said, as he lit his cigarette.

'Finished and framed, my boy!' answered Trevor; 'and, by-the-bye, you have made a conquest. That old model you saw is quite devoted to you. I had to tell him all about you—who you are, where you live, what your income is, what prospects you have—'

'My dear Alan,' cried Hughie, 'I shall probably find him waiting for me when I go home. But of course you are only joking. Poor old wretch! I wish I could do something for him. I think it is dreadful that any one should be so miserable. I have got heaps of old clothes at home—do you think he would care for any of them? Why, his rags were falling to bits.'

'But he looks splendid in them,' said Trevor. 'I wouldn't paint him in a frock-coat for anything. What you call rags I call romance. What seems poverty to you is picturesqueness to me. However, I'll tell him of your offer.'

'Alan,' said Hughie seriously, 'you painters are a heartless lot.'

'An artist's heart is his head,' replied Trevor; 'and besides, our business is to realize the world as we see it, not to reform it as we know it. *À chacun son métier*. And now tell me how Laura is.

The old model was quite interested in her.'

'You don't mean to say you talked to him about her?' said Hughie.

'Certainly I did. He knows all about the relentless colonel, the lovely Laura, and the £10,000.'

'You told that old beggar all my private affairs?' cried Hughie, looking very red and angry.

'My dear boy,' said Trevor, smiling, 'that old beggar, as you call him, is one of the richest men in Europe. He could buy all London to-morrow without overdrawing his account. He has a house in every capital, dines off gold plate, and can prevent Russia going to war when he chooses.'

'What on earth do you mean?' exclaimed Hughie.

'What I say,' said Trevor. 'The old man you saw to-day in the studio was Baron Hausberg. He is a great friend of mine, buys all my pictures and that sort of thing, and gave me a commission a month ago to paint him as a beggar. *Que voulez-vous? La fantaisie d'un millionnaire*! And I must say he made a magnificent figure in his rags, or perhaps I should say in my rags; they are an old suit I got in Spain.'

'Baron Hausberg!' cried Hughie. 'Good heavens! I gave him a sovereign!' and he sank into an armchair the picture of dismay.

'Gave him a sovereign!' shouted Trevor, and he burst into a roar of laughter. 'My dear boy, you'll never see it again. *Son affaire c'est l'argent des autres*.'

'I think you might have told me, Alan,' said Hughie sulkily, 'and not have let me make such a fool of myself.'

'Well, to begin with, Hughie,' said Trevor, 'it never entered my mind that you went about distributing alms in that reckless way. I can understand your kissing a pretty model, but your giving a sovereign to an ugly one—by Jove, no! Besides, the fact is that I really was not at home to-day to any one; and when you came in I didn't know whether Hausberg would like his name mentioned.

You know he wasn't in full dress.'

'What a duffer he must think me!' said Hughie.

'Not at all. He was in the highest spirits after you left; kept chuckling to himself and rubbing his old wrinkled hands together. I couldn't make out why he was so interested to know all about you; but I see it all now. He'll invest your sovereign for you, Hughie, pay you the interest every six months, and have a capital story to tell after dinner.'

'I am an unlucky devil,' growled Hughie. 'The best thing I can do is to go to bed; and, my dear Alan, you mustn't tell any one. I shouldn't dare show my face in the Row.'

'Nonsense! It reflects the highest credit on your philanthropic spirit, Hughie. And don't run away. Have another cigarette, and you can talk about Laura as much as you like.'

However, Hughie wouldn't stop, but walked home, feeling very unhappy, and leaving Alan Trevor in fits of laughter.

The next morning, as he was at breakfast, the servant brought him up a card on which was written, 'Monsieur Gustave Naudin, de la part de M. le Baron Hausberg'.

'I suppose he has come for an apology,' said Hughie to himself; and he told the servant to show the visitor up.

An old gentleman with gold spectacles and grey hair came into the room, and said, in a slight French accent, 'Have I the honour of addressing Monsieur Erskine?'

Hughie bowed.

'I have come from Baron Hausberg,' he continued. 'The Baron—'

'I beg, sir, that you will offer him my sincerest apologies,' stammered Hughie.

'The Baron,' said the old gentleman, with a smile, 'has commissioned me to bring you this letter,' and he extended a sealed envelope.

On the outside was written, 'A wedding present to Hugh

Erskine and Laura Merton, from an old beggar,' and inside was a cheque for £10,000.

When they were married Alan Trevor was the best-man, and the Baron made a speech at the wedding-breakfast.

'Millionaire models,' remarked Alan, 'are rare enough; but, by Jove, model millionaires are rarer still!'

49

ON BEING IN LOVE

Jerome K. Jerome

Love is like measles; we all have to go through it.

You've been in love, of course! If not you've got it to come. Love is like the measles; we all have to go through it. Also like the measles, we take it only once. One never need be afraid of catching it a second time. The man who has had it can go into the most dangerous places and play the most foolhardy tricks with perfect safety. He can picnic in shady woods, ramble through leafy aisles, and linger on mossy seats to watch the sunset. He fears a quiet country-house no more than he would his own club. He can join a family party to go down the Rhine. He can, to see the last of a friend, venture into the very jaws of the marriage ceremony itself. He can keep his head through the whirl of a ravishing waltz, and rest afterward in a dark conservatory, catching nothing more lasting than a cold. He can brave a moonlight walk adown sweet-scented lanes or a twilight pull among the somber rushes. He can get over a stile without danger, scramble through a tangled hedge without being caught, come down a slippery path without falling. He can look into sunny eyes and not be dazzled. He listens to the siren voices, yet sails on with unveered helm. He clasps white hands in his, but no electric 'Lulu'-like force holds him bound in their dainty pressure.

No, we never sicken with love twice. Cupid spends no second arrow on the same heart. Love's handmaids are our life-long friends. Respect, and admiration, and affection, our doors may always be left open for, but their great celestial master, in his royal progress, pays but one visit and departs. We like, we cherish, we are very, very fond of—but we never love again. A man's heart is a firework that once in its time flashes heavenward. Meteor-like, it blazes for a moment and lights with its glory the whole world beneath. Then the night of our sordid commonplace life closes in around it, and the burned-out case, falling back to earth, lies useless and uncared for, slowly smoldering into ashes. Once, breaking loose from our prison bonds, we dare, as mighty old Prometheus dared, to scale the Olympian mount and snatch from Phoebus' chariot the fire of the gods. Happy those who, hastening down again ere it dies out, can kindle their earthly altars at its flame. Love is too pure a light to burn long among the noisome gases that we breathe, but before it is choked out we may use it as a torch to ignite the cozy fire of affection.

And, after all, that warming glow is more suited to our cold little back parlour of a world than is the burning spirit love. Love should be the vestal fire of some mighty temple—some vast dim fane whose organ music is the rolling of the spheres. Affection will burn cheerily when the white flame of love is flickered out. Affection is a fire that can be fed from day to day and be piled up ever higher as the wintry years draw nigh. Old men and women can sit by it with their thin hands clasped, the little children can nestle down in front, the friend and neighbour has his welcome corner by its side, and even shaggy Fido and sleek Titty can toast their noses at the bars.

Let us heap the coals of kindness upon that fire. Throw on your pleasant words, your gentle pressures of the hand, your thoughtful and unselfish deeds. Fan it with good-humour, patience, and forbearance. You can let the wind blow and the rain fall unheeded then, for your hearth will be warm and bright, and the faces round it will make sunshine in spite of the clouds without.

I am afraid, dear Edwin and Angelina, you expect too much from love. You think there is enough of your little hearts to feed this fierce, devouring passion for all your long lives. Ah, young folk! Don't rely too much upon that unsteady flicker. It will dwindle and dwindle as the months roll on, and there is no replenishing the fuel. You will watch it die out in anger and disappointment. To each it will seem that it is the other who is growing colder. Edwin sees with bitterness that Angelina no longer runs to the gate to meet him, all smiles and blushes; and when he has a cough now she doesn't begin to cry and, putting her arms round his neck, say that she cannot live without him. The most she will probably do is to suggest a lozenge, and even that in a tone implying that it is the noise more than anything else she is anxious to get rid of.

Poor little Angelina, too, sheds silent tears, for Edwin has given up carrying her old handkerchief in the inside pocket of his waistcoat.

Both are astonished at the falling off in the other one, but neither sees their own change. If they did they would not suffer as they do. They would look for the cause in the right quarter— in the littleness of poor human nature—join hands over their common failing, and start building their house anew on a more earthly and enduring foundation. But we are so blind to our own shortcomings, so wide awake to those of others. Everything that happens to us is always the other person's fault. Angelina would have gone on loving Edwin forever and ever and ever if only Edwin had not grown so strange and different. Edwin would have adored Angelina through eternity if Angelina had only remained the same as when he first adored her.

It is a cheerless hour for you both when the lamp of love has gone out and the fire of affection is not yet lit, and you have to grope about in the cold, raw dawn of life to kindle it. God grant it catches light before the day is too far spent. Many sit shivering by the dead coals till night come.

But, there, of what use is it to preach? Who that feels the

rush of young love through his veins can think it will ever flow feeble and slow! To the boy of twenty it seems impossible that he will not love as wildly at sixty as he does then. He cannot call to mind any middle-aged or elderly gentleman of his acquaintance who is known to exhibit symptoms of frantic attachment, but that does not interfere in his belief in himself. His love will never fall, whoever else's may. Nobody ever loved as he loves, and so, of course, the rest of the world's experience can be no guide in his case. Alas! Alas! Ere thirty he has joined the ranks of the sneerers. It is not his fault. Our passions, both the good and bad, cease with our blushes. We do not hate, nor grieve, nor joy, nor despair in our thirties like we did in our teens. Disappointment does not suggest suicide, and we quaff success without intoxication.

We take all things in a minor key as we grow older. There are few majestic passages in the later acts of life's opera. Ambition takes a less ambitious aim. Honour becomes more reasonable and conveniently adapts itself to circumstances. And love—love dies. 'Irreverence for the dreams of youth' soon creeps like a killing frost upon our hearts. The tender shoots and the expanding flowers are nipped and withered, and of a vine that yearned to stretch its tendrils round the world there is left but a sapless stump.

My fair friends will deem all this rank heresy, I know. So far from a man's not loving after he has passed boyhood, it is not till there is a good deal of grey in his hair that they think his protestations at all worthy of attention. Young ladies take their notions of our sex from the novels written by their own, and compared with the monstrosities that masquerade for men in the pages of that nightmare literature, Pythagoras' plucked bird and Frankenstein's demon were fair average specimens of humanity.

In these so-called books, the chief lover, or Greek god, as he is admiringly referred to—by the way, they do not say which 'Greek God' it is that the gentleman bears such a striking likeness to; it might be hump-backed Vulcan, or double-faced Janus, or even driveling Silenus, the god of abstruse mysteries. He resembles the whole family of them, however, in being a blackguard, and perhaps this is what is meant. To even the little manliness his classical prototypes possessed, though, he can lay no claim whatever, being a listless effeminate noodle, on the shady side of forty. But oh! The depth and strength of this elderly party's emotion for some bread-and-butter school-girl! Hide your heads, ye young Romeos and Leanders! This *blase* old beau loves with an hysterical fervour that requires four adjectives to every noun to properly describe.

It is well, dear ladies, for us old sinners that you study only books. Did you read mankind, you would know that the lad's shy stammering tells a truer tale than our bold eloquence. A boy's love comes from a full heart; a man's is more often the result of a full stomach. Indeed, a man's sluggish current may not be called love, compared with the rushing fountain that wells up when a boy's heart is struck with the heavenly rod. If you would taste love, drink of the pure stream that youth pours out at your feet. Do not wait till it has become a muddy river before you stoop to catch its waves.

Or is it that you like its bitter flavour—that the clear, limpid water is insipid to your palate and that the pollution of its after-course gives it a relish to your lips? Must we believe those who tell us that a hand foul with the filth of a shameful life is the only one a young girl cares to be caressed by?

That is the teaching that is bawled out day by day from between those yellow covers. Do they ever pause to think, I wonder, those devil's ladyhelps, what mischief they are doing crawling about God's garden, and telling childish Eves and silly Adams that sin is sweet and that decency is ridiculous and vulgar? How many an innocent girl do they not degrade into an evil-minded woman? To how many a weak lad do they not point out the dirty by-path as the shortest cut to a maiden's heart? It is not as if they wrote of life as it really is. Speak truth, and right will take care of itself.

But their pictures are coarse daubs painted from the sickly fancies of their own diseased imagination.

We want to think of women not—as their own sex would show them—as Lorleis luring us to destruction, but as good angels beckoning us upward. They have more power for good or evil than they dream of. It is just at the very age when a man's character is forming that he tumbles into love, and then the lass he loves has the making or marring of him. Unconsciously he molds himself to what she would have him, good or bad. I am sorry to have to be ungallant enough to say that I do not think they always use their influence for the best. Too often the female world is bounded hard and fast within the limits of the commonplace. Their ideal hero is a prince of littleness, and to become that many a powerful mind, enchanted by love, is 'lost to life and use and name and fame'.

And yet, women, you could make us so much better if you only would. It rests with you, more than with all the preachers, to roll this world a little nearer heaven. Chivalry is not dead: it only sleeps for want of work to do. It is you who must wake it to noble deeds. You must be worthy of knightly worship.

You must be higher than ourselves. It was for Una that the Red Cross Knight did war. For no painted, mincing court dame could the dragon have been slain. Oh, ladies fair, be fair in mind and soul as well as face, so that brave knights may win glory in your service! Oh, woman, throw off your disguising cloaks of selfishness, effrontery, and affectation! Stand forth once more a queen in your royal robe of simple purity. A thousand swords, now rusting in ignoble sloth, shall leap from their scabbards to do battle for your honour against wrong. A thousand Sir Rolands shall lay lance in rest, and Fear, Avarice, Pleasure, and Ambition shall go down in the dust before your colours.

What noble deeds were we not ripe for in the days when we loved? What noble lives could we not have lived for her sake? Our love was a religion we could have died for. It was no mere human creature like ourselves that we adored. It was a queen that we paid homage to, a goddess that we worshiped.

And how madly we did worship! And how sweet it was to worship! Ah, lad, cherish love's young dream while it lasts! You will know too soon how truly little Tom Moore sang when he said that there was nothing half so sweet in life. Even when it brings misery it is a wild, romantic misery, all unlike the dull, worldly pain of after-sorrows. When you have lost her—when the light is gone out from your life and the world stretches before you a long, dark horror, even then a half-enchantment mingles with your despair.

And who would not risk its terrors to gain its raptures? Ah, what raptures they were! The mere recollection thrills you. How delicious it was to tell her that you loved her, that you lived for her, that you would die for her! How you did rave, to be sure, what floods of extravagant nonsense you poured forth, and oh, how cruel it was of her to pretend not to believe you! In what awe you stood of her! How miserable you were when you had offended her! And yet, how pleasant to be bullied by her and to sue for pardon without having the slightest notion of what your fault was! How dark the world was when she snubbed you, as she often did, the little rogue, just to see you look wretched; how sunny when she smiled! How jealous you were of every one about her! How you hated every man she shook hands with, every woman she kissed—the maid that did her hair, the boy that cleaned her shoes, the dog she nursed—though you had to be respectful to the last-named! How you looked forward to seeing her, how stupid you were when you did see her, staring at her without saying a word! How impossible it was for you to go out at any time of the day or night without finding yourself eventually opposite her windows! You hadn't pluck enough to go in, but you hung about the corner and gazed at the outside. Oh, if the house had only caught fire—it was insured, so it wouldn't have mattered—and you could have rushed in and saved her at the risk of your life, and have been terribly burned and injured! Anything to serve her. Even in little things that was so sweet. How you would watch her, spaniel-like, to anticipate her slightest wish! How proud you were to do her bidding! How delightful it was to be ordered about by her! To devote your whole life to her and to never think of yourself seemed such a simple thing. You would go without a holiday to lay a humble offering at her shrine, and felt more than repaid if she only deigned to accept it. How precious to you was everything that she had hallowed by her touch—her little glove, the ribbon she had worn, the rose that had nestled in her hair and whose withered leaves still mark the poems you never care to look at now.

And oh, how beautiful she was, how wondrous beautiful! It was as some angel entering the room, and all else became plain and earthly. She was too sacred to be touched. It seemed almost presumption to gaze at her. You would as soon have thought of kissing her as of singing comic songs in a cathedral. It was desecration enough to kneel and timidly raise the gracious little hand to your lips.

Ah, those foolish days, those foolish days when we were unselfish and pure-minded; those foolish days when our simple hearts were full of truth, and faith, and reverence! Ah, those foolish days of noble longings and of noble strivings! And oh, these wise, clever days when we know that money is the only prize worth striving for, when we believe in nothing else but meanness and lies, when we care for no living creature but ourselves!

50

THE KISS*

Guy de Maupassant

There is a chemistry in a kiss that can be enigmatic at any point of time. Sometimes it spells love; sometimes it spells doom. The quantum matters.

My Little Darling,
So you are crying from morning until night and from night until morning, because your husband leaves you; you do not know what to do and so you ask your old aunt for advice; you must consider her quite an expert. I don't know as much as you think I do, and yet I am not entirely ignorant of the art of loving, or, rather, of making one's self loved, in which you are a little lacking. I can admit that at my age.

You say that you are all attention, love, kisses and caresses for him. Perhaps that is the very trouble; I think you kiss him too much.

My dear, we have in our hands the most terrible power in the world: *love.*

Man is gifted with physical strength, and he exercises force. Woman is gifted with charm, and she rules with caresses. It is our weapon, formidable and invincible, but we should know how to use it.

Know well that we are the mistresses of the world! To tell the history of love from the beginning of the world would be to tell

---

*This story appeared in the Gaulois in November, 1882, under the pseudonym of 'Maufrigneuse'.

the history of man himself—everything springs from it, the arts, great events, customs, wars, the overthrow of empires.

In the Bible you find Delila, Judith; in fables we find Omphale, Helen; in history the Sabines, Cleopatra and many others.

Therefore we reign supreme, all-powerful. But, like kings, we must make use of delicate diplomacy.

Love, my dear, is made up of imperceptible sensations. We know that it is as strong as death, but also as frail as glass. The slightest shock breaks it, and our power crumbles, and we are never able to raise it again.

We have the power of making ourselves adored, but we lack one tiny thing, the understanding of the various kinds of caresses. In embraces we lose the sentiment of delicacy, while the man over whom we rule remains master of himself, capable of judging the foolishness of certain words. Take care, my dear; that is the defect in our armour. It is our Achilles' heel.

Do you know whence comes our real power? From the kiss, the kiss alone! When we know how to hold out and give up our lips we can become queens.

The kiss is only a preface, however, but a charming preface. More charming than the realization itself. A preface which can always be read over again, whereas one cannot always read over the book.

Yes, the meeting of lips is the most perfect, the most divine sensation given to human beings, the supreme limit of happiness! It is in the kiss alone that one sometimes seems to feel this union of souls after which we strive, the intermingling of hearts, as it were.

Do you remember the verses of Sully-Prudhomme:

Caresses are nothing but anxious bliss,
Vain attempts of love to unite souls through a kiss.

One caress alone gives this deep sensation of two beings welded into one—it is *the kiss*. No violent delirium of complete possession is worth this trembling approach of the lips, this first moist and fresh contact, and then the long, lingering, motionless rapture.

Therefore, my dear, the kiss is our strongest weapon, but we must take care not to dull it. Do not forget that its value is only relative, purely conventional. It continually changes according to circumstances, the state of expectancy and the ecstasy of the mind. I will call attention to one example.

Another poet, Francois Coppee, has written a line which we all remember, a line which we find delightful, which moves our very hearts. After describing the expectancy of a lover, waiting in a room one winter's evening, his anxiety, his nervous impatience, the terrible fear of not seeing her, he describes the arrival of the beloved woman, who at last enters hurriedly, out of breath, bringing with her part of the winter breeze, and he exclaims:

Oh! The taste of the kisses first snatched through the veil.

Is that not a line of exquisite sentiment, a delicate and charming observation, a perfect truth? All those who have hastened to a clandestine meeting, whom passion has thrown into the arms of a man, well do they know these first delicious kisses through the veil; and they tremble at the memory of them. And yet their sole charm lies in the circumstances, from being late, from the anxious expectancy, but from the purely—or, rather, impurely, if you prefer—sensual point of view, they are detestable.

Think! Outside it is cold. The young woman has walked quickly; the veil is moist from her cold breath. Little drops of water shine in the lace. The lover seizes her and presses his burning lips to her liquid breath. The moist veil, which discolours and carries the dreadful odour of chemical dye, penetrates into the young man's mouth, moistens his moustache. He does not taste the lips of his beloved, he tastes the dye of this lace moistened with cold breath. And yet, like the poet, we would all exclaim:

Oh! the taste of the kisses first snatched through the veil.

Therefore, the value of this caress being entirely a matter of convention, we must be careful not to abuse it.

Well, my dear, I have several times noticed that you are very clumsy. However, you were not alone in that fault; the majority of women lose their authority by abusing the kiss with untimely kisses. When they feel that their husband or their lover is a little tired, at those times when the heart as well as the body needs rest, instead of understanding what is going on within him, they persist in giving inopportune caresses, tire him by the obstinacy of begging lips and give caresses lavished with neither rhyme nor reason.

Trust in the advice of my experience. First, never kiss your husband in public, in the train, at the restaurant. It is bad taste; do not give in to your desires. He would feel ridiculous and would never forgive you.

Beware of useless kisses lavished in intimacy. I am sure that you abuse them. For instance, I remember one day that you did something quite shocking. Probably you do not remember it.

All three of us were together in the drawing-room, and, as you did not stand on ceremony before me, your husband was holding you on his knees and kissing you at great length on the neck, the lips and throat. Suddenly you exclaimed: 'Oh! The fire!' You had been paying no attention to it, and it was almost out. A few lingering embers were glowing on the hearth. Then he rose, ran to the woodbox, from which he dragged two enormous logs with great difficulty, when you came to him with begging lips, murmuring:

'Kiss me!' He turned his head with difficulty and tried to hold up the logs at the same time. Then you gently and slowly placed your mouth on that of the poor fellow, who remained with his neck out of joint, his sides twisted, his arms almost dropping off, trembling with fatigue and tired from his desperate effort. And you kept drawing out this torturing kiss, without seeing or understanding. Then when you freed him, you began to grumble: 'How badly you kiss!' No wonder!

Oh, take care of that! We all have this foolish habit, this unconscious need of choosing the most inconvenient moments. When he is carrying a glass of water, when he is putting on his shoes, when he is tying his scarf—in short, when he finds himself in any uncomfortable position— then is the time which we choose for a caress which makes him stop for a whole minute in the middle of a gesture with the sole desire of getting rid of us!

Do not think that this criticism is insignificant. Love, my dear, is a delicate thing. The least little thing offends it; know that everything depends on the tact of our caresses. An ill-placed kiss may do any amount of harm.

Try following my advice.

Your old aunt,
Collette